ACCLAIM FOR JESSICA KATE

"Combining breathtaking realness, natural humor, and scorching romantic chemistry that leaps off the page, author Jessica Kate has given us a thoroughly modern tale about risk, acceptance, and the true meaning of home. Crackling with electricity and overflowing with heart, *A Girl's Guide to the Outback* is one you won't want to miss. Fair dinkum!"

—BETHANY TURNER, AWARD-WINNING AUTHOR OF *THE SECRET LIFE OF SARAH HOLLENBECK* AND *WOOING CADIE MCCAFFREY*

"*A Girl's Guide to the Outback* is as charming as it is hilarious! Jessica Kate's fresh and unique voice is both humorous and endearing, leaving you no choice but to abandon all personal responsibilities so you can devour every page. This is one of those stories that leaves you looking around for the characters after you've finished reading, because they just *had* to be real."

—BETSY ST. AMANT, AUTHOR OF *THE KEY TO LOVE*, COMING OCTOBER 2020

"Original, heartwarming, full of lovable characters amid a fast-paced plot. Romance readers will love the bicontinental adventure of a sassy, strong-willed woman going across the ocean to win back the Aussie man who holds the key to her career dreams—but also, as it turns out, so much more."

—MELISSA FERGUSON, AUTHOR OF *THE DATING CHARADE*, ON *A GIRL'S GUIDE TO THE OUTBACK*

"This captivating tale from Kate explores a woman's pain and hardship as she questions her faith . . . With believably flawed characters, this affecting tale of deceit and redemption, which questions what it means to forgive, will elicit strong reactions from Christian inspirational readers interested in stories with strong moral themes."

—*PUBLISHERS WEEKLY* ON *LOVE AND OTHER MISTAKES*

A Girl's Guide to the Outback

Also by Jessica Kate

Love and Other Mistakes

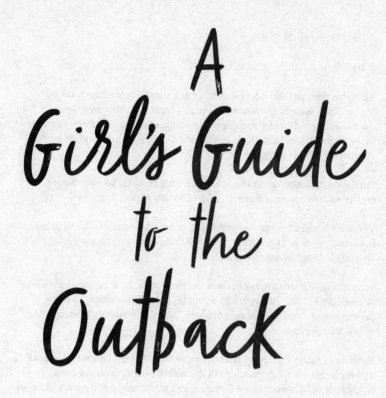

A Girl's Guide to the Outback

A NOVEL

JESSICA KATE

THOMAS NELSON
Since 1798

A Girl's Guide to the Outback

© 2020 Jessica Kate Everingham

Published in Nashville, Tennessee, by Thomas Nelson. Thomas Nelson is a registered trademark of HarperCollins Christian Publishing, Inc.

Thomas Nelson titles may be purchased in bulk for educational, business, fund-raising, or sales promotional use. For information, please e-mail SpecialMarkets@ThomasNelson.com.

Scripture quotations are taken from the Holy Bible, New Living Translation. © 1996, 2004, 2007, 2013, 2015 by Tyndale House Foundation. Used by permission of Tyndale House Publishers, Inc., Carol Stream, Illinois 60188. All rights reserved.

Publisher's Note: This novel is a work of fiction. Names, characters, places, and incidents are either products of the author's imagination or used fictitiously. All characters are fictional, and any similarity to people living or dead is purely coincidental.

Library of Congress Cataloging-in-Publication Data

Names: Kate, Jessica, author.
Title: A girl's guide to the Outback : a novel / Jessica Kate.
Description: Nashville, Tennessee : Thomas Nelson, [2020] | Summary: "Romance author Jessica Kate explores the hilariously thin line between love and hate in her heartwarming new novel"-- Provided by publisher.
Identifiers: LCCN 2019032265 (print) | LCCN 2019032266 (ebook) | ISBN 9780785229612 (trade paper) | ISBN 9780785229629 (ebook) | ISBN 9780785229636 (audio download)
Subjects: GSAFD: Christian fiction. | Love stories.
Classification: LCC PR9619.4.K366 G57 2020 (print) | LCC PR9619.4.K366 (ebook) | DDC 823/.92--dc23
LC record available at https://lccn.loc.gov/2019032265
LC ebook record available at https://lccn.loc.gov/2019032266

Printed in the United States of America

20 21 22 23 24 LSC 10 9 8 7 6 5 4 3 2 1

To God,
For being the Vine
John 15:5-8

Even before he made the world, God loved
us and chose us in Christ to be holy and
without fault in his eyes. God decided in
advance to adopt us into his own family.
—EPHESIANS 1:4-5

CHAPTER 1

Samuel Payton was an idiot.

Kimberly Foster jammed her phone into her pocket and rushed down the sunny Charlottesville street in a Mr. Potato Head costume, peep-toe heels, and murderous rage. It was 10:00 a.m. on a Saturday in June, and she was late for a child's birthday party.

But first she needed to strangle a youth pastor.

The words of her esteemed colleague's voice mail burned in her ears as she shoved open a glass door into the stuffy warmth of Charlottesville's Wildfire Youth Ministries building, stomped over the welcome mat, and beelined for the corridor that led to the offices.

How could Sam do this to her?

She upped her speed. The scent of fresh popcorn leaked through from Wildfire's youth drop-in center, just one thin wall away from this boxing ring they called an office. The birthday party must be close to starting. Her stomach gurgled.

She burst into the open-plan space where two extra-large desks faced one another down amid the clutter of a broken foosball table, drop-in center snacks, and desks for their volunteers. At the workstation closest to the door, one of their newer volunteers straightened the candles on a birthday cake.

Kimberly sucked as much frustration out of her voice as possible. "Where's Sam?"

The woman snapped to attention. Oops. Maybe a teensy bit of frustration had leaked through. The volunteer's eyes darted to behind Sam's desk before she scooped up the cake and escaped.

A broad-shouldered man faced away from Kimberly, silhouetted by the window on the far side of the room.

Her nemesis.

The name tags on their desks had been aligned to stare at one another: *Kimberly Foster, business manager. Samuel Payton, founder.* He'd even been difficult when she made the tags, resisting the title of *founder*. But he'd claimed he even less deserved its alternative, *youth pastor.* Just because he'd never been to Bible college. In the end she'd rolled her eyes, slapped on the word *founder*, and put her headphones on to drown out his complaining.

She took a fortifying breath and yanked a strand of brunette hair behind her ear. It had escaped her classy updo—or at least the updo that had been classy before she put on the potato costume.

"Sam, you'd better have an amazing reason for backflipping on me."

The traitor was going back on his word. His voice mail had been clear: *"I won't be offering my support for this proposal if you take it to the board."*

The last time they'd discussed her idea to open a youth drop-in center in Baltimore just like the one here, he'd been all for it. Well, he'd been reluctant at first. The Atlanta pilot-program fiasco had been tough on everyone. But as soon as she'd promised that Baltimore was less of a risk than Atlanta, he'd come around.

Why, besides his lifelong mission to drive her insane, would he change his mind?

The man swiveled from the window to reveal kind eyes, a streak of premature gray in sandy hair, and a navy blazer over jeans that did little to hide evidence of his marathon-running hobby.

Not Sam.

A blast of heat scalded Kimberly's face from the inside out as Potted Plants 4 Hire's HR manager, Gregory Sampson, walked toward her with his hand extended. What was he doing here on a Saturday?

"Sorry, I'm not Sam—but by the sounds of it, I'm glad of that." Laughter infused his voice.

Kimberly's phone dropped from her fingers and clattered onto a desk. She'd just blasted the good-looking HR manager of a company looking to recruit her. While wearing a potato suit.

She should shrink into her costume and hide like a turtle. Instead, she thrust out her hand to shake Greg's. "Don't be sorry. You're an upgrade. What can I do for you?"

He'd already tried to hire her—twice—to join the team trying to pull his company out of a financial black hole. And she'd refused. Twice. Getting headhunted and offered double her current salary had been an ego boost, sure. But despite Sam's maddening qualities, Kimberly believed in what he was doing at Wildfire with these kids. If she'd had someone like him to show her God's love as a teen, maybe life would've been different.

So, infuriating youth pastor or not, she wasn't leaving.

"You can come with me to lunch. There's a new organic café open in the mall." He smiled the smile of a man who knew he'd just offered a sweet deal. "Not a grain of processed sugar in sight."

Oh, he'd done his research. Her mouth moistened. She licked her lips, and raspberry lip balm teased her taste buds.

"No, thanks."

The wattage on Greg's smile dimmed. "No?"

She mentally groaned. Lunch in Charlottesville's outdoor mall—one of her favorite pastimes—would go a long way toward soothing the rage monster inside right now. But—"I can't accept the job. I'm already late." *And I need to find new and inventive ways to threaten Sam.*

Though a carrot might work better than a stick at this stage. Sam's support for her proposal was vital. If only she was good at the whole carrot thing.

Greg spread his hands, palms up. "No shoptalk. Promise. Just lunch with a friend."

Oh, that spark in his hazel eyes was charming. His smile genuine. His invitation tempting.

"Can't. Sorry." It wasn't fair to get a free lunch from Greg when she already knew her answer to his repeated job offer.

Something shifted in Greg's expression. A flicker of disappointment? A tad odd, to be so invested in a business lunch.

"Okay. Well, then." He deflated more than she'd expected. "Let me know if you change your mind." He left his card on the desk, gave a two-fingered salute, and headed out the door.

Kimberly watched him go, let a moan escape at her fate of sugary party food for lunch, and pounced on her keyboard. The movie-themed tenth birthday bash for Laura, one of the children involved in Wildfire's ministry, started in the drop-in center in 9.5 minutes. Sam's online calendar might tell her where the rat was hiding before she ran out of time.

"He was trying to ask you out."

Kimberly jolted at the deep rumble of a familiar Australian accent.

A dark-haired Captain America strode into the room. His star-spangled costume stretched over the tan skin and impressive biceps that carried two-year-old Andrew Kent and his golden curls. Kimberly's uterus did a backflip of approval. He was dressed as her favorite superhero. Carrying an adorable toddler. Doing his best to make her life miserable.

Samuel Payton.

Trotting along on Sam's heels was Riley Strahovzki, a thirteen-year-old regular at the drop-in center who sported a green dress and a wild red mane reminiscent of the princess from Disney's *Brave*. Of course Sam had offered to pick up Riley and Andrew. That man was a godsend to every time-poor mother in town whose children wanted to be involved in Wildfire.

But for some reason he never extended that same kindness to her.

"What are you blabbing about?" Her hands found her hips. Well, where her hips would be under this itchy potato suit.

"The guy you just shut down. He was trying to ask you out." Sam's tone indicated he had no idea why. He handed Andrew to Riley's waiting arms and held open the door that led to the drop-in center. The buzz of a dozen moms and their kids indicated the party would start any minute.

Sam closed the door behind the kids and smirked, his eyes traveling the length of her. "Must have been the costume." His voice held barely contained laughter.

Kimberly looked down at her potato body and high heels. "You said last month that Laura loves *Toy Story*." The costume wasn't exactly her usual corporate attire, but she'd do anything to put a smile on the face of this ten-year-old birthday girl who apparently shared her love of Woody and Buzz. No matter how many times Kimberly watched those toys reunite with their family, the fatherless eleven-year-old inside her still battled tears. So when the costume store had no Buzz, Woody, or Jessie costumes, she'd envisaged Laura's laughter and said yes to Mr. Potato Head.

Sam popped a strawberries-and-cream lolly from his ever-present Australian candy jar into his mouth, nodding toward the corridor where Greg had exited. "Don't you like him?"

Kimberly stared at him and that delicious costume. His boxing sessions meant the muscles were real, not padding.

Focus, Kimberly.

Hold on—was he being sarcastic? "He was trying to offer me a job, not ask me on a date."

Sam grinned at her. "You leavin' me?"

"You'll have to die or quit for that to happen." Her work in start-up tech companies back in LA had been stimulating, sure. But it had nothing on the smile she was going to see on a ten-year-old's face in about three minutes.

Sam tossed another candy into his mouth.

She frowned. "You trying to speed up that dying process?"

He used the jar in his hand to point at her. "You could use a little more sweetness."

"No one hires me for my personality." A direct quote from her mother. And a fact. People commented on her classic Hollywood sense of style and fast-rising career all the time, but her habit of blurting out whatever was sparking in her neurons meant she'd never been anyone's vote for Miss Congeniality. She'd trade her wardrobe and sharp mind for a softer personality any day of the week, but she played the cards she'd been dealt.

Sam pulled his I'm-too-polite-to-say-what-I'm-thinking face and turned to rummage through his desk drawers.

Not that she needed any reminder that neither her looks nor, apparently, her business brain had any effect on him. She shook off the thought and seized her phone from her desk. "Why aren't you supporting my proposal? It's rock solid." She tapped the small screen and pulled up the file again. "Which part don't you understand?" The board meeting was only three days away, and Sam's support would mean the board approved her proposal for sure. The Australian's infectious passion meant he could sell a wallaby to a jackaroo.

And once he understood how many kids this new drop-in center would help, he'd be even more enthusiastic than she was.

Sam's eyes, the color of fudge sauce—or her foster dog's poop, depending on her mood—focused on her face. His mouth twisted like he knew some joke she didn't. "I understand all of it. And the answer's no."

Her arm, holding the phone in the air, slowly lowered. Stage one of convincing Sam of any of her ideas: The First No. There'd be many more before he capitulated—which happened about half the time—and then her initiative exceeded expectations and he gave a reluctant thank-you. She lived for that quiet "Thanks." If only their process didn't involve weeks of soul-bruising disagreements. "If you understand, why don't you see how awesome it is?"

He abandoned his search through the drawers and came to stand before her, six inches closer than she felt comfortable with—as usual. Her insides tingled, the way they always did when the full intensity of his attention focused on her. Thankfully he always seemed to leave her out of the hug-everyone-I-see thing he had going on. But she could never convince him of exactly where her personal-space boundaries were.

"You told me the Baltimore center would be less risky than Atlanta was." His deep voice held rebuke. "It's more. Support withdrawn. End of story."

Why was Sam the only one who couldn't admit her ideas were brilliant? It wasn't a brag, just fact. She had as much right to take credit for her intelligence as she did for her difficult-to-manage eyebrows. But that didn't change the fact she'd started at this ministry three years ago as an intern, starstruck at the thought of working with the team—and the man—who'd helped spark a Christian revival in West Coast high schools and then shifted their focus to the East Coast. And in two years she'd worked her way up to business manager, with the board making her Sam's equal. He handled the ministry while she crunched the numbers.

But in the past year Sam had demonstrated more than ever that he didn't consider her a part of Team Wildfire.

She stood taller, pointless as it was. He still outstripped her height by at least four inches. "It's completely different. Atlanta had to be shut down, sure, but there were extenuating circum-stances, and we learned our lessons. The cost is only a fraction higher, the location is closer, and the chaplain we'll put in charge of it isn't going to have a breakdown. This time." Unfortunately their Atlanta chaplain hadn't informed them of his impending bankruptcy, nor his fragile emotional state. The man was now recovering with a lot of support, but the fallout at the time had been less fun than a migraine at a Justin Bieber concert.

This expansion plan was her mission to get their partner-ship back on track. With Sam's gift of speaking and pastoral care and her business brain, this ministry could go anywhere. Reach anyone.

If he'd stop fighting her and let her be on his side for once.

"No."

Kimberly's blood pressure shifted into high gear, along with the speed of her words. Why did he put her through this? "The risk factors are way lower. We've already got a major church wanting to be involved, we can offer ten times the support we did last time, we can share resources, and—"

"Kimberly, stop." Sam's hand slashed through the air. "This ministry is not about numbers. It's about helping kids—*these* kids—get to know God. I can't do that if I'm busy running some megaministry that's massive on YouTube but leaves kids like Laura behind. We're about more than just numbers."

Kimberly flinched. Did he think she was wearing this polyester potato for fashion purposes? She'd never leave out kids like Laura. This very party was her idea. Not just a welcome into an age marked by double digits but a rare chance to celebrate among chemo-darkened days. She wasn't great at talking to kids like Sam was, but by golly she could throw a party.

A bead of sweat tickled her neck as Sam continued ranting. "I'm not throwing my donors' money down the drain so that you can expand, expand, expand. That's not what we're about."

"Money down the drain"? Her last thread of self-restraint snapped. "If you're too chicken to take the chance, just say so." She pressed her lips together before she said anything else she regretted. That comment had gone too far, but it was somewhat justified. She'd worked late all this week to get the proposal ready for the board. The project had been months in the making.

Now, all for nothing.

Sam's face hardened. "Save the name-calling for the board meeting, Foster. That is, if you decide to go ahead with the proposal without me."

Kimberly blinked. She could go ahead with the proposal. That hadn't even occurred to her before. Just because Sam didn't support it didn't mean she couldn't present it herself. Though, based on current evidence, her skills at presenting a proposal were lower than today's dip in the stock market.

She spun away from Sam and strode toward the bathroom, thoughts scrambling. This costume was too hot, her mouth too dry.

She needed to think. She needed to hide.

She needed to cry.

CHAPTER 2

Sam dodged a wild uppercut and slammed his right fist into his opponent's ribs. Fourteen-year-old Tariq Ismat laughed and danced away to the other side of the makeshift boxing ring, a thick layer of foam body armor protecting him from the blow.

Police Captain John Walters leaned against the rope—actually a skipping rope tied between a concrete pillar and a bookshelf—and held his fists up before his face. "Keep your hands up, Tariq."

Sam blinked to evict the sweat stinging his eyes and bounced on his toes. Tariq had struggled ever since his family emigrated from Syria to Virginia after his father's death seven years ago. These boxing lessons with Captain Walters were the only time Sam saw the kid smile. Which is why Sam found himself sparring in the captain's sweat-and-rubber-scented basement at—he glanced at the digital clock on the wall—7:14 a.m. this Tuesday morning instead of dozing in bed trying not to think about the board meeting that started in forty-six minutes' time.

Kim was going ahead with her proposal.

He'd never thought she'd really do it without him. They both knew she had as much chance of convincing the board to do something he didn't believe in as Tariq did of winning by knockout.

But the whirlpool in his stomach didn't seem to believe that.

Smack!

A left jab snapped his head back.

He shook the stars off and bounced around the ring. Tariq stood openmouthed as Captain Walters smirked.

"He got you there, Sammy-boy. Distracted, are we?" He folded his arms. "Let another shot through like that, and I'll make you spar with me."

Sam tried not to grimace. The man was a tree trunk wrapped in a brick wall wrapped in muscle. His expression alone could strip the fight from the soul of any man—except his new best friend, Tariq.

Sam smiled at Tariq even as his eye throbbed. "Good shot, mate."

The captain glanced at the clock. "Samuel, aren't you due at Wildfire in fifteen minutes?"

"Yes, sir." Sam tapped gloves with Tariq and ducked out of the ring, then froze. "Fifteen minutes?" His gaze swung to the clock located above a Muhammad Ali poster. Blinked and looked again. Seven forty-five a.m. Curse his dyslexia. Must've been 7:41 earlier.

"You can use my shower." The captain tossed him his duffel bag, which vibrated when Sam caught it. "And your phone's ringing."

He ignored the phone, shook the captain's hand, and dashed up the stairs. The phone call was probably just his sister Jules. Tuesday morning in Charlottesville was late Tuesday night in Australia, and she often rang him for a chat before bed. But that could wait. Five-minute shower, and his Ducati Streetfighter could make it to Wildfire in eight minutes.

So that left two minutes in the office with Kim before the

board meeting. He slowed his pace. That would be two minutes too many.

He sighed and rolled his neck to release the tension building in his shoulders. Kimberly Foster. When she'd first started at Wildfire, he'd found her blunt but talented and dedicated to the ministry. On the occasions he could make her raspberry-scented-lip-balm lips crack a smile, a rush of elation told him he'd earned it. After a few months he'd even had a little crush on her—or at least her confidence and capability.

But in the past year, her single-minded mission had been to turn Wildfire into something it was not. A brand rather than a ministry. One more business conquest to put a notch on her proverbial belt.

And once she achieved that, she'd leave, off to bigger and better things. She'd leave, and their risky financial position would slide into ruin.

Not on his watch.

He finished his shower in record time, threw on his favorite flannel shirt and jeans, and was soon zipping through traffic on his motorbike. He relished the rumble of the engine and tried to focus his brain on the road and the other agenda items for today's meeting.

But Kimberly's words played in his mind like an annoying ad jingle.

"If you're too chicken . . . If you're too chicken . . ."

He shook his head. He'd wanted to support Kim's proposal. He really had. But Kimberly had suggested an investment more than five times his annual salary. He couldn't tell the people who'd supported him for the past five years to put their money into something he didn't believe in. It was too big a financial risk.

13

He'd made that mistake before.

He roared up to the squat brick building that housed Wildfire and parked his bike. Three minutes early. Drat.

His phone buzzed, and he palmed it from his pocket. Three missed calls—and if he was reading the screen right, they'd come seconds apart. All from Jules. Their SOS signal.

In an instant his heart rate was mimicking a cha-cha. Had something happened to Mum? Had there been a farm accident? He hit the redial icon so hard the crack in his phone screen lengthened.

"Hey, bro." Jules's voice sounded tight, even with half a world's worth of satellite bounces between them.

He strove for a calm tone. "What's happened?"

"I need to talk to you about the farm. There's something I didn't tell you."

Sam stumbled into the coffee-scented board room, his ear still warm from the phone and Jules's words reverberating around his brain. He nodded at board members—both seated around the conference table or telecommuting on the projector screen—but processed nothing.

The family dairy farm back in Australia was about to miss its bank repayments. And Jules had been too nice to say it, but this was a direct result of his actions eight years ago.

He seated himself in the office chair with the finicky wheel, the weight of his past pulling on his conscience like woolen garments on a drowning swimmer. The only son was meant to take over the farm—not create more debt and then run off to America while his sister shouldered the burden.

His throat thickened.

Jules must've been struggling for a while now, out there in rural Queensland running the farm with just her and Mum—and Mum unable to do the physical work anymore. And she hadn't told him until the day before the payment was due. Typical Jules.

His focus swung to Kimberly preparing something at the front of the room. Her gaze caught his and she paused, quirked an eyebrow. Were his emotions playing that clearly on his face? Or was she just rubbing in the fact that she was pushing this pitch without him? Her expression gave nothing more away. As usual.

Whatever. There were more important things to ponder than whatever was going on behind that queenly mask she called a face. Like what to do about the property that represented the life's work of four generations.

This repayment wasn't a problem—he'd tap a button on his phone after the meeting, and a chunk of his savings would shoot from his account to the farm's. But looking ahead? Maybe this was the sign he'd been praying for.

He zoned back into the meeting and jolted. Kimberly was giving her presentation. Wearing his favorite light-gray skirt and jacket, the one that flattered all five feet and eight inches of her curves, and with her hair all down and wavy.

Just because she drove him nuts didn't mean he was blind.

A teenage girl's face filled the projector screen. Kimberly gestured to it. "This is twelve-year-old Hayley Washington. Her dyslexia means she struggles at school, but her single mother can't afford a tutor. This is what a Baltimore drop-in center would mean to her."

She hit a button, and the photo turned into video footage.

Hayley, seated on a park bench, tucked her hands under her denim shorts and gave a nervous giggle that sounded tinny through the room's lo-fi speakers. "If I could go to the drop-in center, Mom wouldn't worry about me being alone so much while she works. Annnnnd . . ." She stretched the words out and looked to the person behind the camera, then straight down the barrel of the lens. "And I could get help to study and become a special-needs teacher. I want to help kids like my little brother Trey. He's got autism."

Sam seized a pen from the center of the table and jotted down Hayley's name on a sticky receipt fished from his pocket. He couldn't oppose this plan without making sure he connected Hayley with someone who could help. He, of all people, understood the struggles she faced.

Kimberly clicked to another photo. "This is Ricky Daniels." An eight-year-old with defiant eyes and a rat's tail stared into the camera. She described the young boy's precarious foster home situation, then hit Play on his clip.

Sam shifted in his seat, mouth dry. This presentation was actually good. Telling the stories of the kids with their own voices? It's exactly what he would've done. All this time, she'd secretly taken notice of his methods.

Sam scanned the faces of the men and women of the board—the five around the table and the four on-screen. There were nods. No fiddling. Relaxed expressions.

Oh no. They were considering it.

The tension in his shoulders slithered up his neck and pushed an ache into the base of his skull.

How had Kimberly pulled this off? Three days ago she'd been expecting him to give the pitch. He rewound the past few days in his head. She'd been away all day Monday. She must've headed straight to Baltimore and filmed the footage.

Kimberly continued, telling the stories of more children and teenagers. But for every photo she flashed up on the screen, he saw a different one in his head. Lorna Franke, who'd mortgaged her house to provide Wildfire with a chunk of its seed money. He hadn't found out until years later, and even then by accident.

Don Ward, who'd donated the life insurance payout on his wife so that good could come out of his personal tragedy.

Riley Strahovzki, one of their drop-in center girls, who was caught between her parents in the bitterest divorce he'd ever seen. Wildfire wasn't just an escape for her. It was a lifeline.

How could he face them if he took Kimberly's gamble and lost it all?

Kimberly's voice penetrated his reverie. "And Baltimore would just be the start. Within the next twelve months we would look at expanding to Washington and Pittsburgh."

Sam sat up straight. When had that become part of the proposal?

Her gaze met his. He lifted his eyebrows. She gave the tiniest of shrugs, as if to say, *If you're not on board, I can pitch what I want.*

He huffed. This was way worse than he'd thought. Her desire to expand past Baltimore had been obvious from the start, but so soon? No way.

Kimberly sat down, and former Wildfire employee and new board member Stephanie Walters leaned forward. "So you're confident that Baltimore is more suitable than Atlanta was?"

"Definitely. Atlanta was far from a failure. Had unusual circumstances not played a part . . ."

Her voice faded from Sam's consciousness as he fumed.

Unusual circumstances always played a part. The future was unpredictable. And it was possible to lose everything.

He should know.

"... confident that Baltimore has both the need and the support base to sustain a new drop-in center. We just need to have a little faith." She sent a small smile his way.

"Have a little faith."

He'd said the same words to his father just over nine years ago. And they had sealed his fate.

Thud. Kimberly dropped a stack of papers onto the table.

But in his mind's eye, it was Mum's hands dropping a pile of travel magazines . . . dreams . . . into the bin.

He surged to his feet. "I can't support this."

Every head at the table or on the screen snapped in his direction. He swallowed. "I can't be a part of this. Kimberly wants me to head up the chaplains at every new outreach, but I don't believe in this proposal. It's too much financial risk. I can't do it." The words flew out.

A long pause.

He didn't backpedal. Back in California five years ago, this group had come to him—a guy cooking fries at Sonic and preaching on the weekends—and asked if he wanted to work in ministry full-time. Wildfire had started because they trusted in what he was doing. Some of the board members had changed since then, but the trust remained. He couldn't betray that now.

"Perhaps you two should give us time to discuss it," Steph said, her fingers laced on the table. "We'll call you back in if we have questions."

He stared at her, his breathing rapid and shallow. They would consider this crazy plan, knowing his position?

She waggled her eyebrows at him and nodded toward the door. He scanned the faces of the board members and exited on stiff legs. The answer was written all over each of them.

Kimberly was about to win.

Well, if they wanted to follow her down the road to ruin, he wouldn't stick around to be a part of it. Maybe this was a sign from God that it was time to move on and go home. And not to his run-down rental with its temperamental hot water and loud neighbors.

Time to go back to his real home, nine thousand miles away from Kimberly Foster—though not nearly far enough.

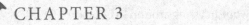

CHAPTER 3

FIVE MONTHS LATER

Julia "Jules" Payton spat dirt from her mouth as she lay in the dust of her stockyards, cool against her goose-bumped skin in the Australian spring night air. Her nose rested only five inches from a steaming cow pat. It didn't stop her from sucking in deep breaths like the ladies on TV in labor.

She eyed the angry mama cow on the other side of the enclosure.

It was hard to tell what hurt the most. Her must-be-broken left foot and ankle, swelling faster than a birthday balloon? The massive egg on the back of her skull? Or the fact that Mick Carrigan had been right?

Please God, let someone come find me.

She dialed Mick for the fourth time and shouted at his voice mail. "Pick up your stinking phone!"

She'd called the ambulance, but town was forty minutes away, maybe thirty if Lead-Foot Larry was on duty. Butch hadn't answered his phone. Not surprising—tomorrow was his day off, so he'd probably drunk himself into oblivion. Sam's phone was out of service, thanks to dodgy reception on the road between here and where Mum was staying on the Sunshine Coast. What use was it having her brother home on the farm if he wasn't here for moments like this?

An owl hooted, unconcerned with the thirty-one-year-old woman lying on the ground.

Jules reached her quivering fingers to the bottom bar of the fence and squeezed it, focusing on the cold metal, the rough texture—anything to try to distract her from the pain. Pressing her lips together, she contained her moan despite no one being around to hear. She focused her eyes on the moonlit trees that lined the Burnett River, which divided the Payton dairy farm from the Carrigan property.

Three kilometers were all that separated her from the infuriating vet who had told her less than an hour ago not to get in a pen alone with a calf and the mother cow they'd nicknamed Psycho. She'd assumed it was just the protective former boyfriend in him talking and ignored his advice. Perhaps a mistake.

Waiting on someone to rescue her was almost worse than the pain. If she could get to her vehicle, she could meet the ambulance and their painkillers halfway. She'd heard old farmhands tell stories of driving through the outback with all sorts of impalements and other horrific injuries.

But when she'd tried to move, she'd passed out. And the only thing worse than being conscious and at the mercy of this ballistic bovine was being unconscious.

Her phone, resting on her stomach, buzzed. She fumbled to hit the Answer button.

"I got your abusive message. What's up?" Mick's voice sounded resigned, like he was too tired to have this fight right now. Understandable, considering she'd roused him from his bed at 2:00 a.m.

21

Jules licked her lips and tasted blood. "I ignored what you said. Psycho got me. You've gotta come quick, and bring some horse tranquilizer or something."

"You what?" Mick let loose a series of words she'd never heard from the usually unruffled man. "Where are you?"

"Lying in the yards. My foot's broken. Just hurry."

"I'm coming. Hold on, Jules." His breathing turned ragged, like he was running. "Stay on the line. I'm coming."

Jules's vision blurred, tunneled. Mick was coming.

She could pass out again.

Kimberly scanned the Washington, DC, café for the gazillionth time, her once-fragrant peppermint tea now cold before her. No Mom. She balanced her covered plate of sugar-free brownies on her knee and tugged her phone out of her handbag. Zippo. Surveyed the street outside for any lost-looking forty-three-year-old tech-company consultants. Zilch.

She closed her eyes and pinched the bridge of her nose.

It'd been tricky to rearrange her morning for this tête-à-tête with Mom, but since the Silicon Valley tech queen's East Coast business trips were rare, Kimberly had hummed with inexplicable anticipation for the entire two-hour drive.

Anticipation because it'd been two—no, must've been three—years since they'd seen each other.

Inexplicable because their intimacy had never progressed past strained acquaintances.

Yet still, she'd hummed.

She swiped to Mom's generic contact icon and dialed. *Call*

Rejected. With a huff she checked her watch again. She was already late for this afternoon's event in Baltimore. The drop-in center hadn't been built yet, but their new chaplain was focusing his time there to garner local church support.

But what if Mom got here just after she left?

Her phone chirped. She snatched it up. A text message. Mom.

Trip canceled. Sorry.

Kimberly closed her eyes and pressed the phone against her forehead. Nice of her mother to let her know.

She took three deep breaths, collected her things, and threw the brownies in the trash on her way out.

She should never have expected today to be different.

Ninety road-rage fueled minutes later, Kimberly stood stage left in an auditorium of three thousand chattering teenagers and stared at Stephanie Walters. "What do you mean he's not coming?" If she sweated any more in this overheated auditorium, her white blouse would turn translucent.

Steph, looking sweat-free despite her fitted black dress, held up her phone. "Your new chaplain quit. On the phone to me just now. I told him we needed it in writing to try to stall for time, and this is what he sent."

Kimberly snatched the phone up and glared at the text message. Two words: **I resign.**

She pinched the bridge of her nose again and winced. It was starting to bruise.

After handing the phone back to Steph, she straightened her skirt. She could wait to fire off her raging questions, like *Why?* and *How could I lose three chaplains in five months?*

Right now someone had to work the problem.

Steph slipped her phone into her clutch. "We need Sam back."

Kimberly flinched. *And it's my fault he's gone.* She tried not to snap. "That doesn't help us right now."

"Right now, I'll handle this talk. But I'm giving you a heads-up about the rumblings among board members."

"Rumblings"? Steph couldn't have sounded more ominous if she'd spoken the words while wearing a black cape and a vulture on her shoulder.

Kimberly straightened her spine. "Sam's not coming back. He's on the other side of the world. I just need more time to find the right fit—" She halted when Steph shook her head. Defensiveness welled up, but she kept her mouth shut. She'd pored over résumés for weeks trying to find a replacement for Sam—and managed to hire someone who seemed nice in his interview but was so difficult to work with he'd been fired in his first week. Next had come a promising mother in her late thirties with a dynamic stage presence and obvious love for youth—who quit two months in when her mother was diagnosed with cancer. This latest hire had seemed like a good fit for the past three months. But now, a third disaster.

"Why did this one quit?"

Steph heaved a sigh. "According to our barely coherent conversation, his wife blindsided him with divorce papers over the weekend."

Kimberly gaped. "That's awful." For both him and—was she selfish to think this?—her. She needed someone to oversee five youth Bible studies and the drop-in center and preach at four engagements in the next two weeks. Plus, the Baltimore center was ready to go pending someone to oversee it. Another hiring decision. Four résumés sat on her desk, but at this point could she trust her own choosing abilities? "Okay, well, the volunteer Bible study leaders can handle things themselves for a few weeks, and if I tweak the drop-in center roster—"

Steph peeked through the stage curtain. Kimberly caught a glimpse of the hordes of waiting teens. "That'll get us through the next month at most. But the board is losing confidence that we can replace Sam with someone appropriate."

Dread sucker punched her harder than the Hulk in a bad mood. *Don't say what I think you're going to say. Don't close it down. Don't close it down.*

She maintained her poker face as best she could and braced for Steph's next words.

"We want you to win him back."

She must've heard that wrong. "What?"

Steph laced her fingers together and held her silence. It'd been a habit of hers during their time working together and allowed her words to hit full potency rather than repeat herself.

Kimberly gave a slow shake of her head. "He's in Australia."

"Yes."

"He's not coming back."

"Convince him." Steph held eye contact, didn't smile, didn't shrug.

The little person inside Kimberly's brain hovered its hand over the big red button marked PANIC. "I have as much chance of that as Bernie Madoff getting a business loan."

Steph winced. "If you don't, the board will consider whether this ministry has run its course. We don't want to be an organization for organization's sake. If we aren't running effectively, we'll disband and divert the money to someone who's doing the kind of good that Sam was. We just haven't seen that in these replacements."

Kimberly stared at Steph, pressure building in her brain. How could she have gone from expanding Wildfire to possibly losing it altogether? "So you just give up? It can take time to find the right person."

"It's November. You've had five months."

Kimberly lowered the volume of her voice but ratcheted up the intensity. "Five months is not a long-term perspective. And Sam is not the only talented youth pastor in the world."

Steph sighed. "I disagreed, for what it's worth. You've hit a perfect storm of circumstances, and that's not your fault. It's just that a number of board members are looking to retire soon from their duties. Many of them donate directly to Wildfire. It's how they got on the board in the first place. If they can't see a strong future, I think they'd just as easily close down and send their money somewhere else as find replacements." She touched a hand to Kimberly's arm, gave a sympathetic squeeze. "Get creative. There's hope yet."

Kimberly watched, frozen, as Steph glided onto the stage and addressed the waiting teenagers. Her throat and jaw ached from the effort of keeping a professional mask in place.

She hadn't poured three and a half years into this ministry to watch it fold now. Images of her future played out in her mind's eye, like a scary movie on fast-forward. No more foosball play-offs against the kids in the drop-in center. No more team meetings with Mrs. Schneider's out-of-this-world cupcakes. No more evening brainstorming sessions with a whiteboard, a truckload of Chinese food, and Steph and Sam. Well, at least Steph.

No place to belong.

She set her jaw. Wildfire wasn't perfect—Sam's refusal to play nice was proof of that—but it was the closest thing she'd had to a family since Dad died more than half her lifetime ago. She, more than anyone, knew these kids needed a place to belong and to learn about God's unconditional love. Because she'd needed it.

We need Sam. If she couldn't convince him to return himself, she at least needed guidance from him on the best person to take over. Probably a few weeks for him to work with the replacement, too, and make sure they had the right person. She'd had three attempts and failed spectacularly to find that Sam Payton combination of enthusiasm, love for God, and ability to speak "teen."

Okay. All business was basically a negotiation. She just needed to find something he wanted and make her deal sweet enough to appeal.

How hard could that be?

 CHAPTER 4

"S amuel John Payton, stop running away from me."

Sam froze halfway through the farmhouse kitchen at the sound of his sister's voice. He eyed the door that led to his childhood home's enclosed veranda and, beyond that, freedom. Four more steps. Three if he stretched.

Tap-tap. Thud. Tap-tap. Thud.

Graceful on crutches Jules was not.

The hallway light threw her shadow up against the wall, visible before she was. Good golly, did she have an electrocuted octopus on top of her head, or was her bed hair really that bad?

Jules hopped out of the hallway sporting her koala pajamas and a glare so toxic it could strip paint. He held up his keys. "Cricket. Do you want me to disappoint twenty eleven-year-old boys?"

She narrowed her eyes. "You finally learned how to lie. Get better at it. You guys never train this late."

"It's a barbie for the parents. I'm bringing the snags." He held up a tray of sausages to prove the point. Funny, he'd missed good ol' Aussie slang while in the States. There came a point where a man tired of explaining that *barbie* referred to a barbecue, not a plastic doll.

He inched toward the door and away from the crazy woman who shared his genetics.

"Not till you agree to help me."

He folded his arms. "I am helping you. I carried you up those stairs. There's twelve of them, if you're wondering. I got your movies and your painkillers. I even lit your favorite scented candle that smells like apple pie and makes me hungry." His stomach rumbled even as he said it. "Oh yeah—and I moved continents for you."

"Call her."

"On second thought, maybe I shouldn't leave you alone. Those painkillers have made you crazy."

Tap-tap. Thud.

He'd hear the sound of those crutches in his nightmares.

"All you talked about for three years was how this woman was some start-up wizard in LA and how she was torturing you with plans for world domination."

He shifted a step back. "That's not entirely accurate."

She followed. "We need some out-of-the-box ideas and world-dominating confidence."

He stared her down, grateful that his extra three inches were able to top her five-ten stature. How could a woman look so fierce in koala pajamas? Her green eyes never blinked as she returned his glare.

But sister or not, a man's love for his sibling could only go so far. "I am not calling Kimberly Foster to ask if she can help us pay our bills."

Tap-tap. Thud. Jules leaned on the crutches, now within arm's distance. "We could use her . . . ideas."

Hell would freeze over before his sister used the word *help.* "So talk to some of the other farmers around here."

Jules set her jaw.

He mentally sighed. She'd never admit to their lifelong friends and neighbors that after four generations of farming Yarra Plains they teetered on the edge of disaster.

But Jules's pride was Jules's problem.

His sister pointed a crutch at him. "You know they'd only give me farming advice. How to grow grass and milk cows is not my problem. My problem is why it's not generating enough money when we're not even in drought. Or flood. Or fire. Or anything else that Mum dealt with for decades. This is a business question. And according to all the ranting I've heard from you over the years, all this woman thinks about is business and how to grow it. Relentlessly."

This is what he got for whinging to his sister.

Jules scratched at the top of her cast. "Didn't she double your donor base within her first six months?"

Tripled it in five months, but close enough. "Yeah, but—"

"Quadruple your volunteers in a year?"

"Sort of, but—" He'd never have told Jules all this if he'd known she'd not only remember but use it against him. Maybe he'd talked about Kim more than he'd thought.

"Sam." Jules put a hand on his arm. "Please."

His armor cracked a smidge. He leaned against the kitchen bench beside him and mustered his final argument. "I'm the last person she'd do a favor for."

Jules inched closer, eyes alight. "I think you're misjudging her. And we could offer to pay her."

He rolled his eyes. "One, why do you take her side? And two, with what? The whole problem is a lack of coinage, remember?" He drew out the last word in that annoying brotherish way he'd done when they were kids.

"You could sell your body."

He snorted. "She's not interested. Believe me." Apart from the whole icky matter of those words coming from his sister's mouth.

Jules set her mouth in a tight line. Then snatched the keys from his hand and dropped them down her shirt.

Sam blinked. "Hey!"

"You want your keys, you ring Kimberly Foster."

"You're a sicko."

"I'm a sicko with keys."

He stared at her. This. Was. Not. Happening.

Jules poked a lamb sausage. "Bet those kids are getting hungry. Wondering where their coach is."

He jammed his hand on his hip.

She waited.

He held out a hand for the keys.

She waited.

He tried his most intimidating I-really-mean-business-and-I'm-definitely-not-bluffing stare.

She returned it. "You said you came back here to help. So help."

He rolled his eyes. "Fine. But if you think I'm carrying you down those stairs tomorrow, you're sadly mistaken."

"The only reason you carried me the first time was because I was too doped up on meds to stop you. Start dialing, buddy."

Sam ground his teeth and pulled his phone from his pocket. He flicked up his clock app and checked the time in Charlottesville. "It's 3:00 a.m. there."

"Promise to ring her tomorrow morning, then."

Don't say it. Keep still, tongue. "Fine."

Jules handed his keys back with a triumphant smile, but she shouldn't have gotten her hopes up.

Because there was no scenario in which this conversation with Kim would end well.

Kimberly stared at Sam's social media profile on her phone screen, as annoyed at it as she was delighted with her present location. She was seated on the couch in Wildfire's drop-in center, the sounds of their annual Christmas party floating around her as her dog shifted its mop of white fur against her wool-stockinged leg and red dress. Today was her last day with the foster dog before he became an early Christmas present for one excited ten-year-old girl. So maybe it wasn't just her lack of progress in finding an appealing deal to offer Sam that caused that constricted feeling in her chest.

Three days, and she had nothin'. Zero ideas on how to entice Sam back across the Pacific. And the social media stalking had provided no fresh insight. She could offer him money, sure, but Sam's habit of donating his wage straight back into Wildfire told her he wasn't motivated much by money. Up until five months ago she would've said he was motivated to spread the message of God's love to as many teens as possible. But then he'd quit over her expansion plan. Did he really hate her that much? Steph had told her a zillion times not to take it personally, but it was kinda hard not to.

His profile picture stared back at her. An action shot of him she'd snapped a year ago, doing what he did best: preaching to a group of teenagers who seemed to hang on his every word. Six of those kids had handed their lives over to God that night.

She looked up from the phone and took in the room. November was early for a Christmas party, especially before Thanksgiving. But this had been the only day that all the board members could attend, so they'd turned it into a combo Thanksgiving-Christmas gathering. Teens lounged around in beanbags and sprawled on the floor, stuffed from the feast now reduced to crumbs. The taste of chocolate pudding—a rare, sugary treat—still lingered on her taste buds. A few parents clustered in groups, cradling cups of punch. And on the other end of the couch, little Laura—now with a dark cap of hair growing back after the end of her cancer treatments—sat with her fingers tangled in Warren Buffett's fur.

It almost felt like Kimberly was at a family celebration. And just as she'd done every Christmas since she could remember, she closed her eyes and pictured a houseful of relatives on Christmas Day. Imaginary brothers and sisters. At least three dogs. Dad alive again. His mystery half brothers and perhaps even some cousins. Grandparents who actually knew who she was. And some kind-hearted stepmother who was the opposite of the woman who'd birthed her in every way.

The perfect Christmas.

Unlike her actual Christmases, which involved a *Firefly* marathon and unending amounts of store-bought pudding in honor of Dad.

"Miss Kim?"

Kimberly's eyes popped open at the sound of Laura's voice. "Yes—" *Sweetheart.* The endearment popped to mind every time she spoke with Laura—with many of the children—but it felt ridiculous to say. It was Sam they adored, not her. With Sam, they'd talk about their day and their families and their problems.

She asked the same questions and got one-word responses.

"Who are you giving your puppy to?"

Kimberly smiled down at the freshly groomed Maltese flopped between them, a huge bow attached to its collar. Laura's parents had said she could be the one to deliver the news. "You."

Laura's gaze snapped to hers. "Me?"

Kimberly picked up the relaxed dog and placed it in Laura's lap. She'd planned to adopt him herself until a Wildfire volunteer mentioned Laura's attachment to him. The house would feel empty, but after a tough year the little girl deserved a win. "I talked to your parents. They said yes. Warren's going home with you tonight."

Laura burst into tears.

Kimberly froze. Wasn't Laura happy? Had she made a mistake? She gave the girl an awkward pat on the back. "Hey. What's wrong?"

Laura buried her face in the dog, who licked her ear in response. "I love him." Then she dropped the dog and flung her arms around Kimberly. "Th-th-thank you."

And just like that, Kimberly's heart exploded into a million pieces. The little girl smelled of strawberry shampoo and turkey dinner. She squeezed her tight and fought the sneaky tears that tried to escape and join Laura's. "You're welcome, kiddo."

Laura pulled back. "Can I name him something else?"

Kimberly smirked. The kids had never appreciated her reference to investor Warren Buffett. "Sure can."

A moment later Laura ran off to show her mom her new pet, Sprinkles.

Kimberly sighed and looked back at the man on her phone. No way was she letting Wildfire go. But the key would be preparation. She wouldn't ring Sam until she could figure out something to offer him—

Her phone vibrated in her hand, and Sam's picture popped up even larger. Her breathing hitched.

Incoming call from Samuel Payton.

CHAPTER 5

K imberly dropped the phone onto the sticky vinyl couch cushion. No no no no no no no. She wasn't ready.

The phone continued to buzz. How could he be calling her right now, as she sat here thinking about him? She hadn't figured out what she was going to say. Her mind always blanked when she wasn't prepared.

The buzzing stopped. She released her breath and inhaled a fresh lungful of cinnamon-scented air.

It started again.

Kimberly picked up the phone and held it out like it was going to bite her. She wasn't ready to talk to him.

Riiiiiiiing.

Not that she'd admit it to another living soul, but Sam's departure from Wildfire had hurt her worse than a wax strip on sunburn. When she'd first joined Wildfire, she'd literally moved across the country for a chance to work with Sam. From the moment she'd seen him preach to a church auditorium of fourteen-year-old punks from the east end of LA—and convert a third of them on the spot—she'd known he was something special. And when she googled his ministry and saw the appalling web copy, difficult-to-use support page, and incorrect email address, she'd known his organization needed someone. Someone who could see an undervalued resource and help it reach its full potential. Someone with vision, patience, and grit.

What they got was her—and two out of three qualities ain't bad.

But over the next several years—especially after she was promoted to be Sam's equal—Kimberly had learned there was something even worse than the unrequited crush she'd carried for Archie Masterson for six years.

Unrequited admiration.

Hopeless love she could deal with. It wasn't like she expected anyone to fall head over heels for her patented brand of blunt honesty and eternal stubbornness. But she'd hoped beyond hope that Sam could respect her as a teammate, even a partner in crime. Not regard her with a suspicion that sliced her soul.

I don't trust you. I don't want you. You have no place here.

He would never have intentionally hurt her, but every rebuff, every microexpression, every argument spoke more clearly than a megaphone. She'd suffered death by a thousand cuts over a period of three and a half years. And now Steph wanted her to "win him back."

Her mind paged through Dad's creative collection of curses, yet none fully expressed this moment.

Riiiiiiing.

Might as well get it over with.

She tucked her legs beneath her, clenched her teeth, and pressed the Answer button. "Hello?"

"I don't expect you to say yes to this." Sam launched into his sentence without so much as a "G'day." "But my sister—Ow! Jules, cut it out."

What on earth was happening over there? Kimberly pressed the phone closer to her ear.

"We wondered—" Sam stopped, like he was choking on the words. "Our farm's having some cash-flow problems. Cash flow's kinda your thing, so we wondered if we could get some . . . advice."

Kimberly blinked. He was calling to ask for her help?

Sam must've taken her stunned silence the wrong way, because he started talking faster than a thirteen-year-old on Red Bull. "This is stupid. You don't know anything about farming. I don't expect you to do this—Ow, *Jules*, I will take away that crutch."

A jostle, a clatter, and a woman's voice. "Hello? Kimberly?"

"Um, yes?"

"I'm Jules, Sam's—"

"Sister." A smile spread over Kimberly's face. She'd always dreamed of having a sibling herself and had forever been curious about Jules, the sister who ran the Payton farm by herself in Australia.

She sounded like the kind of girl Kimberly would like to meet.

"Is there anything we can offer you to get some of those great ideas that Sam loves to complain about?"

A straight talker. Good.

"Yes. Your brother."

A chortle. "I knew it."

Jules leaned away from her brother's grasp as he joined her on the worn leather couch, trying to listen to Kimberly's proposal. This morning Jules had swapped to an *Island Breeze* pineapple-and-coconut candle that now flickered from its place on the bargain TV cabinet Mum had found at the dump shop. The delightful combination smelled of hope.

And if Jules didn't cling to her hope tighter than a baby koala to its mother, she'd implode.

"Six weeks?" She eyed Sam, who leaned in her direction, obviously trying to eavesdrop. She palmed his face away. "I think that sounds fair."

He shook her hand off as his brow furrowed in her direction, the question clear in his expression. *Six weeks of what?* He edged closer and cocked his ear toward the phone. "Jules, what are you doing?"

If she could jump up and run away with the phone, she would. The cast on her leg prevented that, so she used it to her advantage—Sam leaned closer, and she flinched like he'd bumped it. "Ow!"

He leapt away, mouthed *Sorry*, and kept his distance. She scratched her lip to cover a smile and tuned back into Kimberly's voice on the phone.

"—we close down on the sixteenth for Christmas, and I can work long distance for several weeks before that. That'd give me a month."

Sam bounced in his seat. "What's she saying?"

Jules plugged her other ear. "That sounds fantastic."

Sam set his jaw. "What sounds fantastic?"

She shooed him like a fly.

He grabbed the phone from her and pressed it to his ear just as Kimberly said, "See you in a week." The volume was high enough that Jules caught the words.

Beep. Call ended.

She snapped a mental picture of Sam's face. Priceless.

He put down the phone and glowered at her. "'*See you in a week*'?"

Jules struggled to her feet, the worn wooden floor more slippery than she'd like beneath her one socked foot and crutches. "Believe it or not, I've made a deal in the best interests of everybody."

"What deal?" Sam's dark expression demonstrated a disturbing lack of trust in her sisterly wisdom as he stood to face her down.

Jules set her jaw. He had to know she wasn't negotiating on this. "Kimberly's going to investigate our situation and help us get back on the right track. Guaranteed." She poked a finger into his chest. "In exchange for you."

He stared at her, silent, for a full three seconds. "Slavery's not legal, you know." His answer was glib, but the set of his jaw—anything but.

Good thing she'd turned stubbornness into an art form. "You go back to Wildfire for six weeks and help her find and train your replacement. Apparently she's had some trouble filling your shoes. Six weeks, then you can come home or gallivant around the world or whatever tickles your fancy." She paused and let the news sink in. Six weeks, yes, but hopefully longer. As much as she loved having Sam here, she'd never seen her brother so happy as when he was spreading God's love to teens at Wildfire. He'd been born for it. And he was in a rut here.

So maybe some sisterly meddling could get him back on track.

"There has to be another way."

"One that doesn't cost money? No." She folded her arms and

watched him. You could practically see the cogs whirring in his brain, searching for some way—any way—out of this. But he'd have to reach the same conclusion she had: this was their best shot.

He ran a hand over his hair, expression resigned. "Six weeks? And I only recruit and train? I don't run Wildfire or her expansion or anything crazy?"

"Cross my heart."

"Why did she say, 'See you in a week'?"

"Wildfire closes down for two weeks over Christmas. I suggested Kimberly spend those two weeks here, give us a hand while she works out how to free up some more cash."

Sam's expression looked as though she'd invited the Grinch himself.

She added the kicker. "And then she said that up until their Christmas break starts, she can work for Wildfire remotely. So just over a month, all up. That'll give her time to really dig into our situation."

Sam's eyebrows couldn't go any higher. "Why would you suggest that? The plane ticket alone would've paid those wages. And it's still money we don't have."

"I pitched it as a 'Come and see the real Australia' holiday and left it up to her. She agreed in about five seconds. She's paying for her ticket."

He rubbed his hand over his face. "Oh boy."

She tutted at his doubt and used her crutches to hobble into the kitchen so that Sam didn't see the change in her expression. She could only maintain the cheerful facade for so long. This was one hurdle cleared. Only a few hundred thousand more to go.

This girl had better live up to all of Sam's complaining or they were doomed.

CHAPTER 6

J ules hopped down the house's front stairs after Sam returned
to the paddocks and hustled toward the four-wheeled motorbike that sparkled in the morning sun like a golden chariot to
freedom. She'd completed one hard task this morning, and
now she needed an hour without her overbearing brother to do
another.

She glanced around one last time to see if she'd escaped
undetected. Kilometers of farmland sizzled before her in late
November's annual attempt to give every living creature a cracking case of sunburn. Cows mooed. Chickens *buuuurGERK*ed.
And no sound from Sam. Thank goodness.

Because he really wouldn't like what she was about to do.

With eleven hundred acres to roam on, she'd never felt more
trapped than the week since she'd busted her foot. And Sam had
been all "Don't overexert yourself" and "Put down that sledgehammer." Who needed that?

She shoved her crutches onto the black metal rack on the
back of the bike and managed to swing her casted leg over the
seat. Okay, hardest part over. She settled down. The black plastic seat, heated by the sun's over-enthusiastic rays, scorched the
backs of her thighs. Denim shorts were great for being easy to pull

on over her bad leg but bad for hot-seat protection. She hissed her breath between her teeth, flicked the key over, and hit the electric start button.

Nothing. Flippin' fantastic.

Jules maneuvered back off the bike, stood on her good leg, and gave the pull-start cord an aggressive yank. Too aggressive. She wobbled and grasped the handlebars for support as the engine kicked over. *Phew.* That had been close. But at least the engine started.

Movement toward the dairy caught her gaze. Sam. Headed this way.

She leapt onto the bike with all the grace of a three-legged wombat, used her hand to yank up the gear pedal—unfortunately located on the side of her bad leg—and shoved her thumb forward on the accelerator. Kinda hard to see, leaning down with a hand on the gear pedal, but there wouldn't be anything in her way on the driveway. Probably.

The bike zoomed along, and she pushed the throttle till the engine revved. *Vroom.* She yanked the gear pedal up again. *Click.* Second gear. *Vroom. Click. Vroom. Click. Vroom. Click.* She risked a glance back as she cleared the first row of paddocks in top gear. All clear. Sam must've been headed into one of the sheds. Though her Kelpie cattle dog, Meg, raced from the dairy toward her with increasing speed.

She turned her face back into the wind, her old Billabong tank top flapping against her torso, and grinned. Eye-watering speed had never felt so good. The three-kilometer driveway gave her space to open up the engine and take her first deep breath in eight days. And the pleasure of having pulled one over on Sam almost negated the sour taste her present task left on her tongue.

Saying thank you to Mick.

Technically she also owed Mick a "You were right," but Psycho would lactate half-soy extra-foam lattes before that would happen. But she did have to thank him for dragging her unconscious self out of that pen—putting himself within range of Psycho's 560 kilograms of angry cow in the process.

She slowed down at the farm gateway, scooted along the edge of the road for another four kilometers, and headed down the Carrigans' drive with her dog now running alongside her. Hmmm. No need to rush. She eased off her speed as she passed a boom irrigator spraying water onto a sorghum paddock. A mini rainbow emerged from the droplets. She paused to admire it and the sprawling river flats that surrounded her. A thousand shades of brown and green—and even the green had a dirty tinge to it. Dad—technically her stepfather, but the only dad she'd known—used to say he'd never realized how many types of brown there were till he left the US to backpack around Australia. Ironic from a man of his skin tone. But he'd landed a job on their farm as a casual milker, married his lady farmer boss, and spent the next twenty years painting every shade of brown onto his unconventional landscape canvases—sheds, water tanks, gates.

He'd be admonishing her now, if he were here, to quit stalling and get on with it.

A *squark* to her left snapped her attention upward. A cranky-looking magpie eyed her as it perched atop a power line. Jules hit the accelerator. Those black-and-white devil birds could swoop at any moment, especially in spring. She still had a scar on her temple to prove it.

A few minutes later she pulled up in front of the Carrigan family home, a 1960s-era brick affair that she'd practically lived in growing up. A dog yapped inside, probably Mick's ridiculous toy poodle. Meg shot off in that direction.

Clang. The sound came from the direction of the machinery shed. Jules skipped the house and rolled that way. Had Mick returned yet, or was it his dad in the shed? Mick had been temporarily called back to the Gold Coast while she was in hospital. But the grapevine had informed her that he planned to return and keep helping his parents clean up their property before its auction. His father wanted to retire, and with Mick on a different career path, that meant selling.

Another clatter sounded from the shed. Sounded like Mick was fixing something.

Bang.

Or trying to. He'd never been much use with machinery.

"Mick?"

A mumbled curse, then, "Yeah?"

She shuffled around the edge of the shed and viewed the carcass of his old YZ250 motorbike. Yikes. What had he done to it?

"Yes?" His testy tone brought her attention back to where he perched on an upturned bucket, both grease and a sour expression on his face. Almost enough to make his blue eyes, faun hair, and boyish freckles unattractive.

Almost.

She summoned all the humility she could from every molecule of her body. Hopefully it'd be enough. "I just came to thank you. For last week. You know, pulling me out of the pen."

He glared at her and attacked the bike again with a socket drive. "I hope it was worth it."

She blinked. His tone seethed. Tension stiffened her muscles as she snapped out a "What?"

"Your stinking pride or independence or whatever else it was that made you climb into that pen." He rubbed a hand through close-cropped curls, smearing another streak of grease.

Her temperature climbed a notch, but he'd come to her rescue, so a jab to the nose wouldn't be good form. However tempting it might be. She set her jaw. "My pride is the only thing that keeps the bank away from my property. I had my best milker to save."

Mick tossed the socket drive aside. The *clank* of metal on concrete reverberated in the corrugated-iron shed. "And instead you got a busted leg. Like I said, hope it was worth it."

The thud of her heartbeat pounded in her ears. "You wouldn't say that to any man who made the decision I did."

Mick emitted a short, humorless *Ha!* "That's not what this is about. This is a Julia-Payton-values-her-cows-more-than-her-life thing."

Heat flooded Jules's chest, neck, face, and hands. What would he know about fighting for his family's heritage? Persisting through the droughts, floods, fires, loneliness, and bad internet speeds? Mick wasn't going to preserve his father's meticulous fence lines, prized breeders, or the back-paddock tree with a carving of his and Jules's initials. No, he'd chosen his easy life at the coast over his dad's farm, and over her. Just as she'd chosen her lifestyle over him. "You're just mad because I picked them instead of you." She spat the words out.

Oh no. Mistake.

"I'm what?" A series of expressions flashed across his features. Eyebrows up, surprise. Eyes crinkled, scorn. Relaxed back to neutrality. Dismissal.

Something pierced the bubble of emotion inside her. His concern, while annoying, had also been . . . comforting. He'd been worried. Her rigid posture drained away, and she scoured her brain for words that could fix this.

Mick sat back on his bucket and picked up a screwdriver. "Go back to your cows, Jules. Unlike me, they'll be happy to see you."

CHAPTER 7

This was a terrible plan.

Kimberly twisted the strap of her handbag as she stood by a park bench and flickering streetlight and watched the bus that had deposited her here roar off into the night. Though maybe the old diesel engine's struggle into third gear only sounded like a roar compared to the utter lack of other noise. The town of Burradoo at 3:00 a.m. had about as much life in it as the lump of pungent roadkill that lay next to the town's welcome sign.

She scanned the main street in both directions. Lit by a full moon, Burradoo appeared to consist of single-story tin-roofed buildings scattered along both sides of a minor highway, with two notable exceptions: the sprawling two-story pub in the center of town and the twenty-foot-tall fiberglass orange located opposite.

Kimberly blinked at the gigantic fruit.

Yep. It really was a massive orange, topped by a short stem and one leaf. It rested beside a dilapidated shack with the optimistic sign *Tourist Information Centre.* Yikes. Could there be any explanation for this phenomenon besides an abundance of spare time, a lack of amusement, and possibly something nefarious in the water?

A rustle stirred in a bush nearby. Kimberly dragged her eyes from the orange and scanned the park behind her. She'd made the mistake of watching *Wolf Creek* last week as part of her learn-Aussie-culture-via-movies initiative and now had a phobia of strangers who offered to help stranded travelers.

No further rustles. Probably just a bird, not a deranged serial killer. Or a lunatic obsessed with oranges.

She wiped wet palms on the legs of her jeans. Even at this hour she was sweating. But surely Sam wouldn't leave her stranded here till morning. She'd sent her estimated arrival time when she boarded the first bus back in Brisbane twelve hours and two transfers ago.

But who was she kidding? Sam would probably love nothing more than to leave her perspiring on a chewing-gum-covered bench for a few hours. He certainly hadn't sounded enthusiastic about her arrival. But whatever. She should be immune to his jabs by now.

She huffed and wiped her hands again. It had to be at least eighty degrees, and every breath she took carried the weight of humidity. This kind of weather in the final days of November was obscene.

She checked her phone. The Australian SIM card she'd purchased in the airport had worked earlier, so that couldn't be the issue. No service. Terrific. She was in the middle of town, for goodness' sake. She dropped the phone back into her bag.

Headlights swung onto the road a hundred yards away. Kimberly's stomach performed a triple pirouette. Maybe her over-active sweat glands had more to do with a disgruntled Australian preacher than this un-Christmassy weather. She fought the urge to sprint after the long-gone bus.

Eighty yards.

There was no way this could work. Sam had made his feelings pretty clear by resigning. Apparently leaving the ministry he founded was preferable to working with her and her expansion plan. Maybe she should have taken that hint.

No. Think positive.

Fifty yards.

Perhaps in a different setting, such as his home turf, she could figure out what it was that made them clash so much. Maybe they'd work out a permanent truce. Maybe he'd remember everything awesome about Wildfire and come back to where he belonged.

A pinball of fear pinged around her consciousness. *Or maybe he'll confirm that I was the problem all along.*

Thirty yards.

She gritted her teeth and kicked a bottle cap into the street. Stuff Sam and his opinions. All she'd ever done was give Wildfire the best she had to offer: her brain and determination. If he had a problem with that, then she didn't give a flying purple baboon. And if she'd spent the week after he left tearfully watching every sci-fi series in her collection, then that was just a coincidence.

Five yards.

Time for Prayer of Desperation #23. *Oh God oh God oh God oh God oh God oh God oh God oh God.*

The pickup truck crunched to a halt on the loose gravel scattered at the roadside, and a familiar figure stepped out of the vehicle. Kimberly squinted. The darkness and intensity of the headlights as he crossed in front of the vehicle obscured his expression.

Time slowed as he paused in front of her and the yellow light finally illuminated him. Him, his moleskin pants, and the cotton shirt that flexed over his folded arms. He could've passed for Hugh Jackman's younger brother in the movie *Australia*. Her breath left her in a rush.

She'd managed to convince herself in the last six months that, taking into account his irritating personality, she would no longer find the disarray of his hair endearing, his open expression trustworthy, or his ready smile comforting.

She'd been an idiot.

And if that triple threat wasn't enough—"Welcome to Australia."

Oh, that voice. A shiver danced between Kimberly's shoulder blades. It was enough to make a girl throw her passport into the Pacific.

"Thanks." She squeaked the word out and tugged her suitcase off the bench. It slammed into the back of her leg, the plastic wheel catching her ankle bone. She bit back a yelp and hefted it up, eyeing the height of the truck.

"I'll take it." Sam plucked the case from her hands and easily swung it into the truck bed. "Hope you don't mind it getting dusty in the back of the ute."

Kimberly looked at the vehicle. "Ute?"

"The truck. Aussies call them utes."

"Oh."

So far it appeared she was only capable of one syllable at a time. She squinted at the side of the truck—of the ute—and attempted an entire sentence. "Do all utes have landscape paintings on the sides of them?" Hard to tell in the dark, but there seemed to at least be a tree, a lake, and a cow depicted across the side of the vehicle.

Sam crossed back to the driver's side. "My dad was a bit of an artist, and he didn't believe his canvas had to be restricted to an actual canvas."

Kimberly processed the information as she climbed into the truck. She'd known that the man Sam called Dad was actually his American-born stepfather. The artist bit was new info.

She jiggled her knee as Sam fired up the engine and pulled onto the road—the left side of the road. She gripped the door handle.

"Does it freak you out, sitting on the other side?" Sam's question held a hint of laughter.

"Nope."

"Liar."

She acquiesced with a small grin. "How do you swap back and forth? Driving must be terrifying at first."

"The first road I drove on in the US was a fourteen-lane highway in LA. I learned fast. But out here"—he gestured with one hand as they reached the edge of town—"the only things you really need to guard against are kangaroos and falling asleep."

"Legit? Kangaroos?" She sat up straighter and scanned the roadside.

"Yup. There's old mate from last week." Sam pointed.

She'd known him long enough to realize the term *old mate* could refer to almost anyone, from a weird-looking spider in his desk drawer to a head of state on the television. She followed his gesture to the unrecognizable lump at the *Welcome to Burradoo* sign.

"Oh." She deflated.

"Don't worry, you'll see live ones too."

She sat back in her seat and relaxed for the first time since touching down in the southern hemisphere. "Thanks for coming to get me in the middle of the night."

"What's a two a.m. wake-up among friends?"

Friends. Kimberly smiled and rummaged in her handbag for her notebook and its list of Awkward Silence Busters. A little something she'd prepared on the plane, given her less-than-mediocre conversation skills and desperate need to make this work.

At least things were looking good so far. It had been two whole minutes, and not only had she sensed no hint of unpleasantness, but Sam had—for the first time ever—called her his friend. Maybe a different hemisphere did make a difference. Maybe Sam was open to working with her.

Maybe she did have a hope.

Sam rubbed a hand through his hair and eyed Kimberly's dozing form as they zoomed along the dark highway. The radio droned on and on, tonight's topic something about the developmental benefits of teaching young children nursery rhymes. He'd bet the nursery rhyme never said the three little pigs offered to drive the big bad wolf to their home in a 1993 Toyota Hilux and let it stay a month.

Maybe those pigs were smarter than he was. Or at least smarter than Jules. He'd warned his sister this was a bad idea of wolflike proportions. At the time, she'd rolled her eyes and turned up the volume on her episode of *The Ranch*. So now his nemesis lay as relaxed as a cat in the passenger seat beside him, somehow smelling of some fruity girl deodorant and not a day in an airplane. About to "Kim" all over his perfect Kim-less refuge.

No amount of delightful scent could compensate for that.

He'd managed to keep up a friendly facade for the first few minutes until jet lag won out and Kimberly dozed off. Now his smile melted away faster than a rainbow Paddle Pop ice cream on Christmas Day.

Kimberly wouldn't know the first thing about a farm, especially an Aussie one. She wouldn't know that if a cow's nose looked purple it indicated poisoning or how to make an electrolyte solution for a sick calf or a thousand other things. So what on earth was she doing here?

He blasted the air-conditioning on his face. Staying awake during the forty-minute drive was always a challenge, and the heat rising on his neck did nothing to improve his mood.

Kimberly opened her eyes and stretched, her simple gray T-shirt tugging against her form. She looked even better in casual clothes than the office attire he used to see her in.

He focused on the endless white lines on the road and told his brain to shut up.

Paper crinkled as she fiddled with a notebook in her lap. "I was really glad you contacted me about this." Her tone warm as honey, she actually sounded sincere.

Sam pressed his lips together to stop the response that leapt to his tongue and gave a noncommittal shrug. He didn't buy the line about looking forward to an "authentic Australian experience." If she wanted an Aussie holiday, she'd go to the Opera House and Bondi Beach, just like all the other tourists. No, this "holiday" was about more than six weeks of his time. She probably wanted to talk him into a permanent return. And poke her nose into his family business while she was at it.

No sirree.

"Your sister sounds great. I can't wait to meet her. I've already been going over some of the financial information she sent me."

Sam tightened his grip on the steering wheel, lumps of dried mud rubbing between his fingertips and the plastic. Farm vehicles didn't exactly stay pristine.

"And if you want me to look at anything else while—"

"Look, let's drop the act. This was Jules's idea, and we both know I warned her against it." The words burst out with more energy than necessary.

Kimberly stilled.

He cringed as the silence stretched but fought the urge to backpedal. Silence was Kim's favorite method of destroying her opponent. No way would he succumb.

Again, that is.

"Message received." The warmth drained from her voice, leaving the professional detachment he knew so well. *Now* he was talking to the real Kimberly.

"I'm just saying, I know you never stop at 'helping' with one issue. You'll want to reengineer everything." He made an effort to soften his voice and thus the next words. "But if you want my help talking my sister into some scheme of yours, don't count on it."

"Thanks for the vote of confidence." Her stiff posture shouted, "*Jerk*."

Great. As usual, she'd overreacted. But he needed to set expectations.

Silence was better than all the responses that formed on his tongue, and it appeared to also be Kimberly's retaliation of choice. And yet over the next twenty-five kilometers her rigid posture wilted into the seat and her breathing evened out. By the time Sam pulled up at the house, the breaths bordered on soft snores.

He snickered to himself and exited, taking a moment to survey the house with fresh eyes. The wooden structure built by his great-grandfather rested on stumps high enough to allow flood-waters to pass below. Its cream paint and maroon accents stood as evidence of Dad's meticulous attitude toward home maintenance, just as the sagging third step testified to Jules's lack of time to spare. Built in the traditional Queenslander style, the home had a wide veranda that'd been enclosed sometime in the 1960s and a corrugated-iron roof that accentuated the sound of possum footsteps at night. A feature Kimberly would discover soon enough.

He moved to the tray of the ute. She'd probably wake when he dragged her suitcase down.

But when he pulled her door open for her, she was still out cold. Sam paused for a moment. She looked younger in her sleep. Kimberly awake projected nothing but confidence and professionalism. But relaxed in the passenger seat, her perpetual frown smoothed out and her aura of invulnerability melted away.

Which one was the real Kimberly?

Her notebook tumbled from her lap to the dust at his feet. He picked it up, and a word caught his eye. *Jules.*

He stared at the page of neat handwriting for a moment, curious, but with his dyslexia, decoding the letters on a full night's sleep and in daylight would be a chore. With tired eyes and moon-light? Impossible.

Plus it was snooping.

"Hey."

He jerked his gaze up. Kimberly, still blinking sleep from her eyes, pulled her notebook out of his hands. Sam cleared his throat. "It fell out. We're here."

Kimberly glanced down at the notebook and shifted in the seat, her expression embarrassed. "I get tongue-tied when I'm nervous. It helps to write down things I want to say." She pushed past him, scooped up her suitcase, and headed toward the house.

Sam stared after her. That's what the notebook had held—conversation prompts? And Kimberly got *nervous*? The woman was the epitome of poise. And she had a killer stare that, combined with those long pauses before she answered something, was great at making you feel really stupid. As if he needed any more help in feeling stupid.

But had she just been tongue-tied?

He jogged a couple of steps to catch up with her, tugging the suitcase from her hands and sweeping a palm toward the stairs. "After you." As he trudged up the steps behind her, she paused and cooed at Meg, their cattle dog. Everything about her posture softened.

Maybe she really—no. Nuh-uh. He shook off his stupor. They had years of history. He knew Kimberly Foster, and she wasn't welcome here.

CHAPTER 8

"I found her!"

The shout pierced Kimberly's consciousness and dragged her from a dark, calm place. Awareness came in at a trickle. She hadn't been able to sleep. After Sam had pointed her to a spare room and mumbled something about getting the cows in for milking, she'd been too worked up over their argument to rest. Each time she closed her eyes, her overtired mind tossed out accusing questions she couldn't answer.

Why did I ever think things would be different? What am I doing on the other side of the world? What will I do if I fail?

I'm definitely going to fail.

So she'd pulled on workout shorts and an old *Star Wars* T-shirt, sneaked out of the house, and found that adorable cattle dog she'd seen on her way in.

Now, an ache radiated from her neck. Something soft, warm, and furry shifted beneath her hand. She must've dozed off patting the dog. A fly buzzed near her open mouth, and she snapped it shut, cracked her eyelids open, and encountered the smiling face of Julia Payton.

"Hey there, Kimalicious. Nice to finally meet you."

It was like staring at the daughter of Crocodile Dundee. Wide green eyes looked back at her from beneath a battered hat. A braid the color of straw draped over the sleeve of Jules's loose work shirt, and the belt on her denim shorts held a pocketknife less impressive than Mick Dundee's but probably far more practical. She gripped crutches beneath each arm. Kimberly's gaze traveled down to a scuffed-up cast, now more a dusty shade of brown than white.

Jules rapped on the plaster. "Trading this bad boy in tomorrow for a moon boot. Just think how much mischief I'll get into when Sam's not looking."

Kimberly snickered and sat up straighter. What had been digging into her back? She took in the detached garage she'd fallen asleep in. Dirt floor. A stack of various tires behind her. Approximately nine million cobwebs. She jerked away from the tires as *Crocodile Hunter* episodes featuring nasty arachnids sprang to mind.

Jules stuck out a hand and, despite the crutches, managed to pull Kimberly to her feet. Kimberly flexed her hand, crushed from Jules's grip, and tried to shake off the fogginess of sleep. "Hey—"

Jules held up a hand, then turned, put her fingers in her mouth, and let loose a brain-exploding whistle. Kimberly clapped her hands over her ears, wincing, and the corner of Jules's mouth twitched. "Sorry. Sam's just over at the yards looking for you, and I don't think he heard me shout."

Kimberly lowered her hands. "Looking for me?"

"You left your bedroom door open. We could see you weren't in bed. And we couldn't find you anywhere. I must've missed this spot in my first check."

Heat rushed up Kimberly's neck and pooled in her cheeks. "Oh. Sorry. I just came out to pat the dog and must've dozed off."

"Or fallen into a mild coma." Jules grinned. "We've been shouting your name for forty minutes."

Kill me now. Kimberly rubbed her forehead. Not the first impression she'd wanted to make. "Sorry. Jet lag."

"Not a problem. Welcome to Yarra Plains, aka absolute paradise." Jules gestured to the farm around them with a wide sweep of her arm.

Kimberly took in her surroundings properly. The house yard was surrounded with dusty tracks that led to fields on the east side, where a row of trees lined the farm a mile away. Maybe a river? On the other side sat a series of tin sheds—one of them, she assumed, the dairy. Not a barn in sight, and no other man-made structures for as far as she could see.

Kimberly sucked in a deep breath of fresh country air—and wrinkled her nose. Ick. The breeze carried the smell of the dairy. Still, there was something amaz—

A fly dive-bombed down her windpipe.

Kimberly coughed like she was trying to expel a lung. Gross. No choice but to swallow it down. She grimaced and straightened just as Sam stomped around the corner, his moleskins now filthy and an extra button on his work shirt undone.

"Where have you been hiding?" His frown flickered into amusement for a brief moment when his gaze landed on her *Moods of Darth Vader* T-shirt.

Jules waved her brother off with a crutch. "She fell asleep patting the dog. No need to get your knickers in a knot." She glanced at Kimberly. "I'm off to shift the dry cows." She moved toward the four-wheeler parked in the garage.

Kimberly eyed Sam. He took the bait in an instant. "Like heck you are. No motorbikes with a broken foot."

Jules rolled her eyes so hard Kimberly had to choke back a laugh. "It's a *four*-wheeler, not a two."

"Can't change gears with that foot." Sam pointed to the foot pedal on the left side of the bike.

"You're such an old woman. I'll just reach down and use my hand."

"Is that how the front bars got bent? You were leaning down to change gears when you hit that post?"

Jules winced. "Kim can drive me. You wanna come?"

Have a chance to prove herself helpful and spend time with Sam's firecracker sister who probably had juicy dirt on him? "Of course." Kimberly sent her sweetest smile to Sam. "We've got it covered."

"Do you know how to drive that?"

"Would I offer if I didn't . . . ?"

He narrowed his eyes and turned away.

Kimberly muttered the remainder of the sentence low enough that only Jules could hear it. ". . . have every confidence that Jules can either teach me or drive awesomely with a broken leg?"

Jules snorted out a laugh. "Good enough for me. Let's get moving."

Twenty minutes later, Kimberly was chasing cows around a field and had learned the basics of four-wheelers, the Queensland Maroons rugby league team's glorious history, and the fact that Jules Payton was her new favorite person in the world.

". . . and that unfortunately placed leech is the reason why Sam really, really hates swimming in dams." Jules snickered at her own story and then tapped Kimberly's arm. "This is where I hop off."

Kimberly stopped the four-wheeler and seized the chance

to survey the landscape again, keeping one eye out for snakes. Every person she'd told about this trip had warned her about Australia's proliferation of poisonous animals, and Jules had pointed out a deadly brown snake slithering from the track as they drove here.

But the scenery was just too distracting to keep her eyes in the grass. Was the sky this wide and blue back home? "Why?"

Jules pointed up ahead at a dam. "We call that dam the 'turkey's nest' because the walls are built up instead of digging the dam down in the ground. At least three sides are. The fourth's a natural rise. Use that one to get up on top of the others and chase that cow out." A single beast stood atop the dirt wall of the turkey's nest between the water and the fence that ran along the edge of the wall. "My weight"—Jules hopped off the metal bars she'd been perched on at the rear of the bike—"will stuff up your balance when you drive up the slope."

Kimberly eased her thumb back onto the four-wheeler's accelerator. It surged beneath her. She still wasn't great at controlling the speed.

"Careful of the fence," Jules called out after her. "It's electric."

She managed the incline of the wall okay and crept along the top of it—barely as wide as the four-wheeler—in second gear. She glanced across the water to her right. It sure looked idyllic with that giant eucalyptus tree next to the water. And was that—she zeroed in on a flicker of movement behind the tree—a kangaroo? She released the accelerator and just let the vehicle roll. The faun-colored marsupial bounced toward the fence and hopped over it with ease. Kimberly's eyes tracked its progress as it bounced across the next field with impressive speed.

Zap.

Something punched her knee, surged through her body, and zapped her left thumb where it touched the four-wheeler's metal handlebars. Then again. She jerked away, turning the handlebars as her gaze landed on something brown and twisty in the grass. Was that a—"Snake!" She squealed and shoved her right thumb forward on the accelerator. The four-wheeler leapt away from the electric fence and veered right, down the bank. Kimberly clung to the handlebars as the vehicle gave a sickening lurch and then—

Splash.

Water, cool and murky, enveloped her. She pushed away from the four-wheeler, gave two strong kicks, and broke the surface.

"Kim! Kim, are you alright?" Jules's words came from beyond Kimberly's line of sight, past the north bank.

Kimberly blinked the water from her eyes and treaded water. Holy smokes. She'd just crashed the four-wheeler into the water.

Sam was going to kill her. If the snake didn't first.

Jules's head popped over the edge of the bank.

"Snake!" Kimberly waved and pointed with one arm as the other kept her afloat.

Jules—the madwoman—went toward the reptile. Stopped. Threw her head back and laughed. "Stick!"

Kill me now.

Kimberly sank in the water till only her eyes were visible. Could she have made a stupider mistake? And with such an expensive piece of equipment?

After a moment during which she contemplated never leaving the confines of the water, she swam toward Jules and clambered up onto land, her hands and feet sinking into soft mud, leaves, and reeds as she did so. Yuck. Hopefully that leech story wouldn't repeat itself. "I am so sorry, Jules. So, so sorry."

"But are you alright?"

Kimberly waved off her concern, face burning with mortification despite the cool water. "I'm fine." And she was. If only she could convince her thrashing heart that it was true. "I'm so sorry," she repeated.

Jules surveyed the bubbles coming up from the trashed four-wheeler. "Sam can get it out with the tractor."

Kimberly smeared the coarse mud from her palms onto her sodden shorts, dread tightening her throat. "Can you call him?"

Jules shook her head. "No reception out here. You'll have to walk back and bring Sam, the tractor, and the ute."

Kimberly looked back the way they'd come. The house was a couple of miles away. "I'll jog and be back as fast as I can."

Jules offered an encouraging smile. "I'll be here. Actually I'll be under the tree." She pointed toward the only shade in the field, that towering eucalyptus, and hobbled in that direction.

Kimberly stood and inspected herself. Adrenaline still whipped her pulse into a frenzy, and tears lurked in her ducts. She sucked in deep breaths and recalled her mother's voice. *Crying is irrational.*

Water ran in rivulets down her entire body, and mud clung to her hands and legs. She took a step, and her boot—borrowed from Jules—squelched. She looked back up at the house. At least two miles, with a jet-lagged body and wet shoes.

And waiting at the end, an angry Sam.

Oh joy.

CHAPTER 9

Sam wasn't at the house.

A trickle of sweat ran down Kimberly's temple as she jogged from the home to the sheds. The truck was still here, so he couldn't have left the property. She scratched her head, and her already sunburned scalp stung. Mosquito bites on her ankle itched. The mud on her skin cracked as she moved. And this was still the end of November—not even official summer yet. No wonder so many Australians rejected the rural stereotype and elected to live at the coast.

Thud-thud.

The sound of a rhythmic beating came from a tin shed next to what might have been the dairy. She veered toward the three-sided structure with farm machinery spilling out of the open fourth side. "Sam!"

"Over here." He appeared from behind a tractor, sweaty and face as red as her favorite hot peppers. One look at her and he sprinted in her direction. "What's wrong? Where's Jules?" He stripped boxing gloves from his hands as he ran—she must've interrupted a workout.

An imp awoke in the back of her brain. *Shame to have missed the spectacle.*

Where had that thought come from? She rested her hands on

her knees and focused on sucking in air. Must be a side effect of oxygen deprivation. She really shouldn't have skipped those gym sessions over the past few months.

Sam reached her within the span of two breaths, and Kimberly wheezed out the story, along with about a thousand apologies and assurances that both she and Jules were fine. The relief on his face was chased by a very different emotion. He ran his hands through his hair.

"Which side of the turkey's nest?" The way he ground the words out reinforced the ones shouting through her mind: *You're meant to be here solving problems, not throwing four-wheelers into dams.*

She swallowed down any reaction and sketched out the exact spot in the dirt. He nodded. "Keys for the ute are in it. I'll meet you there."

By the time he got the slow-moving tractor down to the turkey's nest, Kimberly had already ferried Jules back to the house and returned. Quite a feat, considering she was driving a manual vehicle with its driver's seat on the wrong side. Taxi service completed, she walked from the truck toward where Sam stood staring at the water, which lay still save the occasional bubble. She grimaced. What was down there?

"I thought you said you knew how to drive a bike." The frustration in his tone snapped her out of her embarrassment and put her on the offensive. It hadn't been intentional, and she'd flown across the world to help him. She needed at least another six hours of sleep before she could deal with this kind of attitude.

She narrowed her eyes at him. "It wasn't just the stick. Your fence also tried to electrocute me. Why's it so close to the edge?"

Sam dropped the chain in his hand and grabbed the fence.

There was a faint *tick-tick-tick* as the current zapped him. "Yeah, that's real agony."

Kimberly blinked. That had to hurt, didn't it? Or maybe it was just the unexpectedness of it that she'd found so unpleasant. Either way, she couldn't let him win. She raised an eyebrow at Sam and put her palm on the wire without hesitation.

Tick-tick-tick.

She kept her face a mask of indifference, but it took effort. The fence felt like a giant rubber band flicking her hand and sending its shock waves up her arm three times every second.

The corner of Sam's mouth tipped up. "It hurts less if you touch the ground at the same time."

She reached down, but he released the fence and grabbed her fingers. She jerked her gaze up, hand captured in both of his. Amusement danced behind his layer of irritation. "Don't believe everything I say. It'd probably knock you off your feet." He released her and turned to look at the water with a mixture of loathing and resignation, then grabbed the hem of his shirt and stripped it over his head.

Kimberly jolted like she'd been zapped again. Oh, mama, but that boy looked good. She blinked to redirect her traitorous eyes. *We're meant to be mad at him.* "What are you doing?"

He picked up the chain. "Attaching this to the bike."

With his hatred of swimming in dams? She didn't need to give him yet another reason to be unhappy with her. Moving quickly, she kicked off her boots and socks and curled her toes against the sharp grasses and stones beneath her tender skin. "Uh-uh. I made the mess, I'll clean it up. And I'll pay for any repairs it needs." She plucked the chain from his hand and jumped from the bank before he could protest.

Splash.

Kimberly popped up, though that was harder with the heavy chain in hand, and paddled over to where the four-wheeler had gone down. She blew out a breath to discourage the water from sneaking past her lips. Its murky brown quality was something she neither wanted to ponder nor consume. "Where do you want me to attach it?"

Sam's brows pulled together. Didn't he think she could do this? Did he *want* to get another leech on his you-know-what? She shuddered and prayed against a similar fate.

Sam crossed his arms across his bare chest. "Back axle. Loop it around and get the hook back through the chain."

"Alrighty." Kimberly eyed the spot where the four-wheeler should be, sucked in her deepest breath, and plunged down into the unknown.

Sam swatted at flies as the bubbles emerged from where Kim had disappeared beneath the water. She'd been down for at least twenty seconds now. He shifted on his feet. Kimberly's brand of "help" so far in Australia had meant "constant irritation." First with not being able to find her this morning, then the bike, and now . . .

Thirty-five seconds.

The bubbles stopped. He tensed. She'd pop up any second now. Capable Kim—there was no way she could be in any real trouble.

An image flashed before his mind's eye of her limp form caught beneath a watery motorbike, hair fanned out in the water around her. Fear slithered a tentacle around his ribs. He checked his watch.

Sixty seconds.

Sam jumped into the water. He landed in close to the bank, despite the risk of leeches in the reeds. Who knew where Kim might pop up, and he could do some damage if he landed on top of her.

Two quick strokes cleared him of the reeds. He sucked in a breath and duck dived.

Thud.

Pain splintered through Sam's skull. He surfaced, spluttering. As did Kim, hands on her forehead. She glared at him. "What are you doing?"

She's okay.

He blew out a breath of relief and wiped the water from his eyes. "Are you pretending to be a fish? How long were you down there?"

"It was tricky to get the chain secured. I went to state for swimming when I was in high school. I was fine."

Something brushed Sam's leg. He flinched. "That would've been handy to know *before* you spent an eternity under water."

"Do you act like this every time someone does you a favor?"

"Throwing my motorbike into the turkey's nest and then scaring ten years off me is a favor? I'd hate to see how you treat your enemies."

"It was an accident, and I offered to pay for it. You going to sulk forever?" She swam past him toward the bank.

He swiveled to follow, retort on his tongue. But a flash of brown on the bank caught his eye. He grabbed the back of Kim's shirt.

She swatted at him. "What is wrong with you?"

"Snake." He twisted his fist in her shirt and tugged her back, keeping his gaze on the spot, not a meter from their boots.

She froze, began to sink, and then kicked again. "For real?"

"It sure ain't a stick." He put on his best American accent for that one.

Her voice came out strangled. "Where?"

"On the bank. Right there." He'd only caught a glimpse, but he'd seen enough eastern brown snakes—just "brown snakes" to most Aussies—to know exactly what it was. The second most venomous land snake in the world and as common in this part of the country as selfies on social media.

Kimberly's body brushed his as she edged back. His skin goose-pimpled with awareness. "Can they swim?" She whispered.

He put himself between her and the reptile and dodged the question. "We'll just climb out in a different spot." He pointed to the adjacent edge of the turkey's nest, the one that ended in a gradual rise rather than a steep bank. "Head that way."

Kimberly beat him to the edge of the water, mainly because he was scanning for any other unwelcome reptiles. The mud on this side was deep, soft and sticky, and by the time he reached the edge of the water, it had swallowed Kimberly halfway up her thighs. She struggled in vain to get a leg free.

He grinned, still floating in the shallows. "Are you stuck?"

"No, I'm enjoying the scenery." She threw her weight forward. The mud didn't release her leg, but it did give her the wriggle room to fall forward. She put her hands out to break her fall. *Splat.* Mud splashed into her face.

He was pretty sure a little puff of steam emanated from her head. He snickered, then chuckled, then abandoned all restraint and let out a thigh-slapping laugh.

A ball of mud slapped him upside the face. He spluttered a moment, then dunked himself into the shallows and washed the worst of it off. "Not cool, Foster."

She'd stopped struggling now and just stood there, arms folded. "You know what's not cool? We made a deal, and I flew to the other side of the world to hold up my end. And so far I've been jet-lagged, shocked by the fence, wound up in this dam twice, scared by a snake, and now I'm stuck in the mud." She scooped up another ball of muck. "And all you can do is be a jerk and *laugh*." She threw the second handful.

Mud rained down upon Sam, and he ducked under the water to dodge it. "Cut that out." He slithered forward, crocodile-style, spreading his body weight across the mud so he didn't sink in. The slop was coarse and grainy, and bubbles of air escaped it as his hands sank in. Gross. What else lurked in the depths?

By the time he reached Kimberly, still crawling on his belly, she'd stopped her rapid-fire assault. She crossed her arms against her chest tightly, like she was braced for something. She practically vibrated with emotion, but when she spoke her voice didn't so much as waver. "Do you just enjoy being mean to me?"

He didn't stoop to a response—not that he could literally stoop from this position. Scooping some mud away from her knees, he indicated his body position. "Spread your weight out on the mud, like this, then move forward with your hands. It's called a crocodile walk."

She didn't move, didn't so much as blink. Just kept glaring at him. He pursed his lips. "Kim."

She shook her head. "I'm serious. You said, 'Let's drop the act,' so I'm dropping mine. Do you have a specific reason for not liking me—"

"I don't not like you."

"—for not liking anything I say or do—"

That he acknowledged with a begrudging nod.

"—or are you just a jerk?" She raised one eyebrow and just stood there. He pressed his lips together and didn't answer. She tilted her head and held her silence.

"It's my fault the farm's in trouble, okay?" The words burst out. Huh. It actually felt good to say it aloud to someone.

She uncrossed her arms. "How's it your fault? You've only been here about six months."

He pointed to the mud. She gingerly lay flat on it and tried to wriggle forward. Still stuck. He scooted around to where her legs disappeared into the mud and dug some more. "This goes back further than that. The farm being in trouble was the whole reason I moved home."

"The whole—So it had nothing to do with the expansion plan?"

"That helped me see it was time to go, but if Jules hadn't called me, I'd still be in the States right now." Probably. Maybe.

He excavated till he could see a shapely calf. Kimberly went quiet. He scooped away more mud. Had she really thought—"Did you think I left because I didn't support your plan?"

"Since you never explained your reasoning to me and the timing was more than coincidental, yes, I did think that." Her voice was terse.

He stared at her a moment. That had bothered her? He scooted away. "Well, I didn't. Try to move again."

She struggled against the mud and inched forward. "So why is this your fault?"

"Less talking, more moving."

"The more you talk, the more I'll move."

Impossible woman. He crocodile-walked forward, keeping ahead of Kim's progress so he didn't have to look at her. This wasn't a story he wanted to tell anyone, especially Kim. She already operated under the impression that he was an ignorant hick.

How insufferable would she be once she learned she was right?

"I'm waiting."

Sam clenched his teeth. *Keep it brief, get it over with.* "My dad helped me out with some cash when I was younger. To start a business. It didn't go well, he lost his investment, and the farm's never gotten back onto its feet." *And Dad spent the last year of his life trying to fix my mistake, and now Jules is paying the price.*

A heaviness settled over him, the same one he felt every time he thought about the situation. As if the grief of losing Dad wasn't enough, Sam had to grapple with the fact he'd cost Mum and Dad their planned trip around Australia together—something they would've done in the final year of Dad's life if Sam hadn't lost that money on his failed café. That kind of guilt ate at a person.

And now it demanded he listen. As much as he believed they'd survive this rough patch the same way they'd survived every other disaster thrown at them, that nagging voice in the back of his mind refused to be quieted. What if this was the time that the worst happened? What if Jules lost everything? All because he was once an overly enthusiastic twenty-two-year-old?

It seemed to be a pattern that ran in the men of the family.

"That's no more your fault than apparently you leaving Wildfire was mine."

Sam paused. She said what? He risked a glance back.

Kimberly struggled to her feet on semisolid ground. Mud dripped from her chin and elbows and ran in rivulets down her legs. He stood as well and grasped her elbow to steady her as they waded through the last section of mud. "What do you mean?"

Finally, dry land. Kimberly stopped walking and tipped her head back a little to look up at him. The brown mask dripping over half her face gave her an eerie quality. "I mean your dad made a choice, knowing the possibilities. That burden's not yours."

He blinked. If he'd known all he had to do to make Kim nicer was fly her to Australia and throw her in the mud, he'd have done it years ago. She was wrong, but it was still nice. And putting "Kimberly Foster" in the same sentence as "nice" . . . This shifted the status quo into new and awkward territory.

He cleared his throat. "If we stomp around, the snake will feel our vibrations and leave. It'll be safe for us to get our boots." Her face dropped. "For me to get our boots," he amended.

Her answering smile looked different when she wore mud rather than makeup. Or was the difference in him?

Sam stomped his feet against the ground and clapped his hands, heading in the direction of their boots. Wrangling a brown snake was easier than wrangling the muddied woman stomping behind him.

CHAPTER 10

S am had ditched her.

Kimberly pulled a UCLA hoodie over her bleach-stained Linkin Park concert T-shirt and stomped through the house yard toward the dairy as early sunlight washed the sky in shades of baby blue and yellow. Had she not been so irritated, she'd have stopped to enjoy her surroundings—the fresh air, the cacophony of foreign bird calls, the way the plants and color palette differed from the Smallville-esque farms back home. But she'd asked Sam yesterday to take her to the dairy with him and had expected a knock on her door at some heinous hour of the morning. Her watch read 5:30 a.m. And no Sam.

What did he think—that avoiding her when they were both on the same farm would actually work?

She passed by the wide track that led to the dairy yard, where the dog barked at cows entering the enclosure. A man she guessed was the employee they'd mentioned, Butch, drove a truck behind the final stragglers, a cigarette dangling from his lips. A pang of nostalgia wedged in her chest. It could just be the scent of his smoke wafting over her, or maybe his thin profile, but he kinda reminded her of an older version of Dad. Dad and Butch probably would've been around the same age—if Dad hadn't died at twenty-nine.

She forced herself to continue. Wouldn't do any good to weird out the guy by staring at him. And she still hadn't found Sam.

She rewound the past eighteen hours in her head. After recovering their boots, Sam had been . . . pleasant. She'd watched him tow the four-wheeler out of the water and load it onto the truck with the tractor. Seeing him make the heavy machinery dance with his fingers on the controls—and his shirt plastered to his skin—certainly hadn't been a trial. And after she'd had a shower and a nap, he and Jules had crammed her between them in the truck and taken her on a grand tour of the property. She'd spent more than two hours enthralled at every childhood story they told of family, adventure, and perseverance. Their lives had been everything she'd ever dreamed of as a kid, and more.

Then, after watching the sun set over the turkey's nest, they'd returned to the house to make spaghetti Bolognese together and laugh at a comedy from Jules's movie collection. Like they were real friends.

She should've known it wouldn't last.

Kimberly stepped into the dairy's brick-and-concrete vat room—which had been included in yesterday's tour—and found her nemesis bent over a large pipe lying next to a vat. He looked up at her, a surprised expression on his face. "I was just about to come over and get you."

She eyed him with suspicion as she tugged down the sleeves on her hoodie. The temperature had dropped a couple degrees in this room—everything in here was wet cement and metal. "Really?"

He leaned against the large vat beside him. "You think I'd be brave enough to ditch you?"

"It may've crossed my mind."

He quirked an eyebrow. "I know not to antagonize a bulldog."

She propped a hand on her hip. "Bulldogs are adorable and strong, so I'll take that as a compliment."

"As it was intended." He grinned at her.

She blinked. Lighthearted banter? That was a nice change from their usual exchange of eye rolls and threats of bodily harm. Though to be fair, all threats tended to come from her side.

Sam attached the hose in his hands to the vat with a ridiculously large spanner, then straightened. "I thought you might still be jet-lagged. I let you sleep in while I got the cows."

"Oh. Thanks." She'd been up since 3:00 a.m. anyway, both jet lag and Wildfire's pressing to-do list ending her rest.

He led her through to the dairy shed. "You ever been in a dairy before?"

She straightened her spine. "Doesn't mean I can't do the work."

"Take a chill pill. I just didn't want to explain things you already knew." He pointed to two rows of metal stalls and rubber piping separated by a three-foot-deep cement trench between them. "This is a twenty-five-a-side herringbone dairy. The bales"—he pointed to a row of stalls—"are lifted by hydraulics to let the cows out. Makes it faster than just opening one gate at the end."

He led her through the yards, explained the milking machines—which resembled four-legged rubber-and-metal spiders—and finished the tour in the vat room, his finger hovering over a big black button. "This is the fun part."

She licked her lips. Big buttons she couldn't press gave her a twitch in the left eye.

"Wanna press?"

She didn't hesitate, just mashed it flat.

The dairy engine roared to life, the suction pump creating a soothing rhythm, like a heartbeat. The heartbeat of the farm.

A little piece of Sam's heritage lodged itself in Kimberly's heart. This was the sound of the Payton family's passion, reverberating all around her. This was the sound Jules and her parents had based their lives around. This patch of dirt had been watered by the family's sweat and blood for generations.

It was a home. And now she was getting a taste of it for a little while.

"You ready?" Sam held out a plastic apron, securing his own with his other hand. She viewed it askance. "It keeps most of the muck off."

Most. Great.

She accepted the apron, tied it on with a grimace, and put her game face on. "Let's do this."

Butch joined them in the "pit," as Sam called the space between the rows of cows, and milked fifteen cows in the time it took Kimberly to get the cups on her first one. These animals were big, at head height, and they *kicked*. If not for the kick bar at chin level, she'd be wearing a rearranged face.

Sam worked beside her, cupping ten of his own cows as he coached her through the process. His focus on her only increased her jitters.

Finally, the cups slurped up onto the cow's teats and held tight. Kimberly moved onto her second cow. "I'll get faster." The words were more to herself than anyone else.

Sam shrugged. "Duh. You're the fastest learner I've ever seen."

Whoa. Okay, first he was being nice, and now an actual compliment? She sneaked a glance in his direction. Was this just part

of a temporary truce, doomed to evaporate in several weeks, or
something more genuine?

Within several hours she learned the basics of both hand and
machine milking, how to chase cows without getting smushed
against the fence, and the best part of the postmilking routine:
ditching their soiled outer clothes outside and coming in for second breakfast. When some neighbor named Mick dropped by to
talk to Sam, Kimberly scooped up her plate of fragrant scrambled
eggs—laid only yesterday—and retreated. She clamped a hot piece
of buttered toast between her teeth as she headed for the sparse
but clean guest room she'd been given. The toast differed from
America's somehow—blander, maybe? But it tasted decent.

Time to get some more Wildfire work done. It'd be an intense few weeks coming up, maintaining her Wildfire workload
remotely while also looking into Jules and Sam's financial rough
patch.

She had just settled in at the ancient desk with a chair stolen
from the dining table when Jules ducked into the room and eased
the door closed. A bite of egg dropped from Kimberly's mouth, hit
her T-shirt on the way down, and landed on her gym shorts. She
fumbled to rescue it from her lap. "Um—hi."

"You any good at sneaking out?" Jules's question was hushed
and muffled against the door where she pressed her face to peek
through the open crack.

"Umm . . ." Kimberly had never attempted it. Too desperate
for Mom's good opinion—what a waste of Saturday nights that
had turned out to be.

Jules pivoted, a crutch beneath one arm, and flicked her gaze
over Kimberly. "Doesn't matter. All you have to do is get me a
ladder."

Kimberly's eyes flickered between Jules and her brand-new moon boot. Jules tapped it. "Mick's mum took me into the doctor while yous were milking."

Based on Kimberly's twenty-four hours here, *yous* was apparently Australia's version of *y'all*.

Jules brandished her single crutch. "One down. One to go. I can't waste this freedom sitting inside."

"Okaaaaay . . ." Had she missed something obvious here? Jules was again dressed in a work shirt—though today's was a green that highlighted her eyes—and denim shorts. She didn't seem to be going anywhere special.

"I'll be honest with you. That good-looking Irishman out there with a stupid tiny poodle is my ex-boyfriend." Jules hopped closer and lowered her voice. Kimberly shut her laptop lid and leaned toward her. Lightning could strike this house and she wouldn't move till she heard this. And what poodle? She hadn't seen a poodle. "And even though our breakup was more than a decade ago, Mick's slightly infuriated with me over how I broke my foot."

Jules paused, a thoughtful finger on her chin. "And maybe the way I insulted him after." She shrugged. "Either way, the kindest thing to do, obviously, is sneak me out the window rather than parade all this"—she did a full body roll—"past him."

Kimberly grinned. "What do you need me to do?"

CHAPTER 11

Kimberly gripped her pilfered ladder with both hands and watched the moon-booted woman above her maneuver from a bedroom window to the top of an old tin water tank. A purple-flowered vine climbed one side of it and rust holes dotted its surface. Kimberly bit her lip. If Jules died climbing from that tank down onto this Kimberly-supplied ladder, then the Wildfire deal would definitely be off.

"So, I told you about my ex." Jules spoke the words crouching on the tank roof, rubbing at her bad ankle. Disturbed dust floated down and tickled Kimberly's nose. She sneezed. "You wanna tell me about Sam?"

Kimberly snapped to attention. "Oh no, we never—I mean, haven't you seen his face when I—We didn't date." Her watering sinuses gave the words a nasally sound. She sniffed. Ugh. That made it sound like their nondating upset her.

Jules grinned and handed Kimberly her crutch. "That's because he's an idiot. It takes a special lady to sneak a thirty-one-year-old woman with a broken foot out a bedroom window."

Kimberly's face heated, but she couldn't help but return Jules's grin as she propped her crutch against the tank. "I won't deny either point."

"You're here for more than help finding his replacement,

81

though." Jules dropped her hat—with perfect aim—and it plopped onto Kimberly's head. She presented Kimberly with her rear as she backed down the ladder, one painstaking step at a time. She didn't put weight on her bad foot but clung to the ladder and shifted her good foot down each rung. The metal ladder moved and dug into Kimberly's hands. She grunted in her effort to steady it, palms slippery in this humid air and morning sun, and Jules seemed to take it as affirmation. "You want him to come back permanently." She paused her descent to look down at Kimberly.

Kimberly gulped. Jules had only just gotten her brother back and obviously needed him here. Would she be mad? "Ahhh . . . What would you think if I was?"

Jules shuffled down two more steps. "I'd be bloomin' ecstatic." She paused again, out of breath.

Kimberly studied her more closely. Had Jules been lying when she said she was up for this? Broken bones took a lot of energy to heal, and this escape route wasn't exactly doctor sanctioned.

Jules shifted her grip on the ladder. "Mum would kill me for saying this when he's just gotten back to 'Straya, but I think he belongs over there." A pause. "With you."

Kimberly absorbed the words, relief flooding her system. Thank goodness. Somebody on her side. "The board's threatening to close us down if he doesn't come back or find us an amazing replacement." A weight lifted from her with the admission. Outside of Steph, she hadn't been able to discuss the burden with anyone. And Steph had already been hounding her with emails this morning, asking if she'd talked about it with Sam yet.

Jules leaned her face against the ladder, still resting. "So you're here to woo him?"

"Woo him?"

"Back overseas. Doing what he's great at."

"Um, I guess." *Wooing* wasn't how she'd describe it, but it summed up the situation.

"I'll help you. Woo." Jules winked over her shoulder and shifted down a step. "Between the sister and the nemesis, he's doomed. Oh—" She halted. "Sorry about the nemesis crack. He just likes to complain, is all. He's an old whinger."

"Believe me, I'm aware of Sam's attitude toward . . ." Kimberly faded off as it became obvious Jules was staring at something over her head.

"What the—?"

Kimberly twisted as far as she could without letting go of the ladder. Jules gave a shout and waved her arm. "Hey! Stop that! Don't—" She scooted down the ladder with surprising speed and grabbed her crutch. Arms free, Kimberly turned to see two guilty-looking dogs dashing away from Jules's indignant rampage. One dog was Meg the Kelpie, the other a white toy poodle that Kimberly could swear was grinning.

Jules dropped her crutch to scoop up her dog and aim a moon-booted kick that missed the poodle by a mile.

"Jules?" Heavy footsteps sounded from the front stairs. Sam and Mick appeared around the corner of the house. Sam's gaze darted from Jules to the window to the ladder to Kimberly. Her cheeks flushed, and she broke eye contact. Jules's ex was a far more interesting subject. The man looked both out of place and completely at home, sporting board shorts, flip-flops, a blue cotton tank, and a battered farm hat that matched Jules's. His skin freckled heavily over his toned shoulders and arms.

Mick's attention, however, was fastened on Jules. "What's wrong?"

"Your ridiculous poodle"—Jules cuddled Meg closer—"took advantage of my poor, innocent Meg."

"Advantage?" The two men's mouths dropped open as one. They spoke at the same time.

"How was that even possible?"

"Nice work, mate."

Mick whistled. The poodle trotted over to his side and offered its paw. Smirking, the man high-fived it and straightened. "See you ladies later." He nodded to Sam and sauntered back to his truck.

Kimberly pressed her hands over her mouth to stop the laugh that threatened. She'd just found an ally in Jules, who was currently shouting threats at the poodle and obviously unable to see the funny side of things.

She wouldn't risk this new friendship for the world.

CHAPTER 12

S am hustled across the muddy yard after a rushed lunch on
Sunday, two days after the incident Kimberly called Poodle-
Gate, as thousands of raindrops launched an assault to breach
Dad's old oilskin jacket. He rounded the corner of the shed and
stopped dead in his tracks.

Kimberly.

Standing on an upside-down bucket.

On top of a hay bale.

On the back of the ute.

She was doing something with the machinery shed's gutter-
ing. A borrowed red flannel shirt—*his* red flannel shirt—clung
to her body, and a stream of water cascaded from her ponytail.
She had to be soaked. How long had she been out here? They'd
all been at church only two hours ago. He opened his mouth
to yell, then stopped. Better not startle her. Instead, he scooped
up some gravel from the sodden ground and tossed a pebble at
the shed roof next to her. It took three throws before she looked
at him.

"Are you crazy? That's not safe!" He had to shout to be heard
over the downpour, rain streaming from the brim of his hat.

She shrugged and pointed to something. He squinted. A rope,

looped around her waist and knotted in the shed's rafters. From what he'd observed of her knots in the past few days, she might as well have made a harness from single-ply toilet paper.

He made sure she was watching and braced, then climbed onto the back of the ute himself. The only part of this situation that was really surprising was that it'd taken him this long to catch her doing something like this. He had to admit, after the three days she'd spent here, the girl had grit. Her body could barely keep up with her ambition. Before this she'd never done a day's physical labor in her life, and now she'd thrown herself into farming like Scrooge McDuck into his money pool. Plus, she'd spent all hours of the day and night completing both her Wildfire work and inspecting Jules's financial data. He admired the work ethic. But it was only a matter of time before her never-give-up attitude led to let's-climb-stupidly-high-things-without-Sam.

He got to his feet in the tray of the ute and touched the wet denim at her knee to let her know he was there.

"Almost done!"

A pile of decomposing leaves—and was that a mouse?—rained down on him from above.

"*Kim!*"

"Sorry!"

She plucked at the knot of the rope cinched around her waist, and it fell away. "Almost there."

The bucket wobbled.

Sam grabbed her legs, but the action threw her upper-body weight over his head, and as he went to step back, his foot caught on something. Kim gave a short squeal as they both tumbled down. Sam landed flat on his back in the ute tray, Kimberly on his chest. The impact knocked the wind from his lungs.

"Sam!" She scrambled off him, eyes wide and face white, and knelt next to where he lay.

His lungs wouldn't cooperate. He fought to breathe in again. *Don't panic, you know it'll wear off soon.*

Raindrops, big and cold, coated his skin. Kimberly's face hovered near, one hand on his shoulder. "Are you okay?"

He pressed a palm against the wet ute tray beneath him and tried to suck air in. Couldn't. He focused his eyes on Kimberly's face, the wet wisps of brunette hair plastered to her skin. Wide eyes searched his. A frown creased the smooth skin of her forehead, and her pink lips pressed into a worried line. He'd always known she was attractive in her classy office outfits. But somehow, now, wearing his shirt and borrowed gum boots, she was . . . beautiful.

Or maybe that was the knot on the back of his head talking.

He ran his thumb along the frown line on her forehead, smoothed it out. "Just . . . winded." He managed to get the words out as oxygen seeped back into his chest. He sucked in a few deep breaths, then pushed himself up and attempted to speak. "Let's . . . out of . . . wet."

She scooted back, giving him room to push himself toward the edge of the tray. Her hand reached for his arm—then pulled back. And again. Was this Kimberly hovering? Despite the ache in his skull, Sam's lips tugged into a smile.

She jumped to the ground, then stood in that downpour watching him gingerly clamber down. He had to give it to her, she never left a mate behind.

They ducked into the shed, the corrugated-iron roof amplifying the sound of the rain. Kimberly flipped a toolbox lid down and sat on it, scooting over to make enough room for him. "You okay?"

When he sat, his coat sleeve brushed her arm, bare to the elbow where she'd rolled the sleeves back. "I'm fine." God would forgive the lie. His tailbone ached and his diaphragm still felt like a punching bag. "You cold?" He shrugged out of Dad's jacket.

She shook her head. "I'd just get the inside of your coat wet."

"In other words, yes." He moved to nudge her away from the wall. She didn't budge, face somber.

He smiled and waggled his eyebrows.

Her emotionless expression twitched, and laughter burst out like sunbeams from behind a cloud. She leaned forward, and he wrapped the oilskin around her shoulders, rubbing her upper arms with his hands to generate some heat. Her cheeks pinked. Was she warmer or embarrassed?

He leaned back, now clad in his blue flanny—flannel shirt to her. Adrenaline still flooded his veins, which probably explained why he was acutely aware of every point at which they touched—shoulder, hip, thigh. He ran a hand through his hair, spiking it up. Time for a distraction. "What were you doing up there?"

"Cleaning the gutters. Jules was worried about the water tanks running low. I was glad when it started raining, but then I noticed the rain spilling over the gutters. They were so blocked, nothing was getting through. So I got up there and cleaned them."

Her voice matter-of-fact, she plucked at splinters in her palm as she spoke. He'd been with her when she acquired them yesterday, when an aggressive cow spooked in the stockyards and they'd both climbed the wooden fence in a hurry.

"Them? As in multiple?"

She glanced up. "You only found me on the last blockage. There were five." A raindrop slid from her eyebrow, traced the curve of her cheek, and disappeared down her neck.

He blew out a breath. "You're insane."

Kimberly shrugged. "The other side of the shed isn't as high. And I made my rope harness. And Jules was worried." She rested her head against the wall and closed her eyes.

Movement caught his gaze. Her hand, resting on her thigh, trembling. He grasped it. "You *are* cold."

She tugged it back, clasped her hands together. "It's just fright. I don't love heights."

He held out his hand, palm upturned. "Let me."

Hesitantly she placed her fingers in his. From the expression on her face and tension in her muscles, she didn't seem sure if he'd help or harm. He flicked a tiny pair of tweezers from the Swiss Army Knife he kept in his pocket and smiled. "Trust me."

Holding her hand as carefully as a newborn chick, he removed a splinter. Hopefully his palm would heat her fingers—her skin was ice. The angle at which he held her wrist brought her face close enough for her breath to caress his cheek. He freed a second splinter. "So you don't love heights and you were up there anyway?"

"I didn't like seeing Jules worried."

He smiled, despite the fright she'd given him. The girls had really bonded during Kimberly's few days here, and only part of it was them swapping embarrassing stories about him.

Splinters gone, he released her hand. "You are a force to be reckoned with."

A smile flickered across her face and she closed her eyes

again, body relaxing beside him. She had to be exhausted. After yesterday's massive workload and then a herd breakout at 11:00 p.m., they'd had less than four hours sleep. "Duh."

He watched her rest for a moment. Occasionally, over the past three years, he'd wondered if there was a whole different person behind those determined hazel eyes, just waiting to be found. Most times she'd been a bulldog personified, tugging the other end of a rope he was trying to pull. He couldn't see anything past the teeth and the snarls. But here, away from Wildfire, he'd caught glimpses of a woman who put her friends before herself. A woman who would give up her vacation to work like a dog and never complain about it. A woman he'd like to have on his side.

That woman heaved a sigh and pulled herself up off the tool-box. "I need to set up the electric tape in the back paddock before I get the herd in. Mind if I take the truck?"

He stood, still grappling with the unusual thoughts racing across his mind. "Go for it."

She sashayed from the shed out into the rain, unperturbed by the wet, the work, or the tumble they'd just taken. Funny, he'd never noticed the graceful way she walked before.

He froze as two thoughts hit him at once. One a reminder. The second not worth contemplating. He pushed it aside as he called, "Kim!"

She swiveled and stepped back in out of the rain. "Yeah?"

"I, um, forgot to ask. How's it going with the financials? Jules mentioned just before I left that she was going to ask you for an update."

Something in her expression shifted. "Uh—give me a day to confirm some things. Then I'll let you both know."

Was it just him, or had her relaxed vibe vanished? He gave a slow nod, his gaze tracing the microexpressions in her face. Lips ever so slightly pursed, eyes a fraction tighter. She waved good-bye, then jogged from the shed to the ute.

A sense of foreboding, together with a ferocious blast of wind, shivered across his goose-bumped skin. What had she found? Were things worse than they thought? He veered away from the questions. No sense worrying about that—things couldn't be too bad. Right? As worried as he got sometimes, in truth this was nothing more than a run of bad luck that they needed a little extra advice to navigate.

But financial concerns weren't the only reason his eyes tracked the ute as its engine turned over and it rolled away. A new aware-ness shouted through his mind till it could not be ignored, though every cell of his being fought to deny it.

There was just no way he could have a crush on Kimberly Foster.

The dairy wouldn't start.

Kimberly hit the big black button that fired up the en-gine harder this time. Nothing. In her six days on this farm—which had been so drama packed they seemed far longer than a mere 144 hours—the dairy had always run smoothly. She hadn't broken it somehow, had she? Out in the dairy pit, Kurt Cobain vented his—and Kimberly's—frustration via the muck-splattered speakers Jules had duct-taped to a metal post. Water sprayed from somewhere in the dairy.

Kimberly set her hands on her hips, one finger still tapping to "Smells Like Teen Spirit." There had to be a way to fix this without alarming Jules, who was two sheds away, working to fix the four-wheeler. The whole time they'd been rounding up the herd together just before, Jules had been worrying. A new load of hay with poor protein quality had her stressed about milk-production levels. Now, another problem. And that wasn't even including what Kimberly's financial analysis had revealed over the past several days. There had to be a way to fix this.

Her music stopped and a moment later was replaced by Katy Perry's "Firework." She frowned. "Sam!"

Squelching footsteps approached the concrete room that housed both vats and the engine that ran the dairy. "Hey, I held up our deal. It's not Madonna." Sam stepped into the room, his brown hair wet and slicked back from his forehead. In fact, his entire body was soaked, right down to the water running from his gum boots.

She averted her eyes from where his sleeves were painted on his biceps. "What happened to you?"

"I just had to pull a calf—and was in the afterbirth splash zone. A thousand showers aren't going to be enough." He shuddered. "The calf wasn't breathing, so Jules came over and gave it mouth-to-mouth. I'm glad the calf's alive, but that's a high price to pay."

Kimberly snorted. Then paused. That was the third time today she'd laughed at something Sam had said. Their near-amicable relationship had lasted five days now. Miracles could happen. She only prayed this fledgling friendship would survive when she did the exact thing he'd asked her not to.

If she plucked up the courage to do it at all.

Sam wiped stray drops of water from his chin. "What's up?" He peered over her shoulder, heat radiating from him.

"It won't start." She backed away to let him look. "Do you know what's wrong?"

Sam fiddled around with something, then shrugged. "I'll get Jules." He frowned. "I hope it doesn't hold us up too long. The cricket kids are coming over for the slip and slide tonight."

You could take the youth pastor out of the ministry, but you couldn't take the ministry out of the youth pastor. Tonight's slip and slide and barbecue was Sam's way of reaching out to both the kids and their parents. A massive sheet of silage plastic had already been unrolled next to the house, with twenty bottles of detergent ready and waiting.

Kimberly might not be an expert at either an Australian barbecue or sliding like a penguin, but at the very least she could ensure Sam was there on time. She indicated the door. "I'll find Jules. And don't worry about being late, I can finish milking on my own if we get held up too long."

Sam appeared to assess her for a moment. "Thank you." The words were quiet and sincere.

Flustered, she opted for her attempt at an Aussie accent to break the moment. "No worries. I'll go find our fearless leader." Wow, that sounded cheesy. Her cheeks burned as she turned to escape.

"I'm here. What's wrong?" Jules swung into the room on her crutch, a garbage bag taped around her moon boot in a vain effort to keep it clean. Kimberly explained the situation, and Jules muttered something under her breath. "Go finish pushing the cows up into the yard. I'll fix this."

Sam ruffled Jules's hair as he walked past, and she swung her wrench at him. He dodged it, smirked, and sauntered out of the dairy. Kimberly's heart twisted a little as she watched the siblings and then followed Sam out. And, like the sucker for punishment that she was, she checked her phone again for any communication from Mom.

Nothing. Well, maybe she should reach out again. She wiped the grit on her fingers against Dad's old Red Dwarf T-shirt, then tapped the screen till she reached her internet messaging app and scrolled for Mom's icon.

Gone.

Kimberly ran her thumb up the screen till she reached the top of her contact list and scanned each name again. Nada. She clicked the screen off and stared at the nothingness rather than the spot where Mom's icon should have been. Her mother must've deactivated her account. Again. Without so much as a "Hey there, daughter, here's how to reach me while you're overseas for the first time and juggling a high-stress career situation."

Kimberly swallowed down the lump in her throat, trying to push her hurt down with it. She'd have to try Mom's work number later and just cop the international call charges. It was the only reliable way to reach the woman.

She closed her eyes for a moment and, nails digging into her palms, dragged her composure into place by sheer force of will and some tricks from her mindfulness podcast. *Focus on the sun on my face, the dust on my fingertips, the crunch of dirt under my boots. Do. Not. Think. About. Crying.*

She opened her eyes again and focused on the scene in front of her: three tractors, meticulously maintained by Paytons past and present, littered the dusty tracks that connected the house, sheds, and dairy. A mural of the back-paddock lagoon covered the brickwork of the dairy's vat room, courtesy of their father. Beyond, green paddocks that'd been fenced by Sam's mom herself stretched for a mile before they hit the wall of trees that lined the Burnett River. According to Jules, that river included a flying fox—which she'd learned was a sort of zip line—over the water that'd been the highlight of their summers. And between the river and the dairy, three hundred cattle lumbered in Kimberly's direction—every single beast known by Jules. The entire property was an outward expression of everything Kimberly had ever wanted: belonging, memories, connection, purpose.

Ahead of her, Sam walked toward the yard gate, oblivious to the jealousy that oozed through her veins. Between Butch, Jules, and Mrs. Payton—due home in a couple weeks for Christmas—Sam had a real family. A real family with a real home.

A home now under more threat than they realized.

In addition to getting her Wildfire work done, Kimberly had spent late-night hours since she'd arrived scouring the six months' worth of financial documents Jules had given her, looking for a way to free up the cash they needed.

Not only was there none, but Jules seemed to be on a downward trajectory that, given the frequency of Australia's natural disasters, would probably lead to foreclosure. But to convince Jules of the need for a change—or even just to confirm her suspicions—she'd need Sam's help. Sam, who'd expressly told her not to meddle beyond finding a short-term fix for their money woes. Who wanted to believe this was nothing more than a rough patch.

Who'd bent over her palm and pulled splinters with such care that her hand still tingled when she thought of it.

How could she keep quiet and watch Sam and Jules lose all they had? Still, Sam's words to her on her first night here swirled in her brain. *"If you want my help talking my sister into some scheme of yours, don't count on it."*

But friends had their friends' backs.

Palms clammy, she hustled to catch up to Sam. He swung the gate open and held it for her to enter the yards. "What's wrong?"

She hesitated. Were her thoughts that obvious? "What do you mean?"

"You have your 'Something's wrong' face on. Last time I saw it was—" He stopped. She finished the sentence in her head: *When you told me about your plan for Wildfire.* "—when Tariq threw up on the foosball table."

She wrinkled her nose as she entered the yards. "If I was pulling any face, it was my 'I'm trying not to also vomit' face. I was the one who cleaned that up. You got to bundle him in the car and take him home."

His lips twitched upward. "Yeah, thanks for taking that bullet."

The moment rested between them. A shared memory, and they were actually both smiling.

Sam relatched the gate, and she summoned the depths of her courage. *Just rip it off like a Band-Aid.* "Sam, can you help me talk to Jules about letting me dig way deeper into the finances? I'm worried the farm's in real danger." She rushed the sentence out.

The smile playing around his lips froze, then drained away.

"Hey, you wombats!" Jules hop-ran in their direction with the assistance of her crutch. "I fixed it. The thingy was hooked up wrong—" She slowed as she reached them, assessing their faces. "This looks serious." She leaned against the gate, where Sam's hand still rested on the chain that latched it.

Sam replied, but the gaze that burned Kimberly's soul never left her face. "We're just talking about the future."

Jules reached over and punched his arm. "Don't be mad at the girl for trying to woo you back to America."

Kimberly shifted on her feet. Uh-oh. This was spiraling out of control. Her stomach tightened as Sam's brow furrowed.

He faced her. "What?"

Jules looked between them. "That's not what you were talking about?"

Sam pressed his lips together before he responded. "We were talking about the farm."

Jules swung her gaze to Kimberly, eyes wide.

Kimberly gulped.

Sam spread his feet and folded his arms, his worried sister on his left and a grimacing Kimberly to the right. *"Don't be mad at the girl for trying to woo you back to America."* What was Jules talking about? The six weeks they'd agreed to—or something else?

But that wasn't the most pressing issue right now. He swished a fly away and fixed his attention on Kimberly, who looked paler than usual in another one of those old sci-fi nerd shirts she seemed to love, this one too big and sliding off her shoulder to reveal the purple strap of her sports bra. He firmed his jaw. "I think Kimberly has your update for you," he told his sister. And if Kim had any telepathic skill at all, she'd get the *Stop interfering* message being broadcast from every atom of his being.

Kimberly took a deep breath and straightened her spine. "The information you gave me on the last six months has left me with a few outstanding questions. I'd like to dig back further to give you a proper assessment."

Jules shrugged. "How much further?"

"Whatever you have."

His sister laughed. "We've been here a hundred and twenty years, so . . ."

Kimberly spread her palms. "Old weather data could be handy. I'll take it."

The smile faded from Jules's face. "That sounds like overkill. You shouldn't need that much to get us out of a sticky situation."

Kimberly licked her lips, shifted her feet, and glanced toward Sam. He raised his eyebrows. *Don't do this.* Why couldn't she help but overcomplicate things? Like Jules had said, their family had been here for 120 years. And they'd remain 120 more—as long as Kim didn't convince Jules to mortgage them to the hilt and gobble up every property around.

"We're not looking for a six-step plan to conquer the world." Sam spoke slowly, like any piece of gravity he could pack into his voice would change her mind. "Just some fresh ideas for a tough year."

Kimberly spread her palms. "That's just it—it shouldn't be a tough year. You're on track for your average yearly rainfall. Milk prices are okay. Your herd's healthy. And yet this downward trajectory . . ."

Sam slid his gaze to his sister. With every word Kimberly spoke, Jules's color deepened. Uh-oh. His sister's trademark passion cut both ways. She leaned forward on the gate. "What are you saying? That it's me?"

Kimberly shifted an inch back. "No, just that—I need to confirm, with your mortgage—"

"Because I've improved things since Mum retired. Our crop yield has increased. I barely lose a calf. Our motorbikes actually have working brakes." Her voice rose with each declaration.

Kimberly's voice dropped to just above a whisper. "I didn't

mean anything personal—I'm just trying to solve the problem you gave me. But I'm concerned the situation might be more serious than you think."

"More serious? How serious? What do you think—"

Sam laid a hand on his sister's forearm. "Ease up, Jules."

She shook his fingers off. "I-I need to go check the vat." She hobbled back toward the dairy.

Kimberly let out a shaky breath. "Thanks."

He turned back to her, jaw set. "I knew you'd make this bigger than it needs to be. This was why I didn't want you to come. Now she's more stressed than ever." He flung a hand in the direction Jules had fled and braced himself for Kimberly's onslaught of maddening logic. Yep, there was that fire in her eyes. She propped her hands on her hips and opened her mouth. So, he beat her to the punch. "And what's this about luring me back to the States?"

She swallowed whatever defense missile she'd been about to launch. "Wildfire wants you back."

"I'm not interested. That's why I moved nine thousand miles."

She looked down at her boots, then met his eye. "*Needs* you back. Your replacements have been useless. The board's talking about shutting us down if we don't get you back or find a replacement they love as much as you."

She thought she had him—he knew it. Everything from the tilt of her chin to the confidence in her gaze. She thought she'd snap her fingers, drop the "Wildfire might close" bomb, and he'd come running back like a trained dog. His fingers tightened on the top rung of the gate. "I never expected Wildfire to last."

His words seemed to hit her like a physical blow—her mouth dropped open and she exhaled sharply. "What?"

"Its success was a mystery to me from the start. I knew its

time was limited. Maybe this is it." He spread his palms. "Meant to be."

She spluttered, "You can't—You don't just—What are you talking about?"

"I mean that Wildfire's your problem. And beyond some short-term assistance, the farm's not your concern. You're on your own." He spun on his heel and left her there.

Alone.

CHAPTER 13

Jules perched on the wooden fence that encircled her house and slammed down her third Coke of the evening. Before her, in that magical light of sunset, twenty preteen boys threw themselves down Sam's slip and slide like it was a human-sized bowling lane. And with them, one shirtless veterinarian with eyes as blue as the first day of summer and a squeal worthy of any eleven-year-old boy as he careened down the slide and knocked over all ten buckets positioned at the end of the plastic.

"Strike!" He leapt to his feet and high-fived every boy there as he ran back to the start of the slide.

How was it that she found that attractive?

She scratched at the itchy skin peeking from her moon boot and didn't try to resist the depression that swept over her. *Dad would have loved this.* He'd have been the king of hospitality—he would've cooked the snags on the barbecue, talked to every bloke that showed up, and probably even gone for a slide himself, despite his bad knee. He would've found a way to cheer her up about Mick. He would've known what to say to decrease her farm stress—and then pitched in to find a solution. He'd been their wise one. Their rock.

But without him she floundered, adrift in an ocean of doubts and worry. And on top of all that, thanks to the three Cokes, she had to pee.

Careful of her leg, she slid from the fence to the ground and began the short walk—now a long, crutch-assisted hop—back to the house. By the time she returned to her spot on the fence, Mick had his shirt on, kombucha in hand, and was perched next to where she had been sitting.

She slumped onto the crutch. There was no energy left in the tank for this tonight. She pivoted to go around him, but he turned. Held out the bottle. "Drink?"

She summoned the last of her spunk and approached him. "You're in my spot."

"I'm next to your spot. And if you're not having it, I'll take the kombucha."

She took the bottle from his hand, condensation cooling her palm. "Now go away." She balanced the bottle on a fence post and pulled herself back up onto the railing.

Mick pulled a second bottle from his pocket and cracked the lid. "What are you annoyed about today?" He emphasized the *today* like this was a common occurrence and took a sip.

"I'm not annoyed every day, you know. Just the ones where I see you." She dragged her eyes from where Mick's North Queensland Cowboys T-shirt clung to his wet skin and focused somewhere near the dairy-bucket bowling pins. Meg barked at the sliding kids even as Butch patted her larger-than-usual tummy. Jules took another sip. "By the way, you're going to be a father."

Mick spit out his drink.

She snickered. "Or at least Killer is." The poodle lapped at water spraying from the hose onto the slip and slide. He must've gotten to Meg long before this week, because you could now feel the pups in Meg's belly.

Mick wiped drips of kombucha from his chin. "That so?" She watched him from the corner of her eye. A smile played around his lips. "Kelpie-cross-toy-poodle puppies?"

She rolled her eyes. The man was downright delighted. "You could at least pretend to be sorry about it. My dog'll be out of commission for weeks, and it's not like I can run around the cows myself. According to Sam, I shouldn't even be driving."

Mick threw her an alarmed look. "You *shouldn't* be driving."

She smiled and sipped her kombucha. She'd kept off public roads, at least. Mostly.

He heaved a sigh that seemed to come from the depths of his soul. "Are you asking me, as a vet, to take care of it?"

She gasped. He wouldn't lay a finger on her dog or those puppies. "No!"

He spread his palms. "I meant I could find people at the Goldie to adopt them."

She grunted. Maybe.

Mick nudged her with his shoulder—still wet from the slip and slide. "This mood seems to be about more than puppies we both know will be adorable. You in a funk about your leg?"

Jules peeled the label from her bottle, the real reason resting on the tip of her tongue but refusing to budge. "Depends. You still mad at me?"

He considered her. "I got over it. But we both know that's not why you look like someone broke all your *That '70s Show* DVDs."

She slurped from the bottle, the fizzy sensation tickling her tongue. "Kimberly basically implied that I can't run my own farm." The words chafed like sand in the undies.

Maybe she would've been better off taking Mick's compromise, all those years ago, to move to a rural center within visiting distance of the beach. She could've worked for another farmer, maybe even dabbled in some youth work like Sam. Those outdoor youth camps had always looked fun.

She shook her head. What was she thinking? She'd always dreamed of running *this* property, carrying on the family legacy, being her own boss. She'd farewelled Mick for the sake of that dream. Lot of good it'd done her.

The sun slipped behind the horizon, and its golden glow faded to something murkier. Mick rubbed the barely-there stubble on his chin, the scratchy sound putting every one of Jules's senses on heightened awareness. "That doesn't sound like the girl I've heard about."

Interesting, considering Sam was the one who'd told him about why Kimberly was here. Jules shrugged. "She didn't use those words, but the meaning was the same."

Mick flicked his bottle cap into the nearby forty-four-gallon drum they used as a rubbish bin. "Business is her thing, right? Even if you're doing fine, it might not hurt to let her take a peek. Times are tough out here. You never know when it might come in handy." He nodded over to where his parents stood talking to Kimberly. "If she's offering you an advantage, I'd take it. Just look at Dad. He didn't expect they'd need to sell so soon."

That was completely different. No amount of business advice could help a retirement-age farmer with a son who didn't want his heritage. An edge slipped into her tone. "They wouldn't have to if you'd stay."

Midsip, he slowly lowered his bottle, jaw tight. Whoops. Her stomach knotted. Not the right nerve to poke. She opened her mouth to take it back somehow, but he shook his head and jumped down from the fence. "You know, you broke up with me so that you could live your life here, on this farm. I can't believe you could do that without batting an eyelid." Her own bottle cap slipped from her fingers. How could he think that decision hadn't devastated her? "But when you hit hard times, you can't look past your own pride to let a friend help." He pitched his bottle into the garbage and stalked off toward a group of men around the barbecue.

Jules slapped her palm on the railing. Why did she have to go and say that? Mick didn't deserve it. After all, she'd chosen her lifestyle over him just as much as he'd chosen his over her. Dad's words, often spoken but now softer after six years of missing him, returned to Jules's mind. *The thing you're mad about often isn't the thing you're actually mad about.*

Her straight posture slumped into a chiropractor's nightmare. Mick wasn't the problem. Kim wasn't the problem. She was.

She'd prided herself on being the only single-woman farmer in the district. She'd worked the land, battled the elements, the isolation, and the fatigue, and won. Likewise, her mother before her had weathered droughts, fires, floods, isolation, cattle sickness, cyclones, the deaths of two husbands, and anything else nature could throw at her. And yet now, according to Kim, in years of good rain and relative peace, Jules was on the brink of disaster after running the farm alone for just a few years?

The admission marked catastrophic failure at every level of who she was.

She sniffed back her emotions and raised her head. No. She hadn't failed until the eviction notice came. And to stop that from happening, she needed her friend's help.

She slid from the fence and went to look for Sam and Kim.

Sam gave a wave to the final car pulling away from the farm-house with one hand and used the other to slap at a mosquito on his neck. Behind him, empty cans clinked as Kimberly scooped up the rubbish from the party. Silent—apart from the occasional yelp when a cane toad startled her.

As she'd been all afternoon.

That milking they'd just done had been the quietest of his life, save that relentless Nirvana she insisted on blasting from the speakers. His extroverted personality meant he usually talked to anyone nearby, even her. But today he didn't even try. If he could x-ray that girl's heart, it'd probably just be one big ball of prickles.

The uneven gait of Jules and her crutch approached from be-hind. "Hey."

"Hey, yourself." He slung an arm around her shoulders, bare except for her loose-fitting tank top. Humidity had been a killer today, and the cool change wasn't due for days yet. "Mick around?" They walked back toward the slip and slide as the insects sang their nightly chorus.

She shrugged. "I think he went home." She glanced between him and Kimberly. "How's Kim?"

He hesitated as he bent to collect discarded bottles of deter-gent. "Quiet." Moonlight glinted off something in the grass. More cans. Sam held his wet shirt out like a pouch and added them to the collection. He really should've thought ahead and gotten a rubbish bag.

"She's right."

Sam snapped his head around to look at his sister. "What?"

She studied the ground by her toe. "Things aren't going well."

He squeezed her shoulders. "Your leg will be better in five weeks. You've had a few years of decent rain. You'll be fine again soon."

She kicked a rock. Actually, on second glance, a dead cane toad. "The interest payments alone are sucking up all my profit. Kim can see that. I keep thinking things will turn around, that it's just temporary, but . . . maybe I need to make some bigger changes. Find efficiencies."

He let the news sink in a moment. Kim had said "downward trajectory." What if Jules really did lose the farm? Grandad's stockyards. Dad's murals. Their childhood cubby houses. Mum's custom-designed dairy. All those memories. Foreclosed and sold to the highest bidder. Nausea hit him in an unexpected wave.

"I want you to work with Kim."

He almost dropped his increasingly sticky shirt pouch. Had she lost her mind? Swallowing his initial less-than-polite reaction, he paced a few steps away to the drum of rubbish and dumped the bottles and cans. "I beg your pardon?"

Jules hobbled a few steps after him. "I've listened to you talk about her for years. I've heard you admit how so many of her ideas have worked. I'm no big fan of risk, so I don't want her running off with some grand scheme. But I need her help. I think the two of you can balance each other out."

Sam let out an incredulous chuckle. "Or become part of a murder story that the local high school kids tell for years to come."

But even as the denial left his lips, reality intruded. Did they have any other choice? If he knew Kim, her assessment would've been thorough—and now even Jules was admitting the truth in it. His sister—the very person he'd expected to object to this as much as he did. The stiffness drained from his spine. No, no other choice at all.

Jules nudged him with her crutch. "It wasn't entirely her fault. Like I said, she was right about a lot of things."

Time to accept his fate. He forced a smile. But he couldn't just let that last comment slide. "Hey." He gave her shoulder a playful shove. "Do you want my help or not?"

She grinned. "I already know you'll give it. You're sweet that way."

Ugh. Done for. And she knew it. Sam rolled his eyes and threw out his final plea. "This is asking a lot. We don't see eye to eye. And she gets mean."

"She's not mean, she's blunt. It's never malicious. Grow a thick skin."

He stifled a groan. He'd do it, of course. And he could deal with the groveling. But his real challenge would be keeping Kim's head out of the clouds and on the ground—a task that had proved impossible time and time before. But this time he couldn't fail.

His family's entire way of life was at risk.

CHAPTER 14

Kimberly hunted for a stray cow along the bank of the Burnett River and plotted her escape. The landscape around her steamed under the late-morning sun, and trickles of sweat ran from her thighs all the way down to her socks poking out from the old elastic-sided riding boots she'd borrowed from Jules. The salty taste of sweat invaded her mouth. She plucked her hat—also borrowed—from her head and fanned herself with it. Why had she ever thought she'd be anything but an outsider on the farm that was clearly in the Payton family's blood?

In the night and morning that had passed since her conversation with Jules and Sam at the dairy, Kimberly had successfully avoided both of them. To think that just yesterday morning she'd thought she and Sam could build somewhat of a lasting truce. She might not have Sam's communication skills or Jules's zest for life, but she'd offered them the best she had: her brain.

But Jules didn't need her, and Sam didn't want her.

A tear leaked from her eye. The effort of keeping her impassive mask on since yesterday had drained every ounce of energy she had. Now, defenses depleted, the dam of emotion threatened to break.

Her phone buzzed in her pocket, and Kimberly sniffed and

pulled it out. Incoming video call. Steph. Chasing an update on Sam, if her five emails and three missed calls were any indication.

She should answer. She needed to answer. But her thumb refused to move faster than a snail's pace toward the green icon.

Before she could swipe, the phone went black. Out of battery. God was merciful after all—well, God and her habit of forgetting to plug it in at night. Kimberly shoved the phone back into her pocket. She should just find some local high school kid to take her place in the dairy, go home, and throw herself into saving Wildfire. She'd only known Jules a week—though it felt far longer—but logically the loss of that friendship shouldn't hurt this much. And Sam . . . If she'd been honest with herself, she would've accepted that situation long ago. But this place . . . She laid a hand on the cream trunk of a gum tree and scanned its branches for koalas. The only highlight of her morning had been spotting one of the fuzzy creatures snoozing in a branch an hour ago. But this tree contained nothing—except the rotting evidence of an old tree house.

Some children fantasized of Disneyland as the place where their dreams came to life. To her, this farm was Disneyland with a flying carpet and fairy godmother to boot. From the smooth dip in the house's wooden threshold—the wood worn down from a hundred years of family life—to the photos taped to the dairy's dusty message board, the life the Paytons had here was more than she could have dreamed of. It was this sense of homecoming that Sam managed to re-create wherever he went—what was missing from Wildfire now. What it would never have again.

She couldn't bring herself to admit her failure to Steph just yet.

She ducked under a low-hanging branch, Meg the Kelpie trotting faithfully at her side. Another tear leaked through. If she went home, she'd miss the birth of these pups. Yesterday, before the argument, Jules had guessed that Meg had three weeks to go and predicted a Christmas birth. She sniffed and wiped the tears from her cheeks. *Stop crying.* Another branch loomed ahead, and she kept an eye on it to make sure she didn't whack her head.

Meg barked. Kimberly scanned the landscape around her. Just the river to her right, trees behind and ahead, and a field of stubble to her left. No cow. "What're you barking at, girl?"

The dog barked again, more insistent.

"Shut it, Meg." Kimberly went to step forward. The twig beneath her foot moved.

Moved?

Snake!

Kimberly leapt back with a shriek as the serpent struck at her. The dog launched forward, seized the snake, and gave it a vicious shake. Kimberly grabbed the low branches of the nearest paperbark tree and scrambled a few feet up off the ground. Could snakes climb trees? She clawed her way up a few more branches, spiky leaves and twigs tangling in her hair. Wrapping her legs tight around the bough, she ignored the rough bark tearing at her tender skin and focused on Meg.

The Kelpie looked to be winning the battle as the snake flicked about uncontrollably. But then it caught Meg's hind leg with its fangs. Kimberly screamed. No. Not this beautiful dog. Not with her in pup.

Meg dropped the snake with a yelp, and the reptile slithered into a hole in the ground. The dog limped away, whimpering with each step.

"Meg!" Kimberly slid down the branch, disregarding the

splinters, and then jumped out of the tree. Her right foot jarred against the ground, shooting pain through her ankle. Not important. Meg. She had to help Meg.

She stumbled toward the dog and scooped her up. Now what? It'd been a long walk down to this part of the river. And brown snakes were deadly to humans, let alone medium-sized cattle dogs.

A sob tore from her throat. How was she going to get help in time?

Sam hunted for Kimberly along the bank of the river. He had an angry woman to sweet-talk.

It'd been sixteen hours since Jules's request that they work together, and he'd asked that he have the chance to apologize to Kimberly before Jules spoke to her. After all, Kimberly's gut had been right, and all she'd gotten for her honesty was an earful from both him and Jules.

Which led him here, dodging tree branches and spiderwebs as he walked along the riverbank. Today's humidity was so high that the air felt heavy as he puffed along, sweat stinging his eyes. He cupped a hand to his mouth. "Kiiiiiimbeeeeeeerlyyyyyyyyy!" She'd left to round up strays just over two hours ago.

He really should have apologized first thing this morning, but Kim had been avoiding him. Guilt pricked his conscience. He'd never thought before that his words had any lasting effect on her. She never seemed to care. But if yesterday was any indication, he'd been wrong. So, he dawdled along, brain focused less on his surroundings and more on composing one fabulous apology. Not only had Kimberly been right, but she'd been courageous enough to speak up when she knew both how he'd react and how it could affect her secret agenda of luring him back to Wildfire. She was chasing an impossible goal with that one, but still, her honesty had taken guts. She needed to know he appreciated that.

A pounding sounded up ahead, to his left, away from the bush surrounding the river. Sam snapped his gaze up and jogged several paces, sticks crunching beneath his boots. He broke out of the riverside bush into a corn paddock. The corn stretched above his head, blocking his view. "Kim?"

"Snake!" The ragged scream came from his right.

Pure fear filled Sam's veins, and he charged in the direction of Kim's voice. Had she been bitten? Antivenom cured most victims, but when the hospital was hours away, those statistics changed.

At the edge of the paddock, he spotted her. A hundred yards away, in the neighboring paddock of rye grass stubble, Kimberly dashed toward the gate. She had some sort of bundle in her arms, and a desperate speed in her legs.

"Kim!"

She changed direction for him.

He reached her in under fifteen seconds, unarmed but ready to distract the reptile if necessary. But Kimberly stopped running, didn't even look behind her, just dumped the bundle in his arms.

Meg.

"She was protecting me." Kimberly's voice sounded strange. Sam pulled his gaze from the limp dog to her face. Torrential tears stormed from her red eyes. "I accidentally stepped on a snake, and when it struck at me Meg bit it and shook it. But it flicked around and got her."

The dog wriggled in his arms. No ill effects yet—but it'd only be a matter of time. They'd lost a dog like this when he was a kid.

Sam adjusted his grip on Meg. Jules would know what to do. "The ute's two paddocks away. I've been walking the bank looking for you."

They ran across the uneven ground, Kimberly's breath coming in gasps. Finally, they reached the vehicle. He jumped into the passenger seat with the dog. At the wheel, Kimberly crunched the gears, and they took off at an unholy speed. The engine screamed.

"Kim, gear change!"

She shoved the gear stick into third, and they fishtailed out of the paddock and onto the track. Kimberly was crying so hard he was afraid to contemplate how well she could see.

"It's my fault," she gasped. "I should've watched where I was going. N-now I-I-I've got her k-k-illed." Another sob. "Jules is going to hate me."

Sam cradled the dog with one arm and used his phone's virtual assistant to google what to do for a snakebite as they bounced along the track twenty k's faster than they should have. Kimberly's right hand squeezed the steering wheel so tight her knuckles whitened, and her hand on the gearstick between them shook. If his arms weren't full of dog and phone, he'd have squeezed it. "It's not your fault, Kim."

She just pressed her foot down harder.

His phone buzzed and the computer voice read him the first of the search results. "*If your vet is some distance away, if practical, you can apply a pressure bandage.*" He pulled his T-shirt over his head and wrapped it as tightly as he could around the puncture marks on Meg's hind leg.

Jules must've seen their speed because she was already running as fast as her crutch would allow when they skidded to a stop next to the house. "What's wrong?" Her face went white when she saw Meg.

"Snake."

"Dunk her in the water trough. Keep her cool. I'll call Mick." She fumbled for her phone in her pocket.

Sam ran for the paddock beside the dairy, where a concrete water trough held hundreds of liters of water and quite a few gross water weeds. Meg kicked and splashed as he lowered her in. "Easy, girl, you'll be alright. Jules is gonna get help." He stroked her ears. The puppies. Even if Meg lived, could the pups survive?

Kimberly caught up with him, wheezing, and slid down into the dirt with her back against the trough. At the sound of her cough, Sam pulled his attention from the dog to the woman. "Hey, are you alright?"

She just sucked in oxygen—too much oxygen. He shifted to hold the dog up with one arm and rub Kim's back with his free hand. "Take deep breaths. Slowly. Don't hyperventilate." Her words from earlier replayed through his head. "This isn't your fault. Jules isn't going to blame you."

She just covered her eyes with her hands, breaths increasing in speed. He squeezed her shoulder. In the three and a half years he'd known Kimberly, he'd never seen her panic. Not even that awful day when a car struck Juliette Berger in front of the Wildfire building and gave her a compound fracture to the leg. Kim had stayed calm, barked out orders, and administered first aid. She did what needed doing, no matter how many kids—and adults— were melting down around her. She was strong.

But the woman in front of him had just blown past Panicville at a hundred k's an hour.

"Breathe, Kim." He shook her shoulder until she looked at him. "In-two-three, out-two-three." He repeated himself until she breathed in time with him. Rubbing her arm, he ducked his head to try to catch her gaze. "I meant what I said. Jules knows that you're her friend and this isn't your fault. She won't be mad."

Kimberly's gaze never even flickered up. Maybe a subject change would help distract her? "She's not even mad about yesterday. She asked me to talk to you about it. For starters, I'm sorry for what I said."

"No, you're not." Her voice cracked on the words. "You said what you really think. You think I make things bigger than they need to be—why? Just for the fun of it? You think I like people being mad at me all the time?" She lifted her face, eyes fierce and red rimmed, hair damp across her forehead. Her raw expression was a punch to the throat. Kimberly Foster, queen of the poker face, sat before him with an expression as naked as hippies at a certain Byron Bay beach.

She pushed her hair back from her face. "Did you know that I cried when I got the Wildfire job, I was so happy? I worked eighty hours in my first week because I wanted to impress you. And you think I'm this monster." She drew in a shuddering breath. "Or a robot. You seem to alternate between believing me cold or straight-up out to get you." She grasped at his fingers rubbing her shoulder and threw them away. Climbed to her feet.

Her gaze landed on Meg, and her face contorted into tears.

He stared at her, shock waves from her revelation reverberating across his brain. Flashbacks of their fights flickered past his mind's eye. Had her anger been a cover for . . . hurt? Her single-minded ambition just a desire to impress?

Each tear on her cheeks flayed his soul. *He* was the monster.

Kim was one of the strongest people he knew. How could he have reduced her to this state?

Kimberly pressed her lips together and swallowed her sobs down with visible effort. "I'll find my own way to the airport." She turned to leave.

Sam rocketed to his feet. "Kim, wait."

She paused.

Meg moved in his arms. He knelt again and lowered her back into the trough but kept his eyes on Kimberly. "I was way out of line yesterday." From the way her gaze darted to his, those weren't the words she'd expected him to say. Maybe if he kept talking, didn't give her a chance to argue, she'd listen. "It took courage to tell us what we didn't want to hear, and that's something only a real friend would do. And the Wildfire thing just took me by surprise. Of course I'll keep my word and help you find my replacement." He hadn't meant to imply otherwise yesterday. He just couldn't take the job himself.

Her shuddering breath was her only response.

It cut like an oxy torch to a human appendage. *He* was the youth pastor. He was meant to help people who'd been hurt like this, not cause the hurt. She was right; he'd regarded her as somewhat of a cross between Godzilla and HAL 9000. Unreachable. And unhurtable.

He'd been wrong.

The uneven crunch of Jules's footstep and crutch approached from the direction of the house. Sam twisted as far as he could to see without shifting Meg as a ute thundered up the two-mile-long driveway behind Jules. It screeched to a halt, and Mick jumped out clad in sweaty workout gear.

He nodded at Jules and strode over to the trough. "Julia."

117

"Michael." Her tone was curt.

From the ute's tray, the poodle barked. "Shut up, Killer." Jules and Mick spoke at once.

Mick knelt next to Sam and scooped Meg up from the water. "Hey, Megs." His voice was gentle. "It's okay. I'm here."

Sam wiped his wet forearms on his shorts—his shirt went with the dog—as Mick headed back to his ute.

Jules's crutch slowed her down, so Mick passed her before she even reached the trough. But she didn't follow him. She headed straight for Kimberly and squeezed her in a hug that, from the look on Kimberly's face, was both unexpected and a relief.

Jules pulled back but kept a hand on each of Kim's shoulders. "You okay?"

"It didn't bite me."

"I know. But are *you* okay?"

The question seemed to surprise Kim as much as the hug. Had it been a while since anyone asked her that?

"I—um . . . Meg—" She just stuttered until Jules spoke again.

"I'm sorry I didn't react well yesterday. But you were right. And if you're happy to put up with lug nut over there, we'd love to hear your ideas."

Kimberly glanced over at Sam. He cleared his throat, tasting sweat and dust. "I hadn't gotten to that part yet."

Jules's gaze sneaked in Mick's direction, then back to Kim. "Sam will explain. We've gotta get into town to the antivenom. I'll see you later." She hobbled off after Mick.

Sam approached Kimberly with slow steps, her expression shifting back toward its usual neutrality the closer he got.

Actually *neutral* was the wrong word. Her inability to meet his gaze gave her away, as did her fingers twisting in the hem of her shirt—a shirt that was now a mess of sweat, dog fur, and mud. She was embarrassed and trying to hide it.

Some pastor he'd turned out to be. He rubbed a hand over his face, grit scraping his skin. "I am truly sorry for the way I reacted."

Kimberly's gaze landed somewhere below his left ear. "Apology accepted." Her voice was quiet, calm. But not confident. She might have forgiven him, but she didn't trust that his attitude had changed. And after all these years, why would she?

All he could do was prove it to her, try and reverse some of the hurt he'd caused. Which meant she had to stay. "Jules told me last night that you were right. She's in more difficulty than I realized. She asked if we could work together to come up with ideas on how to fix it." He offered a small smile. "She thought we might balance each other out."

Kimberly's wary gaze met his own. "Do you want that?"

He offered his right hand for a handshake. She looked at it a moment, then shook it, strength behind her dusty palm and soft skin. He released a breath he hadn't realized he was holding and grasped her hand in both of his. "Not just a truce. An alliance. We're on the same team."

"Team Jules." A faint smile touched her lips, like the word *team* was the piece of triple-chocolate cake calling his name from Mum's freezer.

He nodded. "Team Jules."

CHAPTER 15

Mick's ute screeched to a halt in front of the main-street veterinary clinic and its peeling posters of happy cows. Jules struggled to wrangle her crutch and exit the ute holding Meg, who had grown increasingly weak. Mick's lead foot had shortened the drive to thirty minutes, and Meg had probably been bitten ten minutes before that. They had to get to the antivenom now, or she wouldn't make it.

Mick yanked the parking brake into place. "Give her to me."

She handed the dog over, slid out of the ute, and landed on her good foot. But Mick still beat her to the door of Angel's Touch Animal Clinic. Owner Glen Martin held the unique role of being the town's only farm vet, New Age enthusiast, and Mick's old boss from his high school years.

Instead of barging into the building, Mick halted. She caught up and read the note on the door.

Gone to impregnate 1000 cows. A phone number was scrawled underneath.

Mick huffed and dumped the dog back into her arms. "Very funny, Glen." He grabbed a credit card from his pocket and had the door open in five seconds. The farm vet probably wouldn't return for hours and operated his business from his phone far more than from his office. Jules would square up with him after the next milk check.

They headed straight for the windowless examination room. The medical instruments and eerie quiet gave off a creepy vibe as the harsh fluorescent light contrasted against the darkened hallway and waiting room.

Meg whimpered as Jules placed her on the table. Mick hooked up a saline drip with antivenom. "I know they said it was a brown snake, but Kim wouldn't recognize the differences, and we all know Sam's rubbish at identifying snakes." There'd been a memorable incident when he'd mistaken a baby brown for a nonvenomous common tree snake. "I'll give her a combined dose just to cover our bases."

Jules sniffed and wiped her nose against her sleeve, past caring about minor issues such as the lack of a tissue.

Mick finished setting up the drip, then ran a calming hand across Meg's side. "You realize that face you're pulling right now? Multiply it by a million, and that was me." His blue eyes bored into her conscience.

Jules bit her lip. He must've been totally freaking out during those minutes when she was bloodied and unconscious, the ambulance still far away. "I know. I'm sorry." She stroked the soft tip of Meg's ear. "Please save her."

Mick touched her hand. "I'll do my best. And the puppies—there's a chance. We'll just have to see how it plays out."

The silence stretched. Jules's feet ached—both the booted one and the good one from bearing all her weight. But more uncomfortable was the awkwardness. Things still weren't completely right between them. She cleared her throat. "And about what I said on the slip and slide night—I shouldn't have needled you about your dad's farm. I was just mad at myself. So sorry. Again."

His lips curved. "You're forgiven. Again."

That look on his face—the hint of a smile that seemed to be reserved just for her, the brightness of his eyes—rewound the clock, and she was eighteen again, sitting in the shed with Mick, alternately fixing his motorbike together and kissing.

She broke eye contact, focusing on the dog and keeping the man in her peripheral vision.

Mick's smile widened, though he could not possibly have read her thoughts—could he? "Come on, Jules, let's be friends again."

Don't be a chicken. She forced herself to meet his gaze and shove aside any and all thoughts of making out. "Okay. How's the Gold Coast? Any churchgoing bikini models there?" Sam had flatted with Mick on the Goldie for a while before he went to the US, and she'd heard plenty about just how true the coastal stereotypes were.

"Jules."

"What? I can't ask? Friends are interested in other friends' love lives."

Mick acquiesced with a reluctant nod. "I haven't met any churchgoing bikini models."

"That's not what I was really asking."

He rolled his eyes. "Yes, I'm seeing a girl. No, she hasn't met my mum. Yes, I will skin you alive if you tell my parents."

Intriguing. Jules raised an eyebrow. "Why?"

He stared at her with a mutinous expression. She stared back. He huffed a sigh. "She's a mining company lawyer. The same company that's been plundering Queensland's best farms for years. According to my dad, at least."

122

Jules laughed. "Oh man, you know how to pick 'em. You just can't help but antagonize your family, can you?"

"She also has a great sense of humor, a love for God, and a soft spot for vets."

A hiss sounded from somewhere out back. Probably another feral cat Glen had patched up. Jules narrowed her eyes. "How soft?"

He grinned. "Jealous?"

"Of course not. Just making sure she appreciates what she's got." *And judging whether I need to scratch her eyes out or not.*

Mick ran a hand over his hair. "Well, it's still new, so . . . yeah. What about you?"

"Do you see any studly men getting about on my farm?"

"Besides myself and your brother, no."

She flipped her braid over her shoulder. "That answers the question."

"I guess there's not an abundance of decent blokes under fifty around here."

"Don't forget Jacko Saunders."

Even Meg gave a yip of disgust.

"He still stealing cars on Saturdays and playing the organ on Sundays?"

"Yup."

"I wish you both every happiness." He adjusted Meg's drip.

Jules's throat ached at the sight of her dog lying there limp. "She gonna make it?"

Mick pursed his lips. "We'll keep her on fluids overnight to reduce the risk for her liver and kidneys." He glanced around. "Glen's got a swag here somewhere. I'll stay overnight to make sure she's okay. Moving her now could cause problems."

Jules scanned the room, too, but didn't spot the swag—an Aussie term she'd had to explain to Kimberly the other day. The canvas sleeping bags with thin mattresses were a staple for those who loved camping. Glen probably had his stashed in that fire hazard he called an office.

She caught Mick's gaze and held it. Only a true friend would camp on the floor of the vet's overnight just to make sure her dog was okay. "Thanks."

The word didn't express enough, but for now it would have to do.

CHAPTER 16

So, what would you do if—" Kimberly paused her sentence as she stretched to reach the leaking copper pipe high in the dairy's rafters without losing her balance. Which was hard when Sam—who had his arms wrapped around her legs as he boosted her up—wobbled. Such things were necessary when the farm's only ladder had somehow disappeared. Jules had spent most of yesterday and today in town with Meg—and Mick—and texted them hourly with doggy updates but hadn't responded to their ladder question. "Hold still!" She grasped the pipe with one hand, wincing at the cobwebs, and wrapped plumbing tape around the leak they were attempting to repair.

Or, at the very least, redirect so it wasn't dripping on some exposed wiring Jules hadn't gotten around to fixing.

Sam steadied, his cheekbone hard against her knee, as she finished the job. And her question. "So, what would you do if you had no constraints? Money was no issue, I wasn't at Wildfire, the world was your oyster?" These probing questions had become their little game in the past twenty-four hours since they'd agreed to work together on a plan for the farm. Sam had finally shown a crack in his defenses, and she planned to jam the biggest crowbar into it she could.

"I have no idea," Sam mumbled against her shinbone.

She wrapped the last of the tape around the pipe and dropped her hands to his shoulders. "Done."

He loosened his grip so she slid through his arms to the ground. She landed lightly on her toes, her face inches from his. Heat exploded into her cheeks, and she took a step back. Boy, the sensation of his arms and chest gliding over her body had been— well, not unpleasant.

Not at all.

And that wasn't acceptable. "I, um, need to go get the cows." She spun on the rubber heel of her gum boot and power-walked out of the dairy, jumped on the newly repaired four-wheeler, and sped away.

What was wrong with her? She and Sam were just starting to get along. She'd finally been able to give Steph a kind-of-positive progress report. Any stupid emotions or hormones or whatever they were could not get in the way. She gave herself a stern talking-to over the next hour as she chased the cows from their paddock, puttered along behind the slow-moving herd, and then locked the gates behind the stragglers. When she tied a plastic apron around her waist and stepped down into the dairy pit, Sam turned straight to her. "What would you do?"

"What?"

"If you had no limits? What would you do?"

That didn't even require thought. "What I'm doing now. I mean, at home. Working with Wildfire to help it reach its full potential."

Sam pulled a disbelieving face. "Really?"

She frowned. What was he implying? "Yeah." She picked up the closest set of cups and held the first cup up to a cow's teat. It slurped on, and she moved to the next.

Sam worked beside her, leaning in her direction to be heard over the dairy noise. "So, if you had a gazillion dollars, the brains of Einstein, and the wisdom of Solomon, you would work at Wildfire the exact way you are now?"

Her brain scrambled for an answer that revealed more—but not that much more. "No. I'd also pay someone to run my sugar-free food empire, and I'd freelance as their taste tester. The Wildfire drop-in center has shockingly poor nutrition levels." She hesitated for a moment. Was it the right time to probe Sam about Wildfire? "And I'd use my piles of money to convince you to stay."

Her heart lodged in her throat. Would he close the door on this forever? The work they'd done together at Wildfire had given her a purpose she'd never known while consulting for start-ups in LA, but without Sam's spark the drop-in center felt less like a home away from home for these kids and more like a tutoring center. They needed their leader back.

Embarrassing as it was to admit, the image she pictured as she drifted off to sleep each night was her and Sam at Wildfire again, running the expansion program together. If they were still talking dream scenarios, she'd eventually add some consulting back in on the side, tackle projects that stretched her, like Greg's offer at Potted Plants 4 Hire. But she'd always have Wildfire to come home to.

So first she had to get Sam back.

Sam slid the next set of cups onto a cow, his movements quick with the confidence of hundreds of hours of practice. "You think you'd need piles of money to convince me?"

A spark of hope flamed to life. He hadn't laughed in her face, at least. But what was the key that'd unlock whatever held him back?

She attempted to attach the metal cup in her hand to the next cow's teat. It didn't suction properly, and the beast slammed the kick bar. Kimberly flinched, both from instinct and the muck now splattered on her cheek. The entire dairy reverberated with the impact. She opted for honesty. "Giving it three years didn't work."

Sam went silent for a moment, his hands busy fitting the metal-and-rubber milking cups onto a cow. Kimberly watched him from the corner of her eye. What was he thinking? She didn't mean to imply he was in it for the money—that thought was laughable, and they both knew it. Maybe it hadn't been a great idea to refer to his dislike of working with her. The past days had been new territory for them both. It was obvious that Sam was making a real effort. If she had just screwed that up with some ill-timed humor . . .

This was why she tended to get tongue-tied.

She turned her attention back to the cows. Whatever his thoughts were, they looked serious. Maybe it was better she didn't know.

Sam sprayed iodine disinfectant on the newly milked teats of the cattle, screwing up his eyes as the breeze blew the orange-brown concoction back onto him, and pondered Kimberly's answer to their what-if question. And his lack of one.

He looked over his shoulder toward Kimberly as she struggled to milk the cow in the last stall. "How did you have an answer so easily?"

She managed to get all four cups on a squirmy Jersey cow's

udder, but the suction didn't hold and the whole thing fell off. She huffed, shook the worst of the muck off the machine, and started again. "Answer to what?"

"To what you'd do if you could do anything. What makes Wildfire the thing for you?"

She reattached all four cups. The cow kicked and caught the rubber hose pumping milk to the vat, breaking suction again. The contraption fell off.

Sam took a second look. He knew that udder—cow number 481. A known brat.

He stepped forward, but Kimberly waved him off, set her jaw, and tried again. This time 481 munched on a mouthful of grain and decided she didn't care. The machine held, milk swirling down into the clear plastic "body" of the spiderlike machine and then disappearing into the black hose that went up to the pipes above their heads. Kimberly turned to him with a triumphant grin. He grinned back. She was nothing if not persistent. "So, what makes Wildfire your thing?"

She shrugged. "I dunno. It helps kids, I'm good at business, and it combines those things."

Sam chewed on his cheek and pondered. "Nope, that's not it."

"What?"

He grasped a water hose hanging down from an overhead pipe. Holding the spray against one palm had the double benefit of cooling him down and washing the filth from his hand. "That's not it. Those are good reasons, but that's not what gets you out of bed in the morning. It's not what puts you on a plane to 'Straya."

Jules had given Kimberly a thorough pronunciation lesson last night on how locals said *Australia*.

He jostled Kim with his shoulder. She slid him a sideways look. "Come on. You can tell me." Now that his brain had seized on the thought, it held on tighter than a koala in a gum tree.

She pursed her lips and appeared to consider the question for a long moment. "I guess . . . it's the act of taking something that has potential but is underdeveloped and helping it grow. That's what I did with businesses in LA before Wildfire." She rubbed her cheek against her shoulder, removing the worst of the splattered muck there.

"So, why'd you leave the business stuff for youth ministry?"

She met his eyes. "Don't get me wrong—business is great, and good businesses can really make people's lives better. But in Wildfire I can point to fifteen-year-old kids who now know they're loved and say, 'I helped make that happen.' And that's just"—she shrugged—"what gets me on a plane to 'Straya." The corner of her mouth lifted as she overarticulated the word.

He winked his approval.

She quirked an eyebrow. "Isn't that why you do it?"

Yikes. Back to him and his less-than-satisfactory answer. Should've seen that coming. He opened his mouth to obfuscate—Kimberly's word—when movement caught his attention. A cow tail above Kim.

Lifting.

Sam seized a handful of Kimberly's plastic dairy apron and yanked her toward him. She stumbled forward just in time, bounced off his chest, and almost fell backward. The cow shifted in her stall, lowering her tail again. False alarm.

Sam kept his grip on Kim's apron and steadied her. "Sorry. Thought she was—Sorry."

She blinked, then seemed to register his meaning. "Oh. Yep.

Thanks." He'd brought her half a step closer, and her cheeks pinked. He tucked that information away.

"Um, what were we talking about?"

Sam pulled the dairy's hydraulic controls to release the milked cows. The stalls lifted up and away like a Lamborghini door, and the cows wandered out into the yard. "What gets us out of bed for work. Mine's what you'd expect. Preaching or talking to the kids one-on-one. Getting to articulate the ultimate truths of the universe and put them into people's brains. Nothing better."

She cleared her throat. "I don't think you realize how good you are at it."

He looked at her and raised his eyebrows. Seriously? He'd had no formal tertiary education—barely, in fact, graduated Year 10—and had to rely on audiobooks, a strict preparation routine, and memorization to prepare his messages. Billy Graham he was not.

But Kimberly nodded enthusiastically, eyes latched on his face. "Talking to people the way you do. When you listen to someone, it's like you forget the rest of the world and they're the most fascinating thing in the universe to you. That's why the kids love you so much." She shrugged. "I've never had anyone really ask why I choose the work I do. It's nice to feel that someone's interested."

He stared at her, thoughts scrambling.

Kimberly picked up the length of poly pipe propped in the corner and walked toward the steps out of the pit, then turned back to him. "You don't know how much it means for someone who doesn't have anyone in their corner to really be listened to. It changes everything." Her expression flickered with something— loneliness? "That's why I've stuck by you for so long. That's why

I'll do anything to push you to reach your potential." Her expression turned rueful. "Even when you hate me for it."

She headed up into the yard to chase the next group of cows in. Sam watched her go, mind reeling from the impact of an emotional two-by-four.

This was how she saw him? His gaze unfocused as he replayed her words in his mind. *"That's why I'll do anything . . ."*

Her actions at Wildfire, her decision to come here—everything looked so different through this lens. She seriously had this kind of belief in him?

At least she hadn't pressed him for more information the way he'd pressed her. The truth was, given a gazillion dollars and the brain meld of Einstein and Solomon, he knew exactly what he'd do too. But he didn't have a gazillion dollars. Or a brain that could even read properly. So, he wiped away a glob of cow poop from his forearm and picked up the next set of cups, brain whirring to process this enigma of a woman that maybe he'd never really known before.

CHAPTER 17

Kimberly accidentally-on-purpose dropped a piece of ham from her second brekkie pizza scroll to Meg as she leaned against the workbench of Jules's machinery shed. It was lunchtime on day two of the dog's recovery—her first day home—and Meg thumped her tail appreciatively at Kim's feet as she gobbled up the tidbit. So far the Kelpie's appetite was just starting to return, and though they wouldn't know the true fate of the pups till birth, the signs were positive.

But from the mottled tone of Jules's face, she wasn't having quite as much fun. They'd been in here for the past hour, Jules tinkering with an old Massey Ferguson tractor's finicky battery while Kimberly gathered information from her on the farm.

Kimberly scanned the next question in her notebook and shrugged. They were twenty questions down, only sixteen more to go.

She wiped at a trickle of sweat that tried to sneak down her chest and into her soggy bra. Maybe Jules's face was just red from the heat. "So, is there a reason why you only milk twice a day? I read that increasing it to three times can increase milk production."

An empty soda can flew in her direction. Kimberly ducked. "Ow!"

The voice came from behind Kimberly's crouched position.

She swiveled. Sam stood a step inside the shed, rubbing a red mark on his forehead. He grabbed the collar of his shirt and swiped the dust and sweat from his face.

Kimberly bit her lip. Have mercy. He must've been working without his shirt on again, because his skin glowed with the tan that this Aussie sun perfected a little more every day.

Snap out of it.

Kimberly whirled back to Jules. "What was that for?" Jules was the one who'd asked her to help with a plan for the farm. Why was she bent out of shape now?

If she could concentrate for more than three seconds, she'd get that answer out of Jules. But Sam stopped beside her and crouched to pat Meg. He played with the dog's ears, flopping them over her face and then smoothing them back, making kissing noises the whole time. Kimberly shifted from one foot to the other. Was it wrong that her skin was tingling?

Meg's big brown eyes gazed up at Sam the whole time, till the dog made a quick movement and nailed him with a lick to the lips. Sam fell back onto his rump, laughed, and wiped his mouth on his shirt. The dog rolled onto her back and grinned up at Kimberly as Sam rubbed the animal's belly. Kimberly clasped her fingers together.

I am not jealous of a dog.

Sam clambered back to his feet. "Bit sick of this interview process, are we?"

Now that she'd gotten to throw something, Jules had a slight smile on her face. "More like a Spanish Inquisition." She picked up another can.

Kimberly ducked behind the workbench as Sam plucked the can from Jules's hand and tossed it aside. "Let's try a different approach." The eyes he turned upon Kimberly looked amused. Almost like he'd been waiting for this to happen. But who could have anticipated that thirty-six innocent questions about how Jules could run this farm more efficiently would annoy the other woman so much?

"Let's go for a ride." Sam led the way to the multicolored truck and opened the door. "How'd you like to drive without having to be sneaky about it, Jules?"

A smile peeked through Jules's sourpuss expression. "Mick rat me out?"

"He didn't have to." Sam placed her crutch into the truck bed as she pulled herself into the driver's seat, then slid in next to her, one leg on either side of the gearstick. "It'll be a team effort. I'll do the clutch and gear stick, you get steering and brakes." He patted the seat next to him. "Come on, Kim."

She approached with hesitation—there wasn't a whole lot of room left on that bench seat. The three of them had crammed in there on her first day in Australia, but that had been before. Now her brain was tuned into the Samuel Payton frequency, and she couldn't change the dial.

Sam grinned at her and winked.

She stopped. No way. This was weird.

"Oh, come on." He leaned out the door, grasped her forearm, and pulled her in. With the door shut, the three of them sat shoulder to shoulder . . . thigh to thigh. Kimberly rolled down her window and tried not to think about how, even on a day so hot she felt like a roast duck, the sensation of Sam's warmth against her side was exquisite.

Jules fired up the engine, and Sam shifted the vehicle into first. "Okay, Jules, take us on a tour. Pretend we've never seen the farm before. Take us to all your favorite spots and tell Kim about them."

Delight spilled over Jules's features, and she steered down the driveway. "Mum and Dad got married at the top of that rise in the front paddock. You can see half the farm from there. Then we'll hit the turkey's nest—our irrigation system is pretty nifty."

Kimberly shifted her eyes to Sam's face. Clever boy. Jules would probably volunteer half the information they needed, and a few well-placed questions from Sam would elicit the rest. How did he manage that? She talked to people and they got angry. Sam did it and they had a sudden urge to tell their entire life story. It was like he had a sign on his forehead that said, "It's okay. You're safe with me." Apparently the sign on her own forehead was less reassuring.

He caught her looking at him and offered a smile. She offered one back and mouthed a thank-you. He squeezed her hand and returned his attention to Jules's monologue about why the paddock of sorghum on their left was the fastest growing in the shire.

Two hours later they arrived back at the sheds and Jules left to go check on her chooks—chickens, to the uninitiated. Kimberly leaned against the truck and watched Sam unload a reel of electric tape and temporary fence posts from the truck bed. "Thanks for that. I didn't even realize she was ready to skin me until the Coke can went flying."

He gave her a smile that curled her toes. "That's what I'm here for. We're a team."

"*We're a team.*" A smile broke across her lips at his words.

Sam picked up an armload of equipment she didn't recognize. "Maybe that's how we should divvy up the work for this farm research." He hefted the gear into the back of the ute. "You can read numbers, I can read people. We need to interview some experts, get some shared knowledge behind this. What if I did that and you got the bank statements?"

"Sounds good to me." In fact, what she'd always wanted. "What's all that for?"

"A friend. Who happens to know a lot about farming, if you want to come join the chat. He'll be able to answer some of those more in-depth questions you've been asking."

"Right now?"

"Be there or be square." He tossed a few other random supplies into the truck bed.

Kimberly jumped into the passenger seat, and they motored down the driveway. The radio filled in a comfortable silence, with some Australian rapper laying down a rhyme about an ex-girlfriend. Kimberly whipped out her phone to Shazam the track. Dead battery. She seized Sam's phone from the dashboard.

"Your password still 2–5–1–2?" Irrelevant question. She was already in. She'd first guessed his password—the date of his favorite day of the year in the Aussie dd/mm date format—two years ago, and he'd still never bothered to change it.

"What are you doing?"

"Shazaming this song. I'm addicted to the way the Aussie accent sounds in a rap."

His phone buzzed as it recognized the song.

Sam hit the button to turn down the radio. Weird. Kimberly glanced at him.

Sam held an empty water bottle like a microphone in one hand and rapped Eminem's "The Real Slim Shady" with atrocious lyrical accuracy. Kimberly grinned. He'd rapped once in the middle of a school talk, and the kids had gone wild. She tapped his phone into camera mode. Jules would get a kick out of this.

Sam was halfway through his second chorus when he noticed the camera. "Hey!" He made a swipe at the phone.

Laughter bubbled out of Kimberly as she flattened herself against the door. His seat belt pulled tight and jerked him back. She kept filming. "Watch the road, Eminem."

They made it into town without crashing, and Sam pulled into a trailer park straight from a Stephen King novel. He stopped on the edge of the park beside a camper that rested next to the skeletal remains of a shed.

"This is your farming expert?" Nothing but weeds appeared to be propping up the camper's bottom right corner, which leaned at an unusual angle.

The camper's door popped open. A woman with the aura of a hungry cat stumbled down the steps wearing nothing but a blue cotton tank top—she'd heard Sam call his own a *bluey* yesterday—and shorts. "Is that the sexiest priest this side of Kosciusko?"

Sam hopped out. "Is that the sweetest baker this side of the Daintree?"

Kimberly slipped out of the truck as Sam and the woman exchanged a bear hug. She eyed the supplies in the back of the ute and the angle of the camper. If her hunch was correct, Sam wasn't just here to do reconnaissance. He was here to be a handyman.

"That your girlfriend?"

She snapped her attention back to the woman, who laughed with the bark of a lifelong smoker. Heat rushed through her as Sam glanced in her direction. Her mind's eye flashed back to their comfortable silence as they'd driven together. Her laughter while he rapped. The wrestle for the phone.

Did a part of her—a teeny-tiny part that also thought it was a good idea to poke forks into power outlets—wish the answer was yes?

Sam slung his arm around the woman's shoulder. "Kezza, meet Kimberly."

Kimberly gave a small wave and smile.

"Kim's a colleague visiting from the States, and we're here to talk to your dad. I rang him this morning." He nodded toward the camper. "And I'll take a look at getting you guys level. Might be able to weld something up."

Welding gear. That's what he'd put in the back of the truck.

Kezza propped her hands on her hips. "'Preciate it, but Dad's at the doctor's and I'm on my way out. He should be back in an hour, though."

Sam shrugged. "Gives me time to work on the caravan first." He nodded at a dilapidated mobile home a stone's throw away. "Butch in?"

Kimberly surveyed the home. This was where Butch, the man of mystery, lived? She'd done a few milkings with him, and they'd probably exchanged a total of five words.

Kezza slid into the driver's seat of a car that appeared to be more sticky tape than metal and barked a laugh. "Can't you tell by all the noise?" She threw her car into reverse and backed out with barely a glance behind. Kimberly jumped to the side and started when a voice spoke from behind her.

"I'm here."

She whipped around. Butch, hands in his pockets and a cigarette dangling from his lips. Where had he materialized from? He jerked his head toward his open door.

Sam pointed to the welding gear in the truck. "I'm gonna do

some work on Kezza's van first. You head in and grab a drink, Kim. I'll be a little while."

She widened her eyes at him, attempting to telegraph her thoughts. Small talk with Butch? Was he crazy?

But he just widened his eyes back at her, smiling, and hefted down the welding gear. Butch held his door open for her. She sighed and followed.

Clothes, dirty dishes, and a surprising number of troll dolls littered the home—with the exception of the tiny kitchen. That was meticulously clean and held a plateful of scones loaded with jam and cream. The scent of fresh-baked goods mingled with the aroma of cigarette smoke and the open can of Bundaberg Rum that sat on the bench. The tension seeped out of Kimberly as she inhaled the scents. Most people wouldn't find this particular aromatic combination comforting, but it reminded her of home, of Dad. If you replaced the fragrance of fresh baking with microwaved baked beans, it would've been a dead ringer.

She eyed the scones. "You bake?"

He sipped his rum. "Kez bakes too much for Bonesy to eat." The longest sentence she'd ever wrangled from him. He nodded for her to take a scone, but she spied a stack of comic books underneath a pile of dirty tea towels. Superman, circa 1970s by the look of the cover. "You're into comic books?"

Butch shrugged.

Kimberly picked the top one off the pile and leafed through it, careful not to damage the pages. "A lot of people love John Byrne, but José Luis García-López was one of my favorite Superman artists."

Butch took a long drag of his cigarette. "You draw?"

"My dad did."

"Published?"

She waved the idea away. "Only amateur. But my eleven-year-old self thought he was good enough to do it for a living." She reached for her notebook and pulled out a folded piece of paper. "This is one of his." It'd fallen out of her Bible. She'd found it on the floor this morning and popped it in the notebook for safekeeping.

Most people would think it odd she still took her twenty-year-old children's Bible with her when she traveled, but they hadn't seen the illustrations that Dad had drawn and pasted in it. Mom's religious parents had agreed not to hassle him about custody if he took her to church. He'd spent the long hours in the pews sketching replacement illustrations for her hokey kid's Bible. Fat-cheeked cherubs were replaced with angelic warriors, cartoon-y soldiers with epic battle scenes that probably contained far more gore than was appropriate for any six-year-old. But those bedtimes going through that Bible together were hands-down her favorite memories.

Butch peered at the illustration. This one depicted Joshua standing over the rubble of Jericho, a massive unseen being holding a sledgehammer behind him. A smile broke over his craggy features. "Not bad." He held it up to the light of the window. "Bit like Lee Bermejo."

"That was his favorite DC artist."

Three jam-covered scones later, they'd covered the merits of the Silver Age of comics versus the Bronze Age, everything wrong with Marvel's *Trouble* comic, and whether *The Killing Joke* was the best Batman comic of all time. Plus, she'd told Butch all about her dad's story, from when he gave up a college art scholarship to raise her to his short battle with sarcoma.

A yelp sounded from outside.

Kimberly jerked her gaze to the open window in time to catch Sam slapping at his shirt, welding mask still on his face. He stripped the mask and gloves off and approached the window. "Got any ice? Or water?"

She stood. "You're burned?"

"More like a singe."

Butch pointed to a tap that jutted from a fence post. Kimberly hustled out of the home, and he followed at a slower pace. At the tap, Sam cupped his hands under the water and poured it over a quarter-sized hole in his shirt, a few inches above his hip.

Kimberly swept her gaze over his arms and neck. Tiny red marks peppered his skin. "You're burned all over."

He shrugged. "Part of the job. And I'm a rubbish welder." He grinned. "The new steel support's ready, though. I'll let it cool off, and then we just need to jack up the van and get it in place."

"Then you deserve a scone." They settled in camp chairs on the front porch, and three scones later a man who weighed three hundred pounds if he weighed an ounce rolled up to Kezza's home on a child-sized motorbike.

Sam wandered over and talked to him for a minute, pointing to the corner of the camper and the new steel support. Then he waved Kimberly over. "Bonesy, tell Kim more about the water efficiency we were talking about this morning."

Kimberly shook the man's meaty paw and had to close her mouth to contain her surprise—and her scone—as Bonesy launched into a monologue with the expertise of a university professor.

After three hours of detailed technical discussions, she and Sam said their goodbyes and departed with a covered plate of a dozen more scones. Kimberly checked the time as she climbed into the truck. Two fifteen. Time to get the cows for the next milking. She flipped through the twenty pages of notes she'd taken and tucked Dad's drawing inside the notebook as Sam drove them down the driveway. She'd promised Butch she'd make a copy of the illustration at the Paytons' and bring it to him next time they visited.

Sam rattled off Bonesy's history as they rumbled out of the trailer park. "In the nineties he was the biggest landowner in the district. He went broke during the Millennium drought, then had two heart attacks and a stroke. Kez lived a hard life, and they were estranged, but when he got sick, she moved back in her van and took care of him. He's called Bonesy because before she moved back in with him he was always skin and bones. They've been Butch's neighbors for about ten years now."

Kimberly skimmed her notes. "He's so knowledgeable." Which was bittersweet. Bonesy was a good source of information, but he'd only confirmed her suspicions about the farm's future.

Sam glanced in her direction. "You and Butch seemed to get along well while I was welding. I heard a little bit through the window."

Kimberly snapped her notebook shut. "We both like comic books."

"Your dad drew?"

"Some." She left it at that. Talking about Dad with Butch was fine—therapeutic, even. Butch didn't judge the excessive violence depicted in his drawings, didn't criticize her extensive knowledge of R-rated science-fiction movies—all obtained before she reached double digits. He only laughed when she admitted she'd not tasted broccoli till she was eight but could smell the difference between rum and whiskey at four.

Dad had not been a perfect parent—she knew that. But he'd loved her. He'd sacrificed his own future for her. And he'd spent more time with her than most of her friends' dads combined. But most people couldn't see past the imperfections in her memories through to the beauty of them. She never wanted to see that look of censure in Sam's expression.

Or even worse, the line of questioning could veer toward Mom.

So, she opted for distraction. "Bonesy seemed pretty complimentary of your property."

Sam took the bait. "Too right he is. Did you hear him say he tried to buy Mum and Dad out a couple of times? These are some of the best river flats on the Burnett."

Kimberly leaned back in her seat and listened to him regurgitate all the best facts about the property. Sam's memory seemed to be selective. He left out the fact that milk prices had already peaked in their usual five-ish-year cycle and that the impending collapse of one of the major suppliers wasn't likely to do the market any favors. That, plus a dozen other warning signs, showed that low-level changes like water efficiency weren't going to make a big enough dent in this problem. And she hadn't even gotten to the risk of a natural disaster.

But right now he was smiling and looking at her like she wasn't the devil incarnate, and she didn't quite have the fortitude to shatter that illusion.

Yet.

CHAPTER 18

K imberly was doomed.

She ducked a branch that whizzed past her face as Sam practically floated ahead of her along the riverbank, walking home from an afternoon of tea and Anzac cookies—biscuits, to the Australians—at the Carrigans'. His cheery whistle filled the air, and she sighed.

She should have seen this coming when they agreed to divide up the work. Everyone Sam interviewed delivered the same report—the Payton family owned fertile river flats, secure water rights, and a family heritage that had seen over a hundred years of successful dairying. Now Sam was even more puffed up by Mick's father's nostalgic memories of Jules's farm and its production capabilities, only a day after their conversation with Bonesy had had a similar effect.

But they did not see the balance sheet.

A long brown something caught her gaze, and she jumped on instinct. A stick. She shuddered at the memory of what had happened to Meg—who was now recovering steadily—and hustled to catch up to Sam. Dried gum leaves and weeds crunched beneath her heavy steps. She should've had this conversation earlier. The longer she waited, the higher their expectations built.

But her mind wandered back to last night, when Jules had

closed Kimberly's laptop lid as she answered her thousandth Wildfire email and dared her and Sam to a bake-off. He with his decadent recipes from the café days, and her with the best her sugar-free repertoire had to offer. After extensive sampling of both offerings—and blatant attempts at bribery from both sides—Jules had declared Sam the winner by a narrow margin. They'd laughed, swapped recipes, and eaten way too much. As she'd fallen asleep last night, she'd replayed the evening in her head, polishing each memory to treasure in the future. For the first time in her life, she had real friends. And she wanted to help save their farm.

But it didn't look like she could be a friend and save their farm as well.

They reached the east bank of the river and clambered up onto a platform fixed to a huge gum tree. The shortcut across the river—Sam's famous flying fox. A cable stretched between two riverbank trees, suspending a pulley and handle over the water. A rope ran from the handle to where it was tied at the base of the tree. Sam untied the rope and pulled the handle in close.

Kimberly leaned against the tree trunk, giving a half-hearted smile at his enthusiasm. She'd run the figures for the thousandth time in a fit of insomnia at three this morning. Best-case scenario, Jules's finances would keep her afloat—at a struggle—for another ten years. But given any kind of milk-price collapse, cattle sickness, or large plant cost, and she'd struggle to recover. When you took into account the frequency with which Australia suffered bushfires, cyclones, and droughts, it was hard to imagine her keeping the bank from the door long term. The situation wasn't hopeless—Kimberly had quadruple checked—but the solution required a significant loan.

Sam and Jules were going to hate this—hate *her*—and she wasn't sure she could bear it one more time.

"Okay, I'm going across." Sam gripped the triangular handle of the flying fox and jumped. The cable bounced with the force of his weight and he let out a whoop as he sailed across the water. At the two-thirds mark he let go, doing a backflip as he plummeted into the water. After a moment he resurfaced and used the rope to tug the handle along as he swam to the far bank and climbed the platform. "You ready?" he hollered. He tied the bottom end of the rope to the handle to keep it from dragging in the water, and with a mighty shove sent it flying back her way.

She caught the handle and gave a thumbs-up rather than reply. They'd already gone through this routine on the way over . . . except she'd gone first and landed—barely—on the platform instead of dropping into the water. Thus Sam's insistence to go first this time.

He cupped a hand to his mouth as he called back. "Don't forget, if you don't want to get wet, then just hang on and I'll catch you at the platform. But if you want to swim, the current's not strong, and I checked it the other day for snags."

Which was scarier: swimming in the river with unknown other life forms or literally falling into Sam's arms? After the snake-in-the-dam incident the other day, Sam seemed like the safer option.

But only just.

She stood at the edge of the platform and, one hand on the handle, wiped her other palm against her shorts. Then swapped. How could she tell the man about to catch her that his family's heritage was at such serious risk? Especially given how he'd reacted in the past.

It'd be easy, so easy, to keep her mouth shut and let Sam tell Jules the positive reports from Bonesy and Mick's father. Leave them with happy memories of this month together and hope that something miraculously turned their luck around in the future.

Or she could tell them the truth, risk their friendship, and possibly save their future on this farm.

She jumped. The pulley above her head whirred as the wide river rushed beneath her. Sam's grinning face grew closer and closer until—*bang*—the pulley hit the rubber tires threaded onto the cable as cushioning. Sam caught her on the backswing, arms latching around her waist. She released the handle and her breath, held tight for a moment against Sam's broad chest. He settled her back onto her feet and released her, grinning. "Easy-peesy."

His joy only made this worse. Her returning smile was lackluster at best. His brow creased. "You okay?"

God, give me courage. She drew in a deep breath. "We need to talk about what we're going to tell Jules."

He nodded. They spoke at the same time.

"The farm is going to be fine."

"Jules should take out a mortgage against the cattle and invest."

Sam's smile dropped away. "What?"

Uh-oh. Maybe she should've eased him into the idea a little. "I know Mick's dad was really positive about the farm." She slowed her words and tried not to let the gnawing in her chest seep into her voice as she laid a palm on the gum tree's trunk for balance. "Which is what makes me confident that investing is the best way out of this."

The look he gave her was incredulous. "How is going further into debt going to help us get out of it?"

When he hates this idea, don't take it personally. She kept repeating the refrain in her head as she eased around him, backed down the platform ladder, and explained. "Your production isn't enough to cover costs, not long term when you factor in machinery and plant repairs or a milk-price collapse. But this land can sustain more cattle. An additional loan can supply the cattle and boost what we're feeding them to increase production."

Sam followed her down. "What about the efficiencies Bonesy talked about? Or ideas like having Butch live in the worker's cottage in lieu of part of his wage?"

"All worth doing. But not going to make a big enough dent alone."

He stood at the base of the tree and threw out alternative ideas for another ten minutes. Kimberly pushed all her nervous energy into tapping her left foot and kept her voice as calm as possible. Even when Sam suggested the worker's cottage a third time. It was when he implied she might've "forgot to carry the one" in her calculations that she got a little testy.

Once Sam ran out of alternatives, he just kept shaking his head like a short-circuiting robot. "I can't take that plan to Jules. What if we lose everything?"

All his talk of teamwork, and he didn't trust her one iota more than he had six months ago. Her last thread of patience snapped, and she threw her hands in the air. "So that's it? You're full of big talk about Team Jules, but you won't actually listen to my ideas?"

Sam ran a hand through his hair. "I'm just saying that your idea sounds extreme, and I'm trying to find a middle ground."

Kimberly sucked in a deep breath and tried to let the sting of the comment pass. But failed. *Why don't you trust me? I've only got your best interests at heart. In case you didn't notice, I only stand to lose here.* The words stuck in her throat, soured, and she spat out something entirely different. "I spent this week calculating two-, five-, and ten-year projections to determine the probability of Jules's success if she does nothing, invests minimally, or makes a decent-sized investment." She should have held her next words back, but—"And your opinion is based on, what, a few old farmers that you yapped to for a couple of hours?"

A flash of hurt crossed his expression. They glared at each other until Kimberly's ringtone broke the moment. She hit the answer button. "Jules?"

"Are yous coming or what? The rodeo starts in one hour, and you're not even home yet. I put lip gloss on and everything." Her voice blasted from the phone so loudly Sam must've heard it. He headed in the direction of the truck, leaving flinging branches and trampled twigs in his wake. Kimberly hustled to keep up with him.

When she'd found out about this rodeo yesterday, she couldn't wait for a fun night out with Sam. Now she wished she could give an *I Dream of Jeannie* nod and teleport him to Timbuktu.

CHAPTER 19

Who had he been kidding? Sam gripped the steering wheel of Jules's ute and glared at the road instead of the woman in a cute lacy dress and cowgirl boots beside him.

The woman destined to be his nemesis.

He should be punching his boxing bag right now, not driving to the rodeo. When Jules had waved them goodbye and jumped into Mick's ute like it was the queen's golden carriage, she'd looked so happy. And why shouldn't she? He'd told her only yesterday that she had nothing to worry about.

Big mistake.

Now Kimberly wanted to tell her to take the biggest financial risk of her life, because apparently the farm would be broke in a few short years. It just didn't compute.

Kimberly reached across and hit the radio button, presumably to fill the tense silence. Some awful racket blared from the speakers. She'd already offered a dozen times to take him through her calculations but appeared to have decided now to save her breath. As she should. He had no doubt those calculations would say exactly what Kimberly described—because she was the one who'd done them. If a neutral third party was asked to do the same research, they could reach a totally different conclusion.

He shifted in his seat. Was its lack of lumbar support making

151

his back ache, or was it the way his muscles tightened every time he fought with her?

He sensed her gaze on him. "What?" If it was more about her plan for Jules, he didn't want to hear it. Back by the river she'd pretty much implied he was dumb for not just taking her word for it. His brain flashed back to that day in Year 8 when his teacher had marched him out of class and sat him in special ed.

Rather a sore point.

She opened her mouth to say something, then appeared to think better of it. "Never mind."

He shoved the air-conditioning vents away from his face as the evening's temperatures dropped lower than usual. It wasn't even like he was mad at Kimberly for wanting to make the suggestion to Jules. She was an ambitious person, so to her, ambitious plans seemed normal. Of course she would come up with something like this. But if he could understand her take-no-prisoners approach, surely she could at least try to understand his cautious mind-set. But no, she got angry, like normal, and any hope for a productive discussion went out the window.

A voice whispered in his mind that Kimberly had tried the reasonable route . . . and he hadn't listened. He turned up the radio's punk-rock cacophony and tuned the voice out.

The forty-minute drive to town was completed without speaking to one another any further, even when they met up with Mick and Jules in the dusty paddock where everyone parked. The stands were packed by the time they got their snacks and drinks, and they had to clamber up the stairs and sneak between rows of denim and RM Williams boots to find a space where they could all squeeze in.

Sam angled for a seat by Mick. Hopefully his friend's chilled sense of humor would wash away the bad aftertaste of his encounter with Kimberly. But Jules sneaked in, engrossed in some discussion with Mick about the Cowboys' chances of winning the rugby league premiership next season. Kimberly nabbed the seat by her new best friend Jules.

Sam sighed at the last space. End of the line, next to Kimberly. Great. Now all he'd get for his twenty bucks was a numb butt on these hard seats and a chill from Kimberly's freeze-out.

He took his seat, the metal cold in the night air, even through his jeans. Kimberly sat next to him, silent, eyes on the barrel racers and cowgirl boots daintily crossed at the ankle. She had to be feeling this unseasonably cool night in that dress.

He wrapped his hands around the warmth of his cardboard box of chips—fries to Kimberly—though these were cut thicker than usual french fries. The scent of fat and salt uncoiled the tension inside him. He drenched the chips in tomato sauce—Australia's alternative to ketchup—like it was Noah's flood and he was God. Lifting his first chip, he closed his eyes in anticipation.

But wait. He opened his eyes. He might as well be the first to offer an olive branch, even though all the hostility came from her side. He held out the box. "Chip?" They'd help warm her at the very least.

Her eyes didn't even flicker in his direction. "No, thanks."

He rolled his eyes and stuffed the chip into his mouth. The sweet-and-salty flavor explosion didn't quite trigger the same amount of ecstasy as usual. Consolation prize.

A moment later his phone buzzed.

Jules: **did u two fight?**

Curse her perception. How could he explain this without explaining why?

He tapped in **Creative differences.**

Another buzz. **Well kiss and make up already.**

He snorted. Fat chance. He focused on the lady barrel racers whizzing past at breakneck speed. Vibrations tickled his thigh again.

Jules: **I think usually when Kimba's mad, it's just 'coz her feelings are hurt.**

Huh.

Jules: **For a youth pastor ur kinda thick headed.**

He shot her a look over Kimberly's head. His sister returned the look, wide-eyed.

Was he being thickheaded? He hadn't attacked Kimberly herself. He'd just resisted her terrifying plan of action. Why would she be so hurt by that?

Her words from earlier replayed in his head. *"You're full of big talk about Team Jules, but you won't actually listen to my ideas."*

And last week: *"You think I'm this monster . . . I'd hoped we could actually be friends."*

She did care. She wanted to feel a part of the team. And as usual, it seemed, he was blocking her.

He nudged her lace-covered knee with his denim one. "You know I still think you're on Team Jules. I just favor a different approach to yours, that's all."

The eyes she turned to him held a slight sheen to them. He tightened his grip on the box of chips. He'd expected angry, dismissive, or proud. Not sad.

"You say that because you feel bad." She blinked, the sheen disappeared, and she faced the barrel racers again.

She was sad? Because of what he'd said? The emotions from the day Meg was bitten by the snake hit him again like a bulldozer. Once again, he'd underestimated the effect his frustration had on her.

How could he convince her that he did mean it—without caving to her plan?

An upbeat tune pumped from the speakers. A big love heart popped up on the jumbo screen, beneath the words *Kiss Cam*. Sam's face flashed up on screen, and his heart nearly stopped. But the camera kept moving, till it rested on . . . Mick and Jules. Mick's face flushed a bright red, and Jules grinned. The crowd chanted, "Kiss, kiss, kiss, kiss." Jules plucked the Akubra from Mick's head, held it up between them and the camera, and leaned over to him. Shifting back to see behind the hat, Sam could tell she'd planted a big smooch on Mick's cheek, not his lips.

Good. They'd broken each other's hearts once, and he didn't need them both crying on the phone to him again. But it didn't make Mick's cheeks any less than a shade of Rudolph red when Jules dropped the hat back on his head.

The camera landed on an old farmer and his wife next, who leaned out of their matching deluxe camp chairs for a quick peck. Then a young woman in rhinestone-encrusted jeans and an over-enthusiastic cowboy. A bull that appeared displeased with the notion of going into a pen caught Sam's attention, so it was a moment before he realized one of the next faces on the screen was his own. And the other Kimberly's.

Her face matched Mick's in an instant.

He couldn't help but smile at her discomfort. The crowd, hyped up already, wouldn't let it go. They chanted, jeered, and booed, and that camera just wouldn't give up and choose another couple. Some kid tossed a soggy chip at Kimberly, and

Sam glared at him. Then turned to Kimberly and tried not to sound as enthusiastic as he suddenly felt. "I don't think they're giving up."

She wriggled on the bench. "I guess not."

Perhaps all the enthusiasm was on his side. He glanced toward Jules. She'd wave him off if this wasn't a great idea.

But she grinned, gave a double thumbs-up, then started making kissy faces.

Maybe this was one way he could show Kimberly he was genuine.

He caught her jaw with gentle fingers, and she turned her face to his. He allowed himself a moment of anticipation—and pure terror. Her skin was smooth beneath his fingertips, her pulse fluttering under his touch. This close, the scent of her raspberry lip balm teased his senses, as did the plump curve of her lips. Her eyes, wide and hazel, looked straight into his.

Here goes nothing.

He dipped his head and pressed a gentle kiss to her mouth. That raspberry lip balm did not disappoint, and her lips were even softer than they looked. However, since they did have an audience of about two thousand people, he moved—with reluctance—to break the kiss.

But then her hand slid between his neck and his collar, and her stiff posture relaxed against him. Before he could stop himself, Sam cradled her face with his other hand and said everything his words couldn't convey with the movement of his lips against hers. *I admire your grit. I wish I had your confidence. I want you on my team.*

You're beautiful.

Wolf whistles broke into his consciousness as Kimberly pulled back, just the tiniest bit. He opened his eyes. Hers were half shut, her breathing unsteady, her scent now more intoxicating than it had ever been.

The announcer launched into a spiel about the upcoming bull ride, and the sound seemed to snap Kimberly awake. She withdrew back to her side of the bench, her gaze flicking from him to the bullring, back to him, and then her shoes.

Sam drew in a deep breath and tried to slow his galloping heart rate down. But neither focusing on the bull ride nor pressing his sweating can of soft drink against his cheek had any effect whatsoever.

Had it been this hot earlier? He resisted the urge to fan his face like a menopausal woman. Fair dinkum, it was just a silly Kiss Cam kiss.

Right?

Her phone was ringing.

Kimberly fumbled for the device in the dark. Was Mom finally calling her back?

She reached for the bedside table and encountered wetness. Whoops, that was one of the two glasses of water she'd left there. She groped about, trying not to knock over the four books, pile of research papers, and alarm clock also perched on the table. The clock blinked 2:07 a.m. in red numbers. Great. So it'd been about seventeen minutes since she'd stopped thinking about Sam's kiss and fallen asleep.

There'd been so much to ponder—her intense embarrassment, why they had kissed so long, and which of them had been responsible for that. Most important, how pointless it would be to crush on someone who would never like her back.

Which led to her sleep-deprived state and clumsier than usual fingers. Finally, they closed around her phone.

Not Mom, but Steph. Plus a missed call from her, time stamped a minute ago. Kimberly swiped. "Steph, it's two in the morning."

Steph's voice crackled on the long-distance connection. "Ohhhhh, sorry. Miscalculation. But now that you're awake already . . . you're going to want to hear this."

Somehow she doubted that. Kimberly sighed and kicked back her sheet. "Hold on. Let me go to the veranda. There's better Wi-Fi on that side of the house." She raced past the sleeping household in bare feet, exited the back door, and sat on the steps. Toads croaked from the ground below and the occasional cow mooed in the distance. "Okay, hit me." A fresh breeze kicked up, raising gooseflesh on her arms.

Indistinct music played in the background of Steph's call. Was she in the car? "I'm hearing chatter I don't like. I just came from lunch with a couple of the other board members. They've swung against finding a replacement for Sam."

Kimberly's chest tightened, and she rubbed her eyes. This couldn't be happening, not now. "It's two a.m., Steph; I can't do subtext. What are you saying?"

"You either go all in on Sam or you come home now. Two more weeks and I don't think they'll warm to any replacement, no matter who it is."

Home. Funny thing was, at times her heart felt as at home here as if she'd been born in this house.

"If I got on a plane tomorrow and lost any chance with Sam, do you think I could convince them to stay open?"

"Yes, because you'd get to them individually and unleash that Kimberly Foster persuasiveness that I love. But if you wait till after the next board meeting, I'm convinced they'll lose faith."

Kimberly tapped her forehead against the stair rail beside her. "Okay. I'll—I'll think about it."

Steph signed off and Kimberly stared at the black screen of the phone. This was not a 2:00 a.m. decision—at least, not one she should make alone. She turned the screen on and punched in a number.

Come on, pick up.

"Kimberly?"

She sat up straighter. "Hey, Mom."

She endured the awkward sorry-I-didn't-call-you-back excuses and launched into her predicament, sketching out the situation in the broadest strokes.

"... and that's how I ended up in Australia talking to you at two in the morning."

"Wait—you mean you're there right now? You went to Australia? Kimberly, I think there were more efficient solutions than that. This man isn't irreplaceable."

Tell that to her still-tingling lips.

"I tried, Mom. We hired three other people, but he has this X factor, and the board . . . We—I—trust him. He's the right guy for this. I just have to convince him." *God, please help me to convince him.* The way things were going, it'd take nothing short of an act of God.

"The ones you need to convince are your board. You need to show them you have this place under control by yourself. You don't need some Australian farmer. Seriously, Kimberly, you could be on the fast track to the C-suite if you wanted." Her mother huffed. "Never mind. Who're your top contenders?"

Kimberly rubbed a hand over her face. "Mom, you're not listening. Sam—"

"From what I'm hearing Sam has weakened your position and caused these problems. Cut the dead weight loose."

Kimberly fell silent, save for a sniff. Logic supported her mother's opinion, but her brain rejected the image of a Wildfire without Sam. She sniffed again.

"Are you crying? Honestly, I expected better than this. If you can't handle that little organization on your own, I don't know why the board wants you."

Kimberly cringed. Mom's mantra: toughen up and learn to do it yourself. A phrase she'd heard constantly since moving in with Mom as a grief-stricken eleven-year-old. And an area she still failed in. "I know."

"Change your plane ticket and get back over here, or it sounds like you won't have a job come New Year's."

Their goodbyes as stilted as the hellos, Kimberly sighed with relief as the phone beeped to signal the end of the call. She pressed the phone to her forehead and groaned. Mom's instinct for managing boards and nervous stakeholders was legendary. She should search flights and bus routes.

But her fingers didn't move.

Did she even want a Wildfire without Sam? One day, sure, the ministry would need to run without him—a cult of personality was never healthy. But that day would come after they established a culture and mentored new leaders. Right now the ministry was still toddling about, in need of that special something only Sam could bring.

But how could she convince him? She'd tried logic, tried bargaining, tried the threat of closure. Her mind raced back, first to the day at the dam, second to the day Meg was bitten—two of the first moments when Sam had thawed toward her. Two moments when her guard had come down, if only temporarily.

Maybe going all in didn't just call for a career risk but an emotional one. Her insides quivered, the hurt from Mom's words still rolling in waves through her system.

She just wasn't sure she could take any more punches tonight.

CHAPTER 20

S am screwed his eyes shut and hummed, trying to block out the sound of Kimberly's conversation with her mother. Not that he didn't enjoy the soft lilt of her voice. It just sounded like a private discussion. But as he shifted the pillow pressed to his ear, a few words slipped in.

". . . crying? Honestly, I expected better than this. If you can't handle that little organization on your own, I don't know why the board wants you."

Kimberly's hushed tones sounded again. "I know."

Sam sat bolt upright. Had he heard that right? That was the kind of care she got from her *mother*? He shook his head. If that's what she'd grown up with, no wonder Kim had the prickliness of a porcupine with PMS.

He listened but heard nothing. Was she okay?

Pulling on the high-vis work shirt from the top of his "clean stuff" laundry basket, he slipped through the dark house until he was at the back door.

Kimberly sat huddled on the top step in an oversized LA Dodgers T-shirt and—he assumed, from his angle—the *Battlestar Galactica* pajama shorts he'd seen her in this week. She turned as the hinges squeaked, and whispered, "Did I wake you?"

"Wasn't sleeping well anyway." And that was the truth. When

he wasn't thinking about Kimberly's lips on his, he'd been tumbling her words in his mind.

"You're full of big talk about Team Jules, but you won't actually listen to my ideas."

It was time to admit his hesitation didn't come from reasonable caution. A reasonably cautious person would've agreed to go through Kimberly's figures and hear her out. No, he was bunny-in-front-of-a-semitrailer scared.

He opened his mouth to speak, but words came out of Kimberly's mouth instead.

"That was my mom. She told me to give up on you."

He lowered himself onto the step beside her. Kimberly's mum was right, but hearing it aloud deflated him more than expected. He braced his forearms on his knees, gaze on the moonlit paddocks before them. "And?"

"I don't want to. But Steph said the board's growing doubtful."

The disappointment in her voice cracked something inside of him. Had she asked him to shift Mount Everest by himself, he'd have gone to find a shovel. But to be responsible for other people's investments in him? He laced his fingers together. "I'm sorry for how I acted today. And I don't want Wildfire to end. But this future you envision—I'm not convinced I can do it."

She rested her chin in her hand. "I know." The quiet resignation in her voice tore at him. He'd let her down. Again.

But maybe he wasn't the only thing upsetting her. Time for a subject change—into the mystery of Kimberly's family. "So your mum's a tough cookie?"

She sat up straighter. "How much did you hear?"

Interesting reaction. He opened his mouth to say, "Not much," but she kept talking. "She's not as bad as she sounds. She thinks

Dad made me too soft. She's still just trying to course correct." Her words tumbled over one another in her rush to get them out.

He shook his head. Parenting styles aside, Kimberly's mother was flat-out wrong—about so many things. "The board wants you for a thousand reasons I can't even begin to list." He shifted his gaze from the soft gray landscape to Kimberly's moonlit face. She stared at the steps below, unmoved—till a lone tear slid down the curve of her face. He couldn't help himself; he touched his finger to her cheek and caught it. "*We* want you."

The smile she gave him was sad. She obviously didn't believe him, and he couldn't blame her. No matter how many tears he caught or nice things he said, when push came to shove, he had never let her play on his team.

He grasped her cold fingers in his. "I'm serious."

She swiped at her eyes and took a deep breath, her face clearing of emotion. "Thanks."

Any other day of their partnership—*every* other day of their partnership—he'd have taken that at face value. But these last days had honed his Kimberly radar, which screamed with one clear message: she was shutting him out.

He added his other hand to the one already holding hers. "Your mum tells you not to cry, and I've been willfully ignorant of the hurt I've caused you in the past. But you don't have to hide that part of yourself anymore." He grimaced. How many times had he caused her pain and she'd just hidden the hurt? The dragon lady had an underbelly far softer than he'd ever imagined. "Not that I've given you much reason so far to believe me."

Her breath releasing, she mumbled something he didn't quite catch. "*All in*"? What did that mean?

"If you really want to know, Mom never wanted me. She was

seventeen and freaking out when she had me. If my grandfather wasn't religious and paying for her college, she would've aborted me." The fingers that tucked stray hair behind her ear trembled. "But Grandfather ruled with an iron fist, so I was born and given to Dad, but he died when I was eleven. Grandfather was gone by that time, and I moved in with Mom. I'd hoped by then that she was ready to be more than a school-holiday parent. But we never really connected."

Memories of his own childhood flooded Sam's mind—Sunday baking with Mum, her homework tutoring, her cheers from the sideline at the school athletics carnival. Nausea flooded him at the thought of grieving eleven-year-old Kim living in a strange house with an emotionally distant mother. "She was hard on you?"

She plucked a stray gum leaf from the stair and snapped it in half, then the halves into halves, till her hands were full of tiny brittle pieces. "My dad was artistic like yours, but more into comic books than landscapes." She shrugged. "Mom's all business, a rising star. She thought Dad was too soft on me and that I wouldn't be tough enough to make it in the real world, so she decided to fix that. It's her way of giving me my best chance in life."

A line she'd probably told herself a thousand times to ease the pain. But that couldn't fix the festering rejection that now appeared so obvious. How had he never seen it before?

"Whatever her intentions, that had to have been tough."

Kimberly pressed her lips together. Had she ever discussed this out loud before? He racked his brain for a list of her friends. She'd never seemed especially close to anyone—and obviously didn't have family she could confide in.

Her voice dropped to a low tone. "She dropped that tidbit about aborting me when I was twelve, on Mother's Day. I used to ask her all the time if she loved me—like, obsessively ask. Part of dealing with Dad's death, I guess." She snapped another leaf. "She'd just say 'of course' but never actually use the words 'I love you.' Eventually she got sick of it and tried to toughen me up a bit more." The leaves in her hands were fragments now, darkened by three tear splatters. "I know she must've been scared back when she found out she was pregnant—but I think there were probably better ways to tell me about it."

Her words from earlier tonight replayed again: "*Team Jules.*" The pieces clicked into place—all the way back to the beginning of her time with Wildfire. Her passion for Wildfire's homey drop-in center. Her determination now to save his family's heritage. Her enthusiasm for Team Jules. No wonder she'd looked so hurt earlier tonight. This woman craved belonging the way his lungs craved oxygen.

Words failing him, he slid an arm across her shoulders. She leaned into him, just the tiniest amount.

God, what can I even say to help this? No words came. If only he could convey the truth of how much God wanted her as easily as he could lend his warmth. "You have a right to feel grief over that. And I know the phrase sounds trite, but God loves you. To Him, there was nothing about you that was unexpected or less than delightful."

She nodded, wordless.

"If you're not getting on a plane tomorrow, I'd love to hear your plans for Wildfire again. I can't make any promises, and I definitely can't leave Jules in the lurch. But I'll listen. I promise."

A pause. "Okay. Thanks."

The silence lingered, awkward—at least for him. If only he'd been able to promise her more, say he'd come back to Wildfire, put that spark back in her eyes. But it wasn't on the table right now. So with his free hand he plucked at a splinter separating from the step. "Thanks for telling me."

She brushed the gum-leaf pieces from her palms. "I guess coping with her means I come off a little . . . aloof. Maybe abrasive. At least now you know why."

He gave a gentle squeeze. "I think we've both let our insecurities get the better of us. Thanks for trying to make me listen. You're a real friend."

A hint of a smile softened her lips. "I've always wanted to be your friend."

He couldn't help but grin. "You're a lot more honest at two a.m., you know that?"

An undefinable expression crossed her face. Embarrassment? Shyness? She stood. "Want to see those figures?"

He laughed. "Maybe later in the morning?" There were 2.5 hours left before his alarm was set to go off, and he planned to be unconscious for most of them.

"Oh. Yeah. Right. See you in the morning." She hustled back inside, leaving him on the step with the croaking toads and her dried tear on his fingertips.

He rested his forearms on his knees. So, this was the Kimberly behind those hazel eyes he'd always wondered about. Loyal and determined but wounded by those who should've loved her. He'd waited three and a half years to get a glimpse of the real woman. It had been worth it.

But when the clock struck midnight—or in today's case, 3:00 a.m.—would she disappear?

Kimberly rattled off the final calculation, leaned back in Jules's office chair, and assessed the damage she'd done.

Sam stood a foot away, eyes still on the laptop screen, though, from his unfocused look, he probably wasn't seeing it. Was it his lack of sleep last night that caused that dazed expression on his face or the data dump she'd just unloaded on him?

She'd laid it all out. Every calculation, every variant of the farm plan, every probable outcome and its likelihood. It would've been so much easier on her to have him read it and she just answer any questions—every word she spoke made her own plan sound more ludicrous to her ears, the way he must be hearing it. But Sam had mumbled something about text-to-speech software being on the fritz and talking him through the numbers, so for the first pass Kimberly had to endure the sound of her own voice and Sam's agonizing silence.

But she was taking the risk. An email waited in Steph's inbox with the subject line **ALL IN**.

She grimaced at Sam. "So, what do you think?"

If only this morning's camaraderie could've lasted. They'd spent the milking talking about the time they'd both spent living in LA, and after church they made pizza for an early lunch and Sam bounced his next sermon idea off her. Though why he wanted her opinion on it was a mystery—she was about as suited to preaching as a pig to a career as a dental hygienist.

And now that smile she'd enjoyed for a few glorious hours had turned into something else altogether. Not a frown, exactly. She linked her fingers across her *Babylon 5* T-shirt and allowed herself the rare privilege of openly staring at him. Why did she find the way he rolled his blue work shirt to his elbows so attractive? She diverted her gaze elsewhere.

His brow puckered together in the expression she'd labeled back in the US as *You're so ridiculous.*

But perhaps that had been a miscategorization.

The clock ticked. Almost one thirty. A fly buzzed near the window, probably trying to escape the overpowering scent of Jules's cotton-candy candle. From the direction of the kitchen came the clatter of a crutch hitting the wooden floor and subsequent grumbling.

"Sam?" Kimberly tensed for whatever would come next. *Whatever it is, I'll just listen.* Her sleep-deprived self was bound to overreact and therefore couldn't be trusted.

"Good work." Sam's brow smoothed. "I'm going to go chop wood with Mick and process a little. Maybe we can go over the Wildfire stuff tomorrow?" She gave a cautious nod, and he dropped his hat on his head. "See you at dinner."

Her mouth fell open as he strode away. "That's it?" Her anxiety at his reaction morphed into something different. Something heavier that sank from her tight chest to weigh down her midsection. Could Sam actually say yes? And why did that thought bring zero relief?

He paused in the doorway, quirked an eyebrow. "What did you expect?"

"Some of this." She pushed out of the chair and struck a hands-on-hips pose, raised her eyebrows, and did her best to look down her nose at him. "Plus a lot of reasons why borrowing money is a terrible risk that only a heartless businessperson would suggest."

A smile played around the edges of his mouth. "Pretty sure I promised not to do that."

She searched her brain for a response and opted for honesty. "I'm not sure what to do with this new status quo."

His smile increased. "Get used to it."

She trailed after him as far as the enclosed veranda, then watched through a window as he strode through the yard to where Mick stood with a ute, two axes, a chain saw, and the expression of a boy with all his favorite toys. Her eyes tracked their vehicle until it stopped next to a fallen tree in the east paddock. "It's so weird."

"What is?"

Kimberly stepped back into the kitchen just as Jules dunked her knife into a jar of Vegemite. She wrinkled her nose at the salty scent. The stuff was basically a form of black tar that Australians thought tasted good on toast. "Sam being nice."

Was he a bomb waiting to explode? Did he agree with her idea? Or did he really just need a while to process?

Her phone beeped. Message from Steph: double thumbs-up. Obviously the woman had faith that Kimberly could convince him to return.

Now she just had to deliver.

Jules—allegedly not in a pizza mood, if such a thing were possible—smeared a thin layer of black across her buttered toast, then added slices of avocado and cheese on top. "Was that before or after the big smooch?" She bit her toast and rolled her eyes in apparent ecstasy.

Kimberly slid onto a barstool at the counter and tried to talk her cheeks out of blushing. "It was just Kiss Cam." Or so she'd told herself twenty million times last night. She leaned forward. "And I wasn't the only one smooching. How is the neighbor boy this morning?"

Jules stuck out her tongue. "I kissed his cheek. And I have no idea how he is this morning." She pulled out her phone. "Unless you count this GIF he sent, but I don't know what he's talking about."

Kimberly peered at the screen. A three-second grab of the *Texas Chain Saw Massacre* dude. "He's about to chop up that tree that fell on the fence. With Sam. He's way too excited about using that chain saw."

"He's what?" Jules yanked open the kitchen drawer and rummaged through it. Kimberly leaned over to see what she was after. Binoculars?

Jules pushed past her and hobbled to the window at the veranda.

"What are you doing?"

"I just wanna make sure they do a good job with that tree. If Mick happens to look great swinging an ax, that's pure coincidence."

Kimberly rolled her eyes. Jules never pulled her gaze from the window but swirled her finger in the universal signal for "Go on." "So, isn't that a good thing? Sounds like you guys might be able to agree on something after all."

Kimberly just nodded. The thing was, her throat had just about closed over with nervousness as she squeaked out her plan to Sam. It would've been easier if he'd thrown his hands in the air and stomped out. What if he'd been right? What if she talked him and Jules into this and then it didn't work? Would either of them ever forgive her?

Could she forgive herself?

"I think it's just in your head, Kimberlina. It's not weird." Jules lurched forward until her binoculars hit the glass, apparently liking whatever she saw. "Oh. My. Gosh."

Kimberly smiled at her friend but laced her fingers together and willed them to stop sweating. Last night, when Sam had offered her his friendship, she'd gotten just about everything she'd ever wanted.

But now she had something to lose.

Sam swung Dad's old ax through the air and sank it deep into a block of wood. The impact's vibrations went all the way down to his bones. They'd used the chain saw and tractor to cut the trunk and drag the pieces off the fence and over to the edge of the paddock of rye grass stubble, but the wood would be handy for Jules's fire come winter.

Though that didn't quite explain the ferocity of his swing.

Mick picked up his own block splitter from the tray of the ute. "Maaaaate." He jammed a weather-beaten Akubra on his head as he dragged the word out. "What did that tree ever do to you?"

Sam halved the next block in one chop. Giant splinters of wood flew toward his face, and he jerked back. "Fell on my fence." Technically the fence his mother owned, which penned the cattle his sister owned. But whatever.

Mick lined up his own block. "Shift your grip or you're going to lose a foot. What did Kimberly do?"

Sam tossed the ax aside and bent to grab the chopped pieces of wood, the scent of eucalyptus tickling his nostrils. "What?" He hadn't whinged to Mick about Kim—not now, and not before either.

"Jules is a big gossip." Mick answered the unasked question, then cocked his head in the direction of the house. "The girls inside right now?"

Sam nodded as he deposited an armful of wood into the ute

tray, accumulating approximately six thousand splinters in the process. His friend dropped his ax long enough to strip off his battered hi-vis shirt and toss it on the grass.

Sam glanced at the overcast sky. The morning had been steamy, but a short rain shower an hour ago had broken the humidity and dropped the temperature by about seven degrees. He inhaled a deep breath of the rain-scented air. "Hot already?"

"Just betting Jules has her binoculars out."

Sam smirked and lined up his next block. "Don't you have a girlfriend?"

"I made her up."

Sam's blow glanced off the wood and almost hit his foot. He snapped his gaze up to Mick. "You what?"

Mick pointed a finger at him. "No judging. We were talking about your problems, not mine."

Sam let the thought marinate for a moment. Nope. Still weird. "My problems don't involve imaginary girlfriends."

Mick shrugged. "It was either beg Jules to take me back or tell her I have a girlfriend."

"That's a real logical approach." Sam tightened his grip on the ax. Mick and Jules had broken each other's hearts once already, and Mick was still as committed to the coast as she was to the country. Not good.

Mick gave him a pointed look. "I'm not the one fighting with the girl who followed me all the way from America."

Sam pulled a face. What was he implying? Besides . . . "We didn't fight. This time."

Mick gave a teenage-girl-worthy eye roll. "Do I need to beat it out of you?"

"We're coming up with options for Jules."

"Jules told me."

Just how much had the vet been talking with his sister? Maybe he should suss Jules out. Nothing like focusing on other people's problems to distract from his own.

Sam rolled his shoulders as he formulated his words. His muscles would ache for sure. But that wasn't the reason he wasn't looking forward to the coming days. "Kim told me her plan. It's more risk than I'd like. But maybe we don't have that many options, and I don't know what to tell Jules."

Thwack! Mick landed a blow in the dead center of his block. "How is that a decision? Just lay the options out."

Sam shrugged. "If Kim and I say we agree on a plan, Jules will do it."

A wood chip came flying toward his head. He ducked. "Hey!"

Mick threw a second one at him. It bounced off his forehead. "You're selling Jules short. It's her responsibility, not yours. Who made you king of the farm?"

Sam pegged the wood chip back at him. "I'm not king of the farm, doofus. They're her cattle. It's Mum's land. I just don't want to influence her in one direction and then have it go wrong."

Mick shook his head. "Trust her to make up her mind. You can't control the outcome. Just tell her the truth."

Sam chewed on that thought for a moment. "You gonna do that too?"

Mick grinned a wicked smile and hoisted the ax again. "Eventually. But I'm gonna make her sweat first."

CHAPTER 21

"This is all on you, Kim."

Jules's ominous words carried over the backyard as even the cattle, munching away three paddocks down, seemed to hold their breath.

This was it. Take no prisoners. Winner takes all.

Kimberly stared down her opponent: Mick, who stood in front of the garbage bin with a cricket bat at the ready. The dying sun threw harsh shadows across his face and gave his wink an evil glint.

She weighed the tennis ball in her hand, rubbed her palm over its fluffy surface, a little wet with Meg's slobber. If she bowled the ball too fast, Mick could smash it over the fence for six points, called runs, and win this Girls versus Boys backyard cricket match—that is, if she'd understood Sam's explanation of the rules correctly. But too slow, and he could use the remaining three balls of the game to build up the four runs needed to beat the girls. They needed to get him out lest he win himself, Butch, and Sam unlimited bragging rights and a pass from cleaning up the barbecue dinner that still left its salty sweetness on her tongue.

Technically Butch was playing the role of umpire, though he'd fallen asleep in his camp chair twenty minutes ago after a dinner of barbecue ribs and comic book talk. Well, not a lot of talk on

Butch's part, but his eyes had lit up when she showed him more of Dad's illustrations. Still, Mick had made it clear: whichever gender lost the game dealt with the dishes.

"You can do it, Kim!" Jules leaned forward behind the bin—which substituted for the three sticks known as a wicket—in her position as "wickie" or wicket keeper. If Kim bowled the ball and it hit the bin, the girls would win. If Jules touched the ball to the bin while the guys were outside the "crease"—the line before the wickets—they would win. But if Mick got a good hit in, they were done for.

Sam grinned back at Kim from his spot three feet away from her.

"Do your worst, USA." Mick's taunts carried across the pitch, which the boys had mowed specifically for this purpose. "Show me some of that all-American spirit."

Jules narrowed her eyes at his back. "Oh, we're bringing nationality into this now, Irish boy? 'Cos I've got a few things I could—"

Kimberly clutched the ball in her right hand and brought both hands to her chin as she took two quick steps, swung her arms in the windmill motion she'd been practicing for the last hour, and released the ball at the top of the arc.

The ball's trajectory remained straight. It bounced once and came up high.

Mick took a big step forward outside the crease. Swung. Missed. Jules snapped the ball up with both hands and touched it against the bin.

The backyard dissolved into uproar.

Mick's face dropped, and he sank to his knees with an anguished cry.

"Howzat!" Jules unleashed a victory whoop as she ran-hobbled with one crutch straight for Kimberly. She lifted her from the ground in a hug and swung her in a circle, all balanced on one leg.

Butch woke from his nap with a snort. Even Meg seemed to celebrate with a flurry of barks.

Jules dropped Kimberly back on her feet and grabbed both her hands. "I'm adopting you. Honestly. You now have an open invite to our house for any and every Christmas." Her face was so close, Kimberly could count the riot of flecks in her green eyes.

Kimberly eased a step back and bumped into something solid. She caught a whiff of Sweet Baby Ray's barbecue sauce and cotton-scented fabric softener, mixed with an indefinable quality that prickled her skin into goose bumps.

Sam.

She half turned to face him and Jules, and he held a hand up for a high five. It took effort to pry the fingers of one hand from Jules's grip, but she managed to give him a hearty slap.

The crinkles by his eyes glowed with amusement. "Well done."

The two words shot warmth through her. This is what it felt like to have Sam's approval. She drank it in like a flower in drought. How things had changed in the past two weeks.

"You might think I'm free and easy with my Christmas in-vites," Jules continued saying as if Sam weren't standing there, smelling so good and smiling at her like she was the only person who existed. "But I'm not. Butch has one. Mick's is revoked until he admits that I'm a better spin bowler than him."

Mick dragged the bin back to its usual place. "I'd rather Santa gave me coal."

Jules flipped her braid over her shoulder. "That's happening either way."

"Actually I can still use my invite from Sam. He has equal

Christmas power. Your mum's rules." Mick deposited the bin in its place and sent a triumphant smirk in Jules's direction.

"You have Christmas rules?" Kimberly slapped at a mosquito. Night was coming.

"Penny had to." The rough voice sounded from behind Kimberly, and she whipped around.

Butch shifted in his chair enough to pull a cigarette and lighter from his pocket and lit up as he spoke. "When Sammy was a teenager, he invited fourteen people for Christmas one year. Two were blokes he picked up hitchhiking."

Jules hopped over to Butch, dropped an arm around his shoulders, and squeezed him to her side. "One of them was a real jerk. We never could get rid of him."

Butch grunted, but a glimmer of a smile peeked around his cigarette.

Apparently aware he'd reached his word limit for the day, Jules took over the explanation. "Mum will cater for five guests we invite each per year. Any more, and we have to cook."

Sam returned with the bat and ball. "That was the year my culinary triumphs began. Just wait till you try my double-decker pavlova."

Kimberly's mouth watered at the picture they painted, and not just of Sam's dessert. Christmas traditions. Teasing. Lifelong friends.

Her yearly date with Captain Malcolm Reynolds and the rest of the Firefly gang hadn't ever ranked on the top-Christmases-of-all-time list, but never before had it seemed so depressing. A quake of emotion shook her. She sucked in a deep breath and willed this ridiculous rush of tears to dissipate from behind her eyes. Did these people have any idea of what they had?

Sam caught his sister's attention. "That reminds me, Kez and Bonesy are coming."

Jules hobbled back over to Kimberly and slung an arm around her shoulders. "That puts you at eight. Kim counts as one of mine."

One of mine.

Kim darted her gaze around the scene before her. She needed to imprint this moment in her memory for all those future birthdays and Christmases she'd spend alone. Butch, quiet and relaxed with his cigarette and this makeshift family that had barreled into his life. Jules and Mick's banter—how they maintained this deep friendship despite the energy that vibrated between them, she'd never know.

And Sam. Packing up everyone's dinner plates from the plastic outdoor table with the satisfied expression of a man who'd successfully brought people together—dinner and cricket had been his idea—and was planning to do it again with his Christmas. Kimberly had no doubt that Butch, Kez, and Bonesy wouldn't ever spend any holidays alone while he was near.

She sighed. Lucky them.

Sam pitched a Coke can into the trash—nothing but net—and picked up a stack of dishes. "Time to head inside for the formal part of this evening, Jules."

Kimberly's stomach lurched. Their presentation. She'd managed to quell her nervousness up until this point. But now Jules had dangled the lure of future Christmases.

God, I don't think I can do this. Sam had surprised her by offering to present their findings to Jules himself, but she'd still need to field most of the questions. They were telling Jules that her financial position was far more precarious than she knew. Nothing about this would be easy.

Kimberly's eyes darted around, searching for escape. The detached garage loomed on one side of the yard, offering sanctuary. As the others packed up chairs, she headed that direction. She couldn't do this. Her breaths came shallow and rapid. She couldn't stand there and watch Jules's expression turn from expectation to disappointment or anger. Why had she ever thought this was a good idea?

"You okay?" Sam's voice came from right behind her.

She spun, hand on her heart. "Where did you come from?"

He glanced over his shoulder at the others, occupied with a discussion on this week's Australia versus India test cricket match. "Come on." He tugged her elbow and led her over to the side of the garage, out of sight of the others. She leaned against the worn timber, disregarding the peeling paint flecks probably attaching themselves to Dad's old *Stargate SG-1* shirt.

"You're not backing out on me now, are you?" Sam stood close, voice lowered, leaning on the same wall.

"No, I just, um . . ." She folded her arms tight against her chest as her throat ached. "I don't know." Her vision tunneled onto the vine growing up the posts that held the house up off the ground.

He mimicked her posture against the wall and tilted in her direction until his shoulder brushed hers. "Your plan makes sense. I wouldn't do this if I didn't trust you."

"If I didn't trust you." Obviously that trust had limits, as he hadn't said yes to Wildfire yet. But he'd heard her out, asked questions that showed he'd actually listened, and promised to pray it over. And he'd said yes to this.

She rubbed her arm against a chill that had nothing to do with the weather. "I'm just worried about how she's going to react."

He gave a slow nod. "She might be a bit freaked out at first."

Kimberly bit her lip. He didn't get it. To them she was a short-term friend, that girl from America who visited that one time. But for her—she'd treasure the memories of this month for life. She couldn't spoil it with a bad ending.

"Hey." He nudged her. "What are you thinking? You don't have to hide it."

She cleared her throat. He could have honesty or tears but not both. "She's going to hate me."

"That's not true." He came off the wall and gripped her upper arms, head bent so even her downward gaze couldn't avoid him. "We appreciate what you're doing, and I'm so sorry we ever made you feel otherwise—that *I* ever made you feel otherwise. Both at Wildfire and now."

She met his gaze. Oh, he was close, close enough for her to drown in the hot-fudge depths of those eyes. Was he changing his mind about Wildfire?

He gave her a smile. "You said last week that you believed in me." He rubbed her arms and her chill faded. "This is me saying that I believe in you. We don't have to do this if you really don't want to, but don't back out 'coz you're scared. This isn't all on you. We're a team."

"We're a team." Her dream come true, in three simple words— even if it was only temporary. Plus the added bonus of Samuel Payton, inches away, eyes wide and earnest and his whole attention focused on her.

What mere mortal could resist his plea?

She nodded, taking a deep breath. "Okay. We'll do it."

Sam flashed her a grin. "Good on ya. That's the Kimberly I know."

He led the way inside, waving goodbye to Mick and Butch as he went, and Kimberly followed a pace behind. If God was into bargaining, she'd offer up just about anything for the chance to come here every Christmas. But the Creator of the universe didn't roll like that.

So, she just repeated a prayer a thousand more times as they headed through the door.

Someone needed to play bad cop.

Perched on the worn edge of Jules's couch, Kimberly picked at the cracking leather and shifted her gaze between Sam, pacing the living room as he gesticulated in full presenter mode, and Jules sat enthroned in her recliner. They were now ten minutes deep into Sam's presentation.

From the pinch between Jules's brows, Kimberly could tell they'd lost her enthusiasm. The fold of her arms hinted at disapproval. And the tapping of her good foot probably meant she wasn't even listening anymore.

Kimberly crossed her socked feet at the ankles and scanned Sam, sleeves rolled to his elbows and voice brimming with that trademark Samuel Payton enthusiasm he brought to any presentation—whether he was preaching to three thousand teenagers or telling his sister to buy seventy extra cattle. But was he picking up the same vibes she was?

Jules held a hand up to Sam and spoke over him. "This isn't what I wanted."

He halted. Glanced at Kimberly.

A gust of wind swept through the window and blew out

Jules's Citrus Explosion candle. Kimberly's anxiety levels kicked up a notch. *That is not a sign.* She pushed herself to her feet and stood by Sam. Pep talk outside notwithstanding, she shouldn't kid herself. Sam had made it clear that he'd support her idea and bring it to Jules, but he wouldn't talk his sister into anything. And neither would she. But right now Jules wasn't even considering their idea. The expression on her face was just the adult equivalent of sticking her fingers in her ears and singing *la-la-la-la.*

But good cop was worth at least one more shot.

Jules pushed the footrest of the recliner down and leaned forward to speak. "I wanted efficiencies, alternate feed sources, that sort of thing. I wanted to see if you could find something I hadn't thought of."

Kimberly shook her head and pinned a gentle smile to her lips, even as her heart sped up. "You have this place running as well as it can with these stock numbers. You need more production."

"Which means more debt." Jules said the word *debt* with the same tone one would use for *terrorist.*

She couldn't let Jules lose this place. Sam believed in her for a reason. Kimberly held up both hands in entreaty. "Take my calculations and get a second opinion. And a third and a fourth." She steeled herself and lowered both her hands and her voice to drive her point home. "But don't toss them aside, because the long-term outlook if you maintain the status quo is riskier than taking out this loan."

Jules folded her arms. "I'm not taking out a mortgage against my cattle when there's already one against the land. That's crazy."

Kimberly suppressed a groan. She'd checked all options, and the loan against the cattle was the best way to go. But Jules's stubbornness was formidable. This wasn't the first time she'd stood in her own way. Kimberly had pieced together enough of Mick and Jules's story to know that Mick had offered a compromise ten years ago—a place to live that was both rural for her and within visiting distance of the beach for him. But Jules had envisaged her life one way: on this specific farm. That same stubbornness was rearing its head today.

She zoned back into what Sam was saying.

"—up past midnight all the time getting this ready, and she works like a trooper all day long. The least you can do is listen."

Sam coming to her defense? Another piece of her heart inflated.

Jules leaned back in her chair. "I am listening. But I'm not going further into debt."

Kimberly bit her lip. She could let this slide, let whatever happened happen. But the Christmases at this house sounded too good to let them be repossessed by the bank. Even if what she had to say to accomplish that got her Christmas invite rescinded.

Time to screw up her courage and do what only a true friend could do.

She wiped sweaty palms on her shorts, then leaned toward Sam and murmured, "This is for her own good."

Deep breath. *Here we go.*

To Jules: "You already know that I'm right." The words came out with the detached voice she'd used so many times on Sam.

"Excuse me?"

As a consultant, this tactic had worked on clients again and again. Kimberly visualized wearing her favorite dove-gray skirt and jacket with the white shirt that flattered her neckline rather than this baggy *Stargate* shirt and lavender sweat shorts. *Confidence, Kim. You're the expert.* She clasped her hands in front of her and raised one eyebrow just a fraction. "You knew you needed a push into something you don't want to admit is necessary. That's why you asked my opinion in the first place."

Jules's expression morphed into an amused, slightly incredulous smile. "That so?"

"You're a capable woman. Usually you farm this land alone. You solve the problems. You don't quit. And you only ask an outsider for help when you know there's something you can't do." She plucked the folder containing their proposal from Sam's hands and dropped it in Jules's lap. "Your persistence is how you survive out here. But don't let that turn into stubbornness that bankrupts you."

"I know what's at stake."

Kimberly looked her friend dead in the eye. No, she didn't. Not really.

Back when she'd worked for Mom, they'd taken meetings with clients about to lose their businesses, homes, credit rating— everything. She'd seen people neck deep in foreclosure insist with all earnestness that their fortunes were about to magically turn around.

They didn't. At least not without a change in strategy.

She sucked in a supply of oxygen, released it. If she had to spell out exactly what could happen, so be it. "My job is to put the plan in front of you. I can't make you look at it. But remember this conversation when the bank's coming to padlock the gate and you have to go to the front paddock to dig up your dad's urn."

The temperature in the room plummeted to thirty below zero. Any hint of a smile fled Jules's expression. She stood without the aid of a crutch. Kimberly held her breath and maintained her neutral expression with agonizing effort. Jules articulated each word with careful precision. "Get. Out."

She walked from the room, gait uneven, like she couldn't stand Kimberly's presence for another second. The silence lingered with all the comfort of a belt sander to the face.

Sam shifted behind Kimberly. What was he thinking? She couldn't make herself turn around and look. She managed to keep her voice even. "It had to be done."

And then she sat on the edge of the coffee table and burst into tears.

CHAPTER 22

J ules sat on the burned-out shell of the old Suzuki DS 80 motorbike, tailbone sore from the hours she'd been here, and stared at a moonlit rock with googly eyes and a pipe cleaner smile that rested on the dirt between three dog collars and a turtle cage. She sniffed back the remnants of her tears, salt in her nostrils and mouth. Rubbed at goose bumps as the night breeze wrapped its cold fingers around her arms. Leaving the house in footy shorts and a Brisbane Broncos T-shirt may've been short-sighted. But she'd needed to come to the burial ground of all her favorite things—including the urn that contained Dad's ashes.

She'd made the pet rock that marked the spot to look like Dad in the second grade, and it'd sat on Dad's office windowsill for years. Unconventional tombstone perhaps, but fitting.

Was there really a chance she'd need to dig him up?

Curse this boot on her leg. Were she free from it, she'd go borrow Mick's dirt bike and take out her frustration on the overgrown track Dad had formed with the tractor when they were kids. But no, she was trapped. In more ways than one.

She smacked a fist against the cold metal frame of the bike she sat on. Ow. Pain radiated up the bones in the side of her hand. That was stupid.

She punched it again.

A vehicle rumbled along the track, which was corrugated from the hooves of three hundred cattle. Mick's ute. She'd know that engine anywhere.

Light danced across the bush paddock, reflecting back at least three sets of mystery eyes, as he swung the ute around to park behind her. The engine stopped, and the ambiance returned to cane-toad croaks and the occasional moo.

She didn't turn around when footsteps crunched toward her. Just kept her eyes on the googly ones that stared back, unblinking.

Mick appeared in her peripheral vision, squatted by the front of the bike, and rubbed the decal *80* with a fond touch. His T-shirt and board shorts from the cricket game were gone, replaced by jeans trendier than anyone wore in this entire district and a flannel shirt she suspected was his dad's.

She cast her eyes downward. Crocs. He had his feet jammed into rainbow-swirl Crocs. His mum had unusually large feet.

A giggle bubbled up even as hot tears rushed to her eyes yet again. Blinking them away, she swallowed to try to stop the sensation of her throat closing. On the day that she felt more dread than a mouse outrunning a brown snake, he was here. Despite everything that'd happened between them. He still came.

"So, I talked to Sam." Mick's voice came out gravelly, quiet. "You've been out here awhile."

Probably four hours, give or take. What conversation had Sam and Kim had after she left? That would've been an interesting one to see.

Mick swiped a cobweb from the bike's clutch. "Wanna go for a drive?"

"Wanna go for a drive?" Those had been her favorite words

at the age of fifteen, when they'd flogged his little '86 Pintara around the back roads like they were at the Bathurst 1000.

Still not trusting her vocal cords, she just nodded. Stood up from the bike, let Mick prop it back up against the tree with the collars of Meg I, Bo II, and Nip IV nailed to it, and hopped into the passenger seat of the ute. Mick stowed her crutch in the tray.

Within ten minutes they were humming along Newell Road, which ran treeless and straight for forty-five kilometers. If it weren't for the threat of kangaroos on the road, you could set the cruise control and take a nap. They'd passed the first corner before Mick spoke.

"Wanna talk about it?"

She picked at the top of her moon boot. "Not really."

"Wanna go somewhere in particular?"

"Any direction works for me."

He glanced at her. "Trust me?"

She considered him. "Yes."

He smiled. "Then take a nap. The view will be better when you wake up."

A mystery tour. Sweet.

She reclined her seat and closed her eyes. A nap would be good. Sleep had evaded her recently. The classic-rock tunes playing from the radio lulled her into oblivion.

Much later a radiating ache in her neck and strange sounds pulled her back to consciousness.

Was that . . . ocean waves?

She must be hearing things. She shifted in her seat and drifted back off to sleep.

Jules dragged her eyelids open and swung her gaze around. Empty driver's seat. Big white building on the right, lit by predawn light. And a whole lotta ocean.

Her jaw dropped. "What are we doing here?" She swung her gaze around. High-rise apartments dotted the landscape behind her. The Gold Coast?

And where was Mick?

The clock on the dash read 5:02 a.m. She scanned the sand as she kneaded the crick in her neck. There, at the point where the sand met grass, Mick stretched out on the beach, using his jacket as a pillow.

Jules grabbed her crutch and hopped over to him, careful to not get sand in her boot. Wow, she'd forgotten how good the sea air smelled in the morning. "Oi. Bozo. What are we doing at the beach?"

One eye peeked open. "Watching the sunrise."

"From behind your eyelids?"

"It's my preferred method."

She scanned the landscape around them. Yep, this was the Gold Coast. Mick was insane. That was a five-hour car trip. How deeply had she slept?

"Beautiful, isn't it?" Mick sat up, and Jules not only looked at but *saw* their surroundings.

The skyscrapers of Surfers Paradise rose on their far left, appearing to almost meet the water. A wide bay of white sand curved for kilometers, all the way from the center of the city to where they now stood. The grassy knoll of the headland rose at their immediate right.

"Look." Mick pointed to the horizon, where the freshly risen sun threw its rays onto the water.

Jules had to squint to look at it, but it was worth the effort. "It really does look like gold." If only she'd brought her good camera.

"Nothing like it." He wore the smug look of a cat who'd stolen the cream. Or, in this case, the farm girl.

She narrowed her eyes at him. "I'll admit it looks awesome, but are you crazy? I need to be at the farm right now."

"Maybe some perspective will help you make your decision."

"I don't need perspective, since according to Sam and Kim I have no real choice. I need a strong drink."

Mick spread out his jacket under her moon boot, and she plopped down into the sand. He held up three fingers, folding each one down as he spoke. "You always have a choice. We both know you can't handle a drink stronger than kombucha. And it's been scientifically proven that the beach helps everything."

She rested back on her elbows. Much as she hated to admit it, this was *almost* as beautiful as Yarra Plains.

Mick pulled off his crocs and shoved his feet under the sand. "So talk to me. Why does their proposal have you so freaked out?"

She closed her eyes, a sick twist in her stomach. She couldn't even go there. "I . . . I don't want to talk about it yet. I just need to get home and . . ." And do what? Ignore all the research Kimberly and Sam had done? Stick her head in the sand? But she couldn't go to the bank and take out that kind of money against her cattle. Mum would have a fit—though technically, as the landholder under their share-farming agreement, she had no legal say.

But lawyers couldn't stop a mother's wrath.

They sat in silence, the sound of breaking waves a soothing balm to Jules's frayed nerves. Seagulls flapped overhead, a few mad-keen surfers bobbed out in the ocean, and a haze of salt spray filled the air. Jules rolled fine grains of sand between her fingertips and inhaled deeply. As much as she ragged Mick about this place, there was something about the ocean that revived the soul.

After a few minutes Mick stood up, balanced her crutch, and pulled her to her feet—or foot. She kept her moon boot in the air, well clear of the sand, and gripped Mick's hand for balance. Heat spread from her palm and swept through her body. How could this tiny amount of skin contact affect someone so much? Her bloodstream must be drowning in hormones.

She held her hand out for her crutch. He handed it over and stuck close by as they made their way up onto the grass. "Take a break for one weekend. Get some distance, have some fun, and your farm will still be there when you get back."

She nibbled her lip as they paused before the wide bike path between the beach and car park. Two perky women jogged past, their makeup immaculate and several body parts artificially plumped. "A whole weekend? In the city?"

He nudged her with his elbow as they crossed. "This isn't just a pleasure trip. I've got work for you to do."

She looked from her moon-booted leg to him.

"I've got some potential puppy families, but I wanted to check them out personally first." He grinned. "You won't regret it."

Oh, but she would.

Yet those sweet blue eyes that had searched for her when she was sad, driven through the night for her, and now reflected the sunrise—they were her kryptonite.

How could she say no?

"You'd better buy me some mind-blowing fish 'n' chips."

"Deal."

CHAPTER 23

This place was a disaster.

Kimberly propped one foot on a fallen fence post and surveyed the dilapidated remains of the old worker's cottage on Jules's farm. Sweat already slicked her skin, though it wasn't even breakfast time yet. She'd left the truck and four-wheeler for Sam and Butch, who milked this morning, and instead pedaled out here on a rusty bicycle that had been decomposing in Jules's shed.

She'd remembered this idea as she tossed and turned at 2:30 a.m., and she'd had to check it out right away. The structure was indeed as terrible as she remembered. And it was perfect.

The home's sagging front door opened to reveal an even more depressing interior: the scent of Eau de Dead Mouse, carpet stains from my-gosh-I-shudder-to-even-think-of-it, and paint flaking from the ceiling like dandruff.

She folded her arms and nodded. They could fix this by the time Jules got home. With Wildfire now closed for the Christmas break and her research for Jules complete, she had hours to spare. And the more comfortable Sam felt about Jules's financial position, the more likely he'd be to return to Wildfire permanently. But she'd need his help to pull this off.

She left the house at a fast clip, jumped back on her two-wheeled rust bucket, and rode one-handed as she shooed flies with the other hand.

Jules would need a pick-me-up when she got home, and what better than to find an existing asset revitalized and ready to save her some cash? Butch had already said he'd happily swap part of his wages to live here, so the savings would be immediate.

And with some elbow grease, the cans of paint she'd found in the shed, and a small contribution from herself, they'd be able to pull it off at no cost to Jules.

The growl of the four-wheeler's engine emanated from the other side of the slight rise she now labored to pedal up, and a moment later the vehicle—and Sam—sailed over the crest like a chariot with its king. The breeze played with Sam's hair and navy T-shirt as he approached.

Have mercy. How could a girl keep her head on straight with things like this appearing like a mirage straight from her fourteen-year-old fantasies?

Sam slowed to a stop beside her and grinned. "Nice wheels. Want a lift? I've just gotta lock the cows in, and then I'm going home for second brekkie."

Kimberly eyed the back of the bike. A ride would be far preferable than pedaling these rutted tracks for another mile. But it would also mean sitting on the back of the bike with Sam, his muscles, and three years' worth of a combined crush and dysfunctional relationship.

She needed to get these silly emotions under control.

"I'll be fi—"

"Don't be silly. It's hot enough to fry an egg on your head." He hopped off the motorbike, plucked the bicycle from her hands, and propped it against the fence. "We'll grab it on the way back. Hop on."

She perched on the bars that crisscrossed over the top of the plastic mudguard and wrapped her fingers around the cold metal rather than Sam's shirt—or torso. But when he took off with a jump, physics threw her weight backward. Her flailing fingers snagged the bottom of Sam's shirt as gravity pulled her down, and something firm clamped down on the top of her thigh, anchoring her to the bike.

But not before her fingers registered the sensation of tearing fabric.

The bike came to an abrupt halt, Sam's left hand still holding on to her leg.

Heat gushed into Kimberly's neck and face as she righted herself and stared at the eight-inch tear she'd made in the back of his shirt—and the skin beneath it. "I'm so sorry—"

"Don't worry about it. I took off too fast. Are you alright?" His dark eyes focused on her with such intensity she couldn't hold his gaze.

"I'm fine." She stared at the hand just above her knee.

Sam removed it. "Hop on properly and hold on." He shifted forward so she could sit behind him on the seat.

Oh yeah. Sitting with her body pressed against his back and wrapping her arms around him would really help this situation.

"Unless you'd rather sit in front."

And have *him* wrap his arms around *her*? Good grief. A girl could only have so much self-control.

Kimberly swung her other leg over so she straddled the bike and slid into place behind Sam. She twisted her hands in what was left of the back of his shirt. "Okay."

He reached back, untangled her hands, and pulled them around him.

At least with her behind him, he couldn't see the glow that was surely radiating from her cheeks right now.

Sam set off again, at a marginally gentler pace. "What were you doing out here?"

"Figuring out a surprise for Jules. I think I can pull it off, with your help." She raised her voice to compensate for the rushing wind that tickled strands of hair against her neck. Sam seemed to believe the Honda FourTrax was his Ducati Streetfighter.

"What did you have in mind?"

"Fixing the worker's cottage. Before she gets home. The bathroom just needs a bucketload of bleach, there's paint in the shed, and Butch says he has a trucker friend who can smuggle a flat-pack kitchen along with his load and drop it off tomorrow."

Sam's fingers slid along her forearm and squeezed, the effect almost as potent on her as an actual hug. "That's ambitious, but sweet. It deserves a face-lift. Mum and Trent lived there before his accident." Sam glanced back at her and amended his comment. "My biological dad. He died after a farm accident."

"Oh." She'd never heard Sam mention his biological father before. She'd assumed he and Mrs. Payton had divorced.

"That must've been hard for your mom."

Sam nodded. "I was a baby, Jules was a year and a half. We moved back in with my grandparents, and Gran babysat us while Mum worked the farm with Granddad. Then once Mum married Dad, my grandparents lived in the cottage."

Kimberly filed the time frames away in her head. "When did your mom and stepdad meet?"

"When I was four." Sam slowed the bike's pace, making it

easier to talk. "I don't remember, but Gran talked about it sometimes. Trent was a decent bloke, but they had Jules and me pretty young. They were both immature, and the relationship wasn't easy. Then Mum had to deal with grief, farming, and single parenthood—she turned a bit hard and cynical. But Dad brought joy and beauty back into her world." He cleared his throat. "He was the love of her life." His voice wavered a little on the last word. Kimberly fought the urge to tighten her arms around him and squeeze the hurt away. She knew what it meant to lose a father you adored. Sam squeezed her hand, like he telepathically understood what she was feeling, and why it was so hard to express it. A rush of warmth flooded her, and she squeezed back.

He stopped at the open paddock gate, and she leaned back as he dismounted, missing his heat even on this toasty day. But he didn't walk toward the gate. Instead, he turned and unleashed the full force of his smile on her.

Oh, that dimple. Her thoughts exploded into a glitter cannon of color and sparkle.

"I'm in. But I think we can do better than the paint in the shed. Let's head into town."

Mute, Kimberly nodded. She'd say yes to anything when he used that smile on her. The memory of their rodeo kiss sizzled in her synapses.

Sam turned to fasten the gate, and she blinked to shake off his effect on her.

You're going home soon. And he might not be coming back for long—or ever.

Not if she couldn't convince the board that Wildfire would be worth keeping open without Sam. She was past the halfway mark on her time in Australia now, and the clock ticked louder every hour. Steph blew up her inbox daily. If she wasn't successful in luring Sam back, she might as well not come back at all.

This weekend would give her and Sam some one-on-one time. If she couldn't make some serious progress in convincing him, then her future was in serious jeopardy.

Jules leaned against Mick's ute and surveyed the coastal home before her. Behind the dog-proof fence, children squealed as they jumped into the inground pool.

Thwack. The distinctive sound of a tennis ball meeting a cricket bat. Probably the three boys she'd seen ten minutes ago still playing backyard cricket. A shout arose. A white Maltese dog dashed past the gate, tennis ball in mouth, and a moment later a child flashed past in hot pursuit.

At the gate Mick waved a final goodbye to the suntanned yummy mummy who owned these six kids, loving husband, and fabulous house next to the park. Jules lifted a hand in farewell. Mick waggled his eyebrows at her as he approached, now clad in board shorts and a Rip Curl tank that showed off his surfer's physique.

"Well?"

She grimaced. "I don't think they're puppy appropriate."

Mick rolled his eyes and walked around to the driver's side. Jules stashed her crutch and pulled herself up into the vehicle. Her stomach rumbled as they drove onto the road.

"Want that fish-and-chips for lunch now?" Mick tapped his fingers on the steering wheel to the tune of the pop song on the radio. Her stomach growled again in response. It'd been a long morning of meeting potential puppy families.

Jules rolled down her window to let the delicious sea breeze in. Everyone here seemed to drive with their windows down—unlike home, where they stayed tightly closed to prevent the onslaught of flies, dust, and extreme temperatures. "Did you hear what I said?"

"I'm ignoring you because hunger has obviously caused you to lose your mind."

"How many puppies did you say Meg'll probably have?"

"Can't know for sure, but average litter size for Kelpies is around five."

She eyed the home. The fifth one they'd checked. "I don't think they have room for another living thing in that house."

"They have a six-bedroom house, and they live next to a park. Just say it."

"Say what?"

He stopped at a traffic light and looked at her, those blue eyes seeing straight through to her soul. "You want one."

His gaze was almost as potent as his touch. She looked back at the road. "Do not. They're a ridiculous crossbreed. But if we can't find enough good homes, I might just have to keep one." Despite her best efforts, her lips twitched with a smile.

Mick huffed out a "Ha!" then reached behind her seat and pulled out a plastic bag. He tossed it into her lap as the light turned green.

"What's this?" She pulled out a tangle of fabric and shook it into shape. Two pirate outfits. For dogs.

"I couldn't resist. I have a matching outfit. Last year at the RSPCA Million Paws Walk, all the vets at the practice dressed up to match their dogs and told the kids of our clients to do the same. Donations skyrocketed."

Best mental picture ever. She grinned at the tiny pirate outfits. One for Killer and one for—"You want one too?"

"Killer needs some company." He pulled the ute into a car park beside Currumbin Creek, a sandy waterway that met the ocean. "Let's go. Lunchtime."

They headed across the road to a fish-and-chips shop, and as Mick ordered, Jules slouched in a chair at one of the outdoor tables, head back and eyes closed. She stretched her legs out to the sun. Warm darkness enveloped her consciousness—until a hand glided from her shoulder to her neck, then tugged her ponytail. She shivered, caught his fingers with both hands, and opened her eyes. "Got my food?"

"We're not eating it here. Come on."

He headed to the road, and she hustled to catch up. "Picnic by the beach?"

He waited for her before he crossed, positioning himself between her and the traffic. "Sort of."

Sort of? What was he planning?

He sat her and the food down at a picnic table that offered a great view of the beach. "Just a sec." He jogged down to a wooden shack by the sand, his thongs—flip-flops to their American guest—slapping against the ground.

Jules sneaked a peek at the chips. Had they used enough chicken salt? Only one way to find out. She was one and a half handfuls into her taste test when she heard a "Hey!"

Mick walked toward her, carrying what looked like an overweight surfboard and a paddle. "Quit stealing chips."

She wagged one at him. "You knew the risks when you left me alone with the food."

He scooped up the paper-wrapped cardboard box of lunch and nodded toward the water. She balked. "Are you serious? Paddleboarding?" She waved her foot at him. "Aren't you forgetting something?"

He was already walking to the water, managing to hang on to all three items in his arms. "Don't be a sook." He plopped their lunch onto the sand and positioned the paddleboard two-thirds on water, one-third on land.

She stood where the grass met the beach, one arm gripping her crutch and one on her hip. "I'm not getting my moon boot wet or sandy. And what are you going to do with my crutch?"

He secured the paddleboard in the sand, jogged up to her, and took the crutch. "Just a sec." He ran over to the ute, locked it inside, and jogged back to her. "So, no sand?"

"No sand."

"Right-o." He reached down and swept one arm behind her knees and the other around her back. Jules squeaked as her feet left the ground, her arms latching around his neck. He grinned at her, close enough she could count every freckle where his Irish skin met the Australian sun. "No sand it is."

He carried her down the beach, waded two steps into the water, and sat her on the paddleboard. Jules gripped his neck as she tried to balance and keep her moon boot on the paddleboard at the same time. Mick laughed, breath tickling her ear and doing all sorts of things to her nerves. "You can let go. I've got it." He unfisted her hand from his shirt, his other hand on the paddleboard, and made his way to the back. "Take this." He passed her the fish 'n' chips, picked up the paddle, and managed to launch them while stepping onto the back of the paddleboard and somehow not pitching her off.

"Whoa." Jules clutched the edges of the board in a death grip, lunch safe in her lap, as Mick used a few quick strokes to direct them to the center of the wide, salty creek. Once they were drifting out of the path of the other paddleboarders and swimmers around them, within sight of the crashing waves at the mouth of the creek, Mick balanced the paddle across the board. "You face one way, and I'll face the other, and it'll balance." He nudged her to face the left shore, her good leg trailing in the water, as he sat next to her and faced the right. "Okay, hand over the goods. Or what's left of them."

She gingerly released one hand from the board long enough to pass him the fish-and-chips. He tore open the paper and held the box out to her. "You can let go. You won't fall off."

"Says you." But the irresistible smell drew her fingers to a particularly large battered chunk of fish.

Mick popped three chips into his mouth. "Nothing like eating fish 'n' chips while on the actual ocean."

She couldn't disagree. The fresh sea air, cool water, spectacular views of waves and sand and surfers—it was addictive.

Or maybe that was just the man beside her.

That man ate a bite of fish and nudged her with his leg. "So talk to me. What did Kimberly say that's got you freaking out?"

She licked a grain of salt from her fingers, eyes on the water. Mick had bided his time, but he'd never let her get away with not having this conversation.

She sighed. "Because money stuff might not be my thing, but

I know how many zeroes were in that number. What they're asking me to do is a gamble, and they're telling me it's my best option. Which means my other options are worse." Her next words tasted of metallic fear. "What if I lose the farm?"

"Tell me why that would be terrible."

She swung toward him, and the paddleboard wobbled.

He held both hands up. "I'm not saying it wouldn't be terrible. I'm saying that naming the fear sometimes helps."

"I'm afraid . . ." The worries poured in, faster than she could get the words out. "I'm afraid I'll lose my job. My lifestyle. I'll lose who I am. And I'll—" Sobs threatened, but she swallowed them down. "I'll lose all I have left of Dad." She swiped at her eyes. "I know it's silly—he's already gone, and he's in absolute paradise with God. But I can milk in the dairy and pretend the knocking in the vat room is Dad tinkering with the vat, not the loose drainpipe on the east wall. I can see his murals on the walls. I can take care of the animals he loved. I can fix the tractors he drove, tend the paddocks he and Mum cultivated."

"It's not silly." Mick's voice sounded rough with emotion. She bit her lip. It wasn't the same kind of grief, but she wasn't the only one who missed him.

Mick's hand squeezed her shoulder, and she leaned into his chest. With his arm around her and her forehead resting against his collarbone, she could feel the vibrations of his words as well as hear them.

"It's not silly, but you can't let that hold you back. Whatever happens, God won't desert you. You aren't alone. Trust Him."

She smiled, her cheek brushing the fabric of his shirt. "Since I ended up in this godforsaken place, maybe I shouldn't have trusted anybody."

Mick laughed, the rumble through his chest a comforting sound. "'Godforsaken'?"

"Look at it. Not a cow in sight."

"Take one surfing lesson with me, and you'll never want to leave."

She drew in a deep breath, sat up, and smiled at him. He was righter than he knew.

CHAPTER 24

Kimberly had made a mistake.

She stacked the dishwasher with Sam, muscles aching from the even-harder-than-usual day's work. She, Sam, and Butch had purchased new paint, ripped out the old cottage's kitchen, scrubbed the bathroom, undercoated two rooms, and discovered actual timber floors underneath the mangy carpet. She had paint on her old Wolfmother shirt, splinters in her fingers, and the aftertaste of bleach in her throat. And it had been awesome. They'd worked so well together, Sam had even complimented her quick meal of spaghetti Bolognese before they launched back into painting.

But a whole day was gone, and she hadn't dragged up the courage yet to talk about Wildfire.

She switched on the dishwasher and watched him from the corner of her eye as he stacked pots in the sink. It'd been five days now since she'd taken him through her expansion-plan figures again, and he'd reacted much the same as he had to the farm plan. Quiet nods, thoughtful expression, a promise to think about it.

But this time he hadn't returned the next day to say yes.

Maybe a head-on assault wasn't what this situation called

for. She cast her mind back to that day in the dairy when they'd been discussing their long-term goals and motivations. She could be totally off base, but her Spidey senses had tingled at the time. His answer—"Preaching"—was plausible but vague. Preaching where? Full-time? To what audience? Surely he had some kind of secret dream—one he was afraid to hold up to the light.

Sam had unknowingly nailed hers in his pep talk before they presented the farm plan to Jules: "*We're a team.*" A feeling of belonging, of purpose—of being wanted—had addicted her at that moment more powerfully than any opiate ever could.

What was that dream for him?

She shifted his boxing gloves from the countertop to his gym bag in the corner and fetched a tea towel from the kitchen drawer. "Excluding the obvious options, if you could do anything, what would you do?"

He dunked a pot in suds. "Didn't we play this game the other day?"

She fingered the frayed edge of the tea towel. "You never answered me properly. What's your so-crazy-you-never-say-it-aloud thing?"

"Caribbean island."

"You'd preach to the coconuts. Yesterday I heard you exhorting Rocket the bull on the power of the Holy Spirit."

He smirked. "Meg's received a lot of sermons on discipleship."

She studied his face. "Would you pastor a church? Go on mission?" No reaction. "Attend Bible college?" There it was. Hard to define—a blink, a twitch, a slight shift in demeanor? She wiped the pot he handed her. "I think you'd enjoy it."

The smile he gave had a slight twist to it as he washed a large frying pan. "Now you're making fun of me."

She frowned. Not the reaction she'd anticipated. "Why would you say that?"

He handed her the dripping pan. "You've proofread my emails often enough. Don't think that Bible college would appreciate my unique spelling style."

Oh yeah. Dyslexia. She rubbed the frying pan dry. Surprising to see him balk at this, after watching him thrive at Wildfire for so long. "It would be a challenge. But I've seen you tackle challenges before."

His brow creased, like the thought pained him. His voice came out with a tinge of bitterness. "Kimberly, when I was in Year 8 they put me in the special-ed class." His voice caught, just the slightest bit, and he cleared his throat.

Kimberly jerked her gaze up to his face, but he kept his eyes on the suds. "Seriously? Why? Just because reading's more difficult?" She placed the pan in its drawer with a clunk.

A long moment ticked by before he answered. "My teacher forced me to read in front of the class and realized I could barely do it. She said I had the skills of an eight-year-old." His ears reddened, and she winced. In front of the class? How humiliating.

A part of her heart warmed—he'd trusted her enough to confide in her. But her indignation at his situation bubbled to the top. "How did you get so far without them realizing? This sounds more like a problem with your teachers than you. How on earth did they think special-ed classes would help?" She folded her arms. Did this teacher still live in town? Still teach? She shuddered at the thought.

"I was great at covering it up, and they still didn't understand the cause. Mum pulled me out and homeschooled me. Eventually a student teacher at the homeschooling place suggested I might have dyslexia. When Mum realized that I did, she was so furious at the Burradoo High principal, they had a shouting match in the school car park." His smile turned rueful.

A pang hit Kimberly's chest, both for Sam and herself. If she guessed correctly, before that diagnosis he'd believed that the problem was with his intelligence or a lack of trying. Both false.

And for herself—what would it be like, having such a lioness for a mother? She couldn't wait to meet this woman.

Sam shrugged and handed her the next pot. "The point is the only reason I *barely* got my Year 10 certificate was because Mum figured out the absolute minimum of what I needed to pass and coached me through it. No one even considered that I could go all the way through to Year 12." He tried to end the sentence on a chuckle, but the pain leaked through his tone.

Kimberly resumed her drying, mind whirring. She'd known about his dyslexia for years—he often mentioned it when speaking to students—but she'd never understood how severe it was, nor the depth of the hurt it caused. He honestly didn't believe he could do this—Bible college or Wildfire. This certainly helped explain his risk-averse outlook.

Relief brought a tiny smile to her lips, which in light of Sam's hooded expression, she tried to smother. All this time, and she'd thought their fights had somehow been her fault. But this was his private battle—one he shouldn't have to fight alone.

She searched for the right response to Sam's revelation. "You've come up with out-of-the-box ways to adapt. You have a phenomenal memory. You memorize every sermon by heart, and I've never seen someone retain information from an audiobook the way you do without taking notes." Her words reflected every bit of the awe she'd felt watching him work harder than those around him to give himself an informal education.

He looked at her like he was surprised. "I guess. Thanks. I've never thought about it that way before."

She studied him as he scrubbed at invisible marks on the sink. Every inch of her Samuel Payton intuition shouted that she'd struck a deep, swollen nerve. But in his midtwenties, with no formal experience, this man had preached the love of God to teenagers and thousands had responded. He'd motivated and managed a large team of volunteers. He had such a knack for speaking with people and making them feel *heard*. It was enough to make a girl wanna spin him around, stand on her tippy-toes, and give him a thank-you kiss hot enough to start a kitchen fire. And yet he seemed to believe it had all happened by some inconceivable stroke of luck.

But words were his thing, not hers. How could she ever express that thought to him? The temperature of her cheeks increased just thinking about it. She took a breath and tried. "I think God's given you talents that the world desperately needs."

His scrubbing stopped.

"If He wants you to go to Bible college, and if you want to go, there will be a way to make it happen. Some colleges might specialize in this, or there's part-time, audiobooks, I can proof your writing, whatever. You said the other day that we're a team." Her lips tugged into a hesitant smile. "So, we're a team."

Sam set the scrubber brush down, his movement slow and deliberate.

Kimberly bit her lip. Had she offended him? She edged away, her back bumping up against the kitchen bench behind her. Her brain scrambled to predict his response and formulated half a dozen snappy comebacks to fire his way.

Confidence, Kim. If Sam's mad, that's his issue, but don't you hide. She took a deep breath and smiled at him.

Sam faced her, expression unreadable. His gaze held hers, then dropped to her lips. She stopped breathing. He met her eyes again, pupils wide and black in the dim kitchen light. Her pulse danced the samba in her throat.

He opened his mouth, but no sound came out. After a long moment during which empires rose and fell, he shrugged and said, "Thanks." He turned back to the sink and pulled out the drain plug.

She released the breath she'd been holding. "No problem." She scooted around him to get to the bathroom, mind buzzing. What had Sam been going to say before he thought better of it? And why had she ever thought that he might kiss her?

She shook her head. It had taken them three years to move from *nemesis* to *friend in a crisis.* It'd take another thirty for him to actually move toward anything resembling *admiration.*

And there probably weren't enough years left before the Second Coming for that to turn into *love.*

Sam stepped back and surveyed the wall he'd just painted. The uneven coat of white betrayed the moldy-yellow shade beneath, with drips down the wall accentuating the effect. Maybe it wasn't a great idea to watch Kimberly from the corner of his eye while he painted.

He sighed, dunked his roller in paint, and started again. The morning sun shone through the dirty window beside him, appearing somewhat like the light in an oven. Except today's muggy temperatures meant he was *in* the oven, looking out. In more ways than one.

"Yeeep!" A short squeal came from Kimberly's side of the room where she'd been painting her own wall. He spun in her direction. A big blob of paint covered her right eye.

"Are you alright?" He snagged a rag from the pile of painting supplies as he crossed over to her.

Her face scrunched up with the effort of keeping that eye shut tight. "I closed my eye in time. I just need to get it off before it leaks in." She grabbed at the collar of her tank top, but that would just smear the paint all over . . . areas he shouldn't be looking at stuff smeared on.

He caught her hand and held up the rag. "Let me." Cradling her jaw with his left hand, he swiped away the worst of the paint with the rag in his right. Her pulse beat beneath her soft skin and his fingertips. The scent—and remembered taste—of her raspberry lip balm taunted him.

Only four inches stood between him and her pink lips. That and his conscience.

He'd wanted to kiss her last night too. But what then? Would they date if he went back to work with Wildfire? Would they date if he didn't? Did she even feel the same way about him? What if he moved to go to Bible college?

Bible college. When she'd named his most far-fetched dream, he'd almost laughed. But then she'd listened to his story, voiced both empathy and outrage, and challenged his faith on the topic. When she offered her support, he'd almost dropped the dishcloth on the kitchen floor and kissed her senseless.

No one had believed that something as crazy as him and Bible college was possible. But Kimberly had stood in his childhood kitchen—at the bench where he'd struggled over homework for ten unending years—and not only believed he could do it but seemed shocked that anyone would suggest he couldn't.

In that moment he'd felt ten inches taller. Her faith, both in God and in him, had always surprised him with its ferocity. But last night it had struck his core like lightning.

Snap out of it, man. You two haven't gone a whole week yet without fighting.

He lowered the rag. "Keep your eye shut. I'll just wet this and clean it off better."

She followed him to the sink, and when he turned around he almost bumped into her. Was it the paint fumes making him this heady or just her nearness?

He dabbed her eye clean as gently as he could and stepped back. "All done. Stick your head under the tap and flush your eye out with water, just to check."

"Okay." She bent over the kitchen sink and did so.

Sam scuffed his boot against the drop sheet on the ground. What else could he say to keep her talking to him? "I, um . . . I wanted to thank you. For what you said last night about Bible college. I'm going to pray about it."

Kimberly pulled her head out from under the tap, and he handed her a fresh rag to dry her face. She scrubbed herself dry and beamed at him. "Really? That's awesome."

His breath caught in his throat. *Say something. Anything.* "I mean, I never really thought seriously about it. Like, I really wanted to, but I barely made it out of school, so I didn't think—" He snapped his mouth shut before anything else stupid came out. Deep breath. "I just wanted to let you know I appreciated what you said."

Kimberly's fingers came up to rest on her collarbone. "Oh my goodness. What *I* said changed your mind? Seriously?" The concept appeared to be totally foreign to her.

Another indication that his track record of listening to her wasn't so crash hot. "I know I haven't been great at showing it, but I really respect your opinion."

Her eyes brightened. "Right back atcha." She surveyed their work. "Once we're done here, do you want to hear my opinion on chickens?"

He blinked. "Chickens?"

"Jules's white silkies."

He nodded. The eight birds were fluffy, white and laid eggs so tiny you needed a whole dozen for a decent omelet. And Jules loved each one of them.

"I was considering giving them a bath . . . in food dye." She pulled out her phone and showed him a picture of pink, blue, and yellow adult chooks. "I won't say anything to her, just let her notice when she comes back. She'll get a kick out of it."

Sam grinned. Jules would laugh for a week. "Just let me finish this wall, and I'm in."

Kimberly beamed at him and returned to her own paint roller. Sam watched for a moment, heart rate galloping.

God, please give me some direction soon, because I need to kiss this girl.

CHAPTER 25

"Y ou're doing it wrong." Jules leaned on her crutch and admired Mick's torso and legs poking out from under the ute. Three crazy days, seven hundred kilometers, and ten hours of drive time—and they'd gotten a flat tire only forty-five minutes from home.

Not that she was complaining. Now she had a valid excuse to watch him get greased up under that vehicle, and a perfect view of four inches of skin between his T-shirt and board shorts as he reached up under the ute.

Not that this means anything.

Nope, it surely did not. The man had a girlfriend, and Jules had a farm to save. No matter how many times this weekend he'd sent her pulse dancing.

She shooed a fly and nudged him with her moon-booted foot. "You'll put the jack through the floor pan if you position it there. Get it under the chassis."

Mick shifted the jack to an equally terrible spot.

Jules rolled her eyes and used her crutch to balance as she lowered herself to the road's edge beside him. "I don't understand how you can be genius enough to become a vet, but give you a screwdriver and you're as useful as a stud bull on a vow of celibacy." She ducked under the ute, warm gravel digging into her back.

Mick cut her a look from the other side of the jack. "You just quoted my online dating profile."

She tried not to smile, but her face had other ideas. Mick grinned back, and their eyes held for a moment.

Even if she hadn't had more fun in the last seventy-two hours than in all the hours of the previous year combined, this trip had been worth it for one reason: she had her friend back. At some point between squealing while patting stingrays at SeaWorld and laughing themselves silly trying to sand-proof her moon boot with duct tape and garbage bags, something magical had occurred that Jules hadn't experienced in years: she'd forgotten about her problems on the farm. And it was all thanks to Mick.

For three brief days there'd been nothing but her, him, the beach, and all the novelties the Gold Coast had to offer. They'd even taken the scenic route home and lunched in a cute town called Cockatoo Creek, which she noted with some interest had an outdoor camp for school students. And it had all been amazing.

But now it was time to go home.

Jules shifted the jack to the right spot. "See?"

"My hero." His blue eyes twinkled at her, and his scent—ocean salt and something citrusy—drifted into her space.

"Was your girlfriend disappointed that she missed you this weekend?" She blurted it out before her mouth consulted with her brain, then ducked out from under the ute and tried not to over-analyze why she'd mentioned his girlfriend at the same moment she was tempted to lick some of that salt from his lips.

She clambered to her feet.

"It . . . wasn't a problem."

Why had Mick hesitated in answering? Jules narrowed her eyes. Did that girl appreciate what she had in Mick? If Jules was dating him and he'd been away for weeks, no way would she let him hang out with some old girlfriend for the one weekend he was home.

Let alone not see him at all.

Mick jacked up the ute and set to work loosening the wheel nuts, all without a word.

Hmmm. Something fishy here. She'd sensed it all weekend.

She pushed the thought away. Best not to think about it too deeply. At least he had a girlfriend—otherwise this weekend wouldn't have been possible. She couldn't afford to give him the wrong idea, nor let herself get carried away with a fantasy that would never happen.

Well, not *too* carried away.

This weekend had been great, but three days of traffic, a zillion people everywhere, and no cows in sight had also proved something else: she was not cut out to live in the city. While Mick, with his social personality and obsession with his surfboard, seemed completely at home there.

And in two weeks, once his parents' farm was ready for auction, he'd be going back for good.

She pulled out her phone to distract herself from that depressing thought. "Do you think everything's okay at the farm? Sam hasn't texted me any questions for more than a day."

Mick spun off the final nut and dropped it in the dirt. "Butch is there. They'll be fine."

She bit her lip. The vat better not have broken down again. It had a habit of happening every time she went away, tinging each vacation with anxiety. She couldn't afford to dump any more milk. Then there was her biggest boom irrigator. It had been finicky lately, and—

Her hand rubbed the back of her neck.

"Stop worrying." Mick spoke with his back to her.

How had he seen her worried face?

"I can tell without looking you've got your worried face on."

She folded her arms. "Okay, that's just freaky."

"Not when you have a clear pattern of behavior." He pulled the flat tire free and rolled it toward her, swapping it for the spare. "The reason they've been quiet is they're busy working on a surprise for you."

She straightened. "A surprise? A bad surprise, like something broke and they're fixing it?"

Mick stood up and gave her a see-what-I-mean-about-you-worrying look.

"I mean, yay, I wonder what good surprise they're working on." She injected a dose of cheesy enthusiasm into her voice as her mind raced.

He rolled his eyes and returned his attention to mounting the spare tire. "You'll see when we get there."

Fifteen minutes later they were back on the road, and within an hour they'd rolled into Yarra Plains. But instead of stopping by the house, Mick continued down the track that led to the back paddocks. Jules scanned the landscape.

"What surprise could they have out here?"

They rounded a small clump of trees, and the old cottage came into view.

Jules blinked.

The once overgrown yard had been mowed into submission. But the old weatherboards were still peeling worse than her sunburned nose, and she couldn't detect any further changes.

Okay. Kinda weird surprise, but at least nothing was drastically wrong.

Mick pulled up in front of the structure, shut off the ute, and turned to her. "Close your eyes."

She leaned back. Why did her pulse race at that playful look on his face? "No."

"You're not allowed to look. Kim's orders."

"I'll trip on my crutch."

"I can fix that."

Jumping out, he came around to her side of the vehicle and pulled open her door. He held out his hand for her crutch.

She eyed him with suspicion and held it toward him.

Mick ducked under her outstretched arm, grasped her around the waist, and tossed her over his shoulder.

"Mick!" The name came out as a cross between a squeal and a laugh as his shoulder squished her diaphragm. She dropped her crutch and pushed herself up against his back. "What are you doing?"

"You can't look if you're facing the wrong way."

She poked his ribs—he was the most ticklish person she'd ever met—and he almost dropped her. "Hey!"

Considering her leg, maybe a tickle revenge wasn't in her best interest. She propped her elbows against his back and made several threats against his person if any living human saw her in such an undignified position. Ignoring her, Mick carted her into the cottage and placed her on her feet just inside the door.

"Surprise!"

Jules whirled around as Kimberly and Sam shouted and Butch popped ten party poppers in one deafening *bang!* Tiny colored streamers streaked across her vision as she took in the transformed cottage. Gone were the sagging kitchen cupboards, stained walls, and torn curtains. Instead, a shiny new kitchen, white paint, and teal curtains gave the space a funky, fresh feel. Disbelief and then warmth flashed through her as fast as a grin attached itself to her face.

"What the—How did you—I can't believe you pulled this off!" Jules hobbled to the bedroom, then the bathroom. Same fresh paint and clean surfaces. "Wow . . . Just . . . I mean, wow!" Relief flooded her nervous system. Not only was nothing wrong, but this was so very right.

"If you're open to it, Butch is happy to live here in lieu of part of his wage." Kimberly's smile held a note of caution—with good reason. Jules winced. The last thing she'd said to Kimberly had been *Get out.* "It was Sam's idea."

"But it was Kim's idea to do it while you were away." Sam smiled at the lady in question.

Crikey. She had a renovated cottage *and* Sam and Kim were getting along? What a weekend for miracles. She threw her arms around both of them, squeezing them into a group hug as her heartbeat drummed a victory song. "I love it. Thank you. And I'm sorry, Kim."

Kimberly squeezed her right back.

Mick caught her gaze and lifted an eyebrow. His lips didn't move, but his meaning was clear. *See?*

She smiled at him. Things had turned out more than okay— this time.

If only the future could be so sure.

"I'm being stupid," Kimberly muttered to herself. She jiggled her leg in the plush red seat at Jules's local bank branch on Monday morning. Any minute now, the branch manager would call them into his office to discuss extending Jules's loan. And all she could think about was Sam's gentle touch when he'd wiped the paint from her face, just days ago.

She pursed her lips. His nearness had flustered her so much she'd babbled some nonsense about silkie chickens—although the chicken thing had turned out to be a hilarious idea. Still, Sam had to have seen the way she'd practically melted like one of his candy bars on the dashboard of the truck. What if this silly crush made things awkward and ruined their team dynamic? Affected any chance of him returning to Wildfire?

Jules's hand clapped over Kimberly's jiggling knee, stilling it. "What'd you do that's stupid?"

Whoops, might've said it louder than she thought. Kimberly smoothed her black silk blouse and took a deep breath. Perhaps a modicum of professionalism would help. After all, they were here on official business. "Nothing."

Jules leaned back in her own chair, her gaze still on Kimberly. Jules's version of "clothes to wear to a bank interview" included a kind-of-ironed checked RM Williams shirt and—due to her moon boot—denim shorts. But somehow in this small-town bank, it didn't look out of place. "I don't believe you."

"Nothing we should be focusing on right now, at least." Kimberly nodded toward the door of the branch's interview room.

Jules leaned forward. "All the more reason to talk about it. I need a distraction from my nerves. I'm sweating like a pig." She unbuttoned the cuffs of her shirt and rolled the sleeves to the elbow. "Come on, spill."

Kimberly's face overheated by another degree, already too warm as the building's air-conditioning struggled to keep up with the humidity. She *never* discussed her crushes. Not since the day her fourteen-year-old self had told Mom about Archie Masterson, and Mom responded with, "Don't forget protection."

Jules poked her. *"Spill."*

"I just have a silly crush on Sam, is all." Kimberly rushed the words out, voice low. "But it's nothing."

A wicked grin spread over Jules's face, and she slapped her thigh. "Hallelujah and praise the Lord. It only took you three years." She scooted her chair closer. "I want details. Did this start at the rodeo when you guys kissed? Or before then? Has there been any more kissing? Has he asked you out? Ha—"

"Shhh," Kimberly hissed at Jules and glanced around. Information traveled faster through this small town than data bytes over fiber-optic cables. What if someone overheard and word got back to Sam? "There's nothing to tell. It's just proximity. It's not like anything would ever actually happen."

A landslide of skepticism swallowed up the excitement in Jules's expression. "Why not?"

Kimberly cast another furtive glance around the room. *I've never been so desperate to see a five-foot-three perspiring bank manager.*

But no such person appeared.

She sighed. Looked like they really were going to talk about this. "He'd never think of me that way, Jules. It's taken more than three years to get him to tolerate me as a friend."

Jules's brow cinched together like an invisible hand had pulled a loose thread. "*Tolerate* you? He admires you, always has. Even when you drove him nuts."

Kimberly snorted. He'd considered her about as pleasant as a mouse in his boot.

Jules's hand clasped hers, squeezed it. "I'm serious."

Kimberly cut her a look.

"He appreciates the way you aren't afraid to ask questions and can think outside the box. You have a confidence and tenacity that, to be honest, Sam sometimes lacks. And he knows that. As much as you two have butted heads, deep down he knows you balance each other out. It's why you're a good fit for running Wildfire together. It's why I asked you both to help me come up with a plan for the farm." She nudged Kimberly's knee. "And it's why I don't think it's crazy to imagine he might like you."

Kimberly adjusted the damp neckline of her shirt. Someone needed to do something about this air-conditioning. "We fight all the time."

Jules shrugged. "Sam's overly cautious, and you take it too personally when someone rejects your ideas."

Kimberly wrinkled her nose. Ouch.

"But you're both improving on those things, and the more you do, the better you get along." Jules grinned. "You want me to say something to him? Suss him out for you?"

"No!" Kimberly waved her hand like she was brushing the notion of herself and Sam as a couple aside. "Just forget about it."

A door toward the rear of the branch opened, and a plump man with sweat patches on his shirt approached them. "Julia Payton?"

Kimberly popped up faster than a jack-in-the-box. Saved by the sweaty bald man.

But Jules took a moment to fiddle with her crutch and lowered her voice to a volume only Kimberly could hear. "Don't sell yourself short, Kimbo. You've got something to offer Sam." One lid dropped in a sly wink. "And let me know as soon as there's any kissing."

Kimberly's pulse spiked at the thought. What if there was a chance Jules was right?

She gave her silk top a subtle flap to generate some air flow. Great, now she had to try and concentrate on balance sheets and loan-to-value ratios.

When in the background, her mind would be churning around the enigma that was one Samuel Payton.

CHAPTER 26

This is ridiculous.

Kimberly tugged on a borrowed pair of boxing gloves on Wednesday afternoon and eyed the boxing bag that swung from the rafters of Jules's machinery shed. Threw a fist at it just to see what would happen.

Her hand bounced back off, and the bag barely moved, but a puff of dust rocketed down her airways. She stumbled back from the bag, coughing like a pack-a-day smoker.

"You okay?" Sam's words spun her around, still hacking the dust from her lungs.

Boy, this was a great way to convince a guy to date you. And to think that she—high on the excitement of Jules's loan approval—had thought asking Sam to teach her to box was such a stroke of genius. But maybe a dusty boxing bag in Jules's rusted shed, with its piles of rubber dairy piping, pulled-apart machinery, and spare calf pens, wasn't the most romantic setting she could've chosen.

Kimberly cleared her throat and straightened. "Yeah." The word came out as a croak.

Sam sat his own gloves and catching mitts on Jules's workbench, along with four rolls of material. "You'll need wraps."

She cocked her head. "Like chicken Caesar?"

He rolled his eyes, caught her hands, and tugged the gloves from them. "You need them to stop your wrists from jarring." He tossed her gloves onto the bench, picked up one of the rolls of thin material, and looped the end around her thumb.

Kimberly bit her lip as she watched him work, his quick fingers threading the wrap around her wrist, between her fingers and around her hand with the utmost care. Her gaze trailed up his muscular forearms, past his biceps, and to his chest. Broad, tall, and perfect for hugging pretty much everyone he met. If she took half a step forward, she could close her eyes and lean against his warmth and strength.

But Butch would learn ballet before that would happen, so she redirected her attention to his lips. They curved in a little smile as he secured the Velcro on the first wrap and reached for her other hand. That small smile was Sam's resting face—an expression that made you think he was always contemplating a mountain of gummy bears or something else he found equally delightful.

The only thing better than that *Hakuna Matata* expression was the way it burst into a full-blown smile the instant anyone walked into the room.

Even her.

Sam tapped down the second strip of Velcro. "Those will help strengthen your wrists." He secured her gloves onto her hands and stepped back. "Okay, show me what you've got." He raised his own gloveless fists in a fighting stance and nodded for her to do the same.

She brought her fists to her face and tried to look menacing. Sam's gaze swept from her face to her feet and back again. Purely professional, of course, but Kimberly squirmed just the same.

Who had she been kidding, asking him to do this? She couldn't flirt to save her life. The level of awkwardness on this farm was about to hit new heights.

"Shift your right leg back and stand more side-on." He nudged her foot with his and grasped her shoulders, rotating her till her left shoulder faced him. "It makes you less of a target to your opponent."

Holy smokes, how could she listen with his hands on her arms and his face inches from hers?

His warm breath brushed her neck, and she shivered. Was he lingering, or had her brain function just slowed? She licked her lips. "Like this?"

He took a step back and assessed her. His expression yielded no clues. "Good. Now punch me." He held up a palm.

She hesitated, brain crunching back into gear. "Punch you? Don't we punch the bag?"

"I'm more fun. Take a swing."

She jabbed at his palm with her left hand.

"Now across—your right hand."

His hand slapped against her boxing glove with almost equal force to her punch. Except she was giving it all she had, while he looked like he was shooing flies.

"When you throw a cross, swivel your hips to get more force into it." He placed a hand on her left shoulder and the other on her right hip, twisting her as she brought her arm forward. "That's right. Feel where the power comes from?"

With his hands on her? Yeah, she felt the power.

He ran her through the basic types of punches, then stepped back and pulled on his gloves. "Time to sink or swim. Try to punch me again." No palm in the air this time. Sam shifted his weight to his toes and bounced on the spot, fists held near his cheekbones.

Kimberly hesitated. "What?"

"I'll just tap you, and you try to block the shots like I told you. And you just punch me like normal." He grinned. "If you can land a shot."

"Okaaaay." No way would she take a real swing at him. What if she hurt him?

They circled each other on the concrete floor of Jules's workshop. Kimberly threw a couple of jabs out, but Sam slipped his head from side to side, and her glove met empty air.

She stared. "How do you do that?" Her left hand swung around in a hook, and Sam ducked underneath it and poked her in the tummy.

"Gotcha."

Okay, this was annoying. She shifted her punching level from don't-wanna-hurt-you to a-black-eye-never-killed-anyone.

Sam tossed a soft punch in her direction, basically moving in slow motion. Kimberly froze. What had he taught her? Block, slip, or roll? She dropped to the ground in a crouch, face-to-face with the scuffed-up knees of Sam's old jeans.

He stopped. "What technique was that?" Laughter infused his voice.

She popped up. "Surprise attack." She landed two punches to his midsection.

Huh. No grunt of pain.

She stopped and looked at him.

He smiled. "Oh, I mean, 'Owwwww. Have mercy, Kamikaze Kim!'"

"'Kamikaze Kim'?"

"Everyone needs a boxing name."

"What's yours?"

"Sam 'The Man' Payton." His voice boomed out like a boxing commentator's.

"And that really didn't hurt?"

"You're pulling your punches. And in training we put our hands on our heads and let people punch us in the guts to build up core strength. So no, it didn't hurt."

She cocked her right arm and twisted her hips like he'd showed her. Her right fist connected with his diaphragm and knocked him back a step.

"Ooof!"

"Did that?"

Sam bent at the waist, hands on his hips. He sucked in a big breath. "I must be a great teacher."

She punched at an imaginary speed ball. "Maybe I'm a natural."

He narrowed his eyes. "Maybe you're asking for a dunking in the trough."

She blinked at him. Was her man-starved brain playing tricks on her, or was he flirting?

She threw a few more shadow punches. "I'd like to see you try."

He narrowed his eyes.

No way. He was a gentleman. He wouldn't.

Though if she goaded him . . . *"Burrrrrrk-buk-buk-buk."* She flapped her elbows like a chicken.

Sam was after her in a shot. Kimberly shrieked, threw down her gloves, and tore out of the shed like it were on fire. She got a good dozen strides in before Sam's arms came around her from behind. His arms clamped over hers and dragged her a step closer to the nearest cattle trough, on the edge of the dairy's holding yard. Kimberly squealed, thrashed, and wriggled, but his arms held tight, and he got her inside the open gate and another three steps closer to a dunking.

Arms crossed over her chest, Kimberly gave an almighty shove against him as she dropped her weight. She popped out beneath Sam's arms and threw her weight against his knees.

"Ahhh!" Sam tumbled backward and landed with a squelch.

Squelch?

Kimberly spun around. Fine dust covered the ground beneath them. Except for the muddy patch where earlier Jules had accidentally dropped a forty-four-gallon drum of calf milk from the tractor forks.

Kimberly clapped a hand over her mouth, but a giggle leaked out. "Is it milky?"

Sam's face wrinkled in disgust. "Yes."

Kimberly's laughter couldn't be contained. Tears formed in the corners of her eyes as she gasped for breath.

"Oh, that's done it. I was only gonna scare you, but now—" Sam leapt from the ground, and Kimberly scrambled to her feet. But an arm caught her around the waist, and another scooped up her legs behind the knees.

Three quick steps, and Kimberly glimpsed the murky waters of the concrete cattle trough beneath her. Shrieking, she latched onto Sam's neck and held on in a death grip. "If I go down, I'm taking you with me."

"Worth it." Sam's words were muffled against her shoulder.

She tightened her grip, face pressed against his neck, feet kicking uselessly in the air. "You wouldn't dare."

Sam stepped into the trough, shoes and all, and plopped down into the water.

Kimberly sucked in a breath at the cool water rushing over her lap and reaching her rib cage. Water weeds swirled, disturbed by their presence, and she curled up in Sam's lap to avoid the slimy edges of the tank as she muffled a squeal.

His face stretched into a grin, close enough to feel the warmth of his breath on her cheek. "Gotcha."

She splashed his face as she laughed. "I can't believe you did that."

"Told you, worth it. And I had to wash off my pants, anyhow." He stood, lifting her with him, and stepped out of the trough. Water streamed from both of them. He released his hold on her legs, but not her waist, and she found herself standing toe to toe with him, face tilted up to look into his.

Laughter lurked in every inch of his features as his eyes focused on hers, hands still on her waist.

And he didn't move away.

Electricity shot through Kimberly's nerves at every point where his skin had touched hers. Was this it? What if he kissed her?

Run. Run away. You'll make an idiot of yourself.

Her muscles tensed, and she held her breath. It took every bit of her willpower not to break eye contact, stammer out some glib comment, and scuttle to safety.

Sam's gaze dropped to her lips, and her heart rate found a whole new gear. *Oh. My. Gosh.* Was this seriously happening? She'd never noticed how long his lashes were before, nor the slight bump in his nose. Had he ever broken it boxing?

Concentrate, Kim. This was not the time to be wondering

about a person's sporting history. She had the most ridiculous thoughts when she got nervous.

His fingers brushed her jaw as he leaned forward the tiniest amount.

"Samuel!" An older woman's voice called out.

Sam jumped away like he'd been caught in his parents' liquor cabinet. Kimberly blinked.

A woman moved at a fast clip toward them from the direction of the house. Sam swung toward her. "Mum?"

Kimberly gaped as the five-foot-nothing lady with curly gray hair and a wardrobe that matched Jules's threw herself into Sam's arms. She squeezed him half to death, then pulled back and beamed. Then her gaze landed on Kimberly.

And the smile died.

If Kimberly could see her face in the mirror right now, it'd probably be greener than Shrek's complexion. Both from her jealousy of Sam's family and all the triple-chocolate muffins she'd just eaten. She readjusted the waistband of her workout shorts as she dumped a stack of muffin tins in the sink.

At the dining-room table, Sam, Jules, and their mom were setting up a game of some faster version of Monopoly. It was the first time the three seemed to have drawn breath since Mrs. Penny Payton arrived four hours, one plastic Christmas tree setup, and many muffins ago. The woman—small in stature and big in personality—had grumbled something to Jules about her loan approval, scolded them for their lack of festive spirit, decorated the house, and then commandeered the kitchen. The assortment of sweets she produced was nothing short of Wonka-esque. How was Sam not a diabetic yet? And she'd done it all while talking a mile a minute in that Aussie accent of hers. Kimberly's head was still spinning, especially from the weirdness of seeing Christmas decorations and hot weather together. Weirdly, many of the stars, baubles, and wreaths were still winter themed.

Kimberly blasted hot water into the sink, trying to hear the group's chatting over the rush of the water. She'd sat on the edge of the afternoon's festivities, leaving only when she covered Sam's milking with Butch. Even now she tapped her fingers and willed the sink to fill up faster so she could shut off the noisy water. But the least she could do in exchange for the afternoon's entertainment and snacks was clean up.

"Hey, Kim, you wanna play?" Sam popped his head up and looked at her. "You're the money whiz. You'll kick butt in this game."

She eyed the happy picture they made. Sounded fun. She bit her lip. "I'll clean up, but thanks anyway." Somehow she just didn't fit into that picture.

Sam shrugged and returned to setting up the game. Mrs. Payton's lips tightened for a moment before her expression smoothed out and she handed out the Monopoly money. Kimberly grimaced. Had the woman decided to dislike her already? In her life experience, mothers tended to do that.

Undeterred, Kimberly watched them as she scrubbed four muffin tins, six plates, and a ridiculous number of cups, considering how many people were in the house.

But the amount of washing gave her time to observe and plan. Mrs. Payton seemed like the mother Kimberly had daydreamed about as a little girl—and to be honest, as a big girl as well. She had to get this woman to like her. Maybe she could make a special breakfast tomorrow morning? Something familiar, with a hint of USA? She was mentally comparing her cooking repertoire to the contents of Jules's pantry when her phone rang. Butch.

"There's a cow stuck in the dam. Bring the tractor and the hip lifters." *Click.*

She dried the final cup, placed it in the cupboard, and slipped out the door. Mrs. Payton and Sam were crowing at Jules's downfall in the game, so she didn't interrupt. Let them have their time together without an outsider. Surely that would work in her favor.

Mrs. Payton might be giving out some chilly vibes, but Kimberly was going to warm her up if it was the last thing she did.

CHAPTER 27

S am jiggled his knee and watched the door from his place at the dining table. Kimberly still hadn't returned, the cane toads were in full chorus, and the clock hands were nearing eight o'clock.

Mum dropped into the seat next to him, Jules's laptop in one hand and a plate of Christmas pudding in the other. She slid the plate of pudding before Sam, and the scent made his mouth water. "Could you help me search for cruises, Sammy? The internet and I had an argument last week and aren't on speaking terms."

Sam groaned. "You didn't accidentally reformat your hard drive again, did you?" He forked off a piece of pudding and dunked it in the homemade custard pooling in the bottom of the plate. Yum. Tasted as sweet as it smelled. Mum could never wait until actual Christmas Day to crack into the Chrissy pudding.

She pushed the laptop toward him. "You seem to have better luck at this than me."

He rolled his eyes and started a search, one eye still on the door. Kimberly's phone had gone straight to voice mail, but that was normal. Most areas on the farm got terrible reception.

She was probably fine. It wasn't unusual for one of them to

be caught outside at this time, finishing up one of the millions of jobs that popped up on the farm. But he'd hoped Mum would have the chance to get to know her more tonight.

Just in case he decided to kiss her before morning.

Mum caught his glance toward the door. "How are you going with Little Miss Big Ego? She still plotting to torment you?"

Sam grimaced. He should've known his past whinging about Kimberly would come back to bite him. "She never plotted against me. We just had creative differences. And we're getting along . . . swimmingly." He laced his hands behind his head and smiled at his mother.

She raised an eyebrow. "Oh?"

"I'm going to return to Wildfire." He hadn't officially made the decision till the words popped out of his mouth, but in that moment he couldn't imagine telling Mum any other plans for his life.

Mum pinched a bite of the dessert. "What about Bible college?"

He'd emailed her his thoughts on that topic not long after that conversation with Kimberly.

He gulped. This was the first time he'd said this part of the plan aloud—and his frustrating homeschool days were burned into both their memories. Learning at home with Mum—who wasn't a natural teacher and had almost no resources—had still been better than regular school. But that didn't mean they hadn't both been stretched to the limits of their patience. "I'm thinking of doing it part-time online. They've got flexible options nowadays." An ambitious undertaking, balancing work and study with the extra challenge of dyslexia. But Kimberly's prompting had tacitly given him permission to consider it. He took another bite of pudding and smiled at the thought.

"All while dealing with this girl?"

Sam narrowed his eyes. Hard to tell if she was hinting that she suspected his feelings, or if she was referring to his and Kimberly's tumultuous working relationship. "We've come a long way since we've been out here."

Mum rested her chin on her hand and didn't say anything. Sam's unfurling hopes shriveled a little under her gaze.

"You don't think it's a good idea?"

"You only just got back to Australia."

Guilt weighed on the helium balloons of hope that'd been inflating his chest. He'd left for the US in the aftermath of Dad's death, looking to connect with Dad's extended family and process his grief without a constant reminder of what he'd cost Mum. But that had meant Mum lost her husband and face-to-face contact with her son within a few short months.

Mum laid a hand on his. "I just don't want you biting off too much."

Sam deflated. Was this her well-known desire to keep him in Australia talking, or her doubts about his ability to study? Probably both. No one would question if Kimberly wanted to work and study part-time, not with her genius brain. But him?

Apparently not even his mother thought he could do it.

He eked out a small smile. "We'll see."

Maybe.

Kimberly yawned as she tied a Christmas ribbon around the picnic basket she'd just packed. Her gaze swung to the horizon, visible through Jules's kitchen window. A streak of sapphire ran along the divide between sky and earth.

And she'd already been up for an hour.

Another yawn escaped as she tugged the bow till it was perfect. Sam, Jules, and Mrs. Payton's talking had kept her up until eleven thirty last night. Which meant she'd had less than five hours' sleep. But the sacrifice was for a good cause. She'd needed to prepare this before she left to milk, because Mrs. Payton would surely rise before she returned.

The basket contained fresh-baked biscuits, pancake batter, a glass bottle of freshly squeezed orange juice, half a dozen silkie eggs she'd carefully cleaned, Canadian bacon—known in Australia simply as "bacon," plus Vegemite and Weet-Bix cereal for a traditional Australian touch. She tucked a little note and a bunch of flowers in the top.

The happy thought of Mrs. Payton's reaction carried Kimberly through a long milking with the ever-quiet Butch, during which she was continually tempted to lean against the dairy wall and fall asleep. Her brain was so foggy, she even forgot to bring him more copies of Dad's artwork. By the time she dragged herself back to the house for "second brekkie," she was praying for a good chunk of that bacon to be left and a magical genie to complete the rest of the day's chores for her.

She'd had to lock the cows away in the farthest paddock, so Sam had already left to log some hours on the tractor when she arrived back home, sweating and stinking of the dairy. In fact, the house appeared empty, save for Mrs. Payton sitting at the dining table in a blue button-down and work jeans, fragrant coffee in hand and a laptop in front of her.

Kimberly smiled at the older woman as she entered the room, sweaty socks sliding across the timber floor. "Good morning."

Mrs. Payton set her coffee down, her leathery skin accentuating the frown lines in her forehead. "Morning."

Kimberly glanced at the kitchen counter. The basket sat there, untouched. "Did you see—"

"I only have coffee and a piece of fruit in the morning." Her tone was cool.

Hurt sparked through Kimberly's nervous system. She paused. "Oh. Well, feel free to have some of this for lunch." She headed toward the basket. "I'll just pop it in the fri—"

"I'd like to have a talk with you."

Kimberly froze halfway toward her rejected basket. Mrs. Payton's tone boded no argument. "Okay." She took a seat at the table with trepidation, careful to only perch on the chair in her dairy clothes.

Mrs. Payton pushed the laptop aside. "From what I hear you're a straight talker, so I trust you'll appreciate it when I take the same approach with you."

Gulp. Kimberly laced her fingers together, wiped her expression of emotion, and braced herself.

"I know you're here to take my son away again, and you've already convinced my daughter that this insane mortgage is the only way to save us from financial ruin."

Kimberly raised her hands in surrender. Thank goodness the loan had come through yesterday morning before Jules's mother tried to talk her out of it. "I only—"

"I can understand your motivations—that ministry of Sam's is a worthy cause, and Jules asked for your help and insists that this loan is her decision." She pursed her lips. "But she never would've done it without your interference, and Sam's spent long enough away from his family. I don't want your influence here. Not much point in pretending otherwise."

With every word, Kimberly's Christmas Day fantasies soured. No matter what she'd let herself dream of over the past weeks, this place was not her home, and this was not her family. The Mrs. Payton she'd dreamed of meeting was no fairy godmother, just a mama bear protecting her cubs. From Kimberly.

It seemed mothers were allergic to her.

She forced her lips into a tight smile. "Message received. I'll stay out of your way."

Throat aching with a rush of emotion, she slid a pan onto the stove and tossed a slice of bacon in. That woman could be as rude as she wanted, but she couldn't keep Kimberly from bacon and eggs. Kimberly rubbed dust from her eyes as the fat began to sizzle. This was good in the long run, really. It proved yet again why she and Sam would never work.

Fat from the pan popped, catching her hand with a sharp sting. She hissed and ran her hand under cold water as her thoughts swirled through her mind. Sam was obviously close to his mother, and the woman couldn't stand the sight of her. No way would she be stepping into the middle of that.

This was just the kick she needed to remind herself that any feelings for Samuel Payton would only result in heartbreak.

CHAPTER 28

S omething weird was going on.

Jules eyed Mick as the vet slurped down the last of his kombucha and surveyed his dad's silage wagon. The big green contraption was parked in Jules's machinery shed. Mick's dad needed Jules's mechanical know-how and tools to fix it, and Jules needed Mick's functioning limbs to actually carry out the work. But no one had figured out how to get her in the trailer.

Yet not that problem, nor the stuffy heat in the shed, nor the arrival of the new cattle today was what triggered an icky unease beneath Jules's belly button.

It was Mick.

In the less-than-a-week since their spontaneous trip, she'd rewound their time together through her head. Him rescuing her from Psycho. His anger at her risky actions. Him saving Meg. The rodeo.

He'd mentioned his girlfriend that one time, and she'd grabbed it and run with it. It meant she was safe to revive their friendship without awakening any ancient history. But after their weekend away, doubts battered her brain's wall of denial.

"What if we sent you up in the bucket?" Mick's voice broke through her thoughts.

She pulled her unfocused gaze from a flat tire leaning against the shed to his face. "What?"

"The tractor bucket. Hop in, and I'll lift you up next to the wagon, then climb up and help you in."

She shrugged and swished a fly. "Okay."

Mick tossed his bottle into her forty-four-gallon-drum-cum-garbage-bin and climbed into the tractor cab. Jules pursed her lips as he maneuvered the tractor into position.

The Gold Coast weekend, fun as it had been, was probably a mistake. She'd let her mind drift down a road it had no business traveling, and Mum's return was a great reminder of why. This farm was their home—their legacy. Dad's burial place. She couldn't just ditch it all for Mick and the coast and leave Mum in the lurch. And she couldn't give up who she was—a farmer, a problem solver, an independent woman—to become one of those Gold Coast wives with their fake nails, plastic lawns, and yoga classes. Not even to be with Mick.

Who had a girlfriend.

Tractor in place, Jules maneuvered her bad leg into the bucket, sat on the rusting metal, and surveyed the farm as the hydraulics lifted her several meters into the air. The tractor shuddered to a stop as Mick killed the engine, then used the back of the ute to scramble up and over the side of the wagon. He overbalanced and disappeared over the edge.

Thud.

Jules leaned over to see from the bucket, hovering about half a foot above wagon. Was Mick alright?

And more important, how the devil was she going to get from this tractor bucket into the wagon without jarring her sore foot?

Mick popped up, bits of silage and grain dust speckling his hair and pineapple-patterned T-shirt. "Alright, come 'ere." He tugged her arm toward him.

A rush of energy shot through Jules's system. Uh-oh. Not again.

Mick looped her arm around his neck, bringing her face close to his. She counted the freckles on his nose as he slid one arm under her legs, the other under her back, and hefted her from the bucket into the wagon. Ugh. Even hotter in here.

He kept his arms on her waist until she was steady on her feet, then stepped away and crouched at the front of the wagon. "Okay, Dad said the bearing has collapsed in the bottom beater—"

"Mick, can I ask you something?"

He swiveled to look up at her. "My response to that question has never stopped you before."

"What's your girlfriend's name?"

He dropped his gaze and grimaced.

She clenched her teeth. She'd been an idiot. There was no girlfriend. And that joyful unicorn currently shooting rainbows around her brain could shut up, because any soft thoughts toward Mick were unwelcome here.

"It was a stupid thing for me to say." He brushed his hands clean and stood, only an arm's length away. "Brittany and I did go on a couple of dates, but it kind of fizzled out as I was preparing to come out here. You just caught me at an insecure moment, I guess."

How could something with Mick ever "fizzle out"? She'd had ten years to stomp out this spark, yet it kept flaming to life. She sucked air in through her nose and released it in a hiss between her lips. "So the Gold Coast weekend—did you do that as a friend?"

"I'm always a friend."

"You know what I mean."

His eyes lit with an intensity she hadn't seen for way too long. "I'm always a friend, Jules. But if you're asking whether I'd kiss you right now if I thought for half a second you'd let me"—he edged half a step closer—"the answer is yes."

Her mouth dropped open at his bluntness. Whoa. Where had blushing Mick gone? She cleared her throat. "Then it's a good thing I won't let you." Yet she swayed the tiniest bit in his direction.

He grinned. "Liar."

And he kissed her.

Jules stood stock-still, eyes wide open, as the sweet tang of peach kombucha enveloped her mouth. One of Mick's hands cupped her jaw as the other crept around her waist. At that her eyelids fluttered shut. Of their own volition, her hands slid up his chest, and she leaned into his warmth and his kiss. Mick hauled her tight against him for a heady moment, then pulled back.

Jules caught his jaw with her fingertips and kissed him again. Really kissed him, fingers dragging through the slight curl in his hair. For saving her, for saving Meg, for following her when she was upset, for putting her needs first no matter what she put him through.

And then, with a choked sob, she pulled away.

"Hey." Mick's voice was as soft as his fingers as he traced the curve of her cheek. "What's wrong?"

Jules sucked in air and begged reason to return to her mind. "I can't be with you."

Lines creased his forehead. "Because of the farm? We can work that out, Jules. We're not twenty anymore."

Oh for the love of all that was good, the sweetness in his tone nearly undid her. She pushed against his chest and shuffled a step back, covering her face with her fingers.

"Nothing's changed. My life is here. Yours is not. And there's five hours of outback in between." Focus on the next thing. "So this grinding sound—"

"Forget about the wagon, Jules." Mick's hands turned her to face him. "I can give you time, if that's what you need. We can work out a compromise, something that lets us blend our different lives. But I can't wait forever without knowing."

She folded her lips into a sad smile and pushed his hands away. The man had salt water in his veins. He should never move here. She could never move there. Pain seared her heart till it threatened to cut off her breath. She could barely whisper, "So don't."

What was up with Kimberly today?

Sam trudged up the stairs, his track pants and T-shirt splattered in filth from this afternoon's milking, a day's hard work weighing on every inch of his body. Milking had taken longer than usual, as the first of Jules's new cattle took their time to settle in. But even heavier than his limbs was the memory of Kimberly's behavior today.

Nothing explicit, just an . . . edginess. A withdrawal. He racked his brain for anything he could've said to her in the last twenty-four hours that would be upsetting. Nada.

Was she upset he'd spent so much time with Mum? Nah. Kimberly wasn't the jealous type. Maybe this workload had caught up to her and she was exhausted.

He looked down at himself at the door. Removing boots just wouldn't be enough. He shrugged and pulled his T-shirt over his head, then stepped out of his trackie dacks—Kimberly called them sweatpants—leaving just the shorts he'd worn underneath. Working from the chilliness of 4:30 a.m. to the sapping heat of midday taught a guy to wear layers.

Mum was frowning at the laptop on the dining table when he entered. He smiled. "I'm pretty sure I left you sitting in that exact spot."

Her frown didn't entirely smooth out as she looked up at him. "Hey, darl'."

"What's up?"

"What was the name of the cruise you booked for me this morning?"

He grinned. He'd been particularly proud of finding that deal—though he couldn't really take credit. An email offering a cruise from Brisbane to Cairns had landed in his inbox this morning. Probably Google data mining his search history or something. Either way, the deal had been hundreds of dollars cheaper than any of the other trips he'd researched last night, so they'd booked this morning.

"North Queensland Cruise Lines. Why?"

"I just haven't seen a confirmation email yet."

He shrugged. She'd probably deleted it. Mum and computers seemed to mix as well as wedding dresses and red wine. He took the computer and checked the trash folder. Twenty clicks later, still no email. He frowned. "I'll ask Kim."

Mum hesitated, then shrugged. "Sure."

Sam padded through the house in bare feet and knocked on Kimberly's door. It swung open to reveal her in a pink robe.

He sucked in a breath and tried *really* hard not to ponder whether or not she had pj's underneath.

"Oh." Her eyes darted from his chest to his face, and she folded her arms. "I thought you were Jules."

He opened his mouth but no sound came out.

Idiot!

He spun the laptop to face her. "Can you check this out?" He managed to keep his brain functioning enough to outline the story as she clicked through the inbox, unaware that she'd sent his mind into meltdown.

The strap of a tank top peeked out from her robe. Pj's. He forced out a breath. Good to know.

A line formed between her eyebrows. "Is this the original email?" She pointed to the screen. "Did you click this link to get to the website?"

"Yeah."

The line deepened. "Gimme a minute."

She sat on the edge of her bed and worked.

Sam forced his gaze to wander around the room. Tidy. A single comic book on the bedside table. Some blue Christmas tinsel tacked to the wall, along with a collection of paper snowflakes. Not a whole lot to see, though it smelled of that jasmine body spray again.

She tapped her finger against her chin, then resumed clicking.

He studied the dirt beneath his fingernails.

She huffed.

He leaned his head against the doorframe and closed his eyes. These early mornings wore on a man.

"Did you pay these guys yet?"

Sam's eyes popped open. "Yes." Like fifteen hundred dollars

of Mum's retirement money. An uneasy feeling triggered a wave of goose bumps. "Why?"

Her face twisted into a grimace. "I think it's a scam."

Sam stared at her, then the computer screen, then her again. Chills swept through him. He'd just lost a chunk of Mum's retirement money.

Again.

CHAPTER 29

This was the worst.

Kimberly huddled on one end of the couch in her *Battlestar Galactica* pj shorts and an old sweatshirt of Dad's, nursing a mango smoothie and attempting to focus on the *That 70's Show* episode Jules had on TV. But Mrs. Payton's animated discussion with her sister's voice mail made it difficult.

She dug her fingertips through her hair and massaged her scalp, eyes fastened on the TV but processing nothing.

"Hey." Jules leaned over on the couch till her arm brushed Kimberly's. "What's up?"

"What? Nothing." Kimberly refocused on the now-paused show. "The seventies. Hilarious. Continue."

"Not till you tell me what's going on. Are you worried about Sam?"

His expression while he'd told his mother about his mistake had been nothing short of tortured. And while he'd promised to pay her back, it didn't appear to make him feel any better. When the initial conversation and phone calls to the bank were over, he'd disappeared outside, despite the threat of cane toads and mosquitoes. And that'd been more than an hour ago.

"He'll be okay." If only her brain could believe what her mouth was saying. Her eyes wandered to the laptop screen on Jules's lap, the words *Cockatoo Creek Outdoor Camp* written across the top of the web page. She took a sip of mango-ey sweetness. The rest of her night might not be going well, but this smoothie was like drinking sunshine. "What's that?"

Jules snapped the laptop shut. "We're talking about you. Yeah, I think Sam will be alright. And I think you need to tell yourself that a few more times." She nudged Kimberly with her elbow. "Why don't you go talk to him?"

"Bad idea."

"'Coz Mum told you to stay away from him?" Jules laughed out the words, like a joke, but the expression morphed into shock when Kimberly didn't smile. "Fair dinkum? Yikes."

Kimberly shrugged. "It's fine."

Jules's expression darkened. "She doesn't know when to turn the bossy-mother thing off, even if you're experienced enough to make your own decisions."

Kimberly studied her friend. Was Jules talking about herself or Sam—or both? She stood from the couch, the sticky leather peeling away from her legs. Either way, no part of her wanted to be here when Mrs. Payton decided to join them. Kimberly's bed called—that, and the new sci-fi show queued up on her streaming app. "Thanks. I appreciate it. I think I'm gonna hit the sack."

"Hey." Jules touched her hand and waited to speak till Kimberly met her gaze. "Don't take it to heart. Your worth isn't determined by what my mother or even Sam thinks of you."

Kimberly blinked. Surprisingly direct for Miss Afraid-of-Her-Own-Emotions Jules.

But Jules wasn't done. "I heard you asked Sam the other day what he'd do if he wasn't afraid."

Kimberly shifted her weight between her feet. "I didn't put it like that."

"But it's what you meant. And you were right. So I'm asking you: what would you do if you weren't afraid?"

I'd tell Mom that despite everything, I love her. I'd tell Jules to put Mick out of his misery.

And I'd kiss Sam.

Each of the thoughts reached her throat, then refused to go any further. "I-I'll think about it."

"Actions speak louder than thoughts." Jules nodded toward the door. "Before Mum is finished with her third voice mail message."

Kimberly bit her lip and looked from Mrs. Payton to the door. Sat her smoothie on the coffee table next to a ceramic nativity scene.

And made a run for it.

Sam sat on the roof of the chicken coop, one of his precious bottles of A&W cream soda in hand. His favorite brand was hard to find in Australia. Three empty bottles were piled in the grass below where his feet dangled from the edge of the roof.

Sugar had always been his drug of choice.

He'd thought nothing could twist the knife in his insides like Mum's expression when she threw her travel magazines away after Dad's funeral. Turned out that letting her down a second time came pretty darn close.

He dropped the empty bottle to the ground, where it landed with a clink. The deal had been too good to be true, and he'd followed a link from an email, for goodness' sake. That was a rookie error in this digital age.

Turned out the website even had typos, indicative of the scammers dumping their text into a translation service and posting it for suckers like him. But he'd assumed the letters were only jumbled in his mind. Even if the bank's fraud department could recover the money, that did nothing to restore his shattered confidence. He flopped back onto the cool corrugated-iron roof and stared at the Southern Cross constellation. The stars out here were incredible—almost as incredible as the thought that he'd actually be able to pull off part-time Bible college at the same time as working on the Wildfire expansion. He'd be lucky to pull off one of those things, let alone both.

And to think he could date Kimberly at the same time?

Insane.

"Sam? You out here?"

His head snapped up at the sound of Kimberly's voice. "Over here."

She clomped around the side of the shed in her gum boots, probably worn as protection against the dozens of toads that jumped away with every step she took.

"On the roof." He waved her over to the upturned bucket propped against the wall and grasped her arm to assist her up. "You interested in stargazing too?"

"Not exactly."

He eyed her, sitting so close her leg rested just an inch from his. A glib response was more Kimberly's style, especially when emotions were running close to the surface.

"Oh?"

"I wanted to let you know your mom has options. Depending

on how she paid, Australian banks will sometimes refund the money. I think. It was just a bit of quick research on their banking codes of practice."

"I appreciate it."

"So . . . you okay?"

The words sounded a little strangled. These questions weren't Kimberly's usual style. But then, she'd been full of surprises lately.

He lay back on the roof and contemplated a shallow answer, but opted for honesty. "I've let Mum down like this before. To have done it again . . ." He trailed off.

She matched his posture, lying back on the roof, hands clasped on her stomach. "You didn't let her down. Tons of people get scammed every day."

"I got too excited and didn't take enough precautions. Last time it had even more serious consequences." Though fifteen hundred dollars was nothing to sneeze at. Would he spend his life repaying Mum for his own mistakes that affected her?

"What happened last time?"

He winced. Not his favorite tale. Some little part of her occasionally looked at him with admiration, like she believed he could take on the world. It was unjustified, but nice. And hearing the full story would kill it.

"When I was in my early twenties, I moved to the city and wanted to open a café. Dad gave me the financial backing. He and Mum were close to retirement. They were going to caravan around Australia." He cleared his throat. "I had all these plans for the café. It was so popular. I opened a second store across town and had plans for a third. But . . . after I opened the second location, business didn't go so well. We started to bleed money." He sighed. "Dad worked his guts out for a year to try and recoup some of the cash and then had a massive heart attack."

Cold fingers slid over his. He started, surprised, then squeezed them. "He never got to take that holiday with Mum. And that's on me."

"You couldn't have known." She held his hand for a long minute, then propped herself up on an elbow next to him. "And might I remind you, Mr. Pastor, that carrying guilt around only holds you back from the life God intended? Either take it to Him and get it forgiven, or realize it was never yours to carry in the first place."

He shifted his head on the cool corrugated iron to stare at her. He'd preached that line to thousands of teenagers. Funny how he'd never thought of his own situation in that light. A weight slipped from his soul, and it rose with hope for the first time in years. "Using my own sermons against me?"

She lay back down and smiled in the direction of the stars twinkling above them. "And you thought I didn't listen."

She shivered next to him. He detached his hand from hers and slid his arm under her shoulders. When she shifted her head to let him, then settled in next to him, the movement felt so natural the shock didn't even hit him for a moment.

Oh. My. Goodness. He was lying on the roof of a chicken coop with his arm around Kimberly Foster, and there hadn't been a rift in the space-time continuum or anything.

Maybe the impossible wasn't so impossible after all. A bubble of emotion swelled inside of him, and he rolled with it. "Kimberly?"

"Yeah?"

Here goes nuthin'. "Have dinner with me tomorrow night?"

She turned her face toward him and blinked. "Dinner with you?"

Her jasmine scent teased his senses. He wrapped a strand of hair around his finger. "Yeah. Me. You. Food. A date."

Another blink. "Um . . . okay."

Her face was so close. Her eyes so wide. Lips so full.

He drew in another jasmine-scented breath and leaned his head forward a fraction of an inch.

"I'd better go inside." Kimberly jumped up like an ant had bitten her. He sat up as she scrambled down the bucket. "See ya."

She moved away at a clip just short of a run. Sam kept his gaze on her till she disappeared around the corner of the shed, his arm tingling from pins and needles and the sensation of her skin.

He'd just asked Kimberly Foster out on a date.

Oh boy.

CHAPTER 30

Holy guacamole. Sam had asked her on a date.

Kimberly moved back toward the house as fast as she could without stepping on a toad. He liked her?

His mother would kill her.

What would happen if they both worked at Wildfire?

She'd only brought one dress.

He actually liked her?

Jules was gonna squeal. Then Mrs. Payton would come in wondering what happened. She'd have to find a way to keep Jules quiet.

He really, actually liked her?

Kimberly reached the bottom of the backdoor steps and peered up at the windows, ears straining for sounds of life. No Mrs. Payton. Drat. She'd hoped the woman would be on the phone and distracted while she slipped inside.

Kimberly rested her left foot on the bottom step but just couldn't convince her right one that sleeping inside tonight was worth the wrath of Sam's mom. Her facial muscles refused to relax out of the dopey grin on her face, and if anyone asked what was up, she'd turn red faster than you could say "Samuel Payton is one sexy beast."

There had to be another way.

Kimberly backed away from the house and circled it, folding her arms against Dad's sweatshirt to brace against tonight's cool breeze. The entire home rested on poles that held it six feet in the air—lest the river flooded—which ruled out your basic climb-in-through-a-window routine.

Bingo! Jules's escape. She had a disused water tank beneath her window. Kimberly jogged around to it. The tank's corrugated-iron sides begged to be climbed up. She latched one hand on the top of the tank. Ugh. Was that dried lumpy stuff bird poo?

Big picture, Kim.

She shoved the toe of her boot into a knee-high corrugation and tested if it held her weight. Yikes. These corrugations weren't nearly so easy to climb as they looked.

She wedged her back against one of the house's thick stumps and shuffled up, taking tiny steps. Progress was slow and gave the logical voices in her head a chance to have their say.

He's seriously thinking about staying at Wildfire.

Three feet off the ground.

We fought all the time.

Four feet.

If—when—we break up, we'll be stuck working together. Imagine the fighting then.

She shoved the thoughts aside to deal with the immediate challenge: how to get from this spot onto the top of the tank. Man, that prince that climbed a tower for Rapunzel sure deserved to marry a princess, 'cos this was way harder than it looked.

Maybe she could just reach—

"What are you doing?"

Sam's voice jolted through her system, and one foot slipped. A squeak emanated from her pressed lips as she fought for purchase against the tank. When a hand grasped her boot and pressed it against the tank, she stabilized and released a breath. *Phew.*

Her gaze slanted down to her right and collided with Sam's. If his eyebrows got any higher, they'd pop off his forehead.

"Your mom's not my biggest fan." She grimaced. It'd be impossible to keep it a secret, but still hurt to admit. "This seemed easier."

He cocked his head. "What did she say to you?"

"She's not a fan of the loan idea." A half-truth, but she could only admit so much in one night. "It's fine, but this house is basically in the sky. Do you see any alternatives?"

He appeared to consider that for a moment. "We'll return to the Mum issue tomorrow, but for now do you want a boost?"

"Please."

He placed both hands beneath her right foot. "I've got y—"

A flash of movement on the tank caught her eye. A spider. A black spider. A black spider with a red back.

Australia's poisonous redback spider, made famous by a certain song involving a toilet seat and a lack of lighting. And it ran toward her boot.

Kimberly yelped and jumped away—into thin air.

She collided with Sam on her way down. The impact knocked him to the ground.

Ooof!

They landed in a tangle of limbs and grunts.

Kimberly froze for a moment, cheek in the dirt, torso on Sam's, his arm trapped under her chest. Waves of fright rolled through her, and aches registered from every limb of her body. She closed her eyes. A guy had finally asked her out, and the first thing she did was jump on him and squish him.

Oh, the horror.

Sam gave a low groan. She rolled away from him, heat exploding into her cheeks. "Are you okay?" She inhaled dust as she spoke. Coughed it back out.

"Just peachy." He ran a hand down his body, like he was checking for anything missing or impaled. "You?"

"I'm sorry. There was a spider." She winced at the stereotype. A girl afraid of a spider.

He sat up and reached for her. "But are you okay?"

"I don't know if a date is a great idea." The words rushed out from the dark box labeled *Insecurity* that she normally locked down tighter than plutonium. Sam picked a leaf out of her hair as she sat up, dirt beneath her palms. "We haven't even gone two weeks without a major disagreement. We come from opposite sides of the globe, your mother doesn't like me, and we'll be working together."

Yikes. This emotional-honesty thing was spiraling out of control. Maybe this display of self-doubt would make him run for the hills. And did a part of her want that?

Sam plucked another twig from her sweatshirt, his hair tousled and lightened to the shade of dust. "Do you really think we'd fight that much?"

She dropped her gaze to her hands. "I think we'd get mad. There's a distinct possibility I could threaten to throw out your sugar stash again." His story about his dad threw even more light on his risk-averse attitude. And with that history, it wasn't an attitude likely to change anytime soon. Conflict was inevitable—and with her heart on the line, their arguments could go from upsetting to obliterating.

He didn't respond. She risked a glance up.

Those big brown eyes remained serious, watching her, with just the slightest hint of sad puppy dog. Oh, those eyes. They could make a girl forget the ache in her elbow and the dirt in her hair.

"We might fight," he admitted. Then shrugged. "We would definitely fight."

A little piece of her soul shriveled. She'd made him see reason, curse her own logic. The pangs in her body increased.

"But maybe we can handle it better. Not let a creative difference get in the way of what could be a pretty awesome partnership."

Her chest tightened. "But what if things didn't work out? And then we'd have to see each other every day?" Logic screamed that this was a terrible idea. If—when—this imploded, Sam would be able to walk away with his heart intact. She would not.

"Are you saying you don't want to go out with me?"

I'd love to be your girlfriend. The words whispered through her mind, but throat-closing fear accompanied them. She brushed dirt from her knee. "I'm saying it sounds like an unwise risk." A term that would resonate with him.

A beat. Sam gave a single nod. "Okay. Do you still want help getting through that window?"

The flame of excitement dancing inside her extinguished with a hiss. Even though she'd been the one talking him out of this.

Lights flicked off inside the house. Looked like everyone was going to bed. "I don't think it's necessary anymore."

Sam offered her a hand, but she struggled to her feet alone, heart somewhere in the vicinity of her toes. How had she gone from ecstasy to despair in the space of ten minutes?

It's your own fault, dummy.

She wrinkled her nose at the thought as they trudged toward the stairs.

But it's for the best. I've just saved us both a lot of heartache.

Water in his gum boots would normally rate number one on Sam's *List of Serious Problems*, but as he squelched his way from the dairy to home after the morning milking, the water-and-rubber combination ripping out his leg hairs only ranked at number three.

Kimberly Foster.

How could fourteen letters have him more mixed up than that day his teacher asked him to read aloud a page of Shakespeare? He kicked at a tractor-flattened toad and huffed.

She said yes.

And then she'd talked him out of it. And like a big dope, he'd let her. What was wrong with him?

He reached the base of the steps to Jules's house, yanked off his boots, and jammed them upside down on the handrail posts to drain. Socks followed, left on the handrail for Future Sam to take down to Jules's detached laundry.

Truth was, he'd been more shocked that Kimberly agreed to go on a date with him in the first place than that she'd backed out of it ten minutes later. Because she was right.

He plodded up the stairs, wet footprints following him.

He and Kimberly were just so different. What did he think, anyway—that Kimberly would stay with Wildfire forever, not move on to something else that put her giant brain to proper use?

No, when it came down to it, she was brave and he was afraid. And if he was her, he'd think twice about a date with him too.

He banged his way through the screen door, clomped through the veranda, and entered the kitchen. A wave of lavender-scented warmth met him, along with Jules, facing the microwave with her back to him and . . . sniffling.

Sam paused. Was he hearing things?

Another sniff.

"You okay?"

Jules started, then turned around and glared at him. "What are you sneaking around for?"

"I wasn't sneaking. You were sniffling. Everything alright?"

Jules huffed. "Can't a girl just deal with PMS in peace?" She popped open the microwave and yanked out a heat pack.

Yikes. He held up both palms and headed for his room as fast as his feet would carry him. When he dropped his filthy shirt on top of his overflowing washing basket, it slid off the top and hit the floor. He sighed and scooped up the shirt and the basket, which brought the smell of his dairy clothes way too close to his face. Yuck. What a pong. If he didn't do some washing today, he'd be milking in nothing but boxers tomorrow.

The thud of Jules's door indicated she'd gone to her room, so he pulled on a fresh shirt and scooted back through the kitchen and outside to the small laundry attached to the side of the house.

Something about Jules's reaction didn't sit right. She'd been defensive. And thinking about her problems was a lot more fun than thinking about his, so he allowed his mind to travel down the tangent.

PMS could explain it, sure, but more likely it was a cover for something else. And today's date wasn't anywhere near any significant anniversaries regarding Dad.

No, this had Michael Carrigan written all over it.

He set his jaw. Mick was his friend, sure, but Jules was his sister first. And if Mick had hurt her feelings while she was already stressed out by the farm . . . they'd be having words.

Then again, Jules may've been the heartbreaker. She'd done it before. In which case he should be there to offer Mick a little moral support.

He hauled a pile of wet girly laundry out of the washing machine and tried to ignore the bras. They could be Kim's, or they could be his sister's—and either way it was best not to think about it. If at all humanly possible.

He dumped his washing into the machine, threw in extra washing powder in honor of the calf scours down his left jeans pant leg, and took the stairs two at a time to retrieve his work boots.

Time to pay his friend a visit.

CHAPTER 31

Sam slowed down the quad bike as he neared the remains of the tree they'd cut down almost two weeks ago. Mick stood with a block of wood lined up, ax in hand and a sour look on his face. Jules had promised him all the wood he could chop—looked like he was here to collect.

"Hey, man."

Crack. Mick split the log.

Sam hopped off the bike. "Looks like you've almost got the whole tree done."

Crack.

"Gonna have plenty of wood come winter."

Crack.

"Are you the reason my sister is crying?"

Mick missed the log. He swore as the ax missed his leg by an inch, then glanced at Sam. "Sorry." He hefted the ax back to his shoulder for another swing. "*She's* the reason that she's crying." He paused. "I take it Jules told you to buzz off?"

"She said she had PMS, and I ran like a bat outta hell."

Mick snorted.

Sam shifted his hat to wipe away a bead of sweat. The air hummed with the possibility of rain. "So you told her about the fake girlfriend thing?"

Mick lined up the next block. "Didn't have to. The truth was pretty obvious. When she asked me about it, I laid it all on the line."

"And she didn't take it well?"

"She took it great. Kissed my socks off. Then started crying and said she couldn't marry me because apparently nothing's changed since we were twenty."

Sam rocked back on his heels. "Oh. Wow."

"Yeah."

Crack. The scent of eucalyptus grew stronger with each blow.

Mick wiped the sweat from his forehead. "Subject change. I heard that your mum isn't Kim's biggest fan."

Sam raised an eyebrow. He'd never talked to Mick about it, but apparently someone had. He'd planned to ask Kimberly more about it later but now marked an *Urgent* note on his mental to-do list.

"Oh, come on, mate. You like her. It's written all over you."

"Yeah, well, I'm having about as much success as you." He recounted the sorry tale of last night.

Mick handed him the ax. He tested its weight in his hand. Oh yeah. Talk about therapeutic. Swinging the ax in a wide arc, he sank it deep into a fresh block. The second blow split it through.

"Why do you think Kim really turned you down?" Mick leaned against a fence post and crossed one ankle over the other.

"I told you." Sam lined up his next wooden victim and swung, the impact reverberating through his bones.

"You told me she thought you guys would fight. But you bought that? Come on, you took one look at Jules's face and knew to come hunt me down. Don't take Kim's words at face value."

He blinked. Kim's response had lined up with everything

he'd been afraid of, so he hadn't questioned it. But this . . . this opened up a whole new realm of possibilities.

Sam scooped up an armload of wood and followed Mick's train of thought. "Kim . . . hates rejection. Of her ideas, of anything. She takes it very personally."

"Now we're getting somewhere."

He dumped the wood in the ute's tray. "That doesn't mean she wasn't being honest and she just doesn't want to go out with me."

"Did she say that?"

"What?"

"That she doesn't want to go out with you?"

Sam shoved a heavy block into position. "Do I look like I'm on a date with her right now?"

Mick picked up a second ax out of the ute tray and leaned on it like he had all day. "In what you just told me, she was afraid the two of you would fight. She didn't say she didn't like you. Maybe her comments were more a reflection of what she thinks of herself than what she thinks of you."

Sam stopped midswing. *Lightbulb.* He grinned at Mick. "Ever considered swapping to my line of work?"

The edge of Mick's mouth turned up in a smile. "This is just what I'm telling myself about Jules so that I don't slide into despair. Feel free to apply the same to Kim."

"Women."

"Yeah."

Sam leaned on his own ax and chewed his bottom lip. So, maybe Kim's reaction was more about herself than it was about him.

Maybe.

The question was, what could he do about it? How could he convince this girl to trust him enough to take the leap?

"Speaking of hard decisions, have you decided about Wildfire? You going back?"

Sam sucked in a breath. Wildfire. How could he ask Kimberly to be brave when he couldn't do the same?

He chopped his wood into three different pieces before responding. "I was going to, but—I dunno." He'd been praying about it for weeks. Had three messages from Steph on his phone saying he was welcome to come back.

But every time he went to reply, he froze. And last night had been a harsh reminder of a few realities regarding his competence.

"I don't know what to tell you." Mick put two deep cuts into a particularly thick chunk of wood. "Am I glad I stuck my neck out with Jules? Right now, no. But do I think I'd be better off wondering, *What if?* Also no." He pulled the ax free.

Sam carried the next chunk of wood over and eyed his friend. It was a shame things hadn't worked out between him and Jules. He was a good bloke. "Thanks, man."

Mick didn't respond, just kept chopping.

Poor guy. His sister had done a number on him. Again. But at least he'd taken the risk. He had his answer.

He wouldn't wonder, *What if?*

Sam rubbed a hand over his hair. He needed to think. And he needed to shift the dry cows—those no longer being milked in preparation for calving—to a new paddock.

He nodded a goodbye to Mick and jumped onto the quad bike, thoughts whirring faster than the piece of hay string wrapped around the bike's axle.

He'd prayed about Wildfire every day for the last few weeks but generally along the lines of *Oh God oh God oh God oh God, what am I gonna do?*

Now, drinking in the moisture-laden air, he let himself say the words he'd been resisting for weeks—words more terrifying than *Jules* and *PMS*.

"God, whatever You're guiding me toward, my answer is yes."

"Sam asked you *what?*"

Kimberly winced as Jules's voice reached a pitch only dogs could hear. She climbed inside the next calf pen—a square enclosure made from pig wire—and wrestled the little beasts onto the rubber teats connected to a feeder. Jules flicked on a tap that poured milk from a drum resting on the tractor forks. The calves went nuts over it but couldn't seem to stay on their own teats. One would steal a neighbor's milk, and you'd either get a domino effect or wind up with two stupid calves trying to suck the same teat.

Though she was the girl who'd turned down a date with Sam Payton, so maybe she shouldn't be labeling anyone else as *stupid*.

"He asked me out. I said yes. Then I talked him out of it." Inhaling the sickly sweet smell of the milk, she braced for Jules's screech of "Are you insane?" She'd rather shave her legs with a potato peeler than talk about this, but better that Jules heard it from her than Sam. Her stomach hardened as the pause stretched.

She looked up. No screech. Jules gazed into the distance, an unreadable expression on her face. "I kissed Mick. Like, really kissed him."

Kimberly stared at her friend. Jules wasn't smiling. Even the gold highlights in her braid seemed dull today. "Serious?"

"Then I cried and said I couldn't be with him."

"Ouch." A calf sucked on Kimberly's shirt, and she tugged the fabric from its teeth, rolling the revelation around her mind. Jules had been given a second chance—and said no.

"Yep."

Kimberly muscled another calf toward the feeder and pushed the teat into its mouth. The official end of Jules and Mick—that had to hurt. "I think I need to hear your story first."

It took another two and a half calf pens to swap sob stories. Jules tapped a greedy calf on the head with her hose as Kimberly finished her tale. "So that's it? You're gonna chicken out?"

That stung. Kimberly dropped another calf feeder on the fence and measured her words. "You could say that. Though I prefer to think of it as making a wise choice for the future."

And wise it was. This relationship could never last, and she was already in too deep. She'd admired Sam for years. Now those feelings had morphed into something even more powerful, while Sam simply seemed to be intoxicated by the close quarters they'd been forced into. She couldn't bear to get invested before the illusion fell away.

Jules flicked milk at her. "You and Sam are exactly the same, except he's afraid of messing up Wildfire and you're afraid of him deciding he doesn't want you anymore."

He doesn't want you anymore. Against all logic, tears rushed to her eyes at Jules's words. She tightened her jaw, swallowing the emotion down. What did Jules want from her? Was she holding out for tears and a confession that she was completely unlovable?

The calf stomped on Kimberly's foot, and she shoved it away. Let him go hungry. "I'm not so sure you're in a spot to be giving love advice."

Jules flinched, then directed her gaze to the stream of milk flowing from the hose to the calf feeder. "You're right."

The lack of fight in her tone stabbed a rusty screwdriver into Kimberly's conscience. Ouch.

But she'd also meant it, so she wordlessly climbed out of the calf pen and up into the tractor to shift it, and the milk drum, to the next pen. Jules's words swirled in her mind.

Her friend had said no to Mick. Those two sure looked like they loved each other, but still Jules refused. Yet her friend pushed her to take a step that Jules seemed to be afraid of herself. And the Australian was a much better candidate for love than Kimberly would ever be.

If Jules couldn't make a relationship with as much chemistry as hers and Mick's work, what made Kimberly think she had a snowflake's chance in summer?

 CHAPTER 32

S am took the steps to the house two at a time as he returned from the afternoon milking, his soul lighter than Mum's chocolate mousse.

Amazing what surrender could accomplish.

He toed off his gum boots without having to touch them with his kind-of-clean hands. Kimberly's boots were already lined up at the door. He'd overheard her tell Jules and Mum that she planned to do a late run into town this afternoon for groceries, but perhaps plans had changed.

He stripped off his cotton work shirt as he entered the kitchen, leaving his bluey and KingGee work shorts. The scent of fresh chocolate slice—kind of like coconut-y brownies but less moist—emanated from the stovetop. Where was Mum? She'd be ecstatic to hear that he had some certainty again, even if he still had no idea what his future looked like.

At least he'd stopped resisting whatever God had planned.

His mother's voice emanated from the direction of Jules's room, though slightly muffled.

"—loan?"

Jules's voice: "Kimberly showed me the calculations. If we don't—"

"Kimberly this, Kimberly that. Why are the two of you following this woman like she's the Pied Piper?"

Sam grimaced. They should've kept Mum more in the loop, especially with things progressing so quickly. She'd run this place for decades, and only her failing health had forced her to relinquish control to Jules—and the phrase *kicking and screaming* had almost been literal. She'd never been likely to approve of a plan concocted without her, especially when that plan involved a mortgage. When they were kids Dad had talked her into borrowing to buy the western paddocks, but then the Millennium drought hit, and the debt had almost sunk them.

Frustration laced Jules's tone. "She's an expert—"

"At what? Making Sam miserable? He despised her for three years, finally got sick of her and left, and now she's begging him to come back? I don't think so."

Sam charged toward the hallway and Jules's room. Mum had no idea what she was talking about. He'd been all wrong, and—

Kim.

He froze at the sight of her, standing still with her hand on the bathroom doorknob. The hallway's dim orange light highlighted the crushed expression on her face.

She jolted at his appearance and thrust the door open. "I wasn't eavesdropping. I just came for the bathroom and—" She fled into the tiled sanctuary.

His tongue stuck to the roof of his mouth as he stared at the closed door, shirt still clutched in his hand. What words could even help in this situation?

Well, maybe these ones.

He took three quick steps forward and banged on Jules's bedroom door. The conversation stopped, and the door opened to reveal Mum in her robe and fluffy slippers. Jules, still in her work gear, stood behind her with the expression of someone who'd sucked a lemon. But a smile lit Mum's face. "Hey—"

"What are you doing?"

Her brow creased. "I beg your—"

His internal temperature rose along with his heart rate as Kimberly's expression lingered in his mind's eye. "Kimberly is one of the best people I know, Mum. You've got it all wrong. And she's—"

The bathroom door opened and a blur flew out the door and into the lounge room.

"—right there."

Footsteps and closing doors indicated Kimberly's escape outside.

Mum flushed a little. "Oh."

Jules palmed her face and mumbled something.

Sam clenched his jaw, his latest cavity aching with the tension. "Yes, *oh*. You practically shouted insults about her across the river." He flung his arm out in the direction of the Burnett.

Mum raised her chin. "I thought she was going into town."

"And that makes it okay?" He rubbed his forehead, muscles tense. "She's an amazing person. And she's taught me a lot about myself."

"I didn't intend—"

"It doesn't matter what you intended. You hurt her, you hurt me."

Jules's expression flickered with a smile at his words. But Mum's hands found her hips. "Since when?"

"Since when what?" He licked his lips and tasted dust.

Her raised brows demanded an answer. "Since when is she a

close friend? Six months ago she practically forced you out of the ministry *you* founded. She had you constantly second-guessing yourself. Now you've just gotten settled back home, and she's trying to take you away again."

Kimberly was long gone, but he still checked around for her. "That was my own mistake. She pushes me out of my comfort zone, but that's on me. Wildfire is better for having her in it." He blew out a breath and hung his head. "And this is partly my fault for giving you such a terrible impression of her." Raising his head, he met Mum's eye. "But I misjudged her. All she's done is have more faith in me than I have in myself."

Now that they were out there, the words played on a loop through his mind. *She has more faith in me than I have in myself.* Kimberly was just one of a dozen signs God had given him, all pointing to that little ministry in the US. Only fear held him back, plain and simple.

Mum clasped her hands together, expression somber. "I didn't realize you felt that way."

Sam's hand went to the back of his neck. Should he give Kimberly some time? Try and find her?

Mum touched his arm. "I'll talk to her when she returns."

The image of Kimberly's haunted expression was burned into Sam's brain. He moved toward the window to check if the ute was still there. "At this rate, we'll be lucky if she does return."

Kimberly headed straight for Meg's dog kennel, collected her furry friend, and then almost ran to the feed shed. A twenty-ton truck had delivered a load of cotton seed today, and the soft and spongy pile was the perfect place to cuddle the dog and feel sorry for herself.

She crept inside the shed and a few steps up the pile, sat back into the fluffy gray seeds, and hugged Meg to her chest. The dog licked Kimberly's collarbone, then flopped into her lap to enjoy a pat. The sunset was visible out the open side of the shed, so Kimberly swallowed down her useless emotions in order to enjoy the broad stripes of color across the sky as the insects sang their nightly chorus. No point crying and fogging up her vision.

The dog warmed her body, and she shoved the seeds around to make a comfier cushion for her head. Their fuzzy exteriors stuck to everything and meant she could form a pretty decent lump for a pillow.

Why was she even upset? This was illogical. Sam's mother had just done her a favor. She needed a stronger resolve against this attraction she felt toward him. Besides, this stranger's rejection shouldn't matter. No matter whose mother she was.

And yet Kimberly's fingers itched to dial Mom's number and deliver the I-hate-you monologue that had percolated in her brain for years.

Words whispered through her mind. *"To Him, there was nothing about you that was unexpected or less than delightful."* Sam's words from the night of the rodeo. The truth of the words knocked on the door of her soul, but she could never quite get them to enter.

Footsteps crunched toward the shed, and she pressed down into her hidey-hole. Not that it helped—she was facing the open wall to view the sunset. So when Sam appeared around the corner, in clean clothes and bringing the faint scent of soap with him, she might as well have had a spotlight shining on her.

He paused at the base of the cotton seed pile, his posture tired and face a little lined. "Kim, I can't apologize enough."

She swallowed. *God, keep my voice even.* Her hand waved his comment away. "It's fine."

Thank goodness, her voice came off as cool as a cucumber.

"Nothing about this is fine. Mum was wrong, but I've been even more wrong."

Kimberly shifted Meg from her lap, stood, and attempted to brush the cotton seeds from her shorts, sweatshirt, and hair. Unsuccessful, but she needed to escape this conversation. "You've been fine, Sam." She carefully stepped down the pile toward him, trying to avoid an avalanche of fluffy seeds.

He propped his hands on his hips and contemplated the toe of his boot for a moment. "You want to know why I was so quick to disagree with you all the time?"

She stopped at the bottom and gulped. *Here it comes.* It had been her fault all along—always was. "Because I'm a coldhearted, know-it-all, pain in the behind?" She forced out a laugh with the sentence. *Ha ha, I'm joking, but you don't have to disagree.*

He blinked. "Do you really think that?"

Were those . . . actual tears in his eyes? No. Because that would mean they were for her.

Hot emotion rushed up her sinuses and moistened her tear ducts, but she cleared her throat. Whatever. She turned to go.

He caught her arm and tugged her into a gentle hug, the fresh scent of soap enveloping her.

Hugs were so awkward. She never knew where to put her hands. She spent the whole time panicking she was doing it wrong—did she hold on too many Mississippis? Too few?—and worrying the other person might accidentally see down her shirt.

Sam's warmth seeped through her sweatshirt. His thumb traced some nonsensical pattern on her back, and her skin tingled. It felt . . . like he was trying to talk to her through his touch. *I think you're something more than cold and smart. I care about you. I want you in my life.*

Was that his intention or her wishful thinking?

"Your mum doesn't know what she's missing out on." The words were mumbled into her hair.

Ah. He'd seen past the obvious to why it really hurt. But this was the truth he hadn't yet comprehended. She eased back, not quite brave enough to meet his eyes. "She's my mom, Sam. She knows exactly what she's missing out on." *And when you know me well enough, you'll choose to miss out too.*

Sam cupped her chin and tilted her face up till she met his gaze. Whoa. He was close. And those fierce brown eyes were melting her faster than those rainbow popsicles he loved. Her pulse pounded in her throat.

"So she knows that you bake the best-tasting sugarless food I've ever eaten?" His other hand grasped her arm, squeezing gently to make his point. His proximity gave her a great vantage point to admire the effect of that five o'clock shadow. "Or that you love every animal you see, and they love you back? That you never back down from a challenge if it means you can help someone else—no matter what the cost to yourself? Kimberly, you're one of the most selfless people I've met.

"You could've used your gifts to create a lucrative career, and instead you put up with my attitude for three years and poured all your effort into getting God's love out to those teenagers. You're passionate, creative, and you persevere."

Kimberly stared at him, breathless. He wasn't laughing or anything. Just looking straight into her face with an intensity that seemed to see through to her soul. She closed her eyes. Her face burned where his hand touched it. "That's more nice things in two minutes than I think you've said to me—ever." And she was on overload. One more compliment, and an ugly rush of blubbering would come out.

"I'm an idiot for ever making you think I believed otherwise." The deep timbre of his voice raised goose bumps on her arms. Closing her eyes did nothing to dampen his effect on her. It just heightened her awareness of his warmth, his scent, and—*Oh, that accent*. "The reason I disagreed with you all the time was because I felt threatened."

Her eyes popped open. "Threatened?"

His rueful smile was just enough for his dimple to peek at her. "You're so fearless. You see a mountain and start planning the most cost-effective and time-efficient way to conquer it. Whether you *can* conquer it doesn't seem to even be a question. So when you came to Wildfire and started pushing us . . . me, out of my comfort zone, I was scared senseless."

Now she couldn't drag her eyes from him if she tried. "Why?"

Was it her imagination, or did Sam sway a little closer? "Because life has taught me that when I reach too high, I fall with a big thump. But for you, too high isn't nearly high enough. When you released your expansion plan for Wildfire, I thought for sure you'd exit within a few years and leave me with this giant organization that I'd have no idea how to run. And everything would collapse, I'd lose my donors' money, and I'd disappoint everyone."

She bit her lip. "And if I stayed?"

Sam's brow creased, and she fought the urge to press her

fingers to it and smooth it out. "I never really thought you would. I couldn't understand why someone as talented as you wanted to work with Wildfire in the first place."

Hope flared to life. "But what do you think now? If I did stay? Would you—"

He grimaced.

He still doesn't want to return. She pulled her face away from his hand and stepped back from him.

He caught her fingers. "It's nothing to do with you. Honestly, I'm always waiting for the other shoe to drop. I've got no education. And leading a team of youth pastors is a whole 'nother ball game to preaching."

She let him keep his grasp on her fingers, already hating the increased distance between them. "Well, we're a pair, aren't we? Neither of us thinks we can do what we want to do."

A hint of a smile played around the edges of his mouth. "And what do you want to do?"

She took a deep breath. The guy had just laid it all out in front of her. The least she could do was show a little vulnerability herself. "Date you."

His smile grew. He tugged her closer, slid his hands around her waist. Every inch of her skin came to life.

Don't hyperventilate.

"And what do I want to do?" he asked.

She took a deep breath. "You want to try and to know that God won't be disappointed whether you succeed or fail."

He blinked. "What?"

She talked faster, excitement increasing. Sam could do so much if he didn't let these fears hold him back. "If you're doing something within God's will—something that glorifies Him and that you've prayed about and you have peace over—then He won't be disappointed whether you achieve 'success' or 'failure.'" She made air quotes with her fingers. "What counts to Him is your attitude. The rest is up to Him."

Sam kissed her.

Kimberly froze, hands still in the air from her quote marks.

Sam's hands slid up her back as he pressed another kiss against her mouth.

Her thoughts short-circuited and her eyelids fluttered shut. This. Was. Heaven. Her hands slid up his arms to his shoulders, one finding his jawline.

Sam tightened his hold, pulling her up against him.

Awareness tingled through every one of her molecules. How had she spent three years with this man and not done this every single day? She must've been crazy.

He kissed the corner of her mouth, her cheek, her jaw, and moved to withdraw. But Kimberly caught him with a hand to the back of his head and pulled him back down. So far she'd been too much in shock to do anything other than let Sam kiss her. That had to change. She stepped on tiptoe to wind her arms around his neck and kiss him back.

Sam's fingers dug into her hair. He deepened the kiss for a brief moment. Kimberly's pulse spiked.

Finally, he drew back, chest rising and falling in deep breaths beneath her palm.

Whoa. Her entire body hummed with energy, her lips craved his, and her brain drowned in fog. This was what kissing Sam was like? She needed more. Every day. Forever.

Sam unwound her arms and stepped back, and it almost physically hurt.

"That . . . That . . ." He appeared to have trouble catching his breath or forming words or both. Kimberly's insides twisted.

Please, God, don't let him say it was a mistake.

". . . was something I've been wanting to do for a while." He tugged her closer and pressed a kiss against her cheek. "I'd better go check the cows. See ya 'round, Foster."

Kimberly stood stock-still as he left, gaze frozen on his perfect form. Uh-oh. Her heart had just been stolen.

And she wasn't sure she'd ever get it back.

CHAPTER 33

Kimberly shuffled her feet in her gum boots as she walked back to the house after morning milking, where reality awaited in the form of Mrs. Penny Payton. How exactly was this going to go?

Hey there, Mrs. Payton, I know you hate me, but I've spent the past eighteen hours either kissing your son or thinking about doing it again.

Oh joy.

"Wait up!"

The good kind of shivers raced up her backbone at Sam's call. She paused and looked behind her as he jogged over from the direction of the machinery shed.

Boy, what she wouldn't give to not be filthy right now.

His gaze slid over her form, down to her muck-and-dust-covered boots and up again. The smile lines in his cheeks deepened. "How's it going?"

"Oh, you know. Pretty standard. Had to talk to a colleague about how his mom hates me, so I kept things super professional."

He held up two fingers. "First, I'll deal with Mum. Second—" His grin widened. "I love your definition of *professional*." He came forward half a step, well into her space.

Kimberly's pulse skyrocketed. She'd never been able to flirt to save her life, but maybe the trick was in the right sparring partner. She tipped her head back to keep her eyes on his face as he came closer.

"And I'd like to return to that professional discussion—if you didn't have muck on your nose."

What? She dropped her face and swiped at her nose as heat rushed into her cheeks like firemen to an inferno.

Two fingers grazed her chin and tipped her face back up. Sam's face hovered above hers, smile crinkles around his eyes. "On second thought, I really don't care."

A laugh bubbled up between them as Sam pressed his lips to hers. She caught his cheek, rough beneath her palm, as his hands anchored onto her waist. Her other hand slid around his neck.

She was kissing Samuel Payton.

Out here on the track between the dairy and sheds for anyone to see.

"Stop smiling," Sam mumbled against her lips, his own tugging into a grin. "It makes it really hard to kiss you."

She stood on her tiptoes and kissed him back. "How's that?"

His grin was even more spectacular up close, all warmth and excitement and the intensity of his attention focused on her. "Perfect."

She returned to normal height as he took her hand and turned them toward the house. He intertwined their fingers. "How about we go out to dinner tonight? Check out the finest of what Burradoo has to offer."

Her heart lifted with the joy of a thousand hot-air balloons. "That sounds like something I couldn't miss."

They reached the house—stopping off on the way to admire a semitrailer with the first load of loan-funded hay—and as she lifted her foot for the first step, the door flew open. Mrs. Payton stood there, the Christmas wreath on the door framing her head like a halo. But her hands rested on her hips, and a frown creased her forehead.

Kimberly reflexively pulled her hand back, but Sam held tight. "Mum—"

"Have you seen the weather report?" Her tone was full of concern, not rebuke. Kimberly looked between them, worry climbing up her throat.

Sam shrugged. "No. Why?"

"Cyclone Regina has changed paths. It's headed this way."

"This is a mistake."

Kimberly jerked her gaze up from the phone ringing in her hand, her other palm braced against the torn back of Sam's chair in the tractor cab. Their planned dinner date last night and even church this morning had been swapped for frantic cyclone preparations, including this afternoon's task: storing Jules's new hay.

The tractor hit a bump, and her head smacked the cab roof. Her perch on the wheel arch meant it happened approximately every forty-six seconds. "What's that?"

Sam, one hand on the hydraulics and the other on the steering wheel, directed the tractor like a master puppeteer. He pushed the tractor forks forward until they pierced another half-metric-ton bale of hay from the second truckload of the day. Balancing another bale on top of that one, he lifted them from the back of the flatbed and stacked them inside the shed next to the dairy, which Jules had hastily cleared of machinery.

"If we had time, I'd make a couple of stacks." He ducked his head to see beyond the tractor cab, and Kimberly did the same. "But this storm's coming like a freight train."

Blue-black clouds massed above, and majestic gum trees swayed in violent winds. The tractor wasn't immune—wind gusts rattled the cab and whistled through loose window seals.

The phone kept buzzing, and Sam glanced over his shoulder. "Steph?" The board member was the only person who ever called.

"Yep."

Sam smiled up at her. "Want to tell her I'm coming back?"

Kimberly grinned back at him, but when the call ended she didn't reach to return it. "I'll call her later." Her stomach folded over, half ecstasy, half dread. After Mrs. Payton's storm announcement, the thought of Sam saying no to Wildfire—and to her—had her tied in knots. Her dream dangled before her—them at Wildfire together, as a team. The thing she'd longed for these past three and a half years. Longer, if you counted the lonely eleven-year-old starving for a place to belong. But the cyclone hadn't hit yet. Who knew what was about to go down?

She gripped the back of Sam's chair as the tractor hit another bump. It'd taken three weeks to convince Sam to return, and she only had one left in this country. If he got cold feet, she was done for.

Best be a little more certain before crowing victory to Steph.

She pocketed the phone and jiggled her leg, muscles restless. The nervous energy stemmed not just from her Wildfire concerns—but her fragile hope for a relationship. If Sam changed his mind and decided to stay—even if the reasoning was about his family, not her—the tight knot already in her stomach told her the rejection would hit hard.

Jules's words from days ago echoed through her conscious-ness: *"Your worth isn't determined by what my mother or even Sam thinks of you."*

If only she could convince her churning stomach.

Subject change. Kimberly fiddled with the radio until she hit a station playing Linkin Park. "Why should we do multiple stacks?"

Sam smacked her fingers away but left the station unchanged. "There's less chance of it spontaneously combusting."

Kimberly laughed. He looked at her. She blinked. "Wait—you're serious? There's no such thing as spontaneous combustion."

Sam lifted the next bale. "If the hay has too much moisture when it's baled, it rots inside the bale. That generates heat, and when it's stacked the heat can be enough to make it combust. Dad lost a stack once when I was a kid."

She gulped, visions of a flaming shed in her mind's eye. "Yikes."

"That's why we're putting it in the shed. There's a chance old mate here"—he indicated the farmer inside his truck—"baled in a hurry to beat the rains. We don't want to add extra water to that, so we'll stash it in the shed for the storm. But afterward I'll spread it around in a few stacks and keep a close eye on it."

Kimberly shifted on the wheel arch, an ache emanating from her tailbone and dust in her nostrils. These winds had coated everything in grit. "Just how intense is this cyclone meant to be?" She'd never been in a hurricane back in the States, but surely their location a hundred miles inland would provide some sort of buffer.

"We'll cop the outer edge of it. The wind damage will all be on the coast, but the rain's going to come in fast and hard. The river could flood."

So that's why Jules was moving all the cattle to the west paddocks, farthest from the river. Still, the crop losses she'd sustain if the east paddocks flooded had to be significant.

Numbers whirred in Kimberly's head. What was the maximum loss Jules could take with the added burden of this new loan? She'd already spent a significant chunk of money on new cattle and this hay. As long as her production potential remained high she should be able to dig her way out. But the beginnings of a tension headache niggled at the base of Kimberly's skull.

"Does this happen often?" She ran her research through her mind. She'd covered weather patterns. Cyclones had come up but didn't seem to be a major factor.

"They usually hit farther north. We thought this one would, too, but it changed direction yesterday."

Kimberly rubbed her forehead. "Fabulous timing."

Sam's mouth tightened. "Jules is stressing about it."

Kimberly refocused on him. What stressed one sibling stressed the other. She couldn't have Sam stressed—not already. Iron bands tightened around her chest.

She gripped his shoulder. "She'll be fine."

He grimaced. "Sure hope so." The first raindrops splattered against the window.

CHAPTER 34

The water wouldn't stop, but right now that wasn't Jules's biggest problem.

She knelt by a cardboard box in the corner of the veranda where Meg lay panting. Rain lashed the windows above them, and her knees ached on the worn wooden floor. She'd left Meg alone when her contractions first started, but when they slipped past the hour mark and no pups . . . her decades of farm experience rang alarm bells. That snakebite had increased the risk to Meg and the pups. And dogs birthed much faster than humans—or were meant to.

What a way to spend December 23.

Jules rubbed a hand over her scratchy eyes. For a farmer who'd grown up in drought, the sound of rain on the tin roof at night usually soothed her. But last night she'd just stared at the decaying glow-in-the-dark stickers on her bedroom ceiling.

This could end them.

Footsteps paced the veranda behind her. Her brother's heavy tread. "How long's it been?"

Since floodwaters broke the riverbanks? Fifteen hours. Since Meg went into labor? "Two."

"I'm calling Mick."

Jules shifted from her knees to sit cross-legged, chin in her hand and eyes on Meg. "Okay." The floodwaters, even shallow ones, often proved deadly. There was no way Mick could come himself. But maybe he'd think of an idea she and Sam hadn't tried.

She bit her lip and winced. She'd chewed it so many times, her tender skin was swelling into an ulcer.

Sam paced the veranda behind her, talking to Mick. "—heart feels too fast, and she's just gotten some tremors . . . uh-huh . . . uh-huh." The symptoms could've described either Jules or the dog.

Sam paused and nausea swirled inside Jules. Was it caused by the stress or the fact she hadn't been able to choke anything down since yesterday? She couldn't lose the farm *and* Meg. There was only so much a person could take.

Sam paced back toward her, ear still glued to the phone. "You sure? . . . Well, don't go near the flying fox."

Jules snapped her head up. "Don't tell me he's taking the boat out."

Sam shrugged. "See you soon, mate." He hung up the phone. "He's taking the boat out."

"Idiot!" The word exploded from her lips as she raked a hand through her hair. She'd put him through all this, and still the man would risk his dad's old fishing dingy in floodwaters just to save her dog? "Why do men always think they're smarter than the disaster management people who say not to boat in floodwaters? He should just tell me what to do, and I'll do it." Plus, her eagerness to be in the same room as Mick compared to her eagerness for a gynecological exam. Would he look upset? She'd feel lower than scum. Would he look fine? Even worse.

Sam rested on his haunches beside her. "He thinks it's hypocalcemia. He's coming with calcium and fluids."

Meg stirred at his nearness, panting with another fruitless contraction.

Jules rested her elbows on her knees and buried her face in her hands. A hand rubbed her shoulders. "Kimberly's spent half of today locked in her room going over figures. She swears we're not at the point of no return." His tight tone belied the words intended to comfort, and a sour taste coated her tongue. She knew her brother—inside he was as sick over this as she was. But one of them had to put on a brave face.

Jules dropped her hands but couldn't even fake a smile. "She can't know that."

Sam stayed next to her as they stared at the dog in silence. Water dripped from the ceiling into Mum's biggest pot, and the room steamed with racks of laundry that wouldn't dry. Kind of ruined the festive vibe of the Christmas tinsel lining the room. It'd take them ages to air out the moldy scent.

After an eternity an outboard motor broke the spell. Sam stood. "That'll be Mick."

Jules clambered to her feet. Best make herself scarce. She took a step away—and Meg whimpered. Jules squeezed her eyes shut. The whimper was probably in response to a contraction rather than Jules leaving. But she couldn't leave Meg alone. "Okay, I'll stay."

Sam opened the door, and a bundle of dripping oilskin coat walked through. Mick flicked back his hood. Time slowed.

Sunken eyes. Three days' stubble. No hint of a smile.

A stake pierced her heart. What had she done to him?

Mick and Sam exchanged quiet words, then Mick approached. His resigned gaze seared her soul for an unending moment.

Her tongue moved of its own accord. "I can't believe you came out in this." A gust of wind illustrated her point.

"Of course I came, Jules." Each quiet word stung like a whip. How could she have thought he wouldn't come through—either for her or for Meg? This was the man who'd driven her to the Gold Coast just to cheer her up. The man who'd dragged her broken body to safety in the middle of the night.

The man who loved her.

He fixed his attention on Meg. Jules slunk away, angling to position Sam as a buffer between her and Mick as the vet knelt by the dog and mumbled soothing sounds. Her brother slung an arm around her shoulders, the calluses on his hands rough and warm against her flannelette shirt. They stood like that for twenty agonizing minutes as Mick administered an IV line and then helped Meg deliver. Finally, he gave a whoop. "We have a puppy!"

Sam started forward, but Jules remained still. He crouched a few feet behind Mick, not crowding Meg, and peered into the box. "That is a-*dor*-able."

Mick leaned into the box. "And another."

Jules crept forward till she could lean a hand on Sam's shoulder and squint into the dark box. Two pups squirmed next to one another. One black and tan, one white, both with the finest layer of curly fur. Meg and Killer's pups. Hers and Mick's.

She bit down on that ulcer to keep the tears at bay.

They stayed in their huddle as Meg took care of business. Finally, Mick eased back from the whelping box and stood, movements slow after an hour on the floor. "A big litter. Seven pups."

Seven? Enough for each of the homes at the Gold Coast, plus her, plus Mick. Though—with all that had gone down between them, would he want it? Never mind. She'd keep them both. The coming days would be long and lonely, and the more puppies that filled them, the better.

Mick stretched his back, gaze still on the dogs as he spoke. "Watch her carefully over the next few days. She's not out of the woods yet. And watch the pups too—they might need a bit of extra bottle feeding. Call me if something feels off, though I'll be gone by Sunday." He shook Sam's hand, clapping him on the back like it was the last time they'd see each other for a while.

Or ever.

Centuries passed in the time it took Mick to aim his piercing blue eyes at her. Jaw set, stubble sexier than ever, eyes lined as though he were older than his thirty-one years. He offered his hand. "Goodbye, Jules." The words rang with finality.

The clock ticked. Once, twice, three times. Her mind fled, her body refused to respond. Goodbye? No. Acceptable options: *See you later. Catch ya 'round. Till next time.* But never *Goodbye.*

The corner of Mick's eye twitched. Could he see past her eyes and deep into her soul? Could he see her mountains of resolve collapsing into a raging ocean of despair?

Or did he only see the woman who'd broken his heart—again?

She spun and fled the room. She could face angry cows, mounting debt, and floods.

But she could not say goodbye to Mick Carrigan.

Kimberly leapt to the side of the dining nook and collided with the table as Jules flew past her, down the hall and—*bang*—to her room. An ache pounded through her left hip. Still, worth avoiding being trampled by Jules. Kimberly swung her gaze to the open internal door between the kitchen/dining room and veranda. Mick stood, frozen, staring at the place Jules had been.

His anguished expression scraped across her heart like nails on a chalkboard. *Make it stop.*

Sam slid a hand onto his friend's shoulder. Kimberly looked away. She'd seen flashes of Mick's expression before—a duller, veiled version, but increasingly frequent—on Sam. She walked to the fridge and opened it, viewing the collection of Christmas pavlovas and pudding just for a distraction. The cold blast increased her chill.

Unlike her, Sam had never been good at hiding his emotions. He didn't just worry for his sister, for the farm. No, that particular expression only crossed his face when he was looking at her.

She shut the fridge, collected her laptop, and headed for her room. Her back ached. She'd hovered in the dining nook the past two hours, pretending to work on her laptop but actually listening to Meg's progress. Jules needed her space—the poor woman suffered on so many levels today—but Kimberly couldn't bear to go farther than the kitchen counter away from that beautiful dog.

Now Meg and her pups were okay, and a greater problem loomed: what to do when Sam both reneged on his promise to Wildfire . . . and also broke up with her. Her stomach twisted. No matter that she'd run the figures over and over, nor that she'd reassured both Sam and Jules a thousand times. The truth was that her reassurances were based on the rain stopping soon. And just as the Paytons dreaded Mother Nature's wrath, she sensed Sam's dilemma and feared his eventual decision. If Jules's future looked at all uncertain—especially after taking out this loan—there was no way he'd abandon his sister.

The end, at least for her, was coming. She knew it.

"Can we talk?"

Kimberly jolted, yanked her gaze up. Sam's mother stood at the entrance to her bedroom and jerked her head, motioning Kimberly in.

Shouldn't the woman be comforting her daughter? "Jules—"

"Needs her space. I'm here to discuss my other child."

Kimberly tensed.

"Stop looking at me like I'm the Grim Reaper. You might be surprised."

Kimberly edged into the room, giving Mrs. Payton the same kind of berth she'd award a tiger. Sam's mom had given her a stilted apology for her words the other day, but that didn't mean she wouldn't strike again.

"I wanted to thank you."

Kimberly blinked and sharpened her focus on the other woman's lined face. "Really?"

Mrs. Payton sat on the edge of her bed, which was covered in a rose quilt far frillier than Kimberly would have ever imagined. "You look surprised." She waved Kimberly toward a worn gray armchair resting in the corner. Kimberly perched on the edge of it.

What good way was there to respond to that? "Um—"

A grin broke over Mrs. Payton's craggy features. "My bark is worse than my bite."

Kimberly flashed a timid smile in return and wriggled a little deeper into the armchair. What was this woman torturing her for?

The smile drained from Mrs. Payton's face, replaced by a thoughtful demeanor. "I'll be honest. I dread Sam leaving. Any mother would."

Kimberly tensed. *Here we go.*

"But Sam said something interesting about you the other day." Mrs. Payton leaned forward, arm braced against her knee, and Kimberly's ears perked up. "He said you have more faith in him than he's ever had in himself. And I've watched him second-guess himself for years. But now that's changing. He agrees with getting this loan. He's planning to return to Wildfire and is even talking about Bible college." Her lips tipped upward. "No matter what he's preached, somehow he's spent years falling for the lie that he's the one person in the universe doomed to fail. That's no longer the case." She nodded toward Kimberly. "And I think you played a role in that."

Kimberly's brow crinkled, and she swallowed. Half her mind blasted victory trumpets while the other half gave an Eeyore groan. "But—um—" She bit off her question. Would Mrs. Payton take this badly?

The older woman raised an eyebrow.

Kimberly blurted her fear. "If this gets any worse, don't you think he'll refuse Wildfire?"

Mrs. Payton's expression darkened. "Sam keeps his word."

Bitterness burned the back of Kimberly's throat. "He's also loyal to his family." What did that feel like, to have someone so invested in you they'd alter the course of their life for your sake?

Mrs. Payton conceded her point with a nod.

Kimberly leaned forward. "And a piece of him might hope he's not doomed to failure, but which do you think will win—the new or the old?" The question hung in the air.

Mrs. Payton heaved a sigh, and Kimberly's hopes sank faster than a popped balloon. "Honestly? I don't know."

Jules sat on her first motorbike—her old DS 80—and engaged in a staring contest with the pet rock on Dad's soggy grave as the sun dipped below the tree line.

The rain had stopped yesterday, two hours after Mick left her house for the last time. The floodwaters had retreated overnight. The sun had broken through the clouds this morning—Christmas Eve.

And yet her soul mourned.

A kookaburra made its trademark call from a nearby tree. To an untrained ear—i.e., Kimberly—it sounded like a madman laughing. Laughing at the silly girl with her leg in a moon boot who couldn't catch a break in her farming or her romantic life.

God, I can't do this anymore.

The stress of the last three days had nearly killed her. Yet as agonizing as it had been watching brown floodwaters swallow the paddocks she'd so painstakingly cultivated, worse still was Mick's absence. By instinct, she'd reached for her phone so many times to contact him. When a leak destroyed a painting of Dad's. When she first held her pups. When the floodwaters peaked.

But there'd be no Irish jig to celebrate the end of the flood. Just the dust of his ute leaving in a few short days. And a big, empty farm for her to call home.

She slapped at a mosquito on her arm. This was no time for ungratefulness or heartbreak. The rains were gone—before the damage bill could hit Kimberly's point of no return. Instead of being swept downstream, her cows were safely munching in the west paddocks. The long-range weather forecast looked ideal for autumn planting. The hay would dry out. Production would lift. Her future here would be secure, and long.

And lonely.

"Jules?"

She jolted and twisted at the voice. Mum, squidging her way across the paddock. Jules used the time it took Mum to make her way over to talk some sense into herself. How could she ever begin to disentangle herself from this property? Every waking minute was consumed with it. She read farming magazines for entertainment, dreamed of new tractors at night, and at least 50 percent of her conversations related to rainfall.

And then there was her heritage. How could she remember the twinkle in Dad's eye if she couldn't see the mural he'd painted on the chicken coop just for her? Where would she keep Grandpa's tractor, the one he'd used to teach her mechanics? How would she teach her own children Mum's whip-cracking tricks or how to muster or milk or plow?

Who would she be if not Julia Payton of Yarra Plains, fourth generation on this land?

Finally, Mum reached her. "Hey." She kissed the tip of her finger and pressed it against the pet rock, then perched on a stump beside it. "So you've had *internal crisis* stamped on your forehead for a while now."

Despite her turmoil, Jules snorted. "You picked up on that?"

Mum shrugged, face nonchalant. "Little bit." A grin broke through.

Jules couldn't help but laugh at the insanity of it all. "This week has been ridiculous." Ridiculously awful.

"So talk to your mummy. Have you reached a decision?"

"On what?"

"You tell me."

Jules twisted her fingers together. "Mick wants us to be together. Find a place to compromise on." Her voice wavered on the last word.

"And what do you want?"

Jules opened her mouth, closed it. What did she want? For so long, she'd been certain.

Now not so much.

She cleared her throat. "To stay here, of course. That's why I got the loan. It's what all this is about. This farm is who I am."

"That's not true."

She jerked her head up.

"You're far more than that. I'd hate to see you limit yourself because you have a picture in your head for the future that you can't change."

"You think I should choose Mick?"

"No."

"No?"

Mum reached forward and took Jules's hand in both of hers. "This isn't about Mick. This is about you being open to something new, to God's leading—wherever that may be. Even if it's uncertain. If that's to Mick, great. If it's here, fabulous. But I think the reason you're so exhausted is you're fighting hard to hold on to something that you're not meant to control."

A tear spilled over, then another. "It's so hard to survive out here. Every year brings another challenge, usually another disaster. I *have* to hold on to that picture in my head just to make it."

"And if you let go, what would happen?"

Within a moment she was back on that paddleboard, Mick's arms around her. *Whatever happens, God won't desert you. You aren't alone.*

Mum gave a sympathetic smile. "It hurts to let go. Believe me, sweetie. I've buried two husbands. But sometimes it hurts more to hold on."

"It's not like I don't love it out here." Nothing was more exhilarating than that feeling of battling nature and winning. Clawing a living from this land with little but determination and hard work. "And I don't give up."

Mum rubbed her bad shoulder. "When my shoulder gave out the second time, I was determined to not give up. I was born in that house. Married on this farm, twice. This is where we raised you two. Dad's buried here. A little nerve damage in my arm couldn't drag me away, even if I had to hand the day-to-day running of the farm to you. And you know what God gave me?"

"What?"

"A stubborn daughter."

Jules barked out a laugh.

"Remember how we fought all of a sudden? We got along better when you were seventeen than when you were twenty-seven. I couldn't give up control, and you couldn't stand taking orders anymore. It was Sam who told me to either give you some space or risk permanent damage to our relationship. So I spent some time with Suze."

Jules shifted on the bike. Yes, things had gotten better when Mum took an extended holiday with her sister at the coast, but where was this going?

"I thought I'd hate being at the Sunshine Coast, but this whole new world opened up to me. The people are different, sure, but they're nice. I've seen more growth in the church there in the last two years than I saw in fifty years of attendance here. I have coffee with friends, and we talk about something other than the rain and milk prices. I volunteer at the teen girls' ministry at the local high school."

Jules injected all the levity she could manage into her voice. "You're saying I should retire with you to the Sunshine Coast?"

"I'm saying that sometimes there's more to the picture than we can see on our own. Sometimes we just need to trust and follow."

"Easier said than done."

"Sweetheart, when God closes a door, He closes it. Best not to hold on too long and get your fingers jammed in the process." She stood, brushed the dirt from her trackie dacks. "I'll leave you now to ponder my wisdom."

Jules smirked.

Mum leaned over and dropped a kiss on the top of her head. "Love you, kiddo."

Her footsteps slushed off into the distance.

Jules resumed staring at the pet rock. It was like Mum had put a spotlight on every thought she'd been pushing away for the past few months. Maybe . . . maybe she *could* survive not living here full-time. If she worked at Cockatoo Creek Outdoor Camps, she'd be able to drive up and check the property on the weekends and leave it with a capable manager during the week. And then . . . maybe there was a shot at a future with Mick. If he'd still have her. Goodness knows she'd tried the limits of what any man could take.

She scrubbed a palm across her face. Maybe one day she wouldn't be Julia Payton of Yarra Plains.

Maybe now it was time for her to be Julia the Brave.

She whispered a sentence she never thought she'd say. "God . . . the farm's Yours. Just tell me what to do." She released a deep breath, one it felt like she'd been holding for years. It'd take a long time for her to recalibrate to a new picture of the future—or no picture at all. And who knew if that future included Mick. But she was too exhausted to fight this anymore.

Time to let go.

By the time she got home, everyone else had retired to their rooms and Mum had already stashed presents under the tree. Jules hobbled past Kimberly's room with a purposefully heavy step. Kim probably wasn't asleep yet. She'd want to know about this new development, for sure.

But no one came out to talk.

Jules fell into bed and sank into the deepest sleep she'd had in months. When she woke, it was still dark. What had pulled her from unconsciousness? The childish thrill of Christmas?

She inhaled again. Nope. Smoke.

And a lot of it.

CHAPTER 35

Darkness, warmth, the quiet whir of the ceiling fan. Sam kicked off his tangled bed sheet, barely conscious, and relaxed back onto his pillow. Santa wouldn't come if he stayed awake—or so Mum had said last night, as she'd done for the last thirty Christmases. His thoughts fuzzed, then drifted away as he slid back into oblivion.

Click. Light. Sam's drowsy senses flooded with brightness.

"Sam, the haystack's on fire." Jules's strained voice sounded from the direction of his bedroom doorway.

He launched out of bed before he got his eyes open. Upright, he blinked at where his sister had been, but she'd already fled. He sniffed the air. Smoke.

God, no. Ice ran through his veins.

Clothes? He already wore a bluey and SpongeBob SquarePants boxers. Good enough.

Jules's shuffling step sounded from the kitchen. He ran past her, the Christmas tree stacked with presents, and five fat Christmas stockings. On the veranda, he yanked on his gum boots without socks.

Another light flicked on. Jules's voice emanated from Mum's room. "Mum, fire!" Her head popped out around the kitchen

301

doorjamb. "I called the firies, and the Carrigans are on their way with their water cart. Mick's ringing the neighbors." Her words were controlled, the lines on her face deep.

Sam grabbed Dad's oilskin from its hook. Better the embers landed on the leather than his skin.

Kimberly stumbled out of the hallway, hair mussed and eyes wide. "What's going on?"

On second thought, he'd be fine in the tractor cab. He tossed the oilskin to Kim. "Anyone goes near the fire, they put this on."

Mum rushed into the kitchen. "Sam, don't you—"

He sprinted down the steps before she could finish.

Cane toads jumped away from under his boots—sometimes not fast enough—as he made for the machinery shed farthest from the dairy. Thank goodness he'd parked the tractor there last night instead of beside the haystack.

His view of the hayshed was blocked by the machinery shed in front of him, but there was no mistaking the orange glow in the air, nor the sickening crackle of their last chance burning up.

The heat hit him, even through the tractor cab, as he rumbled around the corner of the shed.

"No—"

His voice failed. Flames danced across the entire haystack, the corrugated iron structure glowing orange. The roof directly over the stack had already buckled. The four-wheeler parked next to the stack had to be a write-off. And Meg. Sam's foot slipped from the accelerator. Mum was no fan of farm dogs inside, and Meg had been well enough to shift the whelping box to the shed last night.

To this shed.

Sam screwed his face up, emotion pounding him like a pro

boxer. He could cry. He just had to keep his eyes open at the same time.

He mashed the tractor's controls forward and plunged the forks into the second-from-the-top bale. Shouted a curse at the searing heat. Yanked the tractor backward and dumped the bales onto the ground. Repeat. Barely audible over the thunderous clamor of the fire, he could just make out the sound of another tractor's engine. Mum towing the water cart with the old Massey Ferguson, most likely.

Two more bales.

Smoke poured into the cab, filling his mouth and nose. Sam stripped off his bluey and wrapped it around his face, holding his breath to try and not cough—his hands jerked on the hydraulic controls when his chest spasmed. He powered forward to the side of the haystack closest to the dairy. The dairy plant was too close to the fire. If they lost the suction pump, the pipework, their ability to milk . . .

Two more bales. The heat intensified. The glass windscreen gave an alarming crack.

He shoved the tractor forward again and yanked out another two. But this time the top bale dislodged . . . and slid backward.

Sam froze. The bale stopped as his heart rate tripled. If that bale tipped, half a ton of flames would smash into the cab. He'd be simultaneously crushed and burned.

With the lightest of touches, he eased the controls forward until the bales touched the ground. He heaved a deep breath and pushed the burning hay out of the way.

Way too close.

On his left, a stream of water hit the dairy. Embers drifted into the air. *God, please let Jules and Kimberly be hosing down the house.* Hundred-year-old timber houses burned faster than a forgotten sausage on the barbecue. He glanced back toward home but couldn't make anything out.

Movement in his peripheral vision caught his attention. Mick. With an extra water cart. Steam billowed as Mick and Mum attacked the burning bales. Mum hobbled forward, hose in hand.

Sam did a double take. No, that was Jules. Mum must be with Kim at the house.

They worked in tandem—the tractor unstacking, scattering, and the hoses trying to douse the flames. Neighbors swarmed with their own water carts. The Rural Fire Service trucks soon followed. Half the volunteer brigade's members were neighbors anyway.

Butch's ute flew up the driveway at an unholy pace only twenty-five minutes after Jules had roused Sam. Yikes. Butch had been staying in town last night. He must've set a new land-speed record to get here so fast.

Glimpses of Mum, Kim, and Butch came periodically—they must've been taking turns manning the house. Jules slipped in the mud. Mick dragged her back to her feet. What state must her moon boot be in with all this soot and water?

When there was nothing left to unstack, push, or roll over in the tractor, Sam backed the vehicle into another shed opposite the burned one. The sky shifted from midnight blue in the west to lighter streaks in the east. But all the increasing light did was show the dairy's scorched side. He sagged back into his seat and unwound the blue singlet from his face. This was it. The farm was done for. Maybe they could've handled a flood or a fire, but not both.

He waited for a wave of rage or despair. Nothing but a numb emptiness. What a merry Christmas morning.

He pulled the bluey over his head and pushed open the tractor door, his arm weighing ten times more than usual.

Kimberly walked over as he descended the steps. Her hair was caught into a messy bun, her jeans splattered in mud, and a cluster of tiny burn marks dotted her LA Dodgers T-shirt. Was her gray pallor from a dusting of soot and ash, her lack of sleep, or their current predicament?

He scanned her locked-down expression. Best guess, all three.

Leaning against the tractor tire, he tried to suck in a deep breath without triggering a cough. Unsuccessful.

Kimberly crossed her arms against her chest while he tried to regain his breath.

After a minute, he swiped his watering eyes and cleared his throat. Plucked at a trio of T-shirt burns where her collarbone met her shoulder and fussed at the red marks underneath. "What happened to the oilskin?" His voice came out gravelly. Must be from the smoke.

"Jules was closest to the fire."

"She has her own."

"Your Dad's was bigger, protected more of her legs. I gave Jules's oilskin to Butch. I was on house duty for most of it, just staying out of everyone's way." She jolted. "Oh! Meg's okay. Jules was worried you'd be upset. Meg got the puppies out before the fire took hold. They're in the garage."

Sam rubbed a hand over his face. *Thank You, God.*

He eased back against the tire, a chill sweeping his skin. He still only wore the blue singlet and SpongeBob boxers, and

Kimberly's grim expression twisted his insides. Meg might be okay, but . . . "How's the house?"

"We put out some spot fires in the yard. Soaked the roof, so it should be okay. A lot of embers came over. We lost the chicken coop, though. No one was watching that."

Smoke coated his tongue as his gaze drifted past Kimberly toward the smoldering wreck of the chicken coop that had sat between the sheds and the house. Gone? One of Dad's best paintings had been on the back of that structure—a silhouetted image of the four of them working in the yards at sunset. He'd painted it at Jules's request.

Sam moved toward the coop on autopilot. The tin roof, a wall, and half the mural had collapsed in; the remaining structure sat blackened and crumbling. One untouched panel of painted wood remained on the easternmost edge.

Sam halted before he got too close. The chickens. The white silkies dyed pink, blue, and yellow.

Kimberly stopped beside him.

"The chooks?"

"I'm sorry."

He kicked a rock and swallowed down the lump in his throat. *Do not cry about chickens.* But his throat ached, and he had to clear it before he could speak. "Any other animals hurt?" A memory flashed through his brain. He tensed. "Jules? I saw her slip. Any people hurt?"

Kimberly pointed to a concrete water trough on the fence line. Jules and Mick sat shoulder to shoulder against it, faces black. "Mick was with her all night. I think her leg's as okay as it can be with her on it so much."

He studied his sister for a moment. Face set but no tears.

Was she in denial, or was there hope that this wouldn't sink them?

"How bad is it?"

"I haven't really had time to—"

He coughed again. The world spun around him. He gripped Kimberly's shoulder, both for support and to make his point. "I know you've been guestimating in your head. Does this push us past the point of no return?"

He'd stacked the hay. He'd even said aloud it should be in multiple piles. The hay wouldn't have been there if not for the loan he recommended. *Say no. Please, please, please say no.*

Kimberly gave the smallest of nods. "It's not necessarily fore-closure. Insurance will likely take too long to hold off the bank, but if you can sell fast enough . . ."

She kept speaking, but Sam's brain refused to take in any more information. His gaze drifted from her to the land around them, his mind's eye traveling to every item he treasured. The dairy whiteboard, ringed with family photos. Granddad's trac-tor. Meg's kennel. The cows. The flying fox. The house.

Dad's grave.

Once again, he'd failed. And it had cost his mother and sister everything.

He kicked another rock. It hit the wall of the chook shed, and the rest of the structure collapsed in. Just like their lives.

The strength left his muscles and he sagged downward till he sat, cross-legged in the dust. The brightening sunrise lit the wreckage around him, and he blocked it out with hands over his eyes. Grit scraped where his palms met his cheeks.

Then tears seeped through and the grit turned to mud.

CHAPTER 36

Sam fought the urge to punch this real estate agent, smash the man's camera, and run off laughing like a maniac. He ran a hand through his hair, fingers quivering, as the man snapped photos of the northern paddocks. An idyllic scene stretched before them under the morning sun—green grass, a gentle hill, a curving river. Three kangaroos bounced along the fence line, over it, and down to the water. This, the highest point of the farm, had never flooded, and the fences remained strong and clean—unlike the tangled mess of wire and tree branches in the eastern paddocks.

Usually comforting, this beauty twisted the knife now living in his chest.

A drip of sweat snaked down his back, dampening his cotton work shirt. Only three days since the fire, and Mum had already listed the property on the market. B-double trucks would cart Jules's cattle to the sales on Thursday. They'd hold a clearing sale as soon as they could properly mop up the fire damage.

And then they'd leave 120 years of family heritage behind.

The man clicked the shutter one final time. "All done."

Sam swiped a fly away as he slid into the driver's seat of the ute. "Let's get you back to your car."

The agent tugged a candy snake from his pocket as they rumbled down the track, his movements wafting strong cologne in Sam's direction. "Lolly?"

Sam shook his head. It wasn't the man's fault that the warroom sessions with Jules, Mum, and Kim had resulted in no better option. Not his fault that the insurance money would come through far too late to save them from foreclosure—though at least it should secure Mum's retirement. If anything, this man was helping them; if they could sell fast enough, they could pay out both mortgages and avoid the stain of bankruptcy on Mum's and Jules's credit records.

But his presence gave Sam someone to hate other than himself. So he tightened his hand on the steering wheel till his knuckles whitened and kept his silence.

He dropped the man off at his shiny Toyota Prado. As the vehicle pulled away, movement caught Sam's eye. Jules, now limping crutch-free but still in her moon boot, heading down the track with a shovel over her shoulder. He rolled forward till he pulled level with her, dust filtering through the open window into the cab. "Watcha doin'?" He tried to mask the tension inside with a breezy tone.

"A job." She kept walking, didn't look at him.

"Want a lift?"

She stopped walking and rested the shovel on the ground, keeping her eyes on it. "I'm going to get Dad."

Loss punched him in the throat again. Dad. His cremated remains buried out with their pet graveyard, near that stand of gum trees frequented by koalas. Dad had never gotten sick of koala-spotting, though over the years they'd grown increasingly hard to find.

Sam cleared his throat. "Hop in."

Jules threw the shovel in the ute's tray and climbed inside. Silence reigned for a long minute as they bumped along the track, now rutted from floodwaters.

His sister stared out the window, looking as empty as he felt. "You talked to Kim?"

"Not since breakfast."

Jules said nothing further. Thank goodness. The atmosphere in his stomach made *The Perfect Storm* look like a pleasant day's sailing—due to something apart from his grief. Kimberly. And Wildfire. Her impending departure this afternoon. And what on earth he would do.

He'd made that deal with Kimberly back in November—in return for her efforts, he'd spend six weeks there recruiting and training his replacement. Then he'd gone and promised a permanent return.

But how could he abandon his mother and sister at a time like this? Much less run the Wildfire expansion after this disaster?

Kimberly's wisdom that night on the chook-shed roof was still something he agreed with—in theory. *"Carrying guilt around only holds you back from the life God intended."*

But in practice, every fiber of his being screamed at him to stay in Australia, to make it up to Mum and Jules the best he could and never, ever attempt anything like this. Ever again.

They arrived at the graveyard, piled out of the ute, and Jules snatched up the shovel before he could reach for it. The stubborn expression on her face dared him to challenge her. He took a step back. She'd planned to do this alone. He'd give her space.

He reached into the ute and grabbed his drink bottle. The muscles in his throat ached as he swallowed a mouthful of water.

They were kilometers from the site of the fire, but he could swear he still smelled the smoke.

Jules thrust the shovel—Dad's old favorite—into the dirt. It barely got a quarter inch into the ground. Sam recapped the bottle and headed over to her, clearing his throat. "Jules—"

"I can do it." The words came out tight.

Sam shifted his weight, and his phone buzzed in his pocket. A distraction. Awesome. They must be in a rare patch of reception.

He pulled it out and noted the caller. Kimberly. His stomach rolled again. Today was her last day.

Where r u?

His eyes slid shut. He put the phone back in his pocket, shoulders slumping. Both options—disappointing Kim or his family—turned his stomach more than a rotten prawn on Boxing Day.

He needed to talk to Kimberly. He just had no idea what he could say.

Jules stabbed at the ground again. Sniffled. The sound ripped apart the shards of calm he'd been clinging to. He threw the drink bottle to the ground, the steam kettle in his brain whistling. "Julia." He stepped over and grabbed the handle. "Don't be stubborn."

Any hint of tears disappeared. She glared at him. "Don't be a *jerk*." She yanked the shovel back with the last word.

He glared back. Clenched his jaw. Kept his grip on the shovel. *What are we doing?*

Just like that, the energy drained from his muscles. He let the shovel go, hesitated a moment, then pulled his sister into a hug. She stayed stiff at first, as she always did. Then rested her head on his shoulder. Squeezed his middle. Pushed back and handed him the shovel.

He took it. "I know you could do it if it weren't for your leg." He drove the shovel into the ground. After about five scoops, Jules knelt by the hole and pushed against his leg. He stepped back. She pawed through the dirt and pulled a dusty black box from the ground.

Sam stared at it. Hard to comprehend that the remains of his six-foot-four father were in that little container. And that they were removing it from the land that he'd loved.

A sour taste spread through his mouth.

He offered Jules a hand and pulled her to her feet. She clutched the box to her chest as they walked back to the ute. He poked his phone into the cupholder as the ute's engine turned over. The phone buzzed again. Jules glanced at the screen. "You avoiding her?"

"No."

"Sure looks like it."

"Shut up."

That enlightened exchange got them to the paddock gate. The silence stretched as they rumbled along one track, paddock posts and then telephone poles skimming by.

Jules sniffed.

Sam slid his gaze in her direction. *God, no.* She couldn't cry. She never cried.

Her face crumpled like a used tissue, and she leaned her forehead against the black box.

A heavy weight pressed against his chest. This was wrong. This never should have happened. This place was home. *How can this be happening?*

The vehicle rattled as he pushed the accelerator down harder and they sped along the rough track. Listening to Jules's shuddering breaths was about as fun as a tattoo to the eyeball. And if his stomach rolled one more time, he was going to throw up.

He skidded to a halt next to the house, exited the ute like it was on fire, and made for his boxing bag. Head down, feet moving fast, vision tunneled onto the dirt in front of him. Everything else faded away—until petite gum boots appeared in his field of vision. He jerked to a stop. "Kim."

She wore Jules's Bintang Beer singlet—a souvenir from Bali—with red denim shorts. That combination, along with her perky ponytail and Hogan's Dairy Supplies baseball cap, would've been a lot more adorable if he didn't feel like a dog for avoiding her the past couple days.

"Hey." Her expression showed concern.

He did his best to wipe any emotion from his face.

"I need to talk to you."

If the pressure behind his eyes built any more, he'd explode. "Is there another ti—"

"I'm leaving this afternoon, Sam. There's no more time."

No kidding. He put his hands on his hips and fought down his roiling emotions.

Her jasmine scent teased him, and she bit her lip, uncertainty written across her face. "I know this timing's horrible. But it's the first thing Steph's going to ask me when I get home."

Home. A place he'd soon be unable to return to ever again.

She rubbed a hand against her other arm. He stared somewhere around the vicinity of her belly button and braced for the words she obviously didn't want to say: *Are you coming or not?*

"You're free from your commitment. If you want to be."

Sam jerked his gaze up to her face.

Her eyes held a sheen, but she blinked and it disappeared. "I know you're worried about your family, and I didn't hold up my end of the deal. Don't feel bad if you need to stay home. But if you want to come . . . you know we'd love to have you."

And beneath her words about Wildfire, the unspoken reality: his decision whether to stay or go would either affirm or end their relationship.

His muscles tightened till it seemed they might snap. "You're still planning to roll out your expansion plan?"

She hesitated, then nodded. He winced at the hesitation. He'd told her a thousand times this situation wasn't her fault, and it wasn't. The fire had been completely unforeseen. Yes, their trajectory had been a downward spiral. But Kimberly had still given them their best shot.

Still . . . "I can't."

She deflated. "You know that—"

"I don't mean that I won't, Kim. I said I *can't*." He ran a hand through his hair. "You know where I just was? Helping Jules dig up Dad." His voice cracked on the last word.

Kimberly seemed to shrink into herself.

He mentally slapped his forehead. *Jerk.* "I'm not saying I blame you. I don't." He sucked in a breath. "I'm saying the thought of standing in front of Jack, of Miriam"—the faces of Wildfire's long-time donors illuminated his mind's eye—"and asking them to trust me with their money . . . Today is seared into my brain. Maybe it's irrational. Maybe I'm not even making sense. But I—"

She placed a hand on his arm. His skin twitched at her touch. "Stop. I get it." Her hand fell away.

Her tone said everything his words hadn't. It wasn't just Wildfire. This was the end of them.

"Steph—"

"I can take care of Steph." Her voice quivered. And the last intact fragment of his heart shattered. Repaying his debt to his family most likely meant crushing Kimberly's dream—meant the end of Wildfire.

He'd told Kimberly weeks ago that he'd never expected the ministry to last, that if it ended, it ended. He'd lied. The thought of those doors closing hurt almost as much as the shovel piercing the dirt around Dad's resting place.

He forced himself to meet her gaze. Her eyes were dry. It was impossible to pinpoint how he knew just how upset she was. Microexpressions? The tension she radiated? Whatever it was, years of knowing this woman told him one thing: intentional or not, he'd just hurt her. A lot. She was just trying to hide it.

And there was nothing he could do.

"Bye, Sam." She walked away and didn't look back.

CHAPTER 37

Jules tossed down a spanner and cupped her hands to shout out to the woman dragging her feet toward the dairy. "Kimba! Over here." Seated on an upturned bucket, she gripped the workbench of her machinery shed and dragged herself upright on her good foot. Crying over Dad all morning had drained every ounce of energy from her cells. But while the grief of losing the farm would take a long time to ease, a foreign sensation had crept through her heart even as she sobbed to the seven puppies licking her fingers.

Peace. And relief. She didn't have to hold on any longer.

There was just one more goodbye that had her nails eaten back to stubs.

The two-wheeled motorbike in front of her gleamed. Mick's old YZ, ready for his parents' clearing sale. Luckily it'd been safely parked next to the house when the fire happened, and even with everything going on, she'd still managed to get it finished in time.

He'd be heading back to the Gold Coast tomorrow. Her chest ached at the thought.

Kimberly walked into the shed at a shuffle, even her sagging ponytail looking glum. Her friend's boundless energy seemed to have burned off on the night of the fire. Her brother's fault, or did it stem purely from them having to sell the farm? Either way, Jules needed to set the record straight.

"Can you drive me out to Mick's?" Jules nodded toward the ute, stomach twisting. But this goodbye was something she had to do.

Kimberly shrug-nodded and helped her heft the motorbike into the tray before they headed off. The radio, tuned to Triple J, blared new Aussie tunes. Kimberly didn't even tap a finger when the station played that Brisbane alt-rock band she'd gushed about last week. Though, truth be told, Jules wasn't tapping any fingers herself. The motorbike felt like a lame peace offering at best, considering what she'd put Mick through. And what words could possibly accompany it?

She rolled down her window to let the stuffy air escape, then twisted the volume knob to quiet the music. She wasn't the only one with problems. "This isn't your fault, you know."

Kimberly shrugged. "Thanks."

She didn't look any better. Jules rubbed paw paw ointment on her lips, chapped from the fire's heat. "Did my brother say different?"

"No."

"But he's not going to Wildfire?"

"No, he's not."

Jules's heart sank. Kimberly must be crushed. And Sam— "He's a dingbat."

A faint smile creased Kimberly's lips.

Jules tossed the ointment into the cupholder. "That idiot is made to preach to kids. And he does it better with you." What would he do now?

"Thanks."

Poor Kimberly. The farm wasn't the only loss of this week. She'd laid it all on the line to try and get Sam back where he belonged. What could Jules say to cheer her friend up? "Wherever I end up next Christmas, you've still got a permanent invitation."

Wherever I end up. Pain pierced her. A Christmas somewhere that wasn't home. Would it hurt as much then as it did today?

"Thanks. I appreciate it." But Kim's words rang hollow. They both knew things would be awkward with Sam if this relationship didn't pan out. And the way it seemed headed . . .

"You're flying out tomorrow morning?"

"Yeah. Bus tonight."

Jules slouched in her seat. "It'll be so boring. You and Mick both gone." Not that she'd be staying herself much longer. Her chest panged again. On some subconscious level she kept forgetting that the farm would be sold. Each time she remembered, pain hit her anew, like rolling waves over a drowning swimmer.

"He's going back to the Gold Coast?"

"Yep."

The silence stretched as they rumbled over the cattle grid, drove up the short distance of road, and turned into the Carrigans' driveway. Kimberly drove slowly, as the driveway's corrugations threatened to rattle out each of Jules's fillings.

Kimberly finally spoke, her fingers plucking at mud on the steering wheel. "It might be too early to ask, but what are you planning to do?"

"I applied for a job at Cockatoo Creek Camp this morning." A cautious smile crept across Jules's lips. It was the first time she'd said it aloud. Speaking of Cockatoo Creek almost felt like a betrayal of Yarra Plains—like one dream was still warm in the grave as she moved on to the next. But she needed something new to look forward to, as well as a new income.

Maybe Cockatoo Creek would be somewhere to heal.

Downshifting, Kimberly dumped the clutch, and the ute shuddered forward. "You did? Are you okay with that? Are you going to tell Mick?"

"Yes, yes, and no." Jules hesitated. She'd been agonizing over this problem for hours—days, really. "I mean, yes—I don't know."

"We're about to drive up to his house, so you'd better make up your mind."

Jules picked at what was left of her fingernails. This was the question that'd been rattling in her brain for days. "The night before the fire, I told God I'd let the farm go if He wanted me to."

"Seriously?"

"I was thinking about going to Cockatoo Creek anyway. And maybe if I was there, Mick might think about giving me a second—okay, third—shot. But then the fire happened."

Kimberly's smile was rueful. "A fairly dramatic answer."

Jules shook her head, urgency in her tone. "No, I mean it's the problem. The fire didn't give me a choice. It looks bad."

Kimberly's nod was slow. "Like he's your consolation prize."

"He's not!" They rolled through the last gate into the flat square of land where the sheds and house stood squat against the muddy landscape. The sheds blocked Jules's view of the house but Killer was barking up a storm.

Kim held up a palm. "I believe you. You're worried he won't?"

"No one would blame him." Jules dragged a hand down her face. "I've been such an idiot. Now it's too late." Her chest tightened as Mick's expression when he said goodbye flashed before her mind's eye.

Kimberly parked the ute behind Mick's shed, still out of sight of the house, and turned in her seat to face Jules properly. "Why did it take you so long?"

Jules rested her forehead in her palm and moaned. "It sounds stupid now."

"Try me."

She waved her hands in the air, like she could pluck the right words from the atmosphere. "I just . . . This is how I pictured my life. Doing what Mum did. I so admired how she never gave up, no matter what. The legacy meant a lot to me." At the look on Kim's face, she halted what she'd been about to say about the farm's connection to Dad. No sense making her feel worse. She shifted conversational gears. "It's just that life out here is such a battle to survive, I had to hold tight to that picture in my head. It took me a while to see that maybe it's okay to let go."

Kimberly steepled her fingers, expression thoughtful. "Would you have gone to Cockatoo Creek even if the hay didn't burn?"

Jules tilted her head, weighing her words. "Of course it's too easy to say yes now. But I really do think I would have. Life out here's been incredible, but it's also lonely and all-consuming. I'd see the work Sam did with those kids and wish I could do something too, but the farm demanded everything I had." She shrugged. "Maybe this is my chance to do that. But I think I've missed the boat with Mick."

Kimberly smoothed a thumb over puppy-inflicted scratches on her hand. "I think this is the same as the farm thing."

Jules refocused on her friend. "What?"

"You've been trying so hard to control the future of the farm. Now you can't control what happens with Mick. Let go and find out." She nodded to something behind Jules. "And I think you'll find out now."

CHAPTER 38

Jules spun her head around so fast she almost threw her neck out. Mick stood ten feet from the ute, arms folded and expression inscrutable.

"How much of that did he hear?" Her voice came out barely above a whisper. Forget butterflies—a flock of emus flapped their flightless wings in her stomach.

"I noticed him there somewhere around 'Cockatoo Creek,' but I think he may've been there longer."

A smile radiated from Kimberly's voice, but Jules's eyes remained locked on Mick. "Stop smiling. This isn't funny."

"You can't see me," Kim protested.

Jules pointed two fingers at the back of her head and one to Kimberly, in the universal "I've got my eyes on you" symbol.

"That'll be real handy when you have kids."

"Shut up." Jules opened the ute door and slid out of her seat. Mick still hadn't moved a muscle. She closed the door and only vaguely registered the ute rolling off to one of the machinery sheds.

She scanned him, from his *Stay Pawsitive* T-shirt to his rainbow crocs and up again. Usually he was easier to read than a fresh edition of *Queensland Country Life*. But as her pulse beat out a panicked staccato, his expression remained a mask of control.

She cleared her throat. "Hey."

"Hey, yourself." Mick planted his hands on his hips. "Let me tell you all the reasons I shouldn't do this."

Shouldn't do this? Did that mean that he would . . . whatever "this" was? Her heartbeat kicked up another notch. "Okay."

He held up one finger, counting off. "You rejected me."

A reluctant nod.

Second finger. "You rejected me again."

She shuffled on her feet. It sounded bad when he put it like that.

Third. "Once I was all set to go home, you come back here and say you changed your mind."

Confound his accurate recollection. She clasped sweaty palms together.

Pinkie finger. "This is all probably a reaction to losing your farm." He held up his thumb. "And there's a decent chance that in a week you'll change your mind." He dropped the hand, then ran it through his hair, ruffling his almost-curls. "I don't know if I can take it a third time."

Jules folded her arms and fought to keep a grin from rising. He'd stayed here long enough to say all that. It was all the re-assurance she needed. "That's rubbish."

"What?" He pulled his gaze up from her boots to her eyes.

She unfolded her arms and took a step forward. "Without think-ing about it, first word off the top of your head, what do you want?"

He smiled that kind of pressed-lips smile he always had when trying to look serious. "That's not fair."

She held up her hands. Her nerves tingled all over. "I'm right here. You would be totally justified in telling me to hit the road. So do it." She waited a beat. He looked at her lips. "I dare you."

The repressed smile turned into a grin as his gaze locked back on hers. "Hit the road."

She turned.

Two quick steps behind her, and he caught her around the waist, his fingers finding that ticklish spot on her ribs. Laughter bubbled up as he spun her to face him. "But not without me."

She kissed him—or he kissed her. Hard to tell which. All she knew was his arms were tight around her, he smelled like fresh air and something spicy, and his lips pulled into a smile as he kissed her once, twice, and a fair-dinkum-I-can-see-through-the-space-time-continuum third time. Her moon-booted foot popped of its own volition, *Princess Diaries* style. It brought a smirk to her lips as Mick leaned back, breathless.

"What?"

"Nothin'. Just happy."

He raised his eyebrows. "Just happy? I was kinda going for ecstatic."

She rolled her eyes and tugged her hand on the back of his neck till they were a breath apart—

A horn sounded. Mick almost jumped out of his skin. Jules laughed, relief and joy cohabitating with her loss in one weird jumble.

The ute rolled out of the machinery shed, a sheepish Kimberly inside.

"Sorry to break up the party, guys, but I've got a bus to catch."

Kimberly's congratulatory smile lasted until they'd unloaded the motorbike, she'd hugged Jules goodbye, and alone in the truck, exited the Carrigan farm gate. Then she ugly-cried all the way back from Mick's. She hiccupped her way through packing. And she sobbed during a shower, the scalding water mixing with her tears.

She had failed, and that failure had not only cost Sam and Jules—it also meant she'd have no home to go back to. Oh, her rental would still be there, but Wildfire would probably soon disappear. She'd fight to save it, but the board likely wouldn't be swayed—not without Sam. And then what would she be left with? LA wasn't home anymore—neither Mom's luxury apartment nor Dad's less-than-respectable neighborhood.

She could take an offer like Greg's for Potted Plants 4 Hire, but the thought pinged away like a repelling magnet. Short-term contract work, a different city every few months? The tender emotional roots that'd begun to sprout from her heart shriveled. No. No home for her there either.

And for every tear she cried for herself, she cried another for her friends. Jules—though hopeful for a new future—still mourned what she had lost. Sam remained guilt-ridden and more gun-shy than ever before. Would he work in ministry again? Would the world miss out on his passion, his enthusiasm, his listening ear? Her insides shredded at the thought.

She even cried for Mrs. Payton, deprived of the land that'd consumed her life for more than fifty years. And what would Butch do if everyone left? This crazy family that'd landed in his life could now leave it.

Kimberly donned her comfy travel leggings and long T-shirt, shoved sunglasses over her gritty eyes, and dragged her suitcase toward the door. She'd farewelled Jules back at Mick's. Butch had given her a silent salute as she left the sheds, which she interpreted as "Thanks for the comic book conversations and best of luck." And Sam . . .

Yeah.

She had the suitcase down three steps when the veranda door opened. Mrs. Payton poked her head out, a red-checked apron tied over her work clothes, face aged another five years in the past five days. The smell of those Australian Anzac biscuits came with her. Ever since the fire, the woman had either worked beside Jules, baked, or slept. It'd take a decade to eat all those biscuits.

The older woman frowned at Kimberly's suitcase. "Sam's down the back paddock."

Kimberly forced a polite smile. "Thanks." She descended two more steps. Sam being in the back paddock was the whole point of sneaking off three hours early.

"He's not driving you in?"

"We've already talked. I'll drive myself. Mick will hitch a ride in with Butch later and bring the truck back."

A half-truth. She and Sam had talked, alright—just not about her accelerated departure time.

Mrs. Payton's frown intensified. Did the woman really care that much? She'd delivered her apology and even surprised Kimberly with that thank-you, but ever since the fire she'd maintained a wide distance. Perhaps she didn't share Jules's "It's not your fault" sentiments. Either way, this reaction came as a surprise. Maybe Kimberly shouldn't have implicated Mick or Butch in the conspiracy.

Another step. Her arms ached from the bag's weight. *Please go back inside.* She didn't have the spunk to go another round with Mrs. Payton right now.

But the older woman leaned against the doorjamb like she had all day. "Does Sam realize you're leaving now?"

None of your beeswax. Another tight smile. She repeated the words with the same breezy inflection she used the first time. "We've already talked."

"This isn't any of my business but—"

Kimberly's suitcase tipped and slid down the rest of the steps. She blinked at it, heaved a sigh, and turned to face Mrs. Payton. She'd had exactly three polite answers left in her. "Look, we both know you weren't my biggest fan. But I'm going now. So what else do you want from me?"

Mrs. Payton absorbed the cheek without so much as a blink. "I want what's best for my kids."

Kimberly cocked her head. *So?*

"You pushed Sam to reach past his fears. He needs that now more than ever."

Kimberly pressed her lips together. What did this woman want her to do about it? She'd flown to the other side of the world and risked heartbreak in the effort to bring Sam back to his calling. It hadn't been enough.

Don't cry, don't cry, don't cry, don't cry.

She dug the nails of one hand into her palm and clutched the rough wood of the handrail with the other. "That's great and all, but he just broke up with me." She—barely—kept her voice even. Just like Mom, he'd seen her at her best and worst, spent incalculable time with her . . . and still decided to push her away. Ninja stars zinged around her heart like a pinball machine, each memory another cut. Kimberly's volume rose as her voice broke. "So can I please. Just. Go. Home?"

Something akin to compassion crossed Mrs. Payton's face. "He's not thinking straight."

Kimberly rolled her eyes and threw her hands in the air. She had nothing left. "What do you want me to do about that?"

"Does he know how you feel?"

Her pitch hit new heights. "Excuse me?"

"If you leave like this, once he comes to his senses he'll think you're long gone. You guys have a good thing. Give him a chance to come around."

Kimberly stared at her. Which part to process first? The fact that Mrs. Payton apparently approved of her? Or that the woman wanted her to spill her guts to someone who'd already cast her aside? Words tumbled out of her mouth, incredulous. "You want me to say, 'Hey, I know you just broke up with me, but I really like you, so just chew on that for a while from the other side of the globe'?"

Mrs. Payton shrugged. "I'll leave that part up to you."

Kimberly threw her a look, then headed down the steps. "I'll drive myself." Rage fueling her strength, she heaved her suitcase into the back of the truck, slammed the driver's door shut, and only dumped the clutch twice as she roared out of the yard.

He was a terrible person.

Sam pushed his next temporary fence post into the soft earth, brushing his cheek against his shoulder to dislodge a persistent fly. If only he could push his problems away just as easily. This partition in the northernmost sorghum paddock didn't even need to be set up until tomorrow morning. Cowardice was the only thing that kept him here.

He'd turned on the Carrigans' borrowed quad bike no less than three times, ready to search Kimberly out and beg forgiveness. And each time he'd climbed back off and returned to his fence.

A figure on a bicycle approached the paddock gate, barely visible past the shoulder-height sorghum at the edge of the paddock. Intelligent thought fled his brain. He'd just spoken on the phone to Butch, who was fixing a broken irrigator in a paddock near the dairy. It had to be Kim. What on earth could he say to her? The energy to argue with her about Wildfire had deserted him, but neither could he make himself get on that plane. He was meant to take her to the bus soon, in what was destined to be the forty most awkward minutes of his life. Why did she make this harder?

But as the figure pushed its way through the sorghum, recognition hit. Mum. He frowned and called out, "Everything okay?" Something had to be drastically wrong for Mum to ride a push bike.

"Kimberly's gone."

Sam's jaw dropped. She'd left without saying goodbye? "Already?" There would be no one last fight. No painful farewell. No awkward hug. Relief flooded in, followed by a black hole of shame.

The reality of Mum's statement sank into his mind like a pebble into a pond. Kimberly was really gone. Barring anything unexpected, he'd likely never see her again.

That pebble morphed into a boulder and settled on his chest. That thought was more awful to contemplate than the dairy's effluent pond.

He had to do something.

Sam did the math in his head as he slipped the electric tape through the insulated loop at the top of the fence post. It'd take Kimberly forty minutes to get to town. The bus had to be some distance away yet—she hadn't been due to leave for hours.

Did she plan to wait in town? Could he catch her? Or was she driving to Brisbane herself?

Puffing for breath, Mum leaned against the four-wheeler, which held his electric tape reel and fence posts. "Why aren't you going with her?"

He opened his mouth, shut it. Every answer that sprang to mind, including the one he'd given Kim, seemed too silly to say aloud to Mum—the woman who'd never been afraid of anything. Mum narrowed her eyes. "Don't give me that look. Spit it out."

"Look at what happened." He gestured around them. How could Mum even ask that? She loved this place the most of all of them—she was the one who'd planned to be buried here beside Dad, beneath the gum trees they'd both loved. "You told us not to take out the loan. Aren't you furious?"

Mum sighed, her posture sagging, and his heart sank. She clasped her hands in front of her. "You know I always tell you the truth. I'll probably always grieve this place. And my feelings toward Kimberly's role in this are . . . mixed." Her voice wavered.

She pressed her fingers to her lips, collecting herself. "If we didn't have the loan and the hay, the fire couldn't have happened. But I know you all had pure motives. And farm or no farm, God still has a plan for our lives, and that hasn't been derailed by this—even if it feels like it. What if this just sped up the inevitable—but while Jules is young enough to pursue something different? While there's a possibility with Mick?" She straightened her shoulders. "There's no point looking back right now, not while there's a future we need to deal with. Specifically, yours." He hesitated. Her frown deepened. "Do *you* think it's Kimberly's fault?"

"No!" He looked at his boots. "I just . . . Kimberly's always reaching for the stars. But I've learned the hard way that when you fly too close to the sun, you get burned."

Mum gave a slow nod. "Your café."

He slapped at the fly again. "The café. The western block."

Her frown turned into a puzzled expression. "What do you mean the western block?"

He was an idiot. No one wanted to bring that up. But too late now. He shuffled his feet. "I remember you didn't want to buy it, but Dad talked you into it. He had all these big plans. Then the drought hit, and you regretted it."

"That was one thing. And we survived it. Why would that—"

"You said you'd never forgive him."

"What?"

"I heard you. One night—I must've been thirteen—you said if we lost this farm because he talked you into buying the western block, you'd never forgive him."

Mum closed her eyes. Rubbed her forehead.

Sam gripped the insulated plastic top of his next fence post. "Well, guess what? I'm the kid who ended up in special ed, then somehow talked Dad into giving me that loan for the café—and lost it all. I talked Jules into getting the loan for the hay and cattle. If I went back with Kimberly, I'd talk my donors into investing their money into an expansion plan that scares the living daylights out of me. And if something went wrong again, forget you forgiving me—I'd never be able to forgive myself."

Mum shook her head. "I should never have said that to your father. If you'd heard everything, you would've heard me take it back almost as fast as I said it."

Sam walked ten paces away and plunged the next fence post into the dirt. "You say what you feel."

Mum trailed after him. "And feelings aren't always right. Sometimes your logic and your spirit need to pick up your emotions and just drag them along until they can catch up."

"What's your point?"

"I'm saying don't let fear stop you from doing what God's called you to do. Don't take responsibility for things you can't control. Dad made the best decisions he could with the information he had. I was proud of him for that." She squeezed his forearm. "And I'm proud of you."

He sighed inside. Every part of him wanted to agree with her, wanted to race after Kimberly and then follow her to Wildfire. But he had responsibilities here. So he just hugged his mother. "Thanks, Mum."

She held on to his shoulders and pinned him with her stare. "You've walked around with your tail between your legs for too long, believing you're doomed to fail and that if your failure impacts anyone else it's unforgivable. Am I right?"

He stared at her, soul naked before her all-seeing mother's vision. "I-I wouldn't use those words. Caution can be a good thing." But Kimberly's words that night on the chicken coop returned to him once more. Could he really label his attitude as cautious?

"Face facts, Sam: this is condemnation and it's fear, and neither of those things is from God. Forget the farm and me and Jules— before the rain and the fire, you agreed to return to Wildfire. Did you believe God wanted you there? That it was the best place to use your gifts?"

He tried to say no. Formed his lips around the word. But it just wasn't true. "Yes." Yes, yes, a thousand times yes. He craved Wildfire like he craved sugar after five days without baked treats. He missed the adrenaline rush of preaching. He missed the light in a teen's eyes when some nugget of truth clicked. He missed the cheerful buzz of the drop-in center in the hours after school.

Mum released him. "Then staying wouldn't just be a mistake. Letting fear win also means you're refusing to trust God. That's a slap in the face to Him." She laid a hand on his chest. "There's a brave man trapped underneath that fear. Let him out."

Sam gripped her hand, hope trying to shout past the clamor of a thousand worries. "But what will you and Jules do? I can't—"

"Sam, your loyalty is one of the best things about you. But what did I just say about trust?" She smiled. "This is us setting you free. You did everything you could for us. Now go use those talents God gave you, preferably with the woman who believes in you."

That suffocating blanket of doubt vaporized as the truth of her words shone through. His muscles, ratcheted to breaking point for oh, so long, drained of tension till he felt as light and loose as a pool noodle. They didn't hold him responsible. Any mistakes he'd made had been long forgiven. And his mother, the person he owed the greatest debt to and who wished for him to stay in Australia—had just offered her blessing.

He was free. And this cycle of fear would be a tough one to break, but the first step would be changing his actions.

And taking a risk.

"She took the ute?"

Mum pulled the reel and remaining fence posts from the back of the motorbike. "So, I may have interfered in one last way." She smiled. "But you'll see. See if you can catch them."

Them? What had Mum done? No matter. Time was of the essence. He kissed her cheek and mounted the quad. "You're a legend."

CHAPTER 39

Five miles was all it took. Five miles for the tears to blind her to the extent that she mistook a mailbox for a kangaroo and executed a wild swerve to avoid it.

The tires screeched as she jammed on the brakes. Loose gravel on the side of the road destroyed any traction she'd had, and the vehicle bumped to a halt only inches from a thick wooden fence post, dust seeping through her open window. Kimberly leaned her forehead against the steering wheel and ugly-cried.

He didn't want her.

Oh, he'd looked torn up alright. At least she could take solace in knowing that Sam cared for her to some degree. But not enough to outweigh everything else. And certainly not as much as she cared about him.

What an idiot she was.

A fresh burst of sobs overtook her. Everything she'd held in from today, from the past several weeks, from six months ago, even from Mom, came out in a rush of salt water and snot.

Finally, she lifted her head and punched her fist on the steering wheel. What had Mrs. Payton meant, telling her to talk to Sam again? How many times could a person hear they weren't wanted? Besides, it wasn't like Sam was oblivious to the way she felt about him. He'd told her what she meant to him all the time. And she'd made it clear when—

She swiped her eyes dry and growled at no one in particular. Crying must've fogged up her brain because she couldn't recall a single time telling Sam what he meant to her.

Surely there was a time when they'd painted—No, she'd chickened out then.

Or when they'd kissed—No, she'd thought it, but then he started kissing her and all coherent thoughts had gone out the window.

Or on Christmas Eve—No, not then either. He'd already been on the verge of a nervous breakdown, and reminding him that his new girlfriend had helped put him in that spot was not a strategy she'd felt wise.

She groped around the floorboard for her water bottle, which had gone flying in the whole is-it-a-roo-or-is-it-a-mailbox drama. Mrs. Payton's other comment stomped into her mind, unbidden.

"Give him a chance to come around."

Did his mother seriously think he would?

No way. Kimberly couldn't go down that path. Only delusional saps convinced themselves that someone who'd said no would magically turn around and say yes. And she was neither delusional nor a sap.

And she would prove it.

Her phone had slid down the side of the seat. She turned off the truck, pushed back the driver's seat, and shoved her hand down the gap. Her finger brushed the edge of the phone. Shimmying down in the seat, she strained to gain purchase on the slick metal and glass. There. She pulled it back up and flicked through the screens till she reached Steph's contact icon. Her scrambled brain couldn't calculate the time difference—chances were it was the middle of the night. Oh well. She'd leave a message. She just needed this settled once and for all.

The messaging app rang once, twice, three times. "Kimberly?"

"Steph." Her voice cracked on the word. She'd hoped to take the professional route, but this was the end of her tether. If she had to blubber the truth to Steph via a glitchy mobile data connection, so be it. "I failed. There was a fire and—"

"I know." Steph's voice held compassion. "Sam messaged us. We've been praying."

"He can't—"

"We didn't expect him to." Her tone carried a note of sadness. Kimberly's last hopes collapsed. No reassurance that they could do it without him. Steph had warned her to either come back early or bring Sam with her.

And like a moron, she'd risked it all on him.

A sob broke through. "I'm sorry."

"Sweetie, come home. We'll fight for this one last time." But Steph's tone lacked the *Braveheart* rallying-the-troops conviction she was known for.

Kimberly ended the call before she embarrassed herself any further. She pressed her hands to her face. This was it. It was official. She'd likely never see Sam again.

Pain robbed her breath.

She'd come out of hiding long enough to hand her heart over to someone—and he'd handed it straight back. No one wanted her. No one even needed her. The childhood rhyme spun through her mind. *Nobody wants me, everybody hates me, I guess I'll go eat worms.*

For about ten seconds on that farm, she'd thought she could be someone different. Someone brave. Circumstances had pushed her and Sam together, and for the first time in many years she'd exposed her vulnerable side.

What a stupid mistake. Nothing was worth this. Hands covering her eyes, knees drawn to her chest, she sobbed till she was dry.

When the storm passed, she stared unseeing through the windshield. *"What would you do if you weren't afraid?"* Unwelcome but there nonetheless, Jules's question from two weeks ago reverberated through her synapses.

I'd track down Sam's sorry backside and tell him that his drive for reaching out to kids is the most attractive thing I've ever seen. I'd tell him that I miss him, I want him to come back with me, and I want to see if we can make this partnership last.

If only she could.

Jules's words returned, stronger this time. *"Your worth isn't determined by what my mother or even Sam thinks of you."* And the unspoken implication: *God wants you.*

But did He? Really? If so, He sure had a funny way of showing it.

A rumble from behind snagged her attention. A rusty, custard-yellow truck flew down the road, its paint job looking like it'd been done with a can of house paint and a broom.

Butch.

Had Mrs. Payton sicced her loyal employee on her? Or was he just on a beer run?

His truck pulled to a stop behind her. Movements as languid as ever, he strolled up to her open window and leaned against it like this was an everyday occurrence. "Gudday." His voice always sounded so scratchy, like he used it so rarely the cogs never quite meshed right.

She flopped back against the seat and looked at him, face wet for all to see. In her broadest Australian accent, she drawled out her response. "Guuuudaaaaaay."

He grinned and took a drag of his ever-present cigarette. "Hear there's rain comin' next Mondee." His pronunciation of the days of the week always ended in *dee* instead of *day*.

She blinked at the choice of topic, then laughed, incredulous. This whole situation was ridiculous. "Did your boss send you?"

He didn't bother with words, just flicked his brow.

"You can tell her that—like I already informed her—Sam and I have spoken. There's nothing more I can say."

He gave the slightest shrug of his shoulders.

"There's not." Her forcefulness rose with her exasperation. Did he think she was a coward?

If he did, he was right.

Another drag, longer than before. He scratched his forehead, dislodging the stained hat molded to his head. Her frustration boiled over. "What? What is"—she mimicked his expression and gesture—"that?"

He met her eyes. "Seems to me you got somethin' you wanna say to someone." He shrugged. "Not sure it's really about Sam."

Lips probably exhausted, he clamped them back around his cigarette.

Kimberly raised her palms. "Who?" Not Mrs. Payton. She'd already farewelled Jules. She knew no one else on this side of the globe—

A mental puzzle piece slid into place, and she stared at him. "You mean my mom?"

Truth was she hadn't just talked to Butch about comic books.

That topic invariably led to Dad, and once that floodgate opened, she hadn't been able to stop it. Tensions between her parents had run high, so she'd never been able to talk about him with her mother. But her long-repressed grief demanded a listening ear, and while Butch barely talked, he had the listening thing nailed. She'd even told him a bit about Mom.

He just shrugged again.

"And tell her what? That she's a terrible parent? That I hate her?" Because, oh, she hated her. Her hands bunched and heat spread through her body. What kind of mother refused to tell her daughter that she loved her? Tried to suppress the grief she'd experienced over her father's death? Paid her little to no attention, even now?

"Tried that with my old man." Butch tossed his cigarette to the ground and crushed it. "After he died, turned out that wasn't the only thing I wished I'd said."

Kimberly stared at him in silence, the implications sinking in. What did she really want to say? If she was brave? *Mom, do you love me?*

Another phrase entered her consciousness, drowning out her eleven-year-old voice. *"Only be strong and courageous . . ."* The old Sunday school verse might've referred to another context, but it trumpeted through her mind with force.

"Will this get Mrs. Payton off my back?"

Butch swished a fly. "Can't ask much more."

She set her jaw. "Fine." Fingers trembling, she swiped her phone screen and called her mother. What was she doing? This was insane. She'd not had the courage to be honest with her mom since that Mother's Day, forever ago.

But desperate times called for desperate measures. Adrenaline

charged her veins. For once in her life, she would be vulnerable—
from the safety of the other side of the phone. Then her heart could
retreat to its cold and dark cave, alone but safe.

"Yes?" Somehow Mom's voice came through strong and clear,
like she was right next to them.

Kimberly's courage failed. "I, um—" She yanked the phone
away and hovered her finger over the End Call button.

A warm hand slid onto her shoulder, giving it a squeeze.
She looked at Butch. His lips twitched in the faintest of smiles
and he nodded to the phone. *You got this.* He might not have
said the words aloud, but she received the message loud and
clear.

She pressed the phone back to her ear. "Mom—"

She gulped in a breath. Here went nothing. "I know we've
never been a normal mother and daughter. And that's affected
the way I relate to other people." Her words came out in a rush
before she lost her nerve. "But I'm trying to get better at it. I'm
trying. So . . . I love you."

She jerked the phone to her lap and slammed her thumb on
the screen's big red *X*. Her heartbeat galloped in her ears. "Sorry.
I—I'm not ready to hear her reaction."

And the radio silence sure to follow this would sting, no doubt.
But as she stared at the phone, a smile crept across her wet face.
She'd done it. She'd taken her first step. Maybe step two would be
finding the courage to hear Mom's response. But a win was a win,
big or small.

Butch squeezed her shoulder again and withdrew his hand.
"Okay."

The phone gave a short buzz in her palm. New message. She
held her breath.

You're just like your dad. Braver than me.

Kimberly's heart expanded like microwaved marshmallows in hot chocolate. Not an I love you, but still . . . progress. Both for Mom and for her. A new future beckoned, filling her with hope—a future where she was secure enough in God to make herself vulnerable to others.

One in which she could love.

She tilted the screen for Butch to see. He grinned back at her and raised his eyebrows. *See?*

The phone buzzed again. Kimberly tilted it back to her. No way this was Mom—it was probably the phone company telling her she'd maxed out her data or something. But Mom's icon flashed up. A pocket message of gooble-de-gook? The woman never messaged her twice.

I'm not like other mothers, but I do love you.

Finally.

She pressed her face to the phone, silent tears coating her cheeks, the screen, even dripping from her chin. Twenty-seven years she'd waited, and finally . . .

Her mother loved her. She had family, such as it was. This could be their start.

Bravery might hurt, but it had its rewards.

Thank You, God.

As she cried out the last of her tears, she could vaguely sense Butch shuffling his feet, viewing the paddocks around them, drumming his fingers on the door. Finally, she lifted her face and gave him a watery smile. "Thanks."

He nodded back toward Yarra Plains. "One more?"

Oh, what the heck. She was leaving the hemisphere. She'd never see Sam again.

Time to be brave.

She started the truck and Butch backed away, a broad grin splitting his features. She threw the gear stick into first and "chucked a U-ey," as Jules would say. Dust kicked up from the wheels and coated her tongue but couldn't dampen her slightly hysterical grin. U-turn completed, she revved the engine to get back to Yarra Plains as fast as possible.

When she was an old lady with a hundred cats, at least she'd be able to say she tried.

CHAPTER 40

Kimberly pushed her hair back from her face as she drove one-handed, urgency pushing her foot against the gas pedal. Humid air rushed past her skin as the truck gained speed. She used the neck of her tee to blot moisture from her face. At least she'd not bothered with makeup, knowing it'd end up drowned anyway. Her pulse tap-danced, torn between joy at Mom's words and trepidation for what lay ahead.

She checked her rearview mirror. Butch dawdled by his vehicle. Why? Sam would be in the fields somewhere. It wasn't like Butch following her home risked any awkward three's-a-crowd encounter. Was this his usual take-it-easy pace? Or did he know something she didn't?

A spec appeared on the horizon, red and blue and coming her way. Sam, on the Carrigans' borrowed quad bike. She eased off the gas, holding her breath. This was it. Five more minutes of courage—

Though, no, that wasn't true.

Jules had been right. The truth was that she was wanted—by God if no one else. That truth might be agonizing to hold on to when rejection slapped her, but letting go and wallowing alone? That was a worse fate. Even if she returned to the US alone, Wildfire closed, and Mom clammed up again, this time she would be different. She would reach out. She would risk vulnerability. If she couldn't find a place to belong, then she'd make one.

And right now, she would tell Sam how she felt about him and be okay—eventually—with whatever his reaction was. And if he'd never really wanted her all along?

So be it.

She pulled the truck off to the side of the road. Sam stopped his bike and strode toward her.

Please God, make me brave. She slid out of the ute, dust in her nostrils and now probably her hair.

"I have to talk to you." They spoke the same words at the same time, then both hesitated. Kimberly used the moment to take him in. Hair tousled from riding the bike at high speed. No Hugh Jackman-esque outfit today, just a loose cotton work shirt with arms rolled to the elbows and short work shorts he called "stubbies" that'd get him laughed out of the state back in Virginia.

And she'd never been so glad—or terrified—to see him.

She held up her hands. "Let me go first." Or she'd never get it out at all. He snapped his mouth closed. "I told my mom I love her. Just now. Just . . ." She pointed back up the road. "Just there."

"That's—well, that's amazing." He scratched his head. "How did she take it?"

"She loves me too." A smile bloomed across her lips.

"That's amazing." His voice came out at a whisper.

Kimberly drew in a deep breath. "I know I'm not always great at showing what I feel, but I'm trying to change that. So what I feel is that I like you. A lot." She ground to a halt. *Eloquent, Kim.* "I—I can't say yet if I love you. Believe it or not, I take risks in business, but I'm cautious with love."

Ugh. That was worse. She'd gone through all this just to tell him she *didn't* love him?

A slow grin grew on his face. "Never would have guessed."

She rushed on. "But I care about you—so, so much. One day I might love you. I think we make an awesome team." Would he think this was just another desperate Wildfire pitch? "And I don't mean work—I mean us."

He nodded.

"So, um, that's it. That's all I wanted to say." Her face burned. Worst. Speech. Ever. But she'd told him what he meant to her. She stood taller. She'd done the thing she'd never thought she could. And God wanted her. Her heart warmed. She'd be okay, whatever Sam said next.

Sam stared wide-eyed at her for an unending moment. Then one edge of his mouth curved upward. He grasped her hand. "I'm an idiot."

A good start. She clasped her fingers around his and grinned. "Do continue."

"I was wrong."

She laughed through a sniff. "Frequently."

"I want to come back to Wildfire."

She couldn't hold eye contact anymore. She buried her face in her hands. If this was going where she thought it was, this was every Christmas, Thanksgiving, and birthday rolled into one. Her limbs tingled and heart swelled. If he kept going like this, she might just defy gravity.

His hands cupped her jaw, pulled her fingers away. "And you are the bravest person I've ever met, and every second I get to spend with you makes me the luckiest guy on the planet." His gaze burned into hers, and the rest of the universe melted away. "I'm gonna need a little while to get Mum and Jules settled into wherever they go. But then I'd love to come back to Wildfire. And, if you're not sick of me yet, to you."

She surged forward and buried herself in his hug. His arms came around her, holding her tight, his stubbled cheek rough against her neck. She leaned her face on his shoulder and squeezed for all she was worth. She didn't count Mississippis. She never wondered where to put her hands. And the words *weird* and *awkward* never materialized in her mind.

She slid her hands up his chest to his neck and laughed as he shivered. He pressed a lingering kiss against her cheek and she tilted her face to murmur in his ear. "I think Wildfire has an opening. Send me your résumé."

He snickered, and the joy of a thousand fireworks exploded in her heart. Rising to her tiptoes, she pressed her lips against his.

And she thanked God for His strength to be brave.

EPILOGUE

FOUR MONTHS LATER

Sam!" Kimberly wound her way through the new Wildfire Baltimore building, dodging toolboxes and piles of lumber, back in her beloved peep-toes and a navy pantsuit. She inhaled the scent of sawdust. The scent of anticipation. Construction was due to finish this month, and they'd open their first expansion site only weeks afterward.

On the other side of the empty space—the tradesmen were out at lunch—Sam walked toward her, hanging up his phone as he came. Back in the comparative cool of an East Coast spring, he'd returned to his lumberjack-inspired wardrobe, and it looked pretty good against the remnants of his Aussie summer tan.

"Got a letter from the Bible college." She pretended to weigh it in her hands. "It's feeling good." He reached out for it, but she yanked it back out of his grasp. "Did you call Jules back yet?"

Sam grinned and backed her toward the wall, hands at her waist. "If I say yes, will you give me that letter?"

She grinned and hid the letter behind her. "Maybe." Her back met the unpainted wall, cool even through her jacket.

He kissed her cheek. "Now?" His warm breath sent tingles through her skin.

"Getting warmer."

He pressed a kiss to her lips, his "Now?" muffled more into a "Nmmmm?"

She smiled against his lips. "Warmer."

His raised his eyebrows and grinned, shifting his lips to the hinge of her jaw. Her pulse skyrocketed and bones melted into something warm and squishy. His lips smiled against her skin as his fingers snatched the envelope from her grasp.

"Gotcha."

A vehicle pulled up outside. He sighed and stepped back as she pulled the letter out of his hands and used it to point at him. "Call. Your. Sister. This letter and I have to go talk to the electrician."

As she discussed extra power outlets with the "sparky"— Aussie slang for electrician—she kept her boyfriend in her peripheral vision. He paced back and forth, phone to his ear. When the electrician left she crossed the space and hugged Sam from behind. He hung up the phone. She laid her head on his back.

"Are you smiling?" She slid a hand up his chest to his face and patted and poked it till he laughed and tugged her around in front of him.

"Jules is engaged."

She grinned.

His mouth dropped open. "You knew? Before me?"

"It didn't take a genius to figure out. Mick's new practice opened last week, and I didn't think he'd waste much time once they finally got in the same town." Not only had Jules, Mick, and their four dogs relocated to Cockatoo Creek but Butch, too, as the outdoor center's new handyman. During their last video chat, Jules had even mentioned that Butch had come along to their new church once or twice. After watching the Paytons lose everything with dignity, he'd figured he'd give their faith a shot too. Kimberly planned to chat his ear off about it when they returned for the wedding—whenever that would be. Mom had even agreed to finally take some time off and come with them to Australia— her first time overseas. "They set a date?"

He nodded.

"Soon?"

"Early July."

"Strewth!" That meant two trips in her future—for both the wedding *and* Christmas. Sam had promised they'd return Down Under for December 25.

He grinned at her use of Australian slang. She took it as encouragement to keep going. "Good on 'em. Faaaaaaaair dinkum."

Sam rolled his eyes. "You know a girl loves you when she memorizes an entire book of Aussie slang just to drive you crazy with it."

She linked her fingers behind his neck, warmth spreading through her. She had a few more words for him—words he might appreciate a little more. "You seem pretty sure of that."

"What?"

"That I love you." In their months of dating, she'd not said it yet, and he'd not pressured her—though he'd said it himself with increasing frequency.

Now his expression turned cautious, though the lift of his lips indicated hopefulness. "Do you?"

She reached up and kissed him, speaking the words against his lips. "By crikey, I love you."

A Note from the Author

G'day!

Thanks for sharing Kimberly and Sam's story with me—and also Jules and Mick's!

Can I make a confession? While I love Sam and Kimberly, it's another character who's my favorite in this book: Mick. I think it's the rainbow crocs that do it. A man who's unashamed to wear rainbow crocs in public, who combines country and surfer culture, and loves someone with such unwavering loyalty the way Mick does just has to get the gold medal.

Another reason why I love Mick and Jules together is because they're kind of an alternate history of my parents. My mum grew up on the beach and my dad in the country. They've been together since seventeen, married at twenty, and have spent the last twenty-nine years compromising on all the places they've lived (and they've lived in a lot of places!). While Mick's and Jules's personalities are entirely their own, their situation is kind of an exploration of this question: what would have happened if Mum and Dad had chosen not to marry at twenty?

It was also just super awesome to get to write about Australia—especially rural Australia. Yarra Plains was closely based on one of the farms I lived on as a kid. Farm life can be tough, so this book is a nod to those who persist, who innovate, and who roll with the punches. Sometimes disaster strikes. But in *Love and Other Mistakes*, God showed me how He's bigger than the mistakes of His followers. Well, He's also bigger than the disasters that throw our lives in an unexpected direction.

A few things I'd like to quickly clarify before I go:

- With Jules being a Queenslander, I had to make her cheer for the Maroons in rugby league's State of Origin. But for the record, and my father's peace of mind, I'd like to state my undying loyalty to the Blues.

- I often roll my eyes at how snakes and spiders are overrepresented in pop culture regarding Australia. And then I filled my book with them, because it was just so funny. It's literally the first question people ask me when I visit the States: "How do you live with all those snakes and spiders in Australia?" For starters, we have antivenom. And guys, America has bears! THERE'S NO ANTIVENOM FOR A BEAR!!!

- For the sake of this plot, I wrote as if Queensland were not in drought. It is. (Again.) Support your farmers, folks. They need it.

- Jules made a reference in her first scene to stories of people surviving in the outback with some horrifying injuries. I'll spare you the details, but if you ever meet me in person, ask me to tell you the story of a man now known as Two Moons. ;)

Can't wait to see where we end up for the next book!

Till next time,
JESS

Acknowledgments

Mum and Dad—the final draft and editing process of this book came at an intense time of my life. All great things happening—but they all came at once! Thanks for always picking up the phone and convincing me to crash on your couch for a week when I needed a break.

My sister Bek—your wedding coincided with the final drafts and edits of this book. Being your bridesmaid was such a special thing. :) One day there'll be a book about a sister's wedding . . .

My brothers Jake and Jack—without you both I wouldn't have any funny anecdotes to tell people.

Abby—no matter how big you get you're always my baby sis. Watching you grow up is one of the delights of my life. You're also one of my best booksellers! Keep it up, bubs!

Marty and Okie—our Great Ocean Road holiday was one of the best trips of my life! As great as author-world is, that trip came between edits of this book, when I really needed a rest. Spending that break exploring the coast with two old mates was awesome. Thanks for such a fantastic week!

David, Matt, Alex and all other past and present friends at work—every time I skip into the building with book news, you get so excited for me. It means so much having supportive friends to work with. David especially—you kept me on task writing that crazy fast second draft of *Love and Other Mistakes*. Thank you!

Hannah Davis and Angela Carlisle—you guys are a constant source of encouragement and joy in this writing life! Can't wait till the day our books are side by side on my bookshelf.

The Just Church community—your enthusiasm for supporting my writing is such an encouragement. In *Love and Other Mistakes* I wrote about emotions of feeling let down by leaders around me. You guys were a big part of that healing process. Being a part of our little church plant has been an experience I'll treasure. Thanks.

My agent, Chip MacGregor—thanks for helping make this book a reality!

My editor, Jocelyn Bailey, and the whole Thomas Nelson team—you're a delight. Thanks especially to Jocelyn for your insightful editorial notes that included a touching personal story . . . and for letting me borrow your line about holding a dream up to the light.

Rachel Hauck and Susan May Warren—your advice early in the life of this book saved me so much (more) rewriting!

The Debut Authors of 2019 Group—I so value having a group of friends to experience this crazy publication journey with!

Thanks to Nicola, KyLee, Trudy, Amanda, Velma and Alex for your input into Sam's experience with dyslexia. You guys have been so generous with your time. Any mistakes are my own.

Jennie—thanks for answering all my vet questions! Again, any mistakes were me.

God—words fail me. You're everything. Thank you.

Discussion Questions

1. What did you think of Sam's reasons for leaving Wildfire? Was he being honest with himself? How might things have been different if he was?

2. At the beginning of the book, what does Kimberly believe of herself? Why? Is it true? What have you believed of yourself that didn't align with the way God sees you?

3. For most of the story, Jules is desperately trying to hold onto something—in her case, the family farm. Have you ever experienced that feeling of trying to hold onto something that's slipping away? How did that affect your relationship with God? With others?

4. Jules and Mick struggle with their feelings for one another and their seemingly irreconcilable lifestyles. Have you ever experienced/seen a difficult choice like this? What did you do? Looking back, what are your thoughts on the situation now?

5. Meg the dog holds a special place in Jules's heart—and she's named after a much-loved dog of my uncle's. Who are the special animals in your life?

6. Sam's mother, Penny, has experienced a great deal of loss—and now she fears her son moving to the other side of the world again. Have you ever been torn between wanting a loved one close by and letting them go?

7. At first Penny assumes the worst of Kimberly. Have you ever misjudged someone and then realized you were wrong?

8. While Jules's romantic life gets a happily-ever-after, she still has to deal with the grief of losing her family farm and feeling like a failure in her chosen career. Have you ever experienced a bittersweet situation? What was God's truth in that experience?

9. Why did Kimberly's mother treat Kimberly the way she did? As a parent or child yourself, have you experienced the effects of "overcorrecting"? How did God heal that hurt in Kimberly? What healing do you think God could also offer Kimberly's mother?

10. By the end of the story, Kimberly must learn to be emotionally vulnerable or risk spending her life alone. Have you ever been scared to open up? Was it worth it?

11. For much of the book, Sam believed that his fear of risk was just a healthy dose of caution. What's the difference? Have you ever struggled to tell between the two in your life? What is God's truth in this situation?

Jessica Kate's heartfelt and romantic debut proves that love always comes in God's own time.

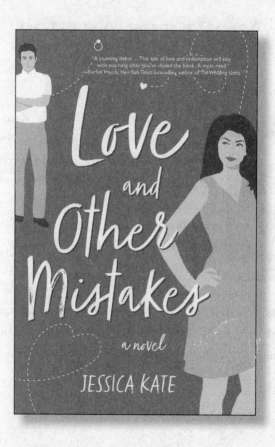

Available in print, e-book, and downloadable audio

THOMAS NELSON
Since 1798

ABOUT THE AUTHOR

Australian author Jessica Kate is obsessed with sassy romances. She packs her novels with love, hate, and everything in between—and then nerds out over her favorite books, movies, and TV in the *StoryNerds* podcast. When she's not writing or discussing fiction, she's hunting the world for the greatest pasta in existence.

©April Hildred - aprilphotography.studio

She grew up on dairy farms on the edge of the Outback and is relieved that all those hours spent milking and daydreaming of being an author have actually paid off. *A Girl's Guide to the Outback* is her second book.

Sign up for her newsletter at jessicakatewriting.com
Instagram: jessicakatewriting
Facebook: jessicakatewriting
Twitter: @JessicaKate05